THE WALLS
BETWEEN US

THE WALLS BETWEEN US

JESSICA DUNKER

Linda Atkins

Thank you so much for supporting a local author!

Queer Space
A REBEL SATORI IMPRINT
New Orleans & New York

Published in the United States of America by
Queer Space
A Rebel Satori Imprint
www.rebelsatoripress.com

Book design: Sven Davisson

Paperback ISBN: 978-1-60864-265-6
Ebook ISBN: 978-1-60864-266-3

Library of Congress Control Number: 2023938543

For the Dunkers, my Po-Po & all of the resilient women in my family

PART I: BLACKOUT

CHAPTER I

He only ever had two people he considered to be family.

On a quiet Sunday afternoon, Akeno could hear the wind chimes ringing on the porch, where a soft breeze blew through the hills. He looks around and pictures it all again. The kitchen smells of roasted chicken, asparagus, and steamed potatoes. Hugh and Sandy must be cooking again. They did this on weekends, like a date.

Akeno is in the next room, reading by lamplight. The old TV is on, but he isn't paying attention to the quiet murmur of voices coming out of it. Sandy sings an old tune, and Hugh says something he can't hear, and the two bubble with laughter as the sweet aroma of baking fills the room. Then it's quiet for a time, until it's too quiet. The TV goes to static, and Sandy and Hugh are gone. He calls their names, but there's no reply. He remembers the cancer, the death, the stroke, and suddenly there's a slam against the front door, and Akeno's eyes open with a start, his shirt soaked in sweat.

Akeno grips the edge of his bed as his eyes move to the door. He heard a noise in the hall, like someone had beaten against the door. He throws off his comforter and stands lopsided, his left hand balancing himself on the bed behind him. He never did find a weapon, but he does have a heavy history textbook on his desk. It's his best defense. He scrambles to find the textbook in the pitch black and grips it tightly between both hands. He waits and listens. He hears nothing.

There isn't the usual hall light spilling in under the door, nor are the streetlamps outside his window lit. Akeno can't see anything in front of him. The only light he has is the moon, but it's only a crescent tonight, and it barely highlights the outline of his window. He strains his eyes to see and his ears to hear, but nothing comes to him. Akeno takes a hard look around the room before leaning back on his bed. His heart pounds as he lays back down and slips one foot, then the other, under the comforter and lets his head fall against the pillow. He still watches the door and waits, his textbook tucked firmly next to his chest. He knows he locked the door, but still he eyes it just to be sure it's still locked. Suddenly he's too tired to move, and his eyes droop closed. Before he knows it, the morning sun shines through the window.

Akeno's eyes flutter open with his hair matted against his head and sweat running down his back, but this time it isn't from the nightmares. It's hot in his room, and he closes the cheap blinds shut. Last night's events are immediately forgotten as he pads his way over to the sink. He catches sight of his pit stains and groans. He instinctively glances at the thermostat, only to greet the blank face of a screen. It's too hot to stay in his room, at least during the day. All he can feel is the afternoon sun heating up the room, especially under all these layers. Akeno strips off the long sleeve shirt until he's down to his black undershirt. He strips off the socks and the sweatpants until he's just down to his underwear. He breathes in the room and takes in the musty smell of dirty laundry and sweat. He needs to get some air.

He starts pulling on a pair of jeans when he remembers the noise he heard last night. He looks back to the door, which is still thankfully locked. It must have been someone residential. It was dark when he heard the noise. Someone must have stumbled in the dark on the way to the bathroom, which he can't believe is still being used by anyone

2

these days after several weeks of not being able to flush.

At first Akeno is stunned to think it's been several weeks, and he peeks at the calendar on the wall. It's been thirty-three days since the initial blackout. Akeno can't believe it's not been longer. It feels like it's been longer. Everything moves day to day, and it all happens so fast that Akeno can't keep track of the days anymore. He wishes someone was here to keep him company at least, just anyone.

He pushes the thought away as he raids his closet for clean clothes. He meant to do laundry sometime this week, but he's pushed it off. Now it reeks, and he'll be lucky to find a clean shirt. After he dresses, Akeno looks in the mirror and grabs the gallon of water sitting on the edge of the sink. He puts a washcloth over the mouth of the jug and tips it over. He lets the water run into the cloth for just a few seconds before putting the gallon back down again. With the damp part of the washcloth, he dabs at his face and scrubs the oil off as best as he can. With another cloth he pulls from the closet, he dabs under his pits and back to dry off the sweat. He crinkles his nose at the smell and tosses it back in the closet.

As he leaves the room and heads down the hallway, he passes a few doors and suddenly stops. He turns around. All the doors to the hall have been pushed open, all of them. The doors stand wide open, the empty spaces inviting anyone to see into them. Akeno's door is the only one that's shut. Akeno's heart rate picks up. All of the doors can't just be left open. He remembers the noise he heard last night. He blanches a few moments and turns away. He steps quietly down the hall and peers into the room nearest him. Nobody's inside. Why would there be? Akeno slips inside and takes a breath. He needs to calm himself down. He needs to think clearly. He needs to stop being so afraid of everything if he expects to survive. He can't be running away from everything.

Akeno peers back out into the hallway and reassess the situation. Someone was here the night before, threw some doors open and deliberately propped them all open, looted the place, and by now has probably left the building. They wouldn't have slept here overnight, at least not on this floor since all the doors are open. Are they looking for something? He looks around the room. Everything is scattered like it was after Kevin moved out, but this room looks specifically searched through. He looks to the room across the hall. It's in the same condition.

Whoever ransacked the rooms must have been looking for essentials. Akeno wonders if they found anything worth eating. All Kevin left was ramen noodles and those chips and fat cakes. There were no fruits, no granola bars, no water bottles. He can't imagine anyone keeping any food in their dorms when the university center fed students on campus. He had never thought to raid the other rooms around him in case someone had stayed behind. All that was in this room was cheap jewelry, clothes, makeup, a mirror, a pair of heels, and a bunch of other odds and ends. He can't imagine what was worth taking from this place. On the wall is a picture of a brunette girl with two other girls. This girl used to live here, and now she doesn't. These useless things are now only a fragment of the person who used to live here.

He glances back down the hallway and slips into another room. It reeks like stale booze and old weed. Pictures of women in bikinis hang above one wall. In the corner he sees a neon Bud Light sign. Nothing like a breath of compensation to heighten Akeno's senses. He leaves the room and heads outside.

He wonders if the scavenger made it to the top floors last night. If the intruder came in from the second-floor entrance, then it would only make sense to raid the first few floors considering how dark it was. Besides, they wouldn't need to hit the top floors yet. The haul from the first three floors should be enough to satisfy one person for a night, but that's assuming this person was alone. He still can't figure out what made that noise? It sounded like someone had beat against his door. He wonders why they didn't break down his door last night. That leads him to believe it must have only been one person.

He shakes the thought from his head. Akeno is alone, too. Could he win in a one-on-one fight? It hasn't come to that yet. Either way, he needs to find out if anyone's coming for him. The best way to do that is to stand his ground, he thinks. He shakes off the feeling and looks around the entrance to his building. He spots a large stick that had fallen from an overhanging tree. He grabs it with both hands and heads back inside.

Akeno makes his way through his hall, checking each room. All's clear. He takes the stairs to the fourth floor and checks the hallway. All of the doors have been flung open too. In spite of his heightened prospects of starving to death on a college campus, Akeno pushes forward and glances into each room. Every room looks the same as the ones downstairs, but Akeno notices there are a few valuable items left behind by the intruder. On several of the desks lie discarded packs of toothpaste, Listerine, deodorant, sunblock, and bug spray. While these scrappy leftovers won't fill an empty stomach, the summer will be a long one without these helpful items, and there's no sense in throwing away personal hygiene products. Akeno grabs a handful of these items in the first few rooms and realizes that he should have brought a backpack with him.

He keeps checking the other rooms. A few doors down, he finds a dusty and crumpled burlap bag in the corner of a closet. He brushes off the dust that floats through the sunlight coming in through the partially opened blinds. Akeno assesses the bag and sees it's purple with gold glitter that flakes off with the dust. He holds it up to the light and sees the words "Glitter is my favorite color." Akeno rolls his eyes. It's no wonder someone buried this in the back of their closet. He throws the bag's straps over his shoulder and makes his way through the rest of the rooms. At least the bag is sizable. It should carry everything he finds. It'll be a good bag to loot the stores with too. It's durable, accessible, and it's purple. He chuckles to himself thinking how it'll match his flashlight. It's been a long time since he's laughed.

When he rounds the corner, he stops short. He heard a noise. What was it? Or is he just imagining things? He steps back around the corner and listens intently. In the next hall are just more rooms and the community bathroom. The intruder, Akeno thinks. They must still be in the building. But he didn't see anyone in the hall. It could be another resident just like himself, scouring the empty rooms for what others left behind.

Akeno peeks around the corner. At the far end of the hall, he sees a flash of movement round the next corner. There's his perp. Without hesitation, he runs after them, a large branch still brandished in one hand. The carpet muffles his footfalls, but he knows he's being too loud. His bag bounces on his shoulder and shakes the contents around. They're going to hear him coming. They're probably waiting around the corner to—

He takes a wide turn, and there's a flash of movement.

CHAPTER 2

The trees lining the narrow campus streets fade into a burnt orange, leaning on red, something like rusting iron. This town is different from the others Akeno is used to. At least it has more trees here and a better smell to the air than the foul pollution he'd become used to growing up on the outskirts of Knoxville.

Johnsville, nestled just outside the western edge of the Appalachian Mountains, is a tourist necessity that people travel to from all over to see the changing colors of fall. Most view autumn as a time for reflection, a moment to take in all of fall's serene beauty. Akeno sees fall as a time of dying, when the birds and bees finally leave with the warm breeze of the changing weather. The trees wither, and the flowers close themselves up until spring.

With all the dying comes midterms, and midterms signal the dawn of the oncoming holidays. It'll be his first year celebrating in the cramped dorms, but at least his roommate will disappear for the break.

Like almost every year, he looks forward to spending them alone. Halloween means binge eating whatever the nearest gas station has to offer: king-sized chocolate bars and a two-liter bottle of Coke. He'll watch cult classics into the late hours of the night on his phone until he falls asleep. He'll pick the movies he's seen too many times while rereading Stephen King.

Thanksgiving means his own personal, pepperoni pizza and wings buffet, and Christmas is whatever discount holiday cookies he can find on the shelves the night before. These treats are considered luxuries, something he waits to afford during this time of year.

His job at the local donut shop is yet another part-time gig that affords him enough hours to pay for food and his phone bill, not that he has anyone to call or text. Nobody has his number anymore, and he's lost everyone else's. The life of a traveler, or so he likes to consider himself.

To the rest, especially the scholarship donors, he's a charity case or a lost cause; either way, he receives enough sponsors to afford a college education. His thank you notes were sent on generic Hallmark cards provided by the college, since all he had was lined notebook paper. He received a few sentiments in return from some of the kinder sponsors: gift baskets with several packs of ramen noodles, a couple of plastic bowls, a plastic water bottle, a key ring, candy, fruit snacks, pencils, notebooks, and an empty picture frame. The picture frame remains empty and stowed away in his desk drawer. These were nice to receive but altogether depressing.

As he walks through campus, Akeno checks his phone and reads 10:36 a.m., battery not fully charged. It must have come unplugged in the night. He sees all of the parked cars crowding the streets and the others hastily driving by, searching for a spot to park in the already packed lots. He notices only a few people on the sidewalk as he makes his way across campus. Most students would have fallen back asleep, content with skipping class for the morning, but something inside Akeno won't let him do that.

He always feels uneasy when he thinks about skipping. His scholarships demand good grades, but more than that, Akeno enjoys the writing process. The deadlines are given far enough in advance and are fluid, depending on the professor. He made a real effort when it came to the short responses and final essays. His grammar sucked, and his spelling always had the red lines underneath, but at the heart of it, his words flowed rather than dampen down. Speaking his mind isn't a trait he'd add to his list of strengths.

Much to the discredit of his high school teachers, he was a quick learner. He learned about Shakespeare from multiple different teachers from several school districts. He would read Romeo & Juliet in one school, but before the final act, he'd be whipped to the next school and start in the middle of watching Hamlet on a shitty projector.

Students who show up to school mid-year, looking like he did every day--worn down, underfed, unbathed, and a little bruised--usually indicated a student who liked getting in fights. He would surprise a few of his teachers, though, who would commend him for his excellent grades and ask about his well-being, but just as he was getting comfortable in one school, he'd be shipped off to another. Thus is life as a traveler.

When he finally makes it to his classroom on the third floor, it's fifteen after. He finds the classroom door open and slides quietly inside. Some students notice his entrance, though Dr. Price does not. Akeno presses his lips together and avoids his peers' stares. They're all sitting in the dark as Dr. Price stands on the other side of the room behind the podium.

He can make out the white glare reflecting off Dr. Price's phone and onto his wire-framed glasses. The other students around him are mindlessly swiping their finger up the screens of their phones. Akeno knows without looking that he has no new messages, no new notifications, no anything. Akeno pulls out a notebook and pen and waits.

After a few minutes of nothing, Akeno sits back and rubs his fists against his eyes. He looks back to the professor, who's still staring at his blank computer screen. He looks to the guy sitting next to him, who's wearing a baby blue Vineyard Vines shirt with his pale yellow shorts. His eyes look glazed over as he fervently texts something on his phone, double taps, swipes left, taps the screen, scrolls up, double taps, swipes right, taps the screen, and texts again.

It's like a ritual, he thinks as he scans the room. *This generation is as mindless as they say.*

"Is something going on?" he asks, his voice quiet.

The guy shakes his head. "I don't know. The power's out," he says, not bothering to look up at Akeno.

They've spoken maybe once before during the semester. He thinks he cheats off Akeno's tests. They all sit in the same seats, but Akeno can't remember his name now. It's been a long time since they introduced themselves during the ice breaker on the first day of classes. He nods like he understands and looks at everyone else. They all seem just as visibly bored as the guy next to him.

Blackouts used to be scary in elementary school, but now they're just inconvenient. The class waits ten more minutes before a girl speaks up from the back of the class. Akeno can tell she's pitched her voice higher than it normally sounds, probably out of nervousness.

"So, can we leave since we're not doing anything?" she asks. "It's been like twenty minutes, and nothing's happening."

Nobody says anything in reply to her comment. Someone's chair slides against the floor on the other side of the room. Akeno looks at Dr. Price, but he merely pushes his glasses up and continues tapping at his phone.

"We'll just make today a review day," he says on the exhale. He removes his glasses and closes his eyes. "Just, uh, go home and study your notes. We'll have the midterm as planned on Thursday. See you then."

He dismisses the class with a wave and goes back to his phone. The class erupts with sound, and several people hold their phones to their ear, waiting for the other person on the line to answer their call.

Akeno slumps over his desk and waits for the rest of the class to leave. American history was his favorite class this semester, though nobody else seemed particularly interested in Dr. Price's lectures on slavery and freedom or the difference between human rights and secular privilege. They scribbled in their notes, sometimes copying the PowerPoint Slides word-for-word, which Akeno found humiliating and depressing, considering they were all posted online. Mostly he saw people on their phones, ignorant to the lecture entirely.

When the class has mostly filtered out, Akeno grabs his bag and leaves the room as quietly as he had entered. Dr. Price is left at the front of the room, his phone still locked in his grip. Akeno walks back through the hall and notices the lights must have been out when he got to class. As he steps out of the building, he closes his eyes against the blinding light of midday and makes his way to the university center for an early lunch, late breakfast.

It seems a lot of classes have let out early. Many students keep their heads down and stride back to their cars. Others like Akeno, without much else to do, decide a quick lunch is in order, as a reward for class letting out early. He has work later today, and it's not like someone could live off donuts alone.

He wonders if the university center has lost power or if it's only the history building. The campus isn't that large; it wouldn't be entirely improbable that the whole university's power is down. He heads straight for the cafeteria on the bottom floor and immediately sees the power is out here too.

The heat lamps are definitely off, so everything that's supposed to be hot is already cold, and whatever's supposed to be cold may already be room temperature. It looks like the only options that are left are sandwiches or salads if the ice hasn't melted underneath the salad bar. He's here now, so he takes his chances. He approaches the cafeteria's front desk, where an older, thin-lipped woman sits hunched on a bar stool.

She extends her hand for his student ID. Akeno already has his card out, familiar with this procedure, though he wonders what she intends to do with it. She takes his card with two fingers and looks at the photo, then at his face, and back again. She scribbles down his ID number in a spiral notebook. She nods and gestures at a clipboard on the desk. Three other students wait to sign their names, their student ID number, and their email. He patiently waits, his eyes staring straight ahead, his mind going elsewhere.

Once he finally gets past the front desk, he checks out his options on the menu board. Chicken and fish are crossed out, and he notices the breakfast bar has been cleared except for the biscuits and muffins, which are probably stale.

He goes for the sandwich station in the corner of the cafeteria. He makes himself a peanut butter and jelly sandwich and takes a seat at one of the tables by the wall-length windows. On the other side of the room, students are still trying to use the drink machine, hopeful that this one comfort might still be working for some magical reason. It's not.

Akeno sits and pulls out his phone. The WIFI's down, but he expected that. He locks his phone and lays it on the table. Akeno takes a bite of his sandwich and feels as jelly spills out the sides and onto his fingers. He places the sandwich back on the plate and sits back in the hard, metal chair, his one napkin already sullied.

He watches as other students filter in and notices a group of athletes roam through the food lines, their heads turning away from each limited option. Their tight joggers squeeze their muscles, the form fitting shirts clinging to their torsos. He was never much of an athlete. For one, he was always too skinny, never made the team in middle school, so he didn't bother to try out in high school. Not to say that Akeno is too skinny.

He had a good face: his straight nose lined the front of his face, centering itself evenly with his cheekbones. His jawline curves faintly just below the ears, which are as average as ears typically go, usually hidden under his coarse hair. He never struggled with acne too badly during his formative years, so his skin has softened around the edges. His lips are full enough to impress a girl and his lashes long enough to make the same girl cry. On the Internet, he read that boys like him are what people considered to be "pretty."

Resuming his focus on the athletes, who he couldn't help but notice sitting across from the cafeteria. It seems like he isn't the only one either. Heads turned when they walked past, if not for their height, then for their status. One athlete points at the chicken on the menu, and the man on the other side of the counter just shrugs, says something with a dull expression. The athlete stalks off, waving his hand at the food in front of him, the others laughing.

The small group makes their way through the cafeteria--shaking hands, clapping backs, and making jokes--and then after the show's over, they take their leave. As Akeno's eyes follow the group out the door, they pass a girl coming in, who walks straight past the woman at the desk. The woman doesn't notice the girl walking past as the group of athletes walk out. Akeno perks up at the sight of it. What will she have to eat now that it's free to her?

13

She walks to the other side of the room, grabs a handful of fruits and several packs of trail mix. She then begins stuffing them in her pockets and backpack, her eyes glancing up only once, catching sight of Akeno. She turns away immediately, as she realizes he's no threat. A woman from behind the counter watches from behind the plexiglass of the bakery, though she does nothing to stop the girl. Sam turns on her heel and walks back out of the cafeteria, never glancing over her shoulder.

Interesting move, Akeno thinks, finishing his sandwich in thought.

They're not supposed to take food outside the cafeteria. That's an easy system to abuse. If every student took several apples from the stand, the cafeteria would run out of apples for everyone else. And she didn't even pay. He supposes he could have done the same thing, or ought to have, but his meals are free already. He supposes if he had to pay six dollars for his measly sandwich, he might consider stealing too.

He should eat something else, but honestly the sandwich was enough. He puts his single plate in the dish line, goes to the fruit stand, grabs an orange and a package of trail mix, and stands there. There aren't any more apples.

A worker walks up to the stand to refill the fruit. She eyes him warily as he continues to stand there. When she's done, she leaves. Akeno quickly grabs one of the apples and walks past the woman at the front desk, feeling rather excited about his act of defiance. The woman at the desk watches him walk out, fruits and trail mix in hand, and turns away, uninterested.

He's outside again, and now the noon sun beats down from up high on his black hair as he makes his way across campus. His next class isn't for another half hour, but he has nowhere else to be. He takes a seat on a bench outside the English building, a spot in the shade. He pulls out his phone and tries to get on Reddit. It doesn't load. He puts his phone away and leans forward, his eyes wandering.

A girl walks by with black hair, dyed black as he notices, and wonders if she knew how much sweat she was going to have to suffer through when she changed her hair color. She catches Akeno's eyes and quickly looks away. He adjusts his bun and sits up straighter. Several people walk by without taking notice of him sitting on the bench. They just walk on without a word to anybody. They're all headed to one place or another, but even if it's the same place, nobody utters a breath as they brush past the others on the sidewalk, their heads bent into their screens.

Fifteen minutes pass and Akeno finally stands, sweat dripping down his temples. He walks into the empty classroom early and takes a seat on the far side of the room. He sits and waits. The lights are still out. People file in, but there are significantly fewer students today. By the time class begins, nine out of thirty-seven students sit restlessly in their seats. A few minutes later, late as usual, Dr. Jennings walks in and sees the class attendance. He sighs but smiles at them warmly.

"Looks like we have a small audience today."

None of them respond, only a short, polite breath of laughter.

"Seems like everyone's using the blackout as an excuse to skip class."

He looks at his watch and flips through his manilla folder of papers. He doesn't say anything for a minute as he flips through the papers and checks his watch again.

"Well, I had planned a short writing assignment to see how everyone's doing with *Macbeth*, but I don't see the use of doing that with half the class gone."

He turns to look at his nine students and smiles.

"Since you guys were dedicated enough to show up, I feel bad for

15

canceling class. Would you guys rather have class, or would you rather I just give you guys the suggested prompts for the next essay to look over on your own time?"

"Own time," the class mumbles. Akeno remains the silent vote.

"Cool, that works out then. Also, I have your last essays graded, so take these home with you and email me if you have any questions about the comments I've made, or if you have any other questions about some of the prompts. Sound good?"

Nobody answers as he passes out the graded essays, and the students leave one by one. Before Dr. Jennings hands back his paper, Akeno can already make out the big, red A next to his name with relief. Akeno takes his essay and smiles. At the top of the paper, Dr. Jennings' barely legible handwriting reads, "Great ideas, here. You're right, Lady Macbeth is the most interesting character. Maybe the play should have been named for her after all."

CHAPTER 3

He falls to the ground in a dizzying blur. His head throbs, and his vision blurs. He probably has a concussion. He reaches up to feel his temple and feels a welt forming. He feels around his hair and scalp. No blood. What was he hit with? Who hit him? Wait, he was running after someone. So it must have been--

Akeno looks up to see a girl standing above him, a large microbiology textbook in hand.

"Who the hell are you?" she shouts. Her eyes are wide, and she looks angry...and afraid. Her rage masks the fear though. Admittedly, he was the one running after her. She must live here too. This is the women's' hall.

"Why did you hit me?" he asks.

"Why were you chasing me?"

"I wasn't," he says. "Or I was...Did you see what happened to all the doors? I thought you might have--"

"What?" she demands. "What are you saying?" She doesn't lower the textbook.

Akeno pushes his hand against the wall and hoists himself up. "Have you seen the hall?"

"What about it?"

"You don't think it's weird?" It occurs to him now.

She lowers the textbook to her side now. "I didn't think anybody lived here still," she mumbles. "Are you in one of the rooms downstairs?"

"Maybe. Was that you last night fumbling around and banging against the walls?"

"I wasn't--," she says. "It doesn't matter. And it wasn't last night. It was this morning."

She reaches behind her and pulls a large military grade backpack around one side. She props it on her knee and stows the textbook away. She also has a sleeping bag, a thermos, a compass hanging from a strap, a watch tucked in one pocket, a pocket knife, and some mace. All that she's missing is a handgun, he thinks. She slings the pack back around her body and tightens the straps around her shoulders. She looks him up and down and smirks. "Nice bag," she says and brushes past him.

Akeno gathers his things that fell from within his bag and drops them back in. The girl pushes open the stairwell door just as Akeno reaches the landing. She's going down.

"Wait," Akeno calls. His voice echoes down the stairwell. "Hey, wait."

She exits through the first floor and makes toward the first-floor double doors. She pushes past them, her curly, earthen colored hair blowing back from the wind from the lawn.

"Wait," Akeno calls again. He's out of breath now. Panting, he bends down with his hands on his knees. The bag falls to his wrist as he reaches for air in his lungs. He definitely needs to pick up cardio again. "Wait."

"What?" she says and turns to face him. "What do you want?"

"I just--" he stands and puts his hands on his hips. He inhales and exhales. "I just want to know why you're here."

"What?"

"I mean, why are you, I don't know, still here? Do you live in this building?"

"Why do you want to know?"

"I, uh, I'm--"

"Exactly," she says. "You're lucky I let you live. Not everybody would give you the chance." Akeno is stunned by the thought but accepts it as fact. Not everyone would have let him walk away unscathed, or at least close to. His head is still pounding.

She walks away and tightens her backpack straps. She walks at a brisker pace, taking one glance behind her shoulder to make sure she's not being followed. Akeno watches as she walks out of sight. He wonders if she lives on campus, since she looks the same age as him, maybe a couple years older. The backpack she carries must be filled with food. Once she's out of sight, he goes back into the building and starts his search again. He shouldn't have asked her where she lives. That's a weird question coming from anyone, especially now when anyone could just break in and--

He lets the thought go. He goes back upstairs and searches through the remaining floors now that she's gone. At the last door on the top floor, he finally drops against a wall and sighs in frustration. He feels the weight of his bag, which is only half filled. He found no food at all, only a few keepsakes he thought he could use--more personal hygiene products, half-drunk water bottles, a few shirts, a couple pairs of men's pants, and a pair of lightly worn men's tennis shoes that fit almost perfectly. Yet the primary issue is still unsolved. He needs food, preferably something with nourishment.

He's given up searching campus for any food. Once everyone left campus, it was a free for all during those next couple of days. It seems more students stayed than he realized, because everywhere he went, people had already taken what was good and ate the rest as fast as they could. All that's left on campus now is a bunch of waste.

Those first few days were more normal than he cared to remember. People still didn't know yet. They were just figuring out what was going on with the world. That's what happens when information isn't as immediate. Everyone thought surely someone would tell them.

Akeno notices the stir in the air as he heads back to his dorm. All the students surrounding him talk about their canceled classes, the amount of homework they still haven't finished, and the apparent city-wide power outage.

Is that true? he thinks. He pulls out his phone and checks the news. No news.

When he unlocks the door to his room, he can hear music coming from within. Kevin must be home. Akeno steps inside, his roommate lounging in bed. Kevin sits, leaning against the white, concrete wall with an open bag of chips and a Diet Coke. His scruff of a beard frames his face as he stuffs one chip after another into his mouth, his eyes glued to his phone.

"What's up?" he says to Akeno as the door slams shut. Their eyes meet, and Akeno turns away. "Have you heard the news?"

"Power's out."

"Yeah, everyone's talking about it,." Kevin says. He dusts off his hands and wipes them against his pants. "I thought, right, classes are canceled, so now I can go home and play *Smite* for the rest of the day. Nope. My PC died last night. Power must have gone out while we were sleeping."

Akeno slides his backpack off and lays down on his bed. As far as roommates go, Kevin isn't a bad one. He's pretty lax and friendly enough, though it's easier for the two of them to put their headphones on and tune the other out.

"What are you planning to do today?" Kevin asks, leaning forward on his bed, his hands coming together to meet in the center of his knees. His eyes are on his forearms flexing as he squeezes his biceps, a natural enough movement for Kevin to perform herself, and anyone else in the room "I heard a bunch of guys were going downtown for a beer, to celebrate."

"I'm not old enough to drink," Akeno says. "So, homework, I guess."

"Yeah..." Kevin says, trailing off. "Well, hey, if you want to put that off, we could go, like, get some pizza instead. Maybe someone there could buy us each a six pack for tonight."

Akeno and Kevin have never gone for pizza, nor have they ever shared a beer together.

"I think I might just spend the day studying," Akeno says, pulling his binder from his bag. "I've got an essay due next week." It isn't due for two weeks, but Kevin doesn't know that.

"Damn, that sucks."

"Yeah, I guess."

"Well, study hard, man. I'm headed out." Kevin slides off his bed and lands with a thump on the ground. He slips into a pair of loafers and heads for the door. "See you later."

As soon as the door shuts, Akeno closes his eyes. Ten minutes pass, and a snore shakes the quiet of the room.

The sun shines in through the uncovered window, blinding Akeno as he sleeps peacefully in his twin-sized bed with the covers half on, half off the edge of the stiff mattress. Minutes later, his arm dangles off the

21

side of the bed, and his eyes creep open. He slides to the edge of the bed and reaches for his phone. He taps his phone screen once to check the time, sighs, and falls back to sleep, his head smothered under an old, stained blanket.

An hour later, his face suddenly feels the hot, late afternoon sun. His eyes snap open as he throws himself out of bed. On the other side of the room is his roommate's bed, the floor strewn with trash and discarded fast food wrappers. Styrofoam cups litter the fallen sheets along with his clothes and a mixed combination of shoes. A pile of shirts and pants hang on the back of his roommate's desk chair. Between the other bits of trash, books, and thin binders on the desk, the clock on his roommate's nightstand is blank.

There's a small sink in the room, and he quickly splashes water on his face and wipes it with a towel. He gurgles a mouthful of Listerine and spits in the sink. He combs his tangled black hair with his fingers and pulls it all back into a bun. He returns to his bed when the sound of the door's lock switching over startles him as Kevin bursts into the door.

"Dude, you are not going to believe this," he says, slamming the door behind him, creating a chaos of noise. Kevin throws himself onto his bed, the springs squeaking loudly from the weight of a former high school lineman. "I went for pizza at Pizza Pie, right? Yeah, their power's out. So I said, whatever, I'll go and get some wings across town at that one place, right? No. The power's out everywhere. The whole city's out."

"What?" he mumbles. He rubs his eyes and looks closer at Kevin

Today Kevin sports a white hoodie, which he immediately peels off, revealing the lines of his waist, the dark hair on his stomach peeking from under his shirt. Akeno blushes and glances away, then back to his roommate once he's thrown his hoodie over his desk chair. Kevin has a plastic bag in his hand and dumps its contents on his bed.

There's a couple of cheap flashlights, a few packages of AA batteries, and a lot of snacks. He glances at the window. There's a long line of cars making their way off campus. He checks his phone and sees an hour hadn't gone by since Kevin left. He checks the news again to see if what Kevin was saying is true. The page can't refresh.

"So, I was driving down the highway," Kevin says. "And like, everybody was leaving. I pulled up to the gas station, and they said their power was out, and I asked why, and they said they didn't know and that nobody in the city has power. So, I was like, okay that's weird, but whatever. I'll get some essentials and then some gas, but they said the gas pumps were down too. So, I don't know. I'm running low on gas, like less than half a tank. How long do you think the power will be out?"

Akeno sits up on the edge of his bed, his head still trying to process everything.

"I don't understand," he says. "How does the whole city lose power?"

"I don't know. That's what I'm saying," Kevin replies with a shake of his head. "Here, take a flashlight." He tosses Akeno a small, purple one. "It's the best I could find."

Akeno flips it on, and a thin stream of light filters out. "You bought these?"

"Well, yeah, they're essentials," Kevin says with a shrug. "They may not work good, but at least they work."

Akeno nods.

"Here, I grabbed a couple other things too," he says, sorting through the pile of stuff on the bed. "I got some Beanie Weenies, some chips, some peanut butter crackers, Gatorade. These things should keep us stable until the university starts working again."

Akeno lays the flashlight on top of his homework. His eyes scan the room and glance out the window again, where several emergency vehicles surge down the road, horns blaring, red and blue lights flashing.

"We've still got the rest of the day, though," Kevin says. "Maybe we'll know something by then. I'm going to go ask Derek. Remember Derek?"

Akeno shakes his head.

"Oh, well he's down the hall. I'll be back."

Kevin leaves the room again. Akeno gets out of bed and slides into his desk chair. He may as well start that essay since there's nothing else to do.

He opens up a blank document and stares at it for several minutes, the title of the essay at the top of the page reading, "Lady Macbeth: the Hero of *Macbeth*." He knows what he wants to write about, but he can't get a clear thought of what exactly he'll say. This was still when he was convinced classes would simply resume, and everything would return to normal.

He gives up and pulls out his history binder, leaving his Lady Macbeth essay blank. He scatters his history notes, his textbook, and all the other papers around him as he works through an outline of government corruption dating back to the Roman Empire. It was his chosen topic for the midterm essay, one that his professor said was an "interesting idea."

After fifteen minutes of staring at his notes, he can't help but let his thoughts wander. Reasonably, this power outage was probably due to one large error: a power tower went down, or a fuse burnt out, or an electrical fire. How could he know? He doesn't know a lot about electrical engineering.

Either way, something happened. his mind races past the worst case scenarios filling his head. He looks back out the window and sees the line of cars still moving off campus. At the end of the line, he sees the blank stop light hanging above all the cars.

A few hours later, he sits in bed reading a book in an effort to block out everything else. He finished his homework and then some. After that, he decided to dive into a new book he found in the library's fiction section. It's about a young girl who runs away from home in search of an accepting and loving family. He just turns the page to chapter six when Kevin's voice sounds in the hall.

Kevin opens the door, and Akeno takes a moment to organize his thoughts as he lays his book down. Kevin looks almost excited as he sits down in his desk chair. Akeno doesn't have to wait long before Kevin launches into a stream of consciousness.

"This is what I've learned: Everyone thinks the world is ending," Kevin says with a laugh and leans back against the wall. "I've heard apocalypse, zombie apocalypse, the Second Coming, global warming, the Second Korean War, a Russian War, a Chinese War, and of course, World War III. Want to add anything?"

"I think people are just overreacting," Akeno says halfheartedly, turning away.

"I did hear someone say the university center will be open for dinner. They got like a generator or something."

"So, we don't need those snacks then," Akeno says with a small smile.

"I mean, I guess not, but now we have snacks for later."

Akeno almost laughs. The university is already finding solutions to the problem. If it was an emergency, especially if it was a war, the school would let everyone know. The government would let everyone know if there was a real crisis. So far, only the news has reported the outage.

25

"Want to grab some dinner?" Kevin asks, breaking Akeno from his thoughts.

He glances at the clock and considers it for a moment. It wouldn't hurt to get something to eat before everything's gone. Better to eat now, even if he wasn't that hungry.

"Yeah, I'll come."

They both grab their room keys and wallets before heading out the door. He shuts off the light switch on the way out, forgetting the lights are already off.

The two of them join the masses heading for the university center. It's still early evening, and everyone's buzzing about dinner. What will the cafeteria have? Can the university get a generator for every building?

"You think they'll have signal?" Kevin asks.

Akeno pulls out his phone. Still no service or any Wi-Fi. Pages still aren't refreshing, meaning there's no mobile data either. "What carrier do you have?" Akeno asks.

"Verizon. Why?" Kevin says. "Thinking about switching plans now?"

"I have Sprint, and I don't have any signal either. I don't even have data."

"So? The power's out. The whole city's out."

"Except signal and data are both based on cell towers," Akeno says. "Power outages don't count for cell phones unless the towers themselves are out, and towers are separated by miles and miles, so say the cell tower is at the top of the mountain. If the tower is down, then that means…"

"Hey, hey, chill, dude. It's gonna be fine," Kevin says, laughing.

CHAPTER 4

Off-campus isn't much better since the days of the blackout marched on.

There was a food truck off campus not far from here, but he doubts that it will have anything that hasn't spoiled or been eaten yet. Small businesses were the first to go in that first week. He assumed they would target the corporations first, but they had everything secured tight, knowing a mob would try for the big outlet stores. Broken glass litters every parking lot of every fast-food chain and dine-in restaurant within a mile of campus, but most of that rotted before people could get to it. If he's going to find food, he's going to have to be creative.

There's a gas station across the street from campus, which is closer to his dorm. There might still be some food and water left there if he looks hard enough. He doesn't like stopping at places close to campus, because that's where everyone gathers to scavenge supplies.

Everyone thinks the students all left, so he's had to be extra careful when going out in the day. He's seen some strange people walking up and down campus with weapons. Most come by vehicle--golf carts, four wheelers, dirt bikes. Unfortunately, he doesn't have anywhere else to live, or he'd have left that first week. He should have been there when Kevin left. He should have gone with him.

His stomach growls. There's a grocery store down the street. He should at least try the store first before he considers the gas station.

More than likely, everything will be taken from the aisles, but there's no harm in looting what's left. He grabs his purple bag from the floor, takes one of the few granola bars he has left, and nearly swallows it as he heads out the door.

He keeps on the road as he's walking through town. He doesn't take the sidewalks. Instead, he cuts through empty parking lots. He starts to get hot as the morning sun turns into the afternoon. He checks the time and sees it's only been twenty minutes since he left campus. He feels like he's been walking a lifetime. Maybe it's because his nerves are on edge, or maybe it's the gut feeling that this trip will be a huge waste or otherwise a terrible idea.

He scans the roads and sidewalks for anyone or anything that he could run into. The last thing he needs is to intrude on someone else's turf. It's a small city, he thinks, but he'd be stupid to believe that gangs aren't everywhere.

Up ahead on the main road, he makes sight of a nasty car crash. The backside of one car is folded to the front seats, and the front of the car behind it is bent up to the steering wheel. He walks past it and sees the crushed car seat in the backseat. He wonders if those people survived. There aren't any bodies in the car. If they had this accident when the power went down, it's unlikely they made it. Maybe it's for the best, Akeno thinks.

A few blocks later, Akeno passes the city hospital. It looks abandoned, but he knows there must be bodies inside. By now the generators are shut off. At one point he could see the glow of the hospital windows at night from his dorm room. Those lights shut off about two weeks ago. He can't imagine what it must smell like in there now. Hospitals never bothered him for the smell, but now it's a graveyard. Were the nurses or doctors there to care for them until the end, or did they

28

leave the hospital to be with their families when they realized the situation turned hopeless? He hopes the staff showed mercy.

The streets begin to blur into suburbs now. Nicer, well-to-do neighborhoods spring up on either side of the highway. They're gated communities, and he knows he can't just walk through their yards. He jogs down the slope of the hill he's on, looks in both directions, and steps onto the highway. Cars rest idly on the sides of the streets. He remembers the traffic piling up on the roads when it all started. It seems like too many people gave up on driving and simply walked the rest of the way home. He can't imagine what the interstate must look like now.

He walks under the shade of one wall on one side of the street, careful to keep his head down but his eyes high as they search for signs of life beyond the community entrances. He had never chanced to go into the suburbs. Houses like that made Akeno claustrophobic. He had lived in a few gated communities before. They weren't anything special. Though the families that fostered him in nice homes were just as nice as the houses they lived in, he learned pretty quickly that those families were also just as empty as their homes were. It was all a facade in Akeno's eyes. When they gave him back to the system, their only explanation for why they couldn't care for Akeno anymore was because "he wasn't the right fit."

A few houses peer at him from behind their wooden fences, the blinds shut and the curtains drawn. Even though the houses themselves look empty, he knows there are still a few families who chose to stay put, probably tuckered down in their bedrooms, just waiting for any news to come. Some of the driveways are empty, Akeno notices. It looks like they packed the family up and left. He wonders if those houses would have any food in them. He knows if the girl was with him now, she would probably scavenge through them and take the most valuable items. She'd leave the jewelry and cash just to take all of the nonperishable foods. She'd probably even set up camp there. Better to live in a nice, big house than a small closet for a dorm room. Maybe they could come here and live in this house together. They'd each get their own room and bathroom, and they'd split whatever food was left.

Akeno stops himself. He shouldn't be thinking of her, at least not in any friendly terms. He doesn't know anything about her. More than likely, she's probably plotting something against him. Even though she said he was the one following her, it's become clear that she was following him. She broke into his building and looted the place and left him untouched. Why? She probably realized he was too easy a target, and if that she wanted anything from Akeno, all she had to do was take it. Akeno stops himself again. He shouldn't worry himself into a frenzy. If she was going to rob him, then she would've already done it. All this isolation has made him lonely and clearly paranoid. He needs to relax. He takes a deep breath and continues forward.

Just as Akeno rounds the corner at the stoplight, the familiar green and white Publix sign gleams in the morning sun. Akeno's not surprised this would be the grocery store next to the suburbs. He's moving out of the shadows of the decorated tree line when he sees a crowd of people gathered at the store.

He stops and scans the crowd. Though he had long hoped to find others who would have information on the blackout, now he avoid crowds of people, seeing how dangerous they could from his vantage point in the dorm. A crowd of people three or more meant a gang, not a search party or a rescue team. He wished he had been braver then. Something inside him tells him to avoid all interactions if he can help it.

He takes a closer look and notices it's really not a crowd at all, but a small militia.

By the doors of the store's entrances stand eight armed men with varying rifles. They're all wearing jeans and a blue shirt like a uniform. All of them wear red hats too, like gang members usually wear bandanas or have matching tattoos. There aren't many cars in the parking lot, only a few to count.

From the entrance, a woman exits the store with bags of groceries and a stroller. A man accompanies her side with his large metallic gun lowered to the ground, his eyes scanning the perimeter. The woman herself doesn't seem the least concerned. She seems content even, as if this is a regular Sunday afternoon for her. They chat amiably, and the man laughs as he opens the trunk and helps her load the groceries in her car. She drives a nice BMW that sparkles against the black pavement, and she drives away, leaving the man to return to his post.

So that does it. He's not going to gain entrance here. He'd probably be shot on sight. He doesn't believe his olive complexion would blend in with the regular customers, even if he is on the paler side during the cold months.

He backs away from the parking lot and heads in the opposite direction, disappointed but not surprised. Surely there would be another grocery store in town, one that isn't guarded. By now, though, he is exhausted from the trip, and his stomach still feels empty

He finds a shady spot under a tree and pulls out the only apple he has left. It's actually the only fruit he has left, other than the browning banana getting squashed in his bag. As Akeno takes the first soft, juicy bite, he relishes in the sweetness of the apple and takes a glance at the world around him.

Of all the places he thinks he would be, the last place he imagined was under a tree, deserted by society itself and left dogging the streets, bent on searching for scraps to survive. It isn't a life Akeno thought he'd lead, but considering how everything has happened, he's lucky to be alive.

Akeno wakes with a start and nearly falls out of bed. Sweat covers his body, and he can feel his heart beating in his chest. Every other hour, he kept waking up from his nightmares. He can't make sense of his dreams now. All he could feel was like someone was chasing him, like if he stopped for a moment that he would be caught and taken away. He pushes the thought away and looks around the room.

Kevin's still sleeping in his bed, his mouth wide open with his eyebrows furrowed together. He rolls over and faces away from Akeno. It's 8:21 a.m. He doesn't have class until ten. His battery sits at fifty-seven percent.

The power must still be out. It's officially been twenty-four hours, probably more.

His eyes close for just a moment when his phone alarm wakes him back up. He stops the alarm and checks the time. It's 9:16 a.m.

"Kevin, wake up," he says.

Kevin doesn't move. He had asked him the night before to wake him up in the morning since his phone died earlier in the day.

"Kevin," he shouts. He throws a pair of Kevin's dirty socks at him. "Wake up."

"Hmm," Kevin says.

"It's almost nine-thirty."

"That's so early," Kevin says. He throws the covers higher over his broad shoulders.

"I'm just telling you. I'm leaving soon."

"Is the power back on yet?"

He walks to the light switch and tries it with a sense of false hope. Up, down, up, down, up. Nothing.

"It's still not on," he says. His thoughts roam rampant in his mind.

"So what now?" Kevin groans.

He doesn't reply. He throws on a pair of joggers and another white shirt. "I'm headed for breakfast, or what's left of it. See you later."

He checks his phone. No signal, no WIFI. No emails, no messages, no calls. Nothing. The news page still doesn't refresh. His silent phone shines dimly in the sunlight. He wonders if anyone else has heard anything new. If there's not been any signal, then probably not. They're all in the dark now.

His mind races faster and faster until a headache forms. He can feel a bubbling ache of anxiety tear apart his insides. Even with the sun out this morning, everything feels much darker. His surroundings dim. The sun no longer brings warmth. A cold shiver passes through him, and he can visibly see goosebumps rising against the hairs of his olive skin. His hair blows in the wind, and he reflexively ties it back in a tight bun. He needs to relax. He'll get through this, just like everything else he's made it through.

When he reaches the university center, he sees flyers posted on all the doors as he heads to the cafeteria. The flyer reads: *The university is currently working on receiving updates about the latest power outage. All classes will resume and remain on schedule. For emergencies, please contact your nearest faculty member or student resource officer. The university is working to find solutions and will continue to update students on the latest news.*

Underneath the flyer is another sheet of paper with the new hours for the university center: 9a.m. - 7p.m. Posted under that is a flyer for the student counseling center.

Akeno reads all three with a shake of his head. At least the university is responding, though not with any information. When he reaches the cafeteria, the woman checks his card, gives him the onceover, and motions for him to sign in again at the clipboard. He sees some of the heat lamps on where the food's being held, but where there are windows providing enough sunlight, the lights remain off. Seems like they're really trying to save on energy now. The grills and machines all sizzle and whir with the usual static of electricity. Everything suddenly sounds so loud in his ears.

At the breakfast bar he gets a plate of scrambled eggs, sausage links, the limpest bacon, a couple biscuits, and a scoop of gravy. He grabs a glass of two percent milk and sits down at one of the tables by the window. He resists the urge to pull his phone from his pocket. He sits in quiet solitude as he watches the others around him mill in and out of the cafeteria.

Some look tired; others look mad. The blackout can't be easy for everyone. A few people have their phones in their hands still, and he notices many regularly pull their phones out, check the screen, and return them to their pockets. It's a natural movement, the way people reach for their phones. It doesn't seem like anyone's found signal though. He doesn't see anyone talking on the phone or texting. The only applications still up and running might be the games on their phones. The only game he has on his phone is Sudoku.

He thinks about the posted flier. The officials must not know anything more than the rest of the students. If phones aren't working, then the university officials are left in the dark just like the rest of them. He wonders about city officials, or would it be the same for them too? Shouldn't the government be involved in this? The governor should at least have released some kind of statement somehow, right? He's never been interested in local politics, but he imagines that's the hierarchy.

All these questions circle through his thoughts as he tries to work it all out. A town meeting would be called, or someone would make an announcement if it was, say, an attack or government breach. People have questions, and right now, he bets a lot of people are scared. Some have probably died. Hospitals need electricity to keep people alive. Then again, they probably have generators too. But what about people living at home on a machine? What happens to them?

It seems like everyone else is just going about their usual routines, himself included. He remembers his history class: Even in times of war, people have to go about their lives as if nothing's happening. Without progress, there's only chaos. Is that why he hasn't heard anything, because the news might incite a panic? Not knowing anything incites panic too. Someone must know something, so why haven't they disclosed that information?

He shakes it from his mind. Again, he's just overreacting. Nobody else is freaking out. He watches as everyone eats quietly, their faces showing their elusive passivity to the situation.

He finishes most of his breakfast and tosses the rest. He walks to class with sixteen minutes to spare. When he gets to the entrance of the science building, he prepares himself for the climb six flights up. Normally he would take the elevator, but this is yet another novelty experience in response to the blackout.

When his foot hits the top landing, he exhales, his calves burning, his chest heaving. He's never felt more out of shape. At least in high school, he had a semblance of athleticism. He could outrun anyone coming after him. Now he could feel his body slowing down. Was it age that made him this way, or is it sitting around all day in a dorm room? A simple life is going to make him lazy, he thinks.

He walks down the hall and hears the familiar sound of static coming from his classroom. Did they get a TV working? The sound blares through his classroom door as he peeks his head around the corner. On the table is a small radio, not a TV, its antenna precariously swinging high in the air. A local signal could pick it up, but only if someone else finds the same radio frequency.

He hurries to grab a seat with everyone else. A few students crowd the radio and listen intently as someone twists the knob. Others sit in the back looking bored as they stare at the radio. He is glad he came to class, if only for the radio.

"Thank you all for coming," Dr. Holden shouts over the loud static. "Our assignment today will be getting this radio to work. If anyone knows anything about radio tech, please apply yourselves. Any volunteers other than the ones at present?"

Everyone else turns a tired eye to Akeno and the few stragglers who just walked in the door after him. They all end up sitting in the back too, other than Akeno.

Suddenly a man's voice filters in and out from the radio, a deep baritone that echoes off the walls. He clasps his hands together in expectation and impatiently waits for the sound to clear up. A student wiggles the dial just a little to get a better connection. He leans forward in his seat, his chin resting on top of his clasped thumbs. It would almost seem like he was praying.

The radio filters in, and a clear voice booms from the speakers. The small group around the radio cheers, and Akeno smiles as everyone makes way for the speaker's sound to reach those in the back. A hush falls over the room.

"--for just the right one to take action. As we know from earlier broadcasting, communications have failed all over the region, and some

36

expect other states to be without power too. We cannot connect to the capital yet, which in our case is Raleigh, but attempts are still being made. Are we the only ones in this mass blackout? If so, why? If not, and the whole nation has gone dark, then I'm not sure I want to know the answer."

Akeno's anxiety is only confirmed by this news. The blackout extends across borders. It's worse than he thought. It's not just the county; it's across states.

He leans back in his desk and scans the room, his arms folding up around his chest. His fellow students' faces turn from smiles to a look of troubled concern. They're listening to everything the man is saying and are just now putting the pieces together. Akeno's heart rate picks up, and for the first time, he's afraid.

"Wait. Does that mean--"

Voices speak over each other.

"Nobody's communicating? Why can't the capital--?"

"Do you think this is statewide?"

"What if it's across the country?"

"You think it's an attack?"

"Everyone, keep listening," Holden shouts louder than the class. Everyone quiets, and those in the back draw closer.

"Update: We've just been able to connect to another radio," the radio man's voice says. "Hello ... Hello? Can you hear me? Hello, can you hear me?"

Static echoes in the background. Akeno thinks they must have several radios on wherever this man is.

"She's a woman from northern Georgia," the radio man says. "So we've finally managed to cross borders...She says she and her family have been trying to contact other family members from across the country...She lives in the woods...She says her family's power is out too...She says she contacted South Carolina!... says it was a man who lost his power yesterday...

"Breaking: Three states have confirmed to have lost power. I repeat, three states are now without power...We have lost power here in North Carolina, the woman in Georgia, and now South Carolina. Another line's coming in!

"Easy folks. We'll return after this break. More to come soon. Tune in to 90.2 AM. Spread the word. Keep your faith. Over and out."

Static.

The classroom erupts in a frenzy.

"So three states don't have power?"

"Has anyone contacted D.C.?"

"Should we be home with our families?"

"My family's in Mich-"

"My family's in Vermo-"

"Can we call from our-?"

"We can't make contact here," Holden says. "There's no speaker to communicate. It's just a receiver radio."

The class is silent as the radio break continues in silence. Akeno worries it won't come back on.

"Has anyone, like, tried a landline?" someone whispers just loud enough for Dr. Holden to hear, who briefly sighs before nodding.

"Yes, we've tried every measure of communication. There's nobody listening."

A chill runs up Akeno's spine, and he shivers. People begin to shuffle their feet with tense anxiety, their faces heavy with dread.

"Has anyone else made contact with family members or friends?" Dr. Holden asks the class. Everyone shakes their heads.

"When's the earliest yesterday someone heard from their friends or family from outside the city?" he asks.

"I texted my mom around 1:30 the night before last," a girl says. "When I woke up around nine the next morning, my signal was out. The message said it was never sent."

"Okay, anyone else? Anyone earlier than 1:30 a.m., two nights ago?"

Nobody answers.

"So early morning, at about 1 a.m., the blackout started. Those who were up late, were your lights working then?"

Everyone shrugs. Dr. Holden sighs and leans against his desk.

"Okay, listen, everyone. For the rest of the class time, I'll have the radio on. If you want to stay and listen with us, you can. Otherwise, class is dismissed. Please, if anyone's able to communicate with someone, please come find me or one of my associates, or anyone really. Find an SRO. Find anyone and tell them. It's word of mouth right now. And radio. We can't go nuclear now."

"Nuclear?" someone shouts from the back.

"It's an expression," he says.

The class looks around, nerves on edge.

"You're dismissed," Dr. Holden says. He lingers by the door as many of them get up to leave, but Akeno stays. "I'm going to find Dr. Jennings," he announces to those remaining. "He tinkers with old things like these. Everyone else, wait here and keep listening. We'll see if we can keep contact with this station or if we can find others like it. I'll be back soon."

He leaves the room, and everyone looks at each other.

"What's happening?" a guy asks.

Akeno realizes now he doesn't know anyone's names.

"He's saying this isn't just us. This is an epidemic," a girl says.

"Will our cars work?" someone asks.

"Yes, cars will work," another says with a roll of their eyes. "They run off an engine. I doubt the gas stations will work though."

"I'm leaving," another girl says.

She takes her backpack and leaves without another word. She isn't the only one either. A few more people leave after a couple more minutes. Only Akeno and two others remain behind. The professor still hasn't returned.

"What about you?" one guy asks Akeno. "Do you have any family around here?"

"Uh, no," Akeno says.

"What about you?" the first guy asks the other guy.

"Mine's in North Carolina," the second guy says. "There's no way I'll make it with the gas in my tank."

They don't say anything else. They listen to the radio's static and wait. Holden returns with Dr. Jennings, and Akeno's thankful for a familiar face.

"Has anything else come through?" Dr. Holden asks the three.

They shake their heads.

"Did we lose connection?"

"No, I think they're just taking a break still," the first guy says.

Dr. Holden takes a seat with the students. Dr. Jennings leans over the desk and starts fiddling with the back side of the radio. He explains to Dr. Holden what he's doing as he works. The other students are growing restless.

Akeno leans his head against his elbows and looks out the wide windows of the classroom. Students and faculty alike rush past each other on the sidewalks. A man outside the building holds a megaphone and calls for the end of the world. A minister stands on the steps of the building opposite and cries for the redemption and salvation in Jesus Christ. Nobody seems to notice either of them.

After a bit of tinkering, Holden decides it's time he brings in the university officials and other faculty members. He says something quietly to Dr. Jennings and leaves. He's gone for at least an hour before he comes back with a few others. Most are faculty, but judging by the look of some of their clothes, at least three of them are university officials.

Another hour passes, and the radio goes dark. Static blares from the radio, and it doesn't seem like it'll catch another signal. Akeno stays behind as the two professors walk the others out with their apologies and emphasis on the information they had already learned before they got there. Despite their words, the officials don't seem impressed. Some of the faculty look just the same. If only they were here when they came into contact with the first man's report.

When everyone else leaves, Akeno starts to feel hopeless and truthfully very tired. Sitting around in a classroom all day listening to static, with his tension rising every moment, that drained him. He's ready to head back as well, but he wants to stay in case he misses anything. He wants to help, but he doesn't know how he could help. He remains faithfully by their side.

Dr. Jennings recommends going to the store for more equipment, but since the blackout, all of the stores had closed the day before and wouldn't be opening until the lights turned back on.

The military has been silent, and he hasn't seen a police officer at all today. Holden had hoped they could get a hold of the police, and when that didn't work, he tried to contact the nearest government facility, but so far, nobody has answered the radio call but the random public. Even the local radio stations had gone off the grid. With the information they had, it seemed like a total blackout, at least regionally.

Considering the lack of response, though, Holden said a nation-wide epidemic is the only answer. He hadn't been meant to hear them say that out in the hall, but whispers carry far when the world is quiet.

When they step back into the room, Holden and Jennings see Ake-no still sitting there and smile. It's time they part ways. Nobody wanted to say it out loud. Moreso, nobody wanted to admit the worst had happened. Akeno gathers his things. It was already growing dark outside from the incoming storm.

Holden says he left something in the break room and hurries down the hall, leaving Akeno and Dr. Jennings in the room. Though they hadn't spoken much the whole time, Dr. Jennings addresses Akeno by name.

"Shouldn't you be trying to contact your family?" he asks. "Are you from around here?"

Akeno shakes his head. "No, sir."

"Do you need a ride somewhere? I live around the area. I can drop you off at your place or a friend's house, or wherever you need to go."

"That's all right. I actually live on campus, so it's not a far walk from here, but I appreciate the offer," Akeno says.

He feels strange talking to Dr. Jennings like a friend, though they've had several one-on-one conversations. He wonders if Dr. Jennings and Dr. Holden will remain in touch, even if they'll keep each other updated on any new information, or if they'll lock themselves away in their own homes with their own families.

Dr. Jennings proffers a sad smile, but Akeno keeps his face neutral as he tries to say goodbye.

"I should be going," Akeno says awkwardly. "Thank you for letting me stay and listen to the radio."

"Good luck, Akeno," Dr. Jennings says with a smile. "Really, stay safe."

Akeno stops and turns. Dr. Jennings stands by the radio, the soft static emitting from its speakers. He doesn't look up again, and Akeno leaves. He assumes Dr. Jennings will take the radio home with him and wonders where he could get a radio like that too.

He walks back to his room as the skies darken and the clouds roll in. The sidewalks are barren now. The preachers are gone. The streetlamps usually blink on at about this time, but nothing offers him any security, walking alone through the deserted campus. He strides past the empty campus buildings, which appear eerily dark. The unlit streetlamps towering above him jut out from the sidewalk like broken teeth. The wind blows and reminds Akeno of the changing season, the season of dying, and a strange sensation runs up and down his arms. He feels as if he's being watched and glances at the darkened windows. What else is there to do but look out the window and wait for help?

He thinks police will arrive soon and guide the rest of the students to a safe location. That must be the protocol. Maybe a church will take everyone in, if they aren't already packed, or if their doors aren't locked to the public. Government agents may come to escort them all away, lead them somewhere remote and unknown. In many ways, it would be easier to go with them, but whatever government agency comes for him, he won't go. He'd rather risk being on his own rather than go back in the system.

Suddenly the rain begins to fall. He walks quicker and expects to see Kevin lying on his bed back in the room when he returns. When he steps inside the building, he shakes off the cold rain and heads for the room. He raps a quick knock and opens the door. Akeno instinctively waits for Kevin's voice to boom out from his corner of the room, but nothing greets him at the door. He sees Kevin's things scattered around

43

the room like he had packed in a rush. There are a few discarded clothes lying about--unmatched socks, a few old t-shirts, some old sweatpants. At first he feels a slight pang in his chest. He just left without saying goodbye. Akeno glances around the room. He didn't even leave a note.

Akeno locks the deadbolt and goes to his bed, where he leans against it in disbelief. He looks around the empty room. Most of the stuff usually scattered around the room had been Kevin's, and now it was all gone, except for a pile of trash carelessly pushed under the bed. He goes to Kevin's desk to check the drawers. Nothing. He opens his own desk drawers to check if anything is missing. Everything's still there. At least that much can be said. He takes a deep breath. Kevin moved out.

He must have finally realized what was going on, Akeno thinks. Who told him? Or did Kevin also tune in to the same radio station? He could have found it using his car radio. He wonders about the man on the radio. He could try and make contact with the station again, but he'd have to find a radio first.

The severity of the situation washes over him in a cold wave, and he finds himself seeing the room differently, its proportions cramped and ill-prepared to become his bunker. No kitchen and no private bathroom. It's just a room with a window that doesn't open. He can't get fresh air in his room unless he goes outside. He's alone and completely defenseless if anyone finds him. He needs supplies. He needs clean water and any food he can find. In every survivor-apocalypse movie, the first thing everyone does is raid the grocery stores. He doesn't think the grocery stores have been raided yet. Maybe a few anxious Doomsday preppers bought all the non-perishables and toilet paper in the store, but he doubts anyone's been there yet.

Akeno checks Kevin's closet, where several new button-ups and heavy winter coats still hang. He thinks Kevin must be stupid for leaving his winter clothes. It's nearly winter as it is. The temperature's starting to drop at night, and it will only get colder.

What if the blackout lasts for the next few weeks? He blanches. He catches himself thinking too far ahead. He shouldn't think that far ahead. Or should he? No, it's only paranoia to think about winter right now. Akeno sits on his bed and runs his hands through his hair. He pulls the hair band out of his bun and lays down. A black halo encircles his head as his thick hair falls around him. He needs to think logically, rationally. What does he know?

The radio said multiple states are without power, meaning multiple regions, multiple counties, multiple cities, multiple power plants. They haven't received any news of an attack, a movement, or an epidemic. People can access information through a radio. Most people have a radio somewhere, so most people should be finding out everything soon. People will panic. They will leave town, go to their families, stock up on everything they need for several weeks, and they will protect their own. That's what people do. That's what Akeno will do.

That night, while everyone else is nestled safely in their homes alongside their parents, pets, and siblings, Akeno finishes off the remainder of the snacks left in the room. Akeno had thankfully saved the trail mix and fruit he took from the cafeteria the day before. He finds a half empty water bottle from days prior under his bed, which he gulps down. When it gets dark, he pulls out his purple flashlight, which Akeno finds still in between his bed and the wall. He tries reading Stephen King again, trying in vain to escape the reality he's facing now, if only to avoid the reality of his fears.

CHAPTER 5

Akeno decides the gas station is his best course of action. He'll only be in there for ten minutes, in and out. He checks his watch. It reads 10:48 a.m. He's never had a watch before. They were always too expensive a luxury when phones always told the time. He looted this one at the campus bookstore.

Actually, he took several. They were locked away in a glass case behind the counter, which he broke into to get the watches. The bookstore was one of the few places left untouched after the blackout. Akeno managed to find some interesting books to read, some of which he'd actually finished .

He needs a better weapon. If the intruder hadn't been her, a petite girl only his height, what would he have done? What if she decided to kill him, despite all that said she couldn't? Plenty of female serial killers existed out in the world, not that he imagined her to be a killer.

He doesn't think she'll come back after their brief encounter, but there's something inside him that hopes she does.

He intends to find a gun soon. He thinks Wal-Mart might have them, but that would be a hike across town. It was only a few miles and something like a ten-minute drive, but to walk all the way there would be a huge risk, especially during the day. He might be able to find food there too, but that's hoping there's any left in the stock room.

A gun could also be used for hunting. That's a better reason to take the risk.

He'll just have to find plenty of bullets so he can do a bit of target practice. Hunting could be the answer to his food shortage. It was time he found a better alternative to feeding himself than scavenging. The mountains weren't far from campus. He could go there, set up camp, and make life an easier one.

He thinks of the girl's military backpack. He wonders if she has a military boyfriend who's helping her learn survival techniques, but something tells him military men aren't her type. Maybe she comes from a military family. Maybe she found that backpack in one of the ROTC buildings. He should swing by there and see if he can find another bag like hers in the locker rooms.

As he makes his way outside, he can barely make out the bright sun peeking through the gray sky. The clouds rest heavy in the air and he knows it will rain. He can smell it. Rain used to be a comforting feeling to him, especially the sound rain makes when it beats against the roof at night. Now something inside him says rain isn't all that great knowing he could be caught in it on foot. Umbrellas aren't good to have. They work like a beacon in the rain. If it rains, he needs a cold shower anyway.

He heads toward the edge of campus. He doesn't see anyone on the streets or on campus. The girl can't be the only one who's chosen to stay, but if any of them are like him--without any food--shouldn't he see at least a couple of them out and foraging around for anything useful? He never sees anyone. Maybe that's the point.

When he reaches the gas station, the door hangs open, blowing unsteadily in the wind. He can hear the metal hinges creaking against its bolts. The gray clouds have become heavier and darker. He should hurry back to his dorm sooner rather than later. He'll wait until the storm passes over, and then when it's dark, he might consider the Walmart trip.

He enters the gas station and sees the mess. Shelves are overturned, and open packages of food are everywhere. Even the trash cans behind the counter have been looted. Animals must have found their way inside and raided the place the same way humans have.

As he walks the haphazard aisles, he notices what was raided in haste and what's been left behind. For the most part, all of the Beanie Weenies are gone. There's a couple of cans in the very back of the shelf, which he grabs and shoves in his bag. He'll need plasticware, if he can find any here, but cutlery is more of a privilege than a necessity at this point.

He scores five cans of Vienna Sausages on the floor, four black bananas (which he leaves), a couple bruised apples hidden behind some empty crates, a torn open box of variety flavored granola bars with two granola bars still left, and a few Payday bars stowed behind the counter.

He goes to the stockroom, where the door has already been smashed in. It looks the same as the front of the store does, but he finds what he needs most: water. Behind a stack of heavy crates, all of which contain two-liter Mountain Dew bottles, he pulls out several of the largest water bottles hidden behind it all.

After a lot of heavyweight maneuvering to get the water out from behind the stacked boxes, he assumes this is why the water was never found. Nobody could move these crates without a dolly. He's surprised the Mountain Dew bottles weren't all taken. They must be low on everyone's shopping lists now.

He finds a couple Gatorade bottles too. They lay in a corner at the back of the stock room, under these massive shelves that still hold plenty of larger boxes stored up high. Holes have been cut into the fronts of the boxes, and if he climbed the shelves, he imagines he could find more to take with him.

He climbs the metal shelves and reaches his hand into the top box. His fingers touch something furry, and he gasps, nearly falling off the shelves. He jumps down from the shelves in a hurry and takes several steps back, his head craning to see inside the box of horrors. Inside is a huge rat, several of them, their beady eyes glowing from within.

He races out of the stock room with a shiver running up and down his spine. He wipes his hand on his pants knowing he won't be able to wipe the germs off. If he gets sick, there's no telling how his body will react. If he comes down with anything severe, he'll most likely die a long and agonizing death by himself in his dorm room.

He pulls out one of the Gatorade bottles he found and takes a long drink. Even though the Gatorade is room temperature, the cool feeling of liquid sliding down his parched throat feels incredible. He unconsciously smiles to himself. He's never tasted anything so desirable. The aftertaste on his tongue leaves a string of goosebumps on his arms.

A short rumble sounds outside, and Akeno recognizes it as thunder. He rearranges the items in his bag before he makes for the door. Just as he steps on the landing, three men block his way. He skids to a halt and almost yelps in surprise at the men's hulking figures. He didn't even hear them outside.

They're wearing boots with their jeans tucked in. Two of them wear jackets, but one of them wears a plain t-shirt that's ripped in a couple places, including the biceps and at the collar bone. He notices the only car in the parking lot is a large diesel engine truck with two smoke stacks on top. It wasn't thunder he heard.

He tries to dodge out of their way, but one of them grabs a hold of his arm.

"What's in the bag?" one of the men asks.

49

"Just some stuff," he says under his breath. The man's grip is strong.

"Some stuff?" another man asks. "What kinda stuff?"

The man with the ripped shirt has already pushed past them and hops the counter. Akeno notices the few packs of cigarettes and tobacco left on the walls' display shelves.

"Anythin' you think we might need in there?" the first man asks.

"There's plenty more in the store. I didn't take all of it."

"I bet there is plenty more. Yer skinny enough," the second of them says with a sneer.

Akeno doesn't know how to respond but instead looks back to the man behind the counter who pockets several packs of cigarettes before eyeing the cases of beer.

"Jason, come 'ere," the man inside says.

The man still holding onto his arm lets go and steps inside.

"Nice meetin' you," he says. He spits brown liquid on Akeno's bag, right where the glitter words are. "See you around, fag."

As soon as the two men are inside, Akeno makes a break for it. He takes off running back toward campus with only a short glance behind him to make sure he isn't being followed.

The rain beats against the windows as Akeno munches on his meager lunch. He's still shaking from the incident at the gas station. He's already escaped danger once when the girl let him go, not that she was a threat, but she could have been. Then he runs into those three, and thankfully they were only looking for beer and smokes. He needs to be more careful. He's managed to avoid everyone for weeks, and today he makes the mistake of feeling safer than he is.

He takes a few moments to look out the window. It doesn't look like the rain may stop any time soon, but for now at least he knows he won't go hungry tonight. He leans back against the cold walls and shivers. His room was hot when he left, but now it's cooled down several degrees. He pulls on a hoodie and closes his eyes. He thinks of putting a bucket under the windowsill to collect fresh water, but he doesn't think that's necessary yet. He heard somewhere that rainwater is actually filled with the toxins of the lakes and oceans. If worse comes to worse, he'll choose the dangers of rainwater over dehydration, but for now, he needs to rest.

The sound of the rain soothes him, and he thinks he'll spend his time thinking of all he's grateful for. That's something he imagines happening right now in the homes of millions across the nation. He imagines families lighting their candles in the dark of the rain and how they sit together in the comfort of their living rooms, each of them with solemn faces as they name off their blessings. He hasn't starved today, he lists first. He has shelter. He has food. He has water. He has no one to betray him. He's not sure if isolation is a blessing or a curse, but for now he counts it as a blessing. Next, he thinks of the small things. He can rest assured knowing he has plenty of listerine, since that's the most of what he's found in the rooms upstairs. He has lots of floss too.

He exhales. This sucks. Even though Kevin talked a lot, he feels a pang in his chest when he remembers Kevin's rambling. Akeno never responded to Kevin most of the time. He usually just gave a nod or a grunt of approval, since that was the only response needed, but he felt included when Kevin was around. He wonders how he's doing now. He hopes Kevin made it home safely. His family seemed pretty cool from what Kevin said about them. His parents were divorced, and he had primary custody with his dad, but his mom has always supported him and his sister. He remembers Kevin saying his dad didn't do much but drink, and Akeno wonders if that's changed since the blackout. He doubts it. He's probably drunk himself to death by now, Akeno thinks soberly.

With his eyes shut, he nods off to sleep. When he wakes up, the rain has stopped and the late afternoon sun is poking its head back through the gray clouds lingering in the sky. He blinks several times and rubs the sleep out of the corner of his eye before instinctively checking his phone for the time. His phone is dead. At this point he just keeps his phone on him for the sake of feeling normal, like the world he's known isn't just falling apart.

He sits up to stretch and peeks outside the window. The world is quiet. There's nothing and nobody outside. As winter starts to set in, Akeno thinks the worst will happen. He doesn't have a fireplace or a heater to keep him warm. He's been wearing several layers to bed, but he's not sure if that will be enough. He could die frozen in his bed. If he stays here long enough, will someone find his body? Maybe someday.

He thinks about his planned outing. Though he has plenty of daylight left, he doesn't see himself getting out again. What if it rains again? But also what if he runs into those men again? They have a truck, and Akeno only has his legs. Besides, if he starts now, he may not be able to get back before dark. With only a flashlight to guide his way, that's a lot to depend on for that far a trip. If he does it at all, he'll need to go around dawn.

In the meantime, Akeno thinks about what's left to do. He could try and find a radio and attempt to communicate with local signals. He found a working radio that allowed him to tune in and listen, but nothing useful has come on so far. He wonders what happened to the one station Dr. Jennings had found. He wonders if they've finally run out of power too. Akeno thinks if he could find a radio to communicate with, he could probably find enough power to fuel it.

There's bound to be some equipment in the communications department. He may even find a camera to document his journeys with. He could be famous one day once this whole incident is over. He'll submit his pictures and videos to a credible producer, and then he'll make millions. He'll be the hero of his own movie. Akeno leans back and smiles, until the smile fades from his face, and he's left alone to his thoughts.

Without any further delay, he grabs his purple, glitter bag and heads out the door. He avoids the urge to lock the door. If anyone breaks in, he's screwed, so he just has to hope nobody does. There's not a lot to take, but it's everything he's saved up over the weeks.

As he walks down the hall, he feels sweat slick his back under his three layers. He has a sudden memory of sitting in the back seat of a car, his back drenched from the soft interior of a beat-up Toyota Corolla. He sees a woman's short cropped blonde hair in the driver's seat. She looks back and gives him a sympathetic frown. Akeno isn't too sorry, though. The woman eyes him through the rearview mirror, her eyes boring into his. She's earnest in what she says next: "They don't know what they're missing, Akeno. We'll find a suitable home soon." Akeno shakes the memory. That was long ago, not anything worth remembering. He keeps walking.

When he reaches a cluster of buildings, suddenly Akeno can't remember which building he's looking for. He hasn't been in all the buildings yet, and he can't guarantee he'll be able to find what he's looking for. He reads the sign on the front of the building, which gives no indication of which building is which, so he chooses one at random. He walks inside and stares at the foyer. There's student art hanging on the walls and cases of pottery and sculptures on display. He steps out. He tries the second, which has nothing on its walls except for the flyers advertising different clubs and advanced classes: "Take the summer Shakespeare class," "Find the right residence hall for you," "Poets Society meets Tuesday and Thursdays in room 304." He leaves. He goes in and out of several more buildings, and he begins to grow frustrated. It'll take him all day to find the right building.

When he enters the seventh building, the walls show no sign of anything being displayed. He's about to leave, but something tells him to check around a little more thoroughly. He searches the lower floor offices, which are all just departmental offices, and heads to the second floor. It's then when he realizes he's in the right building. A student-made movie poster glints in the sun from the windows. The lights around the poster should be blinking, but despite the blackout, the golden frame surrounding the poster shines bright from the window opposite the wall. Akeno almost smiles.

He remembers the first time he took a girl on a date to the movies. He didn't even have a car, so she drove, and it was romantic. The two of them held hands during the movie, and she kissed him when she dropped him off at his house. He hasn't seen that girl since that day though. That same week, he was put back into the system and shipped off to another home. He frowns now. A lot of his memories are never always like this poster, half shining in the light but you know the lights all around it are broken.

He makes his way past the poster and tries each door. Each door had been manually locked with a standard key. He peers into the small window on each door, but every room looks just like any other classroom or lecture hall. There must be an equipment room somewhere, along with its key. When he reaches the end of the hall, he goes up another floor and peeks into all the locked doors again, until he comes across a door in the center of the hall. There isn't a window, and he can guess what this room might be. It has to be the equipment room.

He hurries back downstairs and finds the main office. It's locked too and eerily quiet. This door has a large window looking into the office. He notices how the desks look so ordinary. A moldy ham and cheese sandwich lies half eaten on the desk in metallic tin foil. There's an open can of soda and an empty bag of chips on the floor. The desk chairs are all pushed back except one. He looks around the short interior hallway. There's a fire extinguisher locked inside a glass case on the wall. With three layers of clothes on, he uses his elbow to break the thin glass to the extinguisher. He grips it with both hands, and with both eyes closed, he turns his head away and smashes the office window. There's a loud crack, but the glass doesn't break.

You're kidding, Akeno thinks.

He beats the glass over and over, each hit making a dull thud, until finally the sound of glass breaking rings in his ears. Large shards of glass rain down on his feet as his arms shake. He shakes off the glass and drops the extinguisher on the tiled floor. It resounds through the hallway as he steps through the mess. He reaches his arm through the sizable hole and unlocks the door. He pulls the glass out from his jacket sleeve and opens the office door.

He thinks someone must have heard all the noise he's made. He needs to hurry before anyone else shows up. He scatters the bits of papers and trash on one desk as he searches for a ring of keys. He imagines they would look like janitor keys--the kind with the large ring and several gold, silver, and brass keys hanging and clanging against the ring. He opens drawers, the ones that are unlocked. He looks under desks, in the bookshelves surrounding the room and even on top of the door frames. He starts to kick in the desk drawers, his frustration now com-

55

ing out full force with every swift kick. He didn't manage to break any of the drawers open, and after about fifteen minutes of searching, he takes a seat in one of the desk chairs and twirls around the room. He's sick of this. He wishes just something would go right for once. And he has to piss.

He stands and strides out of the room, his feet crunching again on glass. He makes his way back through the hall and heads to the nearest bathroom. He finds the women's room first, hesitates, and then rushes inside. The toilets here are actually clean, Akeno thinks, except the water has begun to mold on the inside of the toilet bowls. Once he relieves himself, he instinctively tries to flush and remembers it doesn't work. He goes to the sink and remembers it doesn't work either. He thinks he should invest in some hand sanitizer next. Just as he's about to leave, he takes note of the janitor's cart in the bathroom. His eyes light up as he searches through the cleaning supplies and hears the distinct sound of keys. He finds them hooked to the side of the cart and smiles at his good luck.

Akeno races back down the hall, his bag flopping by his side. When he reaches the third floor, he races back to the plain door in the center of the hall. He really hopes this isn't just a janitorial supply closet. He checks the lock and tries to match it with one of the keys, but he can't make any of the thirteen keys out to be the door's specific key. He sighs and begins trying every one of them. He's shaking now, partially from the anticipation and partially out of fear. He thinks someone must have heard all the glass breaking. What if someone finds him here completely unarmed with a full set of keys. He knows what he'll do. He'll throw the keys and run. It doesn't take a genius to run away.

Finally, on the eleventh try, the lock clicks open, and Akeno can't help but cry out in excitement. Inside the small and cramped room are many shelves, bins, and boxes. Akeno doesn't know much about technology, at least not anymore than anyone else, so he picks through the larger objects in hopes of finding anything that could be useful. It all looks like a mess of wires and black boxes to Akeno. Everything he touches looks outdated even, like all of it from the '90s. He's sure there's a newer radio lying around here somewhere as he picks up some of the older models for inspection. There's a few that look just like the one Dr. Jennings used, but he can't be sure. He's not even sure why he came here knowing nothing about radios. He should at least have an idea of what he's doing. After everything that's happened, Akeno needs to find a way out of here. He can't stay here all winter. There has to be more people like him out there, just someone looking for a place to stay and some food to eat.

"What are you doing here?" a voice booms from behind him.

Akeno drops the radio he's holding and turns on his heel. He half turns, half falls over himself as his heart rate picks up and his skin warms from the shot of adrenaline coursing through his body. Then he realizes who it is. In the doorway is the girl from before. She's wearing her backpack, but this time her hair is tied back. He sees sweat stains at her pits and beads of sweat on her forehead.

"Uh--I could ask you the same question," Akeno says, his voice wavering.

She raises her eyebrows. There's a short silence as she shifts from one foot to the other.

"What are you looking for?" she asks.

"Nothing," he says. "I mean--actually, I'm looking for a--a--radio."

"No shit," she says. "Do you even know what you're doing?"

Akeno doesn't say anything as she steps into the room.

"Move," she says. He steps out of her way and takes her spot at the doorway.

She opens and closes a few of the boxes, throws a few things around in one of the crates, and looks on the shelves and on the table. She doesn't seem to find what she's looking for and looks to him.

"What did you take?"

"I didn't take anything," he says.

"Then why are you here?"

"Same as you."

"You didn't answer my question."

"Neither did you."

She says nothing. "Fine. Have fun. There's nothing here anyway."

"Which type of radio were you looking for?"

She doesn't answer.

"Hey," he says. "Hey, hold on a minute. Hey, wait."

"What?" she says. She stops at the stairwell and turns around. "Why do you keep following me?"

"Why won't you just talk to me?"

"Why would I want to?"

Akeno doesn't reply. He shifts his weight and looks at her. She has freckles, he now notices in the sunlight coming from the window. Her hair isn't just brown either. It has a dark undertone to it, and her brown eyes have flecks of yellow in them.

"Don't follow me," she says and continues down the stairs.

He waits a few moments before he hears the door of the building slam shut. Akeno goes to the window and watches as she looks both ways before making her way back across campus. He watches until she's out of sight, as she heads for the other side of campus. There's only a couple of residence halls in that direction. She must be staying in one of them. He wonders if there are others there too. He thinks not. She seems like the type of person that likes to be alone. Besides, if there were others, she's never with any of them.

He goes back into the storage room and looks around. If she didn't find anything, he's doubtful he will either. Or maybe she was bluffing just so she could come back and get what's good later. He considers it for a moment before he closes the door behind him and leaves the door unlocked. If she wants to come back, then fine. She's welcome to anything he finds. Maybe she can figure out what's going on, and he can bum off any information she gathers.

He can't count on that though. He should visit the library and look up radio engineering. It would be a first step in the right direction. He can't keep waiting for someone to come save him. He thought he learned that lesson a long time ago, but there's always hope that he'll be wrong one day.

As heads down the stairs, he checks the time. His watch reads 5:32 p.m. He still has time before dark. He passes by several academic buildings, including the empty courtyard. All of the benches and tables intended for students now stand empty. The trash cans have been over-turned, probably by animals. Bits of paper blow in the wind, scattering the trash all across campus. The trees wave in the wind, but Akeno isn't sure who they're waving to. He feels unsettled. Something pricks up at the back of his neck. He still feels like he's being watched.

It only takes a few minutes before he reaches the library. Normally he would cross through the grass to avoid the heavy flow of human traffic on the sidewalks, but now he walks the concrete and tries not to step on the cracks like the rules state for that one kid's game. When he played as a kid, he used to step deliberately on all the cracks.

He averts his gaze from his feet to the library in front of him. The whole building is made of glass. It's the newest building on campus, so it looks a lot nicer than the rest of the buildings. The university spent millions on this project, but now it just stands sullenly in the middle of campus, the sun glaring off the windows so it blinds whoever looks at it. In front of the library is a fountain. It usually runs throughout the year, especially when it's warm outside and the students like to dip their feet in it. Now the pool's water rests stagnant, and it's filled with debris from the trees overhead float. The automatic doors to the library are closed, but it doesn't take much effort to pry them open. He sees the exit doors are cracked and wonders what it would feel like to be trapped inside a library. It's not the worst place to be trapped.

Once he's inside the library, a chill immediately shoots down his spine. The library is covered in shadow. Some of the window's blinds are cracked but not many. There's hardly any natural lighting in the room. On the left side is the check-out desk. To the right are the couches, chairs, tables, and blank-faced computers. A few of the chairs are overturned and papers are scattered everywhere. It looks like the students here left in a rush. Akeno picks up one of the papers and turns it over. It's a chemistry worksheet, and Akeno scoffs. He barely passed chemistry, and he doesn't regret it now. He wishes he took courses in communications rather than science.

When he looks around the room, he imagines what it used to look like before the blackout. Students would be piled in at the desks, their headphones in, their heads bent. Everyone would be ignoring each other, because during midterms, it's all about the grades, about their GPA, about the exam's curve every student hopes to receive. Akeno realizes none of the academic process prepares them for a nationwide shutdown.

He walks to one of the computers and presses a few keys on the keyboard. If the university center had a generator, could he take the computer there, start up the generator, and just search how to make a radio work? Or if that works, he could try contacting someone by email or through another online server. It's not a bad idea, but Akeno knows nothing about how generators work or anything about how to make a computer work without the convenience of the campus wifi.

He hates to admit it but remaining undecided his freshman year seemed like a smart move ten months ago, but now he's regretting every decision he's made. He wishes he had taken courses that would be useful to him now. He knows he shouldn't be so hard on himself, but he can't help but blame himself for being so ignorant. If only he had done more. The only solution now is to learn information the old fashion way. He needs to find the technology section, and hopefully there he can find several books on how to...

A noise breaks his concentration, and his ears perk up. It sounded like papers being rustled somewhere behind him. He waits and turns around. He scans the lobby and picks up an anatomy textbook sitting beside the computer. Holding it at the ready, he tiptoes behind one of the desks and peers around it. He doesn't see anyone immediately, but he knows there's someone there. He feels his blood go cold. He knows he isn't being paranoid, not this time at least. He heard someone. Someone's following him. They want to steal his supplies, kill him, eat him, or worse. He doesn't have the time to imagine worse. He edges around the desk and looks to the right side of the room, then the left. Nobody there.

He straightens his shoulders and looks around with his head held high. If he meets anyone's eye, he wants them to see him in a position of power. He remembers the way the girl looked at him and how he felt smaller when her brown eyes connected with his. He's determined to make his attacker feel the same way.

"Who's there?" he calls out. He regrets it immediately, but it's better to be blunt. He wants them to know he knows they're there. He waits. "Come out, and I promise not to hurt you. I know you're there."

The room is still. He lowers the textbook.

"Fine, but if you choose to come out when my back is turned, I won't hesitate to break your fucking neck."

He doesn't know the first thing about hand-to-hand combat, but he trusts the sound of his threat and all the Asian stereotypes that protect him. Akeno swallows and exhales slowly. Remain calm, he tells himself. Just walk straight out the door. Act like you found what you were looking for. Act like you know what you're doing. He pulls his bag tighter around his shoulder and heads straight for the door, his eyes scanning the room. He slips through the crack in the exit doors and walks faster as he heads away from the building. He doesn't bother to use the sidewalks this time and doesn't glance behind his shoulder until he's past the few trees that block the library's view of him. Once he's sure he's not being watched or followed, he makes a dead sprint back to his room.

CHAPTER 6

He dreams of thick, gray clouds forming in the sky above tall trees. He doesn't know where he is, but he's alone. He knows he needs to find shelter soon before the skies open up into a torrent. As he's looking for a cave along a cliff, he finds a bear's den. The bear is asleep, and underneath it lies what looks like an indigenous woman. She's brown-skinned with long, black hair, not unlike Akeno himself. She stares up at him, her breathing still but noticeably still alive. When Akeno steps forward to help the woman, she puts her fingers to her lips and points to the bear. She shakes her head and motions for Akeno to leave. He backs away from the cave, the bear still lying on top of her thin frame. She begins to cry, but she continues to wave Akeno away, to save himself before the bear wakes up. Akeno turns and runs, and suddenly he falls off the cliff and wakes up from his nightmare.

He is drenched in sweat when he jumps awake in bed. His whole body is shaking, and he looks around, only to realize where he is and that he's safe. He leans his head back against his pillow and closes his eyes, the pleading face of the Indigenous woman still ingrained in his mind. Who was he?

With a heavy push against the bed, he slides off the thin sheets and goes to the sink. He looks in the mirror, his thin fingers gripping the edge of the sink until his knuckles match its white color. He looks into his own eyes, the color of obsidian. He had always wished his eyes were at least brown like so many others. At least that way he could pass as normal, but instead the black of his pupils matched the black of his irises, and it's no wonder why people felt so uncomfortable around him.

His stomach growls at him, and he wishes he could soothe the pain he feels, but for now, his diet will continue as is until he can find a decent grocery store that isn't guarded by gunmen. He takes a bottle of water from under his bed, where he stores the rest of his supplies. He chugs it all in just a few seconds and takes up a second bottle. The least he can do is stay hydrated if not well fed. In his bag he finds the last can of Vienna Sausages and eats one before setting the can aside. He feels like he might vomit, though what he could throw up is essentially just water and bile. He lays back against the bed and looks out his window.

There must be someone out there who can help him. While he doesn't see the girl as a threat to his safety, he counts her as a rival rather than a friend. They both need food and water, and the only supplies available to them are from the same supply. Whatever they each find is theirs, and that only reduces the number of supplies the other can have. Akeno remembers his dream. Unlike the bear and the Indigenous woman, the girl and Akeno are the same species, which means they should be on an equal playing field, but he knows that's not his reality. He bets the girl could probably waltz right by those armed soldiers at Publix, take whatever she wants, and leave without a bat of an eye. He, on the other hand, well, he turned and left before he could convince himself to make an attempt at diplomacy with those men.

An hour later, Akeno shuts his eyes and falls back asleep. He has another dream. He's walking along a river, his feet bare, and his back shirtless. His hair is down, and his feet are careful to step along the rocks leading down the bank. He knows where the snakes tend to hide, where the crawdads like to pinch toes, and he knows exactly where he is in the forest he finds himself. As he peers into the river, he notices his face for the first time. It's not brown this time, but it's white, and he has blue eyes instead of black. Then he gasps when he sees his hair. It's not black, but rather, it's short and blonde. He feels at his face, and he can feel the high cheekbones and angular jawline he used to wish for as an angsty, self-resenting teenager.

He backs away from the river's edge and heads deeper into the woods. Suddenly there's an echoing boom and a rumbling. It sounds like thunder, but it grows steadily louder, as if the storm is following right behind him. He breaks into a run, but the sound seems like it's coming closer and closer...

His eyes snap wide open to a rumbling sound just outside his window. He wipes the sleep from his eyes and leans over his bed to peek out of the blinds he keeps shut. He sees a black mass pressing its way through the streets. He rubs at his eyes again so his vision can adjust to the dark, only to notice the black mass has lights, headlights actually. Who's come to save them? That's his first thought, but something in the pit of his stomach drops down to his waist and settles in a knot of fear and anxiety. He's not sure where the feeling originates, but his gut instinct immediately tells him to run far and fast away from the lights.

Without a second thought, he jumps down from his bed and feels the cold and dusty tiles beneath his feet quiver beneath him. The whole room feels unsteady as he packs everything he has in his bag— food, clothes, a blanket, matches, and other odds and ends. He pulls on a heavier coat over his hoodie and throws his bag over his shoulder. He pulls on his tennis shoes and breaks for the door. He slips on the edges of the steps outside the dorm in his haste to make a break across campus. He can't see anything in front of him except for what the moon shows. All he sees are shadows and the sidewalk beneath his feet.

As he's running, the tremors from the street only force Akeno to run faster. He feels like he's in a real-life nightmare, the ones where no matter how hard he runs, he only feels more out of breath. He can feel his lungs aching and his breath catching at his throat when he starts seeing spots in his eyes. The adrenaline isn't enough to keep him awake, or it's the shock of seeing a militia plowing down the streets that makes him lightheaded. Akeno glances over his shoulder only to see gaping darkness behind him. Somehow this sight makes his heartbeat faster as he picks up the pace. He's not sure where he's going, only that he's running away from the road and the lights and the military waiting for him at the bottom of the hill.

Just as he rounds a corner of a building, he recognizes the field before him as the courtyard. He runs straight through the grass and past one building. He rounds the corner of another building when he suddenly collides into someone else. He can feel their limbs grab hold of him and swing him toward the wall. He feels a small hand gripping at his arm, and he looks up to see a hooded figure staring straight at him. As if by instinct, Akeno kicks out and the other person cries out in pain. It's a girl's voice.

He escapes her grasp and backs away from the other figure silhouetted just faintly against the background of the building. Akeno can just make out a smaller, more feminine figure. He sees a ponytail and a hulking backpack.

"Wait, you're--"

"Shut up," she says, rushing to place a hand over his mouth. Headlights grow against the building next to them. "They're headed this way. Come on."

She grabs the front of his shirt and pulls him after her. Her feet barely make any sound as she pads through the grass and Akeno stumbles clumsily behind her.

"Where are we--"

"Shut up."

She leads him around another building and under an awning where an emergency exit door leads up a flight of stairs. This must be where she lives, Akeno thinks. It's one of the nicer apartment style dorms on campus.

"Where are we going?" Akeno asks. "We need to get out of here."

She doesn't respond. She only rushes faster up the stairs with Akeno trailing behind her.

"Hey, look, I think we need to leave campus. They'll just search the buildings, and then they'll--"

"Stop talking," she snaps at him. "I'll explain in a minute."

She pushes through another door that leads to the roof of the building. She runs to the edge and kneels down. Akeno follows, and she yanks him down, then points at the building across from them. It's hard to make out, but now that Akeno has had time for his eyes to adjust to the dark, he can see the campus laid out before them in dark angles. The headlights he saw earlier roll up to the same building Akeno was living in. In the silence of the night, he can hear people beat down the doors to his dorm as they enter inside. The same happens to all the other buildings. Beyond the foot soldiers, other vehicles with headlights park alongside the first, and Akeno realizes the massive vehicle he saw was a tank.

The girl exhales, and he thinks she must be evaluating her options. She knows the campus more intimately than he does, that much is clear. His best bet of getting off campus would be to follow her. He knows the campus is surrounded by a patch of woods, several neighborhoods, and the main street. Akeno isn't sure which would be the safest option or what other threats lie ahead. All of them contain threats, but which contained the least amount of danger?

"There are some neighborhoods that look deserted, but--" Akeno whispers to the girl.

"I know a place," she says. "Listen, you have to follow me, and you can't say anything. If they hear us and come after us with dogs, we're as good as dead. Do you understand?"

Akeno can't think of anything else to do but nod. Then she grabs his hand, and they make a break down the stairs and quietly slip out the side door. They run across the grass, then pavement, then grass, then more pavement until they reach a spot where they pause. The moon's just barely shining down now from the clouds that cast wavering shadows on the ground. They must have reached the woods close to campus, but why have they stopped?

"Shit," she mumbles under her breath.

They both nearly stop breathing to listen to the sound of breaking glass and loud footsteps that pervades campus.

"They're searching the place," Akeno says.

"I know."

Neither of them moves, and he imagines it's because both of them want to run, but at the same time, they want to stay too. Maybe being found wouldn't be such a bad thing. It's what they've wanted all along right? It's been several weeks, and Akeno still hasn't received any more answers than the day of the blackout. Now would be the time to ask. Now what would be the time to ask for food, water, and shelter.

"Where should we go?" Akeno asks. It's an open-ended question. He'd rather not decide. Besides, he can't imagine he'd make it very far without her, especially since she's leading the way. He's still not sure where he is. He holds his breath waiting for her answer.

"Maybe we should make camp," she suggests.

He nods, his exhale coming out in one long breath. He checks down at his watch. The one he's wearing doesn't glow, so he pulls open his bag. He can see the one that glows like a beacon in a storm. Akeno pulls it out and holds it up between them.

"It's 11:48 p.m. Almost midnight," he says. "Do you think they're going to search the whole campus tonight?"

"I would if I were taking prisoners."

"If it's the military, then I don't think they're taking anyone hostage."

"Then why come at night? Wouldn't it be better if they had come during the day? We don't even know if they're Americans. It could be anyone. That could be the cause of all of this."

"It's unlikely this is a war-related event, but--"

"Do you trust them?" she cuts him off. She sounds affronted, as if she might just leave him there if she thinks he does side with them.

"No," he says plainly. "I don't."

"Then let's keep moving. There's a neighborhood just over this ridge."

They don't speak for the rest of the hike uphill from the university. Every now and again, Akeno turns to see if anyone's following them. His bag bangs against his side and pulls against his shoulder. The girl looks back at his bag and raises her eyebrow.

"What's in the purse?" she asks.

"Some supplies," he says.

"Like what?"

"Clothes and the rest. Does it matter?"

"It's just making a lot of noise," she says and pauses. "I could put your stuff in my bag."

Akeno notices the size of her backpack. He's surprised it doesn't

69

weigh her down, considering how packed it is. Does she think he's stupid? She'll just take his stuff and run. Then again, he packed more clothes than his bag could carry. The girl pauses and kneels down next to Akeno. She unzips her bag and extends her hand.

"Don't worry, I'm not going to take your food," she says. "If I wanted to rob you, I'd have done it already."

He shrugs. She makes a point.

"So what's your name?" Akeno asks as he unpacks his bag.

"Sam," she says. "Yours?" She takes the hygiene products and the food and stows it all away in different pockets.

"Akeno. Is 'Sam' short for something?"

"No," she says and zips up her backpack. "Let's keep moving." She stands and leads the way forward.

All right, Akeno thinks. Probably for the best anyway.

When they finally reach the ridge, Akeno hides his labored breathing and places his hands on his hips. He joins the girl standing at the edge, where she looks down over a neighborhood of dark houses. Some of the homes have a glimmering swimming pool in the backyard. As a kid, he had always wanted a home with a swimming pool, but now it seems superfluous, almost as if those who had one had to announce how much money they had.

"Do you think anyone's on guard there?" she asks.

"Probably." He remembers the sentries on duty outside the grocery store. "Do you think they'll have guns?"

"Not here," she said.

Akeno thinks they do but doesn't have a chance to speak up when Sam suddenly slides down the ridge with careful and deliberate steps. Akeno hesitates at the top before sighing and moving along after her. When they hit the grass at the bottom of the ridge, they make a break for the high wooden fence that separates them from the homes.

"Give me a lift," she says.

"What if they have a dog?"

"It would've barked at us by now. Give me a hand."

"How am I going to get in?"

"Trust me."

"This isn't a good idea."

"If there's anywhere the militia won't be searching, it's behind this fence. Trust me."

He doesn't trust her, not exactly anyway, but if she does have any intention of leaving him behind, she wouldn't have brought him with her. Why did she bring him with her? He suspects she sees him as a threat, as someone who could have given away her position on campus. She could see him as a prop, as she does now. He supposes if she leaves him here on the other side of the fence, that isn't the worst way she could abandon him. He'll simply turn around and head back for the woods, where he'll find a tree to hide in until dawn. Then he can reassess where he is and make his choice of action from there.

He bends low and locks his fingers together. In the waning light of the moon, he thinks he can make out a smile on her face. She steps into his hands, and with one swift movement, he brings her up high to the top of the fence. She grips the edge of the fence and seems almost surprised when she glances back down at him. He thinks she's as light as she looks. He holds her propped up at his neck as she swings one leg, then the other, over the fence and jumps down. Akeno waits a moment. His legs ache from the hike, and he knows lifting her will cause him some pain later. He doesn't remember the last time he's worked out. He shakes out his limbs and waits for Sam.

For a second he thinks she must have left him. It would be easier for her to slip unnoticed through the streets with only herself to worry about. She didn't pack for two, but one. Now she has enough food for two, and she could easily find an abandoned house to lock herself in for the night. She could probably...

Something flies over the fence and lands with a soft thud. It's a rope. He takes the rope in one hand and pulls. The rope tightens. She must have tied it down to something on the other side. With two hands, he grabs the rope and walks himself up the fence. He mimics her same movements when she climbed: throws his legs over the side, then the other, and jumps. He lands on the grass, breaking his fall to a soft thud, the rope falling silently behind him. In front of him, Sam unties the rope from the side of the house. What she's tied it on, he can't see. He wraps the rope up without any wasted time and stashes it back in her bag. She gestures for him to follow.

They move a few houses down, crossing each backyard with ease. There isn't any fencing between the homes, only the one large fence separating the outside from within. In several backyards are treehouses, swing sets, kiddie pools, and forgotten toys. He can't imagine being a child and going through any of this.

Akeno can't help but notice the unlit streetlamps lingering above the houses, as if they might just bend down and snatch anyone from the street in the night's cover. He used to be afraid of the dark. He remembers a man's booming voice from his childhood, one whose name he chooses to forget, and hears, "Men aren't afraid of the dark." The memories that follow are ones he turns away.

Sam stops at the corner of a house and puts a hand out to stop Akeno.

"I think there might be a man over there," she whispers. She points to the street corner.

Akeno squints through the darkness and just makes out a figure by a mailbox. There's what looks like a stop sign next to a bus sign. There's also an empty bench. The man patrolling the corner has something in his hand, and Akeno knows it's a gun. He can feel his heart beating. If they're seen or caught, it's over for them.

"Let's go back the other way," she whispers, barely audible.

They turn back and make for the other side of the house when a man appears at the other corner. He's just a black silhouette from a distance. Suddenly there's a flash of light, and the two of them are blinded by a bright white light.

"Over here!" the man yells, pointing at them with the flashlight.

Footsteps beat against pavement, and flashlights start clicking on all across the neighborhood, sending huge beams of light into the sky like signals. Akeno considers the militia on campus and wonders if they can see the lights from there. If they notice the lights, will they come looking around the neighborhood? Undoubtedly these people will turn them in as criminals, as potential thieves, rapists, plunderers, kidnappers, or murderers.

"This way!" the girl shouts and grabs Akeno's sleeve. She runs back to the side of the house they were just on and breaks across the space that reveals them to the streets. The man that was standing by the mailbox runs their way and chases after the two of them as they push through gates and fences. Akeno hears more footsteps approaching from the sides of the house. Flashlights inside houses flicker on and shine out the windows. This was a more effective way of seeing who's inside, Akeno thinks, not that it's much help now.

Sam makes a break for the street, and Akeno follows. She's faster than him though. Her feet hit pavement before he reached the end of the yard. Just as he passes the front doors of two homes, a body collides with his, and the two hit the ground. Something crunches underneath them, and Akeno thinks he's broken something. That's it for him, he thinks. It's over.

"No!" he hears the girl yell. "Let go of me!"

Akeno tries to stand up, but the body on top of him buries their knee in Akeno's back, forcing his face against the ground. The same person grabs his arms and yanks them back, ties his hands with a zip tie, and presses him harder against the ground.

"Tie her!" a man yells from a distance. "Bring them here."

The person on Akeno yanks him up and shoves him forward. "Don't run, or I'll shoot," a man's voice says in his ear. Akeno nods to affirm his understanding and walks. Several bodies now collect together under the flashlights' glow. Most of them are men, though there are some armed women. Sam walks sullenly forward, her hands tied behind her back. Someone already has her backpack and shuffles through it. Akeno wonders what will happen to them, what they'll do now that they've been captured. They didn't have much except what was in their bags. Best case scenario: Their captors take all they have and force them to leave. Akeno doesn't want to think of the worst case scenarios. They're too many to number.

The group leads Akeno and Sam to a house one block over with flashlights illuminating the whole street like a landing strip. It's in the middle of a row of other houses that look more or less of the same design. Large windows peek out from both stories, and Akeno can make out a few faces peering down at them until a larger shadow closes the curtains. Akeno thinks there must be children in the house, not exactly a great place to bring two hostages.

Two men by the front door rap three times and another man opens it. The group leads Sam inside first, then Akeno. The two of them step

74

into a nicely decorated foyer with fake fruit lying in a bowl on a side table and a picture of a family on the wall. An intricate fake, crystal chandelier hangs above the staircase. Akeno looks down and sees he's standing on a dark green runner that muffles his footsteps. In the beam of the flashlights, Akeno can make out the floating dust circling through the air. The house needs to be cleaned. Despite its size, the house feels more quaint than grandeur.

"Sit them in here," a man says from the other room.

Akeno and Sam are pushed into the next room, where a man stands facing a dimly lit, gas fireplace that casts shadows all around the big, empty room.

"Please, have a seat," the man says, not bothering to face them directly. He's holding a glass of whiskey, Akeno thinks. No ice.

They take a seat on the edge of the couch, where they sit tied and restless as the bodies fill the room and surround them. Once everyone's filed in, two stand by the partition doors, now closed, and Akeno can barely make out the shuffling footsteps of another man in the corner of the room behind him.

"Are you going to tell me why you're breaking into my neighborhood?" the man asks and finishes his drink. The man half turns, expecting an answer.

Akeno takes note of the man's profile. He has a sharp nose and an angular face, though Akeno thinks if the lights were brighter, he could see the bags under the man's eyes, along with the wrinkles on his temple, and the tired, downward expression of his lips. He wears a button-up, as if it wasn't in the middle night, as if maybe he had just left a nice dinner. It seems this man views the power outage as a matter of inconvenience rather than a dark national mystery.

"Do you even know where you are?" he says, now turning to fully face them, though his face softens, as if intimating a warm, fatherly expression. "Welcome to Oak Hills. Sorry for the cuffs. I didn't realize you'd be kids," he says. He leans against the fireplace and places his head in his palms. "We didn't know *who* we'd be dealing with when one of our watches spotted you climbing down the ridge. You wouldn't believe the people who have tried coming in here to disturb our peace."

"Who are you?" Sam demands suddenly. Akeno's eyes widen as he shrinks away from the booming of her voice. "What do you want?"

"You may call me Mr. Callahan," the man says. "We can skip the formalities, since we just have a few questions for you"

"If it's just a few questions, why not untie us?"

He shrugs. "You know we can't do that. It's just a precaution."

"That's not our motive," she says. "We were just trying to find a place to sleep. A group of people raided campus tonight, breaking down doors and invading the place. We had to run."

Akeno knows she's considering whether to tell them it was the military that raided campus. She must think they'll turn them in just as Akeno bets they would.

"I'm glad to hear you're safe," Callahan says. "I'm sure you wouldn't mind telling us what you two wanted from our neighborhood specifically?"

"Just shelter," she repeats.

"Isn't there other housing off campus, though? You know, the smaller homes where all the parties are held. I'm sure a pretty girl like you has been to a few parties on that side of town."

Sam pauses, her expression blank.

"Everything's locked up," she says, though he knows it must be a lie.

"And what about you?" Callahan asks Akeno, his eyebrows raised. "Are you two together or something?"

"Uh, no, we're not together. I mean we're friends. We're both students at Mountain State, so…yeah."

"Why didn't you two just go home?" Callahan asks with a gesture of his hands. "I mean, two kids like you must have family close by, someone to do your laundry on the weekends and give you a proper home-cooked meal."

"I guess not everyone has as great a home as this to go to," Sam says with a tilt in her tone. The man cocks his head as he tries to read her meaning, but she just smiles.

"Is that true?" Callahan asks Akeno, his eyes boring into his for the truth. Akeno doesn't know anything about Sam's family, but he can speak on his own.

"I'm an orphan," Akeno says, keeping eye contact with Callahan. From the corner of his eye, Akeno can make out the slight shift in weight where Sam flinched from the news.

Callahan nods, though Akeno can tell he's hesitant to believe anything they've said.

" So, you don't have a place to stay, and for the past forty-three days, you two have been staying in a dorm room?" Callahan chuckles. "That's a lousy situation to be in."

Suddenly Callahan's tone changes, and Akeno can feel the tension in the room. He chances a glance at the men by the door, who shift uncomfortably where they stand.

"We weren't sure who had stayed in their homes since most people left the city," Sam says, now taking a different approach. "We didn't think anyone would be living here, especially not any families." She's using a softer voice now, a more delicate and feminine approach.

Callahan doesn't seem the type to warrant violence without cause, but even he can recognize that voice of pleading innocence.

"You're mistaken if you thought any of us left our homes," he says with finality. "Our neighborhood issues door-to-door house calls to ensure the safety of our residents, and we've all chosen to stay together as one." Callahan smiles. "I see your reasoning, though. Not everyone has neighbors they consider to be family. Not everyone is as compliant."

Callahan emphasized the word "compliant," leaving Akeno with an unsettling feeling in the pit of his stomach. A shiver runs up Akeno's spine and down through his fingers. He feels his fight or flight instincts kick in. They have no idea what they're getting themselves into, but whatever it is, they need to get out. Now.

"Thank you for your cooperation. But for the time being, we're going to keep you with us, at least until morning," Callahan says.

"Are you fuc—"

Callahan raises his hand for silence as Sam finishes her sentence.

"We need to confer and consider your stories, which by all means seems reasonable," Callahan assures with a false air on confidence. "But we've had others who we mistakenly believed to be allies, and they eventually turned on us. You must understand. Please," he says, gesturing to a man on the other side of the room. "Would you lead these two to their room downstairs? They should find comfort in resting for the evening."

The man steps forward and takes grip of Akeno's and Sam's arms to hoist them off the couch.

"You can't do this! You can't keep us here!" Sam shouts. She resists by sliding onto the floor, but the man simply bends down and grips Sam's arm harder until she cries out, "Where's your wife and kids, huh? Where's your family? I hope they can hear me! I hope they're wide awake and listening in to what kind of monster you really are!"

There's a swift movement and a loud crack. Sam's head turns to the side from the impact. Akeno can make out a little stream of blood coming out of her nose. Sam only smiles. She turns and spits the blood in her mouth onto Callahan's face. "Fuck you," she says.

Callahan pulls a white cloth from his pocket and wipes the blood from his face with a solemn grin. "Get them out of here," he says.

The man drags Akeno and Sam back through the foyer and into a short hall, the cold threat of a gun now at their backs. At the end of the hall is a laundry machine and a dryer with an empty basket resting on top. There's another room off to the side of that, but they don't get that far. A man opens a door, grabs Akeno's wrists, and cuts the zip. Akeno flexes his wrists as blood rushes through his veins to the tips of his fingers. He shoves Akeno to take the first step. With Akeno leading them down a flight of stairs, he catches sight of a few others already in the basement, five in fact. He pauses on the stairway as all eyes focus on him. There's a couple camping lanterns on the floor, their dim flames exposing the faces among the shadows of what looks like beds. They're lying on spare mattresses that were once white and comfortable. Now they are dirtied and strained, some with what looks like dried blood and piss. They must have heard the commotion upstairs.

"You'll be waiting here until further notice," the man says from the top of the stairs and slams the door. A latch clicks at the top, but the footsteps don't recede. Akeno notes they have someone standing guard at all times of the night. He knows Sam figures the same as she turns from the door and looks to Akeno with a glimpse of worry.

Akeno and Sam face the room. They all raise up from their mattresses, their eyes glaring at the two newcomers. There are no shelves or storage items in the basement, no spare appliances or holiday decorations packed in boxes like most homes have crammed into their storage room. In the cramped quarters of the basement, Akeno notices the odd pathway made from mattresses. If Akeno walked the aisle, in just a few steps, Akeno would be standing directly in front of the back wall, where a large man sits upright like the basement sultan. His legs are crossed beneath him, and his face remains expressionless, though a little curious. He has one of the lights closest to himself. The man's massive size intimidates Akeno more from height than from build. In fact, everyone looks a little skinny, Akeno notices, himself included. A woman lying next to him sits up, though remains on her mattress with a thin blanket covering half her body, her face gaunt and angled in the light.

"Who are you?" the man asks nobody in particular. "Why are you here?"

Sam doesn't answer right away, her eyes on the man across the room and the on the woman next to him.

"Uh, my name's Lee," Akeno says with some hesitation. He doesn't know why he lies, but somehow it felt right to lie in this situation, just in case. "And uh, this is my friend--"

"Sam," she finishes. At first he's surprised that she gives her real name, but for some reason he doesn't think that's her real name after all. It wouldn't bother him any if she gave him a fake name in the beginning. Probably for the best anyway. "I speak for myself." She gives a side glance to Akeno and steps down so she's on the same step as Akeno. "And you are?"

"You can call me Jay," he says, a little gruffly. "What did you do for them to bring you here? What did they say?"

"We hopped the fence just looking for a place to crash," Sam says. "We didn't realize there would be men with guns here, not really the type, don't you think?"

Jay gives a small grunt of laughter. "We didn't either. They confiscated our guns, and I wouldn't be surprised if they're using them now."

"Nine millimeter?" Sam asks.

The man grins and nods. He crosses his arms, baring two full sleeves of tattoos. The woman on the bed sits up straighter and smiles, to which Akeno notices she's missing a tooth on the bottom row. Blood stains her teeth, and he wonders if she lost it in a fight with the soldiers upstairs. She looks just as intimidating as the man with her, but for what reason, Akeno can't pinpoint. There's something about that careless grin that puts Akeno on edge.

"When we got here, they had a few hunting rifles, all pointed down at us from the windows of the houses. Seems they're adding to their artillery," Jay says.

"I doubt they know how to use any of them," Sam says with a snort and takes a seat on one of the mattresses closest to the stairs. Akeno follows, watching as Sam gets comfortable. He takes a seat next to her, since there doesn't seem to be any other mattresses. She gives her a hard glare, and he moves himself so he's sitting against the front wall facing the staircase.

"Bastards," Jay mutters. "You got a cig?"

"I wish," Sam says with a roll of her eyes. "A joint would be good too."

The room erupts in laughter, and the guard upstairs bangs heavily on the door. The room quiets with a lingering smile. Akeno notices the change in attitude from the room, the change in voice and tone from what Sam used upstairs to the person she is downstairs. She knows how to work a room, and Akeno wonders if she chooses her attitude based on what she thinks will work. Does she put on the same facade for Akeno?

"Now they did leave us that," he says with a chuckle. "But then they wouldn't give us a lighter."

"Bastards," Sam says.

The room laughs again, and the guard bangs on the door again.

"If you don't care to share, what brought you here?" Sam asks, leaning on her elbows.

She looks so comfortable, Akeno thinks. He pulls his knees to his chest and watches her carry on conversation like these people are old friends. She reminds him of someone he used to know a long time ago, but now he can't remember who that was. She's someone Akeno can imagine being friends with in high school, if he ever stayed long enough to make friends. She's someone people feel comfortable with, even if they're just listening.

Jay turns to the woman next to him and grins. "Ah, well, the usual-looting, partying, drinking up the rest of some guy's liquor cabinet. We didn't even know people were still living in this neighborhood. We thought, even if they were, I didn't think they would've done anything. I mean it's the fucking apocalypse these days, so we find a house, empty of course, and these people come knocking on our doors dead of night, haul us outside, and we're surrounded."

"Numbnuts up there told us we were unwelcome," the woman says with a snicker. "He said 'unwelcome.'"

"Yeah, it was something simple, but they took it to heart," Jay says. "Said they needed to take us back here and locked us up."

"How long have you guys been here? Is this your whole crew?" Sam asks.

"No, it's just me and Amy and Mike," the man says, gesturing to the woman and then to another man on one of the mattresses closest to the woman. He had already laid back down, his eyes closed. "We've been here a few days. Mike's still sobering up."

Akeno knows that look on Mike's face. It wasn't just alcohol they were partying with. Akeno looks to the other two people in the room, another man and woman. They look like they're together.

"Who are you guys?" Sam asks the other two, nodding in their direction.

"Doesn't matter," the man grunts.

"Well it matters if we're all down here together," Sam says, annoyed. "Why, you don't trust us with your names?"

"I don't trust anyone I meet in a basement," the man says.

Akeno notices the lilt of an accent. The lighting in the basement isn't bright, but Akeno could make out the couple's dark features, brown skin. They sound Hispanic, and Akeno wonders what the people upstairs thought of them when they were caught.

"What'd they get you for?" Akeno asks quietly.

"We didn't do nothing," the man says. "They find us outside the fence and bring us in. We weren't breaking in. We are not criminals."

"So why were you loitering outside the fence? Sam asks, cocking her head to one side, as if she's bored.

"Looking for our daughter," he says, pulling his wife closer. "She don't come home. We thought we could look for her here. Sometimes she comes to see a boy."

"Did you ask for the boy when they found you?" Sam asks.

The man shakes his head. "They don't listen."

"So why are they keeping you here? How long have you been here?" The man shrugs. "Maybe a week."

"They were here when we got here," Jay says.

There's a dull silence in the room. The Hispanic woman begins to softly cry, and her husband consoles her. Jay and Amy watch the couple hold each other with a look of mild sympathy. Mike snorts in his sleep.

"Well we're getting out tonight," Sam says with finality. She sits up and brushes off her hands, now caked in dust from where she was leaning on the mattress. "There's no reason for any of us to be here. We'll just explain we're all leaving together and won't be back."

"We've tried," Jay says, quietly. "They're not letting us go."

"Let me try," Sam says. "Trust me."

CHAPTER 7

Akeno and Sam sleep for a few hours before the basement door finally opens, where light floods in from the top of the stairs, and the guard comes halfway down the steps, carrying food on a tray--several slices of bread and a spoonful of butter on each slice, though not a lot. The man hands out the bread, and Akeno wonders where they get their supply of food. Do they have a nearby grocery store that they taper off for their neighborhood? He recalls the militia guarding the Publix on the other side of town. He wonders if Callahan has a deal with them.

"The two of you are wanted upstairs," the guard barks. He points to Akeno and Sam, and then back behind his shoulder with one thumb. He reminds Akeno of a youth league coach, baseball more likely.

Akeno picks out his one slice of bread and hands the tray to the others. The bread's stale. He scarfs it down. The others do the same, none in complaint. The guard snatches back the tray after it's been passed back to Akeno.

"Let's go," he says at the top of the stairs.

Akeno and Sam step gingerly into the hall, where they're flanked by someone behind and in front of them. They're headed down the hall. As they approach the foyer, Akeno sees sunlight streaming across the golden-brown floors. When they reach the foyer, Akeno takes in the space around them. Now that there's some light to see by, Akeno notices the staircase going upstairs has a small landing, where a white banister is decorated with garland and mistletoe. In the corner of another room sits a skinny Charlie Brown Christmas tree sparkling with different colored lights. He hears something from upstairs and spins around to see the small hands of a child gripping the bars of the banister, looking almost sad.

Once the two are seated back on the couch by the fireplace, Akeno chances a look around the room. The room's exceptionally empty. There aren't any photos or remnants of personality left on the walls. Akeno can make out where pictures and other personal effects were once hanging by the tiny holes marked along the plain, gray walls. The fireplace is on like it was last night, and Akeno feels himself relaxing in the warmth of the room. The fireplace mantel has been cleared of any personal items, except a small, wooden box. The only sound is the ticking clock in the room. It almost sounds like a countdown, as if at any moment a bomb will set off and bury the house. Nobody else is in the room with them.

Two doors open wide, and Akeno jumps at the sound of Callahan striding into the room. He wears a different outfit from last night, and Akeno wonders who does his laundry. Who irons his shirts? He wonders if the neighborhood takes care of that for him.

"Sorry to keep you waiting," Callahan booms, closing the doors behind him. "We've just had breakfast, and that mimosa hit harder than I thought."

He's in a chipper mood, Akeno thinks.

"I hope you both don't mind the breakfast we served. The bread was stale, but I'm sure you haven't had that in a while, have you?"

Akeno sits quietly, his eyes on the rug. Sam's chin is tilted up, but he can't see what she's looking at or where.

"We've spent plenty of time discussing you, your stories, your prospects. We think you must be telling us some truth, but not all of it," Callahan says, his feet now pacing the floor in front of them. "We thought about what strengths you possess, about your character, your morality. Then we thought you might be godless atheists. Colleges convert people, you know, and the Lord says we must turn lost sheep in the direction they need to go. We thought what use you could be to the world at large if--"

"What does that have to do with letting us go?" Akeno snaps and then suddenly blanches.

"It all matters," Callahan says tersely. "I don't appreciate being interrupted. Don't do it again." He eyes Akeno but quickly turns away. "As I was saying..."

Sam nudges Akeno in the side and gestures to the door. He takes a deep breath and sits back from the edge of the couch.

"As I was saying," Callahan continues. "After much deliberation, we've come to a decision. You," he points to Sam. "May take your leave, but I know you don't have anywhere to go. You can stay here under our guidance and protection in exchange for your service. You can help the other women with their chores. We'll arrange a room for you, where you can live with privacy. The choice is yours."

He eyes Sam without taking a moment to glance at Akeno. Sam looks baffled, her eyes wide as fumbles for an answer. Akeno doesn't think she's ever stuttered before. She must not have seen this coming. With nowhere to go, this would be a good place to stay in for a while, especially for her. He thinks about how she doesn't have a good family, how this could be a chance for a community. The houses, the streets, the food, the kids. It's all right here. Akeno saw this coming, expected it even.

"What about Akeno?" Sam asks, and Akeno snaps to attention.

"He will stay here, but not with us. He'll be moved elsewhere, where he'll be working to serve his time."

"Serving time?" Sam demands. She slides to the edge of the couch, but something in the man's gaze tells her to stay seated. "So like what? You got any plantations around here in this tiny ass suburb, huh? Or downstairs in the basement making your clothes like a sweatshop? Is that what you mean?"

"He will wherever he is helpful," Callahan states calmly, his jaw clenching. "He'll be staying with the others. This blackout means our numbers need to stay together. We need to resume a functioning society, one that works--"

"Yeah, where everyone else works while you sit here and operate your own slave trade?"

"You disrespectful bitch," Callahan spits. "I give you the opportunity to live here with us, where you'll be well-fed and well cared for, but you just run your mouth. You haven't known what discipline is, and that's too bad. We'll be forced to discipline you ourselves."

He swings back his hand but stops, his eyes darting to the double doors. Sam doesn't flinch. She only smirks as voices echo from the basement, and Akeno hears several feet running to the stairs. There's a brief silence, and they all go still.

"What's going on?" Callahan demands and goes to the door, just as footsteps are heard from the other side. The door swings wide, smashing Callahan's face on the edge of the door. He reels back as Jay and Amy storm into the room with two of the guard's guns. Akeno and Sam jump from the couch, Sam's grin wider than Akeno's ever seen it.

"Let's go!" Jay shouts and turns to punch one of the men running into the room.

Callahan pushes himself against the wall, his nose running with blood. He leaves bloody streaks against the wall and makes for the fireplace. He's going for the wooden box. Akeno moves faster and reaches the mantelpiece before he does. Callahan pushes Akeno, and the box falls from Akeno's hands and clatters to the floor. A gun slides across the hardwood floor and into the corner of the room. Sam makes a break for the gun as Callahan pushes himself from the floor, stepping on Akeno's hand as he does.

Akeno cries out and reaches for Callahan's ankle with the other hand. Callahan trips and busts his elbows against the floor. Sam doesn't hesitate when she lifts the barrel of the gun to his forehead, her face grim.

"Don't move," she says, her hand steady.

Callahan's face melts into fear. Sam's face contorts with rage, her fingers readjusting its grip. It's unlocked, cocked back, and her finger rests on the trigger. Akeno can't tell if she's seriously willing to fire the gun or if she's bluffing. She moves behind the couch and over to the doors, where Jay and Amy are both waiting. Mike appears by their side, a rifle in hand. "Let's go," Mike calls. "There's more coming."

Sam doesn't take her sight off Callahan until all of them are out of the room. Jay shuts the double doors behind him and knots a rope through the door handles. Just as Jay steps away, the doors shake erratically from the other side. Callahan's anger echoes through the foyer and up the stairs as he shakes the doors. Akeno glances up at the landing, where a woman peers down, her eyes wide and her wan face pale at the sight of them. Sam peers up and notices her too. The woman eyes the gun in Sam's hand and runs in the other direction, out of sight.

"We've got to move," Sam says.

Amy hands Sam her backpack as Jay ushers everyone else to the back door. The Hispanic man and his wife wait by the entrance, their faces anxious and scared in the kitchen of a foreign home. The counters are spotless, Akeno thinks, as they race through the room and onto the back patio. Two men lay unconscious, one with blood spilling slowly from a wound on his temple.

Glass breaks from the other side of the house, probably from the front door, as all of them leave the house and across the yards.

"There's another entrance to the neighborhood over here," Jay shouts behind him.

Sam runs at pace behind Jay and Amy. Akeno follows behind them, and the Hispanic couple aren't far behind Akeno. Mike keeps falling back from the crowd, his arms pumping helplessly at his sides, already out of breath. He doesn't look well, and now in the morning sun, Akeno can see the all too familiar signs of addiction on the man's face. His skin too thin, his peeks too pale, his eyes bloodshot, and his frame looks worn. There's scabs on his arms and around his neck. He slows more and more as the houses pass.

"Mike!" Jay yells, coughs, and stops short. Amy and Sam keep running, throwing their heads back and watching as Jay falls back to help his friend. "Come on, Mike. We're almost there. Don't let those sons-of-bitches get ya."

"I can't, Jay," he wheezes. Akeno slows, willing himself to help Jay carry the man on, but more men with guns round the corner of the house behind them.

"Come on, buddy. You've got more left. You gotta push, man. You have to. Come on!" Jay shouts, tugging at Mike's loose shirt. "Come on, man," he says, now pleading.

Mike turns to see the men barreling across the yard, their guns pointed.

"Go," Mike breathes. "Go!" he shouts at Jay. "Make sure Amy's alright. Get the rest of these people outta here. I'll hold 'em off."

"No, Mike, you can't—"

"Go!" Mike turns and fires the rifle at random, hitting a nearby shrub.

"Mike, no!" Jay yells.

Mike shoots off another two shots, his stance more grounded than Akeno thought possible, considering his weak condition. He reloads, shoots, reloads, shoots.

"Go!" Mike yells at Jay.

Mike fires another few rounds in a rhythm, working the pump furiously as he takes shots at the men chasing the group. Akeno grabs a hold of Jay's arm and pulls him along. Jay finally moves at pace with Akeno as the two of them run to catch up with the others, who are already two houses ahead of them. Behind them, the steady reloading of the barrel ceases as another gunshot echoes out into the neighborhood. Akeno glances behind him, just as Mike's body takes the impact. Mike's knees crumple underneath him as two more shots pass through his chest. He slumps over, and the men who shot him run right past his fallen body.

Akeno's ears ring. He looks beside him at Jay, whose face runs with tears, his hand frantically swiping at his eyes. Jay rushes past him and stops at the fence next to the Dumpsters. Next to the piles of garbage is the other entrance to the community, which is locked with chains and a padlock. Nobody's going in or out that way.

Amy and Sam are already helping the Hispanic couple climb the Dumpsters to jump the fence. They help Jay up, and Sam calls for Akeno. His ears just catch her voice breaking through the din of the gunshots firing at Akeno, bullets ringing off the Dumpsters. Sam grabs Akeno's wrists as he slams into the green siding, his fingers clawing for the edges to pull himself up. Another shot rings against the siding, and Akeno feels himself shaking as he's pulled to the top.

Jay's over the top, and Amy follows. Sam jumps next, and Akeno follows last, landing clumsily next to Sam. His ankles give way from the fall, but the adrenaline coursing through his body doesn't allow him to feel any pain as he pushes himself up and into a sprint. They race across an empty field, its grass withered and dry. Dirt flies up all around them as they flee the prison behind them.

They don't stop until they reach a road on the other side, which leads into a quiet, more recluse sect of woods. Akeno listens for gunshots, running feet, or the sound of an engine. All is quiet. It doesn't seem like they're being followed. Akeno feels his insides burning, his lungs aching, and he feels nauseous. In his mind's eye, he sees Mike's body lying on the ground and immediately releases everything he has in his stomach, which isn't much. He leans against a tree, bile rising up out of his stomach and realizes for the first time that he's crying.

Sam watches from a distance, her cheeks red, her breath coming in shallow takes. Jay and Amy hold each other, as Jay recounts what happened, his voice breaking. Amy is crying too, her chin resting on top of Jay's shoulder, her hand soothing his hair as his body shakes. The Hispanic couple stand off to the side, their backs against a tree, their eyes watching the distance, the gates of Oak Hills still clearly in view.

Akeno needs water. He realizes now that he left his "Glitter is my favorite color" bag back in Oak Hills. Too late now, he thinks. He points to Sam and points to her backpack, motioning for water. Somehow, he can't find the words to speak, his chest still heaving. She pulls out a bottle of water and tosses it to Akeno. He chugs half the bottle and realizes the Hispanic couple has nothing with them. He glances at Jay and Amy, who both have backpacks. Wherever they found their stuff, they must not have noticed Akeno's bag and probably didn't know what the Hispanic couple had brought with them, if anything.

"Here," Akeno says. He hands the bottle to the couple.

The man takes it reluctantly, but the two drink greedily.

"We should keep moving," Sam says softly. "They might follow us."

Jay doesn't say anything, but he nods. Amy hands him a bottle of water from her bag. The Hispanic woman says something quietly to her husband in Spanish. He replies and looks up, his face solemn.

"Thank you for saving us," he says. "We're very grateful, but we must go our own way. We still have to find our daughter."

"Your daughter isn't in there," Jay says, pointing to Oak Hills. "And even if she is, you'll never get her out. She's stuck there now. You'll never find her."

"Maybe or maybe not," the Hispanic man says. "But we must go now. Let this be known. This is not over." He turns to leave, his wife tucked safely in his shoulder. "Your friend," the man says. "Our lives will forever be indebted to him. May God rest his soul." He makes a Catholic cross on his chest and kisses his fingertips.

Jay nods, swiping away the tears from his eyes.

"Thank you," the Hispanic man says to Amy, Sam, and Akeno. "I wish you safe travel."

"Good luck," Sam says, raising a hand to wave.

The man nods, and he and his wife walk back toward the main road, their heads bent forward. Wherever they live, they must be headed back to recoup. Akeno hopes their daughter is safe, wherever she is. Akeno bids a silent farewell, knowing he'll never see them again.

CHAPTER 8

The four of them walk the long, winding road up the hillside until they come to a crossroads. One leads higher up, the other plateaus and goes back down. The road climbed higher until they couldn't see the other side. The trees surrounding them stretched their shade overhead. The leaves have nearly browned, a few red and orange just hanging on by a thread at the end of the branches. Fall was well underway, and winter would be here soon. Where would they be then?

Jay turns to Akeno and Sam. "Where you two headed?"

"Wherever it's safe," Sam says, shielding her eyes from the sun peeking in through the fingers of the trees overhead.

"There's a small town called Sweet Valley if you follow this road," Jay says, pointing ahead. "I wouldn't risk it. Take the backroads until you reach the hills. You should be safer there. That's when the mountains start to form. Not many people live out that way."

"And you?" she asks.

Jay looks around, his expression blank.

"Ah, we'll probably lift a van, clear it out, and hopefully find a spot to park before the gas runs out," Amy answers, her face showing a forced smile, the gap in her teeth showing.

Sam nods with a soft smile. "Good luck."

"Same to you."

The party splits ways. Jay and Amy take the road going up but veer off course as they disappear into the treeline, probably to make camp. Akeno thinks they should be considering the same. They walk along the road and pass what looks like a driveway leading up into the woods. The mailbox is stuffed with mail and a dead mouse.

What a joke, Akeno thinks.

The two walk in silence until finally the sun begins to set below the horizon. They find the signpost pointing in the direction of the town. Six miles, the sign reads. They take the adjacent road and find themselves nestled in the backroads. He doesn't see a house for miles, but they pass several hidden driveways. It should be a decent place to camp if they stay outside the view and property of the homes tucked away in the trees. He imagines they're the sort of people who know how to preserve jellies, jams, pickles, and whatever other vegetables or meats could be boxed in a cellar for years to come. If everyone else returns to savagery, at least these mountaineers, distanced from the world of tomorrow, would survive the apocalyptic cataclysm. Maybe they can break into a cellar, if they want to risk being shot.

"We can make camp here," Sam says and stops in her tracks. "The houses are spaced far enough apart from how many driveways we passed. I think we'll be safe here."

They're on the side of an unlined road. Sam hikes into the woods, uphill, and sets down her backpack in the dirt and small buds of grass. Akeno follows, and when he looks down, they can still see the road, but from where they're positioned, he doubts anyone from the road could see them in the dark.

They haven't seen any cars pass, Akeno thinks. Not that he expected to see any at all, but they could never be too careful. Others might be hiking through these hills like they are. After all, there is a small town close by. Anyone could be living back here.

"What about a fire?" Akeno asks.

"We shouldn't need one," Sam says. "It's not cold enough to risk it anyway." There's a brief pause. "You don't have a sleeping bag."

"No," Akeno answers meekly. She said it as a statement, but he answers it as a question.

"Where's your ugly, purple bag?"

"It got left behind."

She doesn't say anything as she unrolls her sleeping bag, one very clean and seemingly unused. She digs out a few other supplies, including the rope, which she slings over a tree branch and ties it to fashion a levy. She ties her backpack to it and pulls the levy up, testing the rope's strength.

"So animals won't get in," she explains to Akeno.

"Is there anything I can do to help?" he asks.

"Not really."

He's never been camping before, but he always imagined it would be a lot more fun than this. It was kind of lonesome. No folk music, no storytelling, no wind even.

"It's just for the night," she says, reading Akeno's expression again. He wonders if his face gives away too much. "Hopefully we can find a barn or some empty house tomorrow."

"Where are we going?"

"Nowhere," she says. "Survival doesn't have an end destination. This isn't a field trip. I thought you knew that." The tone in her voice grows angry, but Akeno notes more abject disappointment than blame.

"I guess you don't know much about me at all."

She doesn't respond and continues to set up camp. She pulls another jacket over herself and sees Akeno standing sheepishly to one side.

"What?" she demands.

"Nothing."

"Well don't just stand there looking at me like I'm to blame."

"I'm not."

"Whatever."

"Okay, I get it. I fucked up. I should've brought a sleeping bag," he says.

"It's not like you had anywhere to carry it if you had."

"Then I'm sorry."

"For what?"

"I don't know, you're mad at me, so you tell me."

"We're fucked!" she shouts. "We almost died. Then we escape. We have nothing to live on; you don't have anywhere to sleep." She laughs a nervous and strained laugh. "I don't get how completely underprepared you were. You didn't even have a backpack. You had this stupid bag stuffed with random shit, and now we don't even have that."

"Who do you think you are?" Akeno shouts. "I fucked up? It was your idea to sneak into their neighborhood. You told me it was fine, and the minute we got across that fence, people were after us. You keep saying, 'We will do this' or 'We will do that.' Who says I want to stick around with someone like that?"

"You're free to leave," she says, quieter now, gesturing to the open road. "Nobody's stopping you."

A heavy pause hangs in the air.

"Why am I here?" Akeno asks, stepping closer. "We've had two encounters, and you decide to drag me along on your journey for 'survival.' Hell, you talked more to Jay than to me. All you've said is how useless I am."

"Does that make you jealous, *Lee?*"

"Whatever. As if you didn't lie about your name too."

She scoffs. "Sam is my real name. Nobody thought 'Lee' was your name. You're a shit liar, and you didn't have to lie to them."

"Again, why am I here? I'm obviously no advantage for whatever plan you had when you brought me all this way. You knew when we left campus that I didn't have anything special."

"I thought you'd be more prepared than this," she says, gesturing at the emptiness of his hands. "You seemed like you knew what you were doing in the radio room. By the time we were on the hillside, I didn't want you going back to campus and snitching."

"Sorry to disappoint," he says. "And I wouldn't have snitched." He looks around at the sorry camp they have set up. "Now that everything's out in the open, guess I'll be on my way then. I want my food back."

"Oh, you mean your bags of chips?" She marches over to the hanging bag. "Your beans, your weird assortment of canned fruit. None of this is going to last long anyway," she says, throwing the bag of chips at him, along with a bottle of water and fruit snacks.

"Hey," a voice shouts from the road. Sam and Akeno didn't hear the low rumble of an engine until now, when a woman in an old, rusty pickup truck shifts gear so the truck sits idling. "Need any help?"

Akeno peers closer at the woman. She's clean, her hair mostly brushed and hanging in a long, blonde ponytail. She wears a blouse and a heavy overcoat, no plaid, no jean jacket. She appears in her late thirties, her smile a perfect row of teeth.

"We're good," Sam calls back, her arms crossed.

Akeno spins around and glares at Sam.

"Actually, I could use a ride," he shouts back at the woman.

"Well hop in," she says, waving him in. "You kids shouldn't be staying out here so late at night. You don't want to be out here when the sun sets, trust me."

Akeno grabs the food from the ground and carries it in his shirt like a makeshift kangaroo pouch. He jogs down to the truck and opens the passenger side door.

"There's a small seat that pulls down in the back, if your friend wants a ride too, as long it's not too far, wherever you're going."

"We don't have anywhere specific to be," Akeno says, dropping his supplies on the truck floor. He glances back over his shoulder, shading his eyes as he sees Sam just standing there, forlorn in the trees.

"I'm just over the ridge here," the woman says, pointing. "I've got an empty barn, if you need a place to sleep tonight. No sense in letting you both freeze out here."

Akeno eyes Sam with a smirk. Her hands are still holding some packaged food. She stares down at him with disbelief.

"Come on," Akeno says, gesturing with a wave. "We can make a fire."

She stands there for a moment longer and audibly sighs, shaking her head as she shoves everything back into her backpack, unties the rope, and jogs down to the truck. Akeno's shit-eating-grin is still plastered on his face when she pushes past him to the backseat, letting the backpack thud against the floor with a resounding crunch. Akeno hops into the front seat and slams the door shut.

"Good thing," the woman says. The engine revs up as it glides down the road.

"It's a good thing I picked you two up," the woman says after a minute. "There are all kinds of crazies running around the backwoods. Kids go missing all round these parts here recently. Since the power outage, it's like it's a full moon every night."

Akeno doesn't want to know the horror stories these woods hold.

He's had enough of those in his lifetime to satisfy his curiosity. There's a lull as the engine hums down the road, but the woman doesn't seem to miss a beat when talking to them.

"I'm Jennifer, by the way," she says. "But only my mother calls me that. I'd prefer if you called me Jean. Everyone else does. Mind if I ask what your story is? You don't have to share if you don't want, but I figured you two must have something interesting to tell. There's not much TV anymore, so I'm kind of reaching for straws here."

She laughs a little awkwardly. Akeno can understand. All of this is strange.

"Not a lot to tell," Akeno says plainly.

Sam sits in the back with her arms crossed, her face turned resolutely towards the window and away from Akeno.

"We went to college in Johnsville," Akeno says. "We left there and thought we could make it out here."

"Oh, college students," she smiles. "But you two look so young."

"We get that a lot," Akeno says. "We're actually siblings."

Sam's ears perk up, but she doesn't give the truth away.

"Awe, that's so sweet, but you're, uh--"

"I'm Japanese," Akeno says. "My name's Lee. This is Sam. Her parents adopted me when I was seven. I was seven, right, Sam?"

"Six," Sam corrects. "You were six, because you still had those ugly bangs and a cleft lip that dripped when you drank your juice."

"Yeah, you're right," Akeno says genially. "Good thing I had that surgery and got my haircut. I can't say she would love my hair being this long."

"Is that where you're headed now, your parents' house?" Jean asks.

"Yeah, but they live in Charlotte, so it's going to be a while before we reach them. We weren't sure if we should have left campus, but finally it was time to start the trek."

"That's so far. Y'all don't look ready for that long of a journey on foot."

"Yeah, but we figured the trip's worth it. We thought by now the power would snap back on, but it's been so long, so..."

"Better late than never. I'm sure they miss you."

"I bet they do," Akeno says. "We have a pretty big family though, so I'm sure they're busy. We have two older brothers and a younger sister at home. She's African."

The woman coos with affection as Akeno glances back at Sam with a loopy grin. "Yeah, we're really proud of our diverse family. Do you have any kids?"

"Oh, no, honey," she says. "I mean I tried with my late husband, but we never made it there. Then he was diagnosed, passed about a year later. Now I'm just too old to be having any children." She laughs, her breathy airy, and Akeno's mood shifts. He tries to lighten the air.

"That's a shock. I didn't think you were older than thirty."

She blushes and waves his compliment away with a hand. He notes even her nails look nice compared to his own.

The truck hits a bump, and Akeno realizes they've switched from pavement to a gravel drive. At the top of the hill rests a small house, and to the left sits what looks like an abandoned barn. The roof has holes, and the brown siding is peeling. The draft must be cool, but at least it's shelter. The land itself is beautiful. The fields stretch for miles. The yard needs mowing, but Akeno doesn't judge. He imagines himself finding a spot under a tree and reading a good book. It's serene now, a place of refuge. It feels like home.

Akeno compares this place to his old house, where Sandy and Hugh used to live. It was quiet there, like it is here. They didn't have as much land as this, but their small house in the woods was quaint and remote from all the trouble he used to have living in the city. There weren't any neighborhood kids trying to recruit him or stragglers trying to sell him a joint at the park. He remembers the cows that lived behind Sandy and Hugh's house and how Hugh would take Akeno down there to look at them over the fence.

Akeno used to want to live in the country, wanted so badly to stay in the place Sandy and Hugh had together, but since their passing, he hasn't visited the old house. It must have been looted by now, either by relatives or strangers. After the burial, he packed everything he had and moved out for college. It was the only thing Sandy and Hugh had convinced him to do, so he did it, and he's been staying on campus since then. One year later, and this is where life has led him. Sandy and Hugh would be shocked. He's glad they're gone now. He wouldn't want them going through this shit show.

"All right, here we are," Jean announces. "It's not much, but it's home."

"It's perfect," Akeno says with a soft smile.

She drops Akeno and Sam off at the barn. The two exit the truck, their feet shaking up loose dirt. Sam shakes off her shoes and eyes the barn with loathing.

"I've been meaning to rebuild that barn, but I just never got around to it," Jean says. "I've got some extra blankets in the house. I'll be right back with 'em." She drives the short path to the house and parks next to the porch. She takes her time getting out and unloading the truck with what looks like groceries. As soon as she's inside the house, Sam grips Akeno's arm.

"Are you fucking crazy?" she seethes. "You just blindly followed a woman back to her creepy house in the middle of nowhere."

Akeno shakes off her grasp. "Better than staying in the woods. You heard what she said, about the crazy people roaming the night."

"And how do we know she's not a crazy person?"

"Do you see any imprisoned children?" Akeno asks. "If you don't want to stay, fine, but you chose to come."

"You chose for us."

"What 'us?'"

The front screen door of the house slams against the door frame, signalling Jean's return. Sam doesn't respond as Jean approaches, all smiles.

"I found a few pillows too," she chirps. "I know it's not much, but I hope it helps."

"This is great, thank you," Akeno says and takes the blankets. He hands them off to Sam, who takes the pillows as Akeno holds the blankets.

"I hope you don't mind staying in the barn," she says apologetically. "I'd offer the spare bedroom, but it's mainly being used for storage right now."

"No, the barn's fine. We really appreciate your generosity."

"It's no thing," she says, waving them away. "Anyway, I've got just enough for a small pot of stew. I'll let you know when it's through. Make yourself comfortable. Let me know if you need more blankets."

By now the sun dips just below the horizon, but somehow the light still reaches the small hill they're on. She leaves them both to unpack their things, and Akeno notes a small lantern hanging by the door of the barn. Sam drops everything down on the barn floor and tosses her bag against one of the barn pillars. Akeno pulls down the lantern and realizes he doesn't have any matches.

"Give it to me," Sam says. She reaches in her bag and takes out a lighter. As the wick burns, she hands the lantern back to Akeno.

From the glow of the light, Akeno can make out the emptiness of the barn. There's a lot of shadows, which Akeno doesn't like. The empty rafters above them don't show signs of any birds or bats, but Akeno knows there must be rats and mice hiding in the eight empty stalls and the leftover straw.

He doesn't know much about farming, but he imagines himself a boy growing up in the fields, riding horses, and plucking fresh eggs from the chicken coop. He almost smiles at the image of himself, a little Asian boy, wearing overalls and cowboy boots in the American South. There isn't much else but humor in that image.

"Was that true?" Sam asks, as if reading his mind. "About you being from Japan?"

"No," Akeno says, breaking himself from his wandering fantasies. "I'm only half, or at least that's what the state says. My mother's side." He adds the last bit as an afterthought.

Sam doesn't say anything. "Do you have any family? You told Callahan--"

"No," Akeno interjects. "I mean, I guess what I said was true. I don't have a family anymore. The couple who adopted me already passed."

Sam doesn't say anything for a while. She takes a seat on the ground, her back against one of the stalls.

"What about you?" Akeno asks. "Any family?"

"No," she says with finality. There's a brief pause.

"Not all families are great," he says quietly, repeating the words she used.

She pauses, then asks, "Did you like the couple who adopted you?"

"Yeah, I did," Akeno says. "Sandy and Hugh were the only foster parents I actually liked, and really, they were old enough to be my grandparents." He chuckles. "They were sweet. They always made me feel at home. They lived on a farm kind of like this, didn't have any animals though, or this much land."

"Oh, yeah?" she asks. "That must have been fun."

"It kind of was. I didn't like it at first. I grew up in different places, mostly in and around Baltimore. Then somehow they found me. Apparently, they didn't want a younger kid. They wanted someone in their teens. When I found out they lived on a farm, at first I thought they were just wanting cheap labor, but it turns out they were just lonely. They only had a couple of kids, but one of them died in an accident and the other overdosed. Like I said, I think they were just lonely."

A pause.

"Did you love them?"

"What?"

"Did you love them?" she repeats.

"I mean, well, yeah. I guess so. I miss them sometimes. Like today, seeing this barn and the fields. It reminds me of them."

"I bet they loved you too," she says with a smile. "It seems like it."

"Maybe," he says.

"When did they pass?"

"Well, she had cancer for years, but it was in remission. Then it came back, and soon after, that was that. She died in early December and Hugh followed shortly after. This was last year. It feels like an eternity now."

She's quiet for a time. "I'm sorry, I mean, you know."

Akeno nods. "I was only with them for about a year and a half. It wasn't very long, but it was some of the happiest times I can remember."

They don't say anything for a while. He almost feels sorry for bringing it all up, but he dismisses it and asks, "What about you? Care to share your life story?" He laughs and hopes it breaks the tension.

She laughs too, and Akeno feels more at ease.

"I have three older brothers and a few half-siblings," she says. "They live with our dad."

"And your mom's side?"

Sam shakes her head. "She just lives with her piece of shit boyfriend and smokes crack. Draws welfare and harasses her kids for money."

"That kind of family?" Akeno asks. "I've lived with a couple of those. One was on crack; the other dealt meth at the park they took me to."

"Damn," Sam laughs. She can't help it. "Meth, at the park?"

"Yeah, in the middle of a park too." He laughs. "That was definitely the wildest home I stayed in. Lots of partying. I was eleven. That's when I had my first beer."

"Oh, is it a competition now?" she chuckles and gives a long sigh, thinking. "Well, I had my first cigarette at ten, compliments from my mom's *first* piece of shit boyfriend after the divorce."

"Ten? Wow, that's late. Had my first cig at nine with my foster siblings. They were in middle school."

"Wow, smoking, you little rebel. How'd it go?"

"I threw up," Akeno says and bursts with laughter. The sound echoes in the barn, almost scaring the both of them. They laugh again.

"What about your parents? Do you know anything about them?"

"Nothing about my dad. He and my mom were never together, or so she said. She died when I was eight. I was told later that it was an overdose. I don't have any other family, so they put in foster care. I guess I was the few who never made it out."

"I'm so sorry to hear that," she says, her eyes falling on the floor. "Do you remember her? Do you have any pictures?"

Akeno shakes his head. "I used to have a few pictures of her and some of us together, just some mementos they gave me after it happened." He shakes his head again. "I lost the pictures years ago. I ran away at fourteen, got lost, ran into some thugs who robbed me of all I had and my shoes. The pictures were in the bag I took."

Sam looks hurt as she reaches a hand out. He bats it away with a small smile.

"It's okay. It was a long time ago. I still remember her face, and I remember the pictures. They're burned into the back of my head it seems. I think I look like her, more or less."

Sam offers a smile in return. The two sit around the lantern for the next hour swapping stories and memories. Akeno and Sam remember some of the worst, yet some of the funniest, moments of their lives. There isn't much Akeno's proud of, but at least he can make others laugh. He doesn't try to imagine living Sam's life, and neither does she try to empathize with his. Both of them have stories left unspoken, ones they'd rather not share, and by the time the lantern's oil runs low, they've exhausted themselves. For just a moment, they remember what it's like to feel normal.

About an hour later, Jean enters the barn to find the two resting side-by-side, their eyes closed, their backs to the stalls. Sam's backpack is tucked firmly between her legs, her arms circled around it. Jean's lips tighten and doesn't bother to wake them, but Sam's eyes flutter open before Jean can slip outside.

"Is dinner ready?" Sam asks, rubbing her eyes. "What time is it?"

"Little after seven, if my kitchen clock's still working right," Jeans says. "You two could still sleep. There will be plenty of soup in the morning."

"No, we should get up. Hey," Sam says, nudging Akeno with the toe of her boot. "Wake up. Dinner's ready."

"I'll meet you both at the house," Jean says.

She leaves the barn when Akeno wakes up. "What time is it?"

Sam's already standing, her things still packed in the backpack. "We should probably leave after dinner. We can still make some good time in the dark. Probably best to travel that way if there are people out looking for kids. It's easier to fight when you aren't asleep."

"Fair point, but aren't there coyotes out at night?"

"I've got a hunting knife."

"Yeah, and I don't."

"Just snatch one from the kitchen during dinner."

"Should I raid the rest of her house for things I don't have?"

"If she actually cares about our wellbeing, then she shouldn't mind."

"I can't believe you'd rather go camping than sleep in this barn."

"I don't trust this place," Sam mutters.

The two make their way to the main house, where candles and lanterns light the rooms so a yellow light pours from the house. The lighting doesn't shine far, but Akeno thinks it must be seen from miles on the hilltop. Akeno can see the other lights a couple miles away on the neighboring farms, just tiny specks of light in the distance.

"Do you think it's safe that she has all her lights on?" Sam asks, reading his mind again.

"Better to say this house is occupied than for strangers to assume it's not," Akeno says. "Nobody knows she lives alone."

"I bet her neighbors do. Small towns like these know everything."

"Let's hope her neighbors are friendly then."

Akeno pushes open the front door and steps into the warmth of the living room. A fireplace burns in the center of the far wall, and Akeno can't remember a time when he's seen an actual fireplace in a home. Usually, they're just the fake gas kind, like the one in Callahan's house, but this one smells different, like pine or burning sage. It's sweet but coarse, and Akeno can't help but feel comfortable. He wishes Sam would ease up on Jean. He'd rather stay in the barn, if he had a choice.

"Stew's all done," Jean calls from the kitchen, as the screen door slams shut behind Akeno and Sam.

Inside the kitchen is a small wooden table with four rickety chairs. All around the kitchen hang stitchings with cute phrases: Home Sweet Home, Home Is Where the Heart Rests, Growing Up on a Farm Works the Hands and Heart. Other display ornaments lay scattered on the tops of cabinets, the counters, and any other empty space that could showcase the small trinkets Jean has collected over the years. Through all the decorum, Akeno's surprised not to see any photos on the walls. Even if she's never had any kids, it's weird that there aren't any of her and her husband. Maybe she's still grieving, Akeno thinks. He glances at Sam, but she doesn't seem concerned about the stuff in the house as she pulls a chair from under the table.

"What's in the stew?" Sam asks dubiously.

"Chicken, beans, green beans, tomatoes, and onions. Not to mention a variety of my garden-grown spices," Jean says with a smile. If she noticed any of Sam's attitude, she doesn't show it.

"I don't like onions," Sam says, and Akeno kicks her chair as he takes a seat.

"What?" she mouths in silence.

"I like onions," Akeno says. "Thank you for dinner. You didn't have to share what's yours. We really appreciate it."

"Oh, it's no trouble," Jean says. "It's not like I can store leftovers anyway."

"Good thing we happened to be along," Sam says.

Akeno doesn't know what she means by that, but when Jean sets the stew in front of Akeno, he forgets everything else and digs in. Sam sniffs the soup first before taking a bite. She puts her spoon down.

"Do you have a bathroom in the house, or is there like an outhouse here?" Sam asks.

Jean forces a laugh, though without much humor. "Yeah, darlin', it's just down the hall and to the left."

Sam leaves the table, scraping her chair against the floor, her bowl of stew untouched.

"Thanks for the stew," Akeno says, his mouth full of chicken and beans. "It's really good. I haven't had a home-cooked meal in a while."

"Hey, instant mac-and-cheese is my favorite snack. I haven't seen much of it at the store these days. Mostly, we just trade in town, hence the garden outside. Good thing we've had some stuff stored away in the cellar, otherwise I'd have gone hungry weeks ago."

"What kind of food do you store?"

"The usual--sweet apples, beans, peas, jams, those things--but after a while, the taste gets old after eating so much of it, so it's nice to have neighbors who have other food to swap." She glances back over her shoulder and smiles playfully. "Your sister seems kinda moody. I take it she doesn't care much for strangers."

"She's just like that sometimes. I wouldn't worry about it. She's just tired."

"Well, that barn may not seem like it, but it's pretty cozy in there once you get situated. I hope you two can sleep better in there than out in the cold."

"You said something earlier about crazy people and disappearing kids. What's that all about?" Akeno takes another bite of his stew, the warmth of it settling in his chest.

Jean sighs, then shrugs as she leans against the stove. "I can't even be sure that they're taking kids, but at night you can hear screams. I don't know what's going on. I've never actually checked it out myself, but my neighbors say people have gone to investigate and what they find is stuff from nightmares."

"Like what?"

"Ripped clothing, blood, tangles of hair, children's shoes. I don't ever want to know what happens when those screams ring out, but it makes me sick thinking about it."

Akeno lays his spoon down and winces. "That's awful. Shouldn't someone stop them?"

"We don't know who they are or if there's more than one. There are sick people out there, Lee, and I just hope you two never get mixed up with them."

"Kinda hard to avoid them when the world's gone dark."

"You're right. I was actually going to mention it to you both in the morning, but there's this place out in--"

"Your toilet's backed up," Sam announces, interrupting Jean, who tightens her lips and goes back to stirring the stew. "So, thanks for offering us a place to stay, but I think it'd be best if we were on our way. We don't want to intrude."

"Oh, you're not intruding. I was just about to say—"

"It's all right. Thanks for dinner," Sam says, pulling Akeno to his feet. They're at the door when Jean comes barreling into the room.

"Wait," Jean calls frantically. "I mean, as I was explaining to Lee, there's people out there--"

"We'll be fine," Sam says, pushing the door open.

"You can't!" Jean shouts. She pushes Akeno and Sam aside and blocks the door. "You can't leave."

"Yes, we can. Move!" Sam says, stepping forward.

"Listen here, you bitch," Jean says, pulling a kitchen knife from her jeans. "I've waited my turn. I've waited so long to get off this hill. You don't know what it's taken for me to survive this long out here, but I won't do it for another day. I've been waiting for my chance to leave this place, and I'll be damned if one of you brats doesn't come with me for my chance for a better life."

Jean's face contorts with rage, her one hand gripping the knife, the other digging into the palm of her hand. Sam looks to Akeno, searching for a response, but suddenly Akeno's head feels dizzy, his eyes heavy.

"Sam, I--"

Sam's face shifts from angry to enraged. "You roofied the stew?" she shouts at Jean.

"You don't understand," Jean shouts back. "I need someone to take with me. They won't let me in without any kids. Families are first priority."

"What the hell are you talking about?" Sam demands.

"Sanctuary," she says, her eyes growing wide. "They've got power there and running water. It's the only place in the U.S. with any form of stability. The soldiers said they won't let women my age in unless I've got kids."

Sam pulls a hunting knife from her boot. "Listen, you crazy bitch. We can have a knife fight right here, right now, but my knife's a lot bigger than yours, and I will not hesitate to gut you. Now move the hell out of our way!"

"Please," Jean says, her voice taking on an edge of desperation. She sounds almost pleading now. Strands of hair fall from her ponytail as she reaches out to take his hand.

Akeno stumbles back, out of reach, his head swimming. He feels as if he's going to be sick. Sam should just leave without him. He tries to tell her this, but a spew of spit falls from his lips. Sam grabs hold of his other hand and pulls him upright. Just then, Jean lashes out with the knife, just barely missing Sam.

"Are you—" Sam's words suddenly shift into anger and she swipes her hunting knife into a large arc , not aiming to miss as Jean jumps back. Jean lunges again, misses, and Sam swings, once, then twice, her radius much wider than Jean's kitchen knife will reach.

Akeno crumples, his legs weak. He forces himself to stand. When he does, his mouth opens wide, and a spew of vomit dirties the hardwood floor. The fire cracks, and his ears ring as Sam shouts above the din of noise in his head. Through blurry eyes, he watches as Sam lunges again and again, backing Jean against a wall. Jean makes a final sweep like she's going to throw the knife when Sam pulls a gun from behind her back, hidden beneath the backpack, and points it at Jean.

"What?" Jean asks, confused.

"Drop the knife," Sam says and cocks the lever back.

Jean drops it. "You've had a gun this whole time?"

Sam shrugs. "You wanted a knife fight, didn't you?"

Jean's left expressionless as Sam hurries back to Akeno and pulls him from the floor, his shirt covered in vomit. She drags him to the door and lurches him outside, where the cool air hits Akeno's face and sobers him up enough to stand.

"You can't leave," Jean shouts after them.

As they race through the yard with the lights from the house guiding their way, suddenly a gunshot rings out from the porch.

"She's going to shoot us," Sam says with apprehensive shock. "God, please don't let her shoot us."

Sam pulls Akeno around the side of the house. A shot is fired and hits the side of the barn. Another shot rings out, and Akeno can feel the spray of bullets smashing into the yard, flinging up dirt and grass against his ankles. Akeno feels like he might be sick again, more from the rush of fear and adrenaline than the drugs leftover in his system. Jean will need to reload at some point. They need to get to cover, but there's nothing but a wide open field. Akeno can see that Sam's looking all around for something, anything, to shield them.

More shots ring out, but this time it's from the direction in front of them, where the house at the bottom of the hill glows brighter with the door flung wide open, the yellow pouring out into the night like a lighthouse.

"There, head there," Akeno manages to spit out.

"Hell no," Sam says and heads right. "They think we're shooting at them."

Shots continue to buzz the air as Sam and Akeno make a break over a low fence and off into the woods. Akeno can only hear the high pitched whine in his ears, along with their muffled footsteps breaking against the tall grass. The two continue to run until they've reached another fence. Sam clears it easily enough, but Akeno finds it hard to lift his legs any higher or move another step.

"I need water," he breathes. "I need to rest."

"We can't rest now. They're right behind us."

"I just need a few seconds."

He can't hear anything beyond the blood rushing to his head. He feels like he might pass out again. He thought vomiting up the stew would help, and it did, but now all his energy feels as if it's been sapped from him. Akeno has one leg on the fence, as Sam helps heave him over to the other side.

"Get on my back," Sam says. She shifts the backpack to her front and pulls one of Akeno's arms over her shoulder. "I need you to jump on and hold tight. Can you do that for me?"

Akeno grunts but does as he's told. He feels heavy--his limbs, his head, his chest. He can feel Sam making good pace beneath him. He doesn't know how she's managing to carry everything on her own. He berates himself for ever getting them into this situation and hates himself for not being able to carry his own weight. He can't imagine where he'd be without Sam. Probably dead, probably bleeding out in the back of Jean's truck, headed to a place that isn't a Sanctuary at all. He closes his eyes, and the world disappears.

CHAPTER 9

Akeno awakes to the rising sun blinding his eyes from over the horizon. He blinks a few times and shields the light with one hand. He turns his head to the side and sees Sam asleep beside him. She's facing him, her head tilted down into the comfort of the sleeping bag, her hoodie tied tight around her face, her hands tucked under her head.

He glances down and notices he's wearing a gray hoodie that isn't his. He doesn't move, just so he doesn't wake her up, and looks around to see where they are. From this angle, it looks like they're nestled along a thistle of trees. Behind them, an earthen wall rises high above them. They must have come from downhill.

His head spins as he tries to recall last night's events. He remembers bits and pieces, up until the point where he passed out on Sam's back. He thinks they were running away from a cabin. Someone was chasing them with a gun. He remembers how he and Sam talked about their families in the barn, how they went to dinner. All of the rest is a blur.

He lies awake for a few moments, the adrenaline and anxiety returning to him. He breathes in and out, in and out, steadying himself as he checks their surroundings. Sam's backpack is behind them. It looks like she was using it as a pillow. He pulls one arm out and opens the zipper, finds a canteen, and takes a long drink of what's inside. It is water, but there's not much left. He saves the rest for Sam.

He puts his arm back under the cover of the sleeping bag. It's a little snug with the both of them in it, but it's so warm. The biting chill stings his face, and he pulls the hood tighter around his cheeks. Akeno fiddles with the smart knot Sam must have tied to keep his own hood on through the night. Suddenly his eyes close again, and he doesn't wake until he feels the warmth of Sam's body leaving his side.

Akeno peeks one eye open, then the other. He catches Sam pulling off the hoodie she's wearing in preference for a windbreaker. He feels a bit of embarrassment as Sam's head turns to face him. "Good, you're up," she says as Akeno rubs his eyes. "How's your head?"

"Fine," Akeno says and reaches up to pull down the hood. As he does, he feels something crusty dried into his hair, pulls his hand away, and sits up to better examine it. "What the hell? Is that blood?"

"Shit, here, I've got more bandages." She kneels down and pulls out a roll of gauze and tape. Her first aid kit has a few other bottles and packets too. She unscrews a small bottle and dumps two pills in her hand, hands them to Akeno. "You should take these. It'll help with the pain. I'll change your bandages."

"My head's not bleeding now. It's just...Was I bleeding before? What happened to my head? I don't really remember--"

"You really don't remember?" She laughs. "I guess that's kind of a good thing. You'd be pissed at me otherwise. Those roofies really knocked you out." She hands him the pills and the water bottle he drank from earlier.

"Why would I be pissed?" he asks, swallowing the pills and taking another long sip of water. The water's lower than it was earlier that morning. She must have drank some already. He still leaves some water for later.

"Well," she laughs again, the sound refreshing to Akeno's ears. "I slipped when you were still on my back. We fell face first. I mean I managed to catch myself, but you fell off my back and hit your head against a tree root, or I think that's what it was. By the time I found this place, the bleeding stopped. I bandaged you up, but I couldn't get all the blood out of your hair."

Akeno feels around his face and realizes there's a smearing of dried blood that had run down his face in the middle of the night. "And you woke up to this? It looks like I was shot. How did you not scream?"

Sam chuckles as she kneels to check the bandage on his head. "I've seen worse. You're fine. It's just a small gash. It must have reopened when you turned in your sleep, though. It soaked through the night. Here, I've got some alcohol to pour on it."

He leans down some so she's eye level with his head. She unwraps the bandage and puts it to the side. There's more blood on it than Akeno expected. He blanches at the sight of his own blood and turns away. She doesn't give him any warning before the alcohol burns at his wound, and Akeno cries out as she dabs at the wound.

"Relax," she says. "Here, hold on to this." She hands him a large flashlight hidden under the folds of the sleeping bag. He grips it as she finishes her work.

"So what happened to my old jacket, the pullover?" Akeno asks, wincing as she rewraps his wound.

"You vomited on it," she says with a wan smile. "You remember that?"

"The taste of it," he mumbles.

"I cleaned the rest off your pants and from where it got on my backpack, but the jacket was ruined. I tossed it in some bushes about a quarter mile that way," she says, nodding with her head. "If they found it there, they would've followed another direction than the way we came."

Akeno has to admit, he's mildly impressed. She knows what she's doing, what she needed to bring, what to do in an emergency. She wipes his face up with a damp cloth and untucks strands of hair from beneath the bandage. She sits back on her heels to examine her work.

"There, now if anyone asks, you've been shot and you lived. That's a good sob story if we ever need one."

"Thanks," he says. A pause. "What happened to Jean?" he asks coldly, his face then softening. "Is she--"

"Dead? No, I doubt it, though it'd be easier if she was. She's probably still out there looking for us."

"I'm sorry I didn't listen to you sooner. We should've left when you said."

Sam waves it off. "You couldn't have known."

"You did."

Sam shrugs. "I didn't really know until I looked around her house. I knew she wasn't who she said she was."

"How? When?"

"When I used the bathroom," she says, rolling her eyes. "I peeked into the other rooms. That spare room she talked about, it was a child's room, two twin beds and a collection of family photos that weren't hers."

"Wait, she didn't have kids."

"You're right," Sam says with a chuckle.

"You're saying she didn't even live there. Whose house was it then?"

Sam shrugs again. "I don't know, but unless she's a black woman in disguise, then it's not her house. Odds are, the family left, or they were killed. Either way, she lied."

Akeno sits back for a moment, digesting this information.

"And then she roofied you, so it was pretty clear she was fucking nuts. Did you hear anything she said in the kitchen? The part about needing us to get to some Sanctuary place?"

"Didn't she say something about soldiers?"

"Yeah, she said that. She must have been near campus recently. She had that truck and those groceries, and I doubt she traded any canned goods with her neighbors for that much food."

Akeno grunts but doesn't comment as Sam continues.

"If she came across some soldiers, and they told her about it, it must be a government-run program they're advertising. Probably all a big scam to get people to go to some internment camp somewhere."

Akeno nods, pulling the backpack closer as Sam rises to her feet, now pacing the ground in front of them. Akeno searches for something to eat, finds a granola bar, chews it slowly. His head pounds as he eats, but he's grateful for the food filling his stomach's lining.

"She was saying how families are first priority and how she was too old to get in, which is laughable. She's hardly forty," she says, leaning against a nearby pine tree. She yanks down some pine needles and turns them over in her hand, her eyes focused on the bristles as they break in her palm.

"Where do you think this place is?" she asks. "If there is a Sanctuary. Do you think it's nearby, and if it is, was that what she was talking about when she said there were missing children? Do you think people are kidnapping kids to get in this place? I mean I know it's crazy right now, but you'd think--"

Sam continues to ramble on for a few more minutes, asking Akeno questions but not allowing any room for answers. He thinks she's asking the right questions, but Akeno can't answer any of them. As far as he's concerned, he's not shocked the government has already set up a community exclusively for certain people. It all sounds like Oak Hills, like something Callahan would think up, but no. If the woman isn't completely out of her mind and did talk to the soldiers on campus, then it must be something legitimate. They very well might be recruiting.

A thought occurs to him. He can't prove it, but it's a thought, nonetheless. He wouldn't be surprised if the blackout and this newfound Sanctuary were both orchestrated by the same people. For the country to completely lose power all across the nation and then somehow a couple months later, the government has an ideal community set up for people to seek admittance. Is there an application process? Akeno thinks darkly. Are they requiring proof of citizenship, a birth certificate, their tax forms, their former employer's contact information? Akeno almost scoffs at the prospects.

Akeno holds his tongue, though, and doesn't mention these theories to Sam yet. He wants to learn more information before making any conclusions. It'd be best if they can do some recon first. If Akeno has learned anything in school, it's that a biased opinion can change the outcome. The last thing they need is to have a bias on what's happening right now. For better or worse, they need the facts. This Sanctuary could be a place Akeno and Sam want to find themselves in, but not by caravanning with people they can't trust. It would be a solution to many of their immediate problems, Akeno thinks, but he knows better than anyone that one solution won't fix all their problems. In fact, one solution might create more trouble than it's worth.

"Where do you think we can find more information?" Akeno asks, breaking in on Sam's monologue.

"Uh, I don't know," Sam says. "That's what I was just saying. Should we go back to campus? Do you think it's safe?"

"No," Akeno says. "No, I don't think it's safe, but we do need more information. Campus isn't any safer right now than it is wandering the woods. Like you said, Jean might still be out there looking for us. She might even have recruited some others to help her. We don't know who she's in league with."

Akeno slides out from under the sleeping bag and pushes himself into a standing position. He head spins from the sudden movement, but he steadies himself and leans against the cliffside, one hand outstretched to balance him.

"So you think we should go back to campus?" she asks. "I'm asking because by now we should know that making decisions on our own isn't going to work out." She smiles. "I guess our judgment fucked us both, right?"

Akeno smiles in return. "Yeah, I'm sorry earlier about yelling at you. And thank you for saving my life, literally. I wouldn't be here without you."

"Don't worry about it," Sam says. "I owed you one anyway. I did drag you along with me. It's kind of my fault you're here."

"No," Akeno says with a soft laugh. "I chose to be here. I'm glad I chose you to go hiking through the woods with, even if you did drop me on my head."

"You're heavier than you look," Sam says, stepping closer, patting his chest. "Must be all that muscle underneath."

"You're telling me about muscle. Your legs carried us both uphill. That's seriously impressive. It couldn't have been me."

"So..." Sam starts with a laugh. She points downhill, and for the first time, Akeno notices a haphazard path through the leaves and dirt. "I tried covering it up so we wouldn't be tracked, but I, uh, dragged you uphill on your back."

For the first time since they've met, Akeno releases a loud laugh, his one laugh that sounds like a wheezing scream, his back arching as his chest lifts up to the sky. Sam can't help but laugh too, more at the absurdity of Akeno's coughing as tears stream down his face. For a minute, it's like they're just friends hanging out with nothing else to hold them back.

"Sorry," Akeno says finally, wiping a tear from the corner of his eye. "My laugh is really ugly, but I needed that. Thank you."

"Anytime," she says with a wistful smirk.

As she starts to pack up camp, she recounts her trip through the woods with him on his back and emphasizes all the good parts with her hands. Akeno listens as he helps roll up the sleeping bag, his laughter sometimes overtaking him again. As they're ready to head out, the two carry on easy conversation as they hike down the hill, as if they are on a regular, winter camping trip. Their easy lulls in conversation don't feel forced, Akeno thinks. He was wrong about Sam. She looked so intimidating the first day they met, and Akeno has to admit she's shown a side of her that's pretty frightening. The way she holds a gun, the way she had a knife fight with Jean, the way she talks to strangers, like she doesn't have anything to lose. Akeno admires her for that. She might be careless, or oftentimes too flip, but Akeno trusts she knows what she's doing.

When Sam and Akeno find themselves back on the lonely road winding through the woods, they both pause and look in either direction. They both knew what they needed to do--head back to campus and search for more answers. It's what they least wanted, but facing the small town ahead--where they didn't know anyone and probably where Jean knew most of them--sounded like the worst course of action.

Their intention is to get as close to campus as possible and see if they couldn't reach out to the locals for more information. They would start at Sam's dorm room on campus, since it was on the edge, and they would work their way in. They would only talk to people they felt were trustworthy. There are bound to be people wandering close to campus once the military had arrived in town. Akeno wouldn't be surprised if a small commune hadn't built up on campus. Maybe more people his age would come out of hiding.

Akeno isn't sure what could happen once they reach campus. What if they come across someone like Jean again? Akeno isn't one to dwell on the "what if" questions, but he figures they should be prepared for the worst, just in case the worst does happen.

Sam, at first, resists the idea of going back. Even if they had to pass by some small town to get to the mountains, they could make it. But realistically, living in the mountains wouldn't have worked, Akeno said, not because Sam couldn't make it as a hunter, but because Akeno couldn't have made it. He didn't bring any supplies with him. If they're serious about living in the woods, and that's hoping they find an abandoned winter cabin, it would be impossible to make it there through the winter without any extra provisions. Sam knew the odds.

The two head back in the same direction they had come, though this time keeping to the woods. They wouldn't change being spotted from the road again. They talked quietly, their conversation easing the time between here and there.

Sam had enough wit to pack a pair of sunglasses, but as for Akeno, the top of his head burns from the high noon sun. The wound on his head hadn't bled at all, which is a good sign, but he leaves the bandage there as Sam recommends. It could be a good story if they need one.

Traveling all day tends to wear on the body, so they break for lunch earlier than they had planned. They have dried fruit and canned beans for lunch, thanks to Akeno's contribution. It's a good meal, but somewhere deep inside, he misses the cafeteria food, which means Akeno's stomach has turned desperate. Eating in the cafeteria feels like years ago, and Akeno finds it strange he's here, now, with Sam. It doesn't feel unnatural, though, not in the way he would have thought before when he first met Sam. If anything, he's come to admire her more in the past two days than he did before he knew her. Akeno thinks if they can survive the past forty-eight hours together, then staying together for the long run makes sense.

As Sam polishes off the last bite of her beans, she says, "What was your major? I mean, you know, before the blackout."

She tosses the can aside, and Akenos thinks he should pick it up, but then he remembers there's no waste removal now. Does the environment matter anymore? Without all their pollution from the factories and cities and cars, wouldn't Earth have a chance to heal? The thought gnaws at the back of Akeno's mind when he realizes Sam is speaking to him.

"Uh, well, I never declared a major. I didn't really know what I wanted to study yet," he says, finishing only half his beans. "Do you want the rest of this?" he asks.

"You're not hungry?" she asks. "Are you feeling okay? How's your head?"

"No, no, it's not like that. I just, uh, nerves, I guess."

She takes the can and swallows the last few bites leftover. "I wouldn't worry. We're just asking questions. We're just like everyone else."

Akeno nods. "You're right."

There's a brief pause as Sam takes a drink of their water, which is almost out. She hands off the bottle to Akeno. He drinks the last sip.

"What was your major?" he asks.

She blanches at first, then considers the question. "Well, the thing is, I was never a student." She's about to laugh, then stops herself. "I mean, I knew people who went to school in Johnsville, but I never actually enrolled."

Akeno sinks back onto his hands, his mouth agape. "You're kidding," he says. "Why were you staying on campus then?"

"I already told you. My family's not great. I needed to get away, and I figured campus was going to be empty. Sure enough, it was, except for you. I never saw anybody else."

"I never saw anyone else either."

"I guess it was just us then. The whole campus all to ourselves." She gives Akeno a playful grin. "Could've been our realm had we worked together sooner."

"Yeah, it was a ghost town. You had me scared shitless when you bust down all those doors. That was so creepy. Why didn't you just close the doors when you were done?"

"What are you talking about?" she asks. "You mean back in the hall you were staying in, where we first met?"

"Yeah, that one."

"Akeno, I never opened all those doors. I thought you had done that."

Akeno's face turns white, his eyes blank as the thought turns over in his head.

"I don't—" He can't put the words together.

"Jesus," she says. "That wasn't you?"

"No, that's why I was running after you. I thought you were some guy that had..."

They both stop, take a breath, exhale.

"It could've been anyone," she says. "Just anyone."

"I heard them, though. They woke me up when they stumbled down the hall. It was the middle of the night. I doubt they could see."

"And trip over their own feet? I guess they could've been drunk."

"Unless they bumped into someone else by accident."

"You're saying there was more than one?"

"It's just a thought."

They pause again, mulling it over.

"Alright, that's enough of that," Sam says, wiping her hands on her pants. "Let's get moving. I don't like all these horror stories when we're in the middle of a forest."

"Too scared?" Akeno teases. "I've got more stories."

"You and me both," she mutters. "If we make good time, we should be close to campus by nightfall. We can make camp and start asking questions in the morning."

"What about Oak Hills? Don't we have to pass it along the way?"

"That's what I'm saying. If we keep pace, we can go around Oak Hills so we aren't seen by anyone. I doubt they'll go outside their pretty little fence, but just in case."

By mid-afternoon, they've made good time. They're back where Jean had picked them up. Akeno didn't realize just how far they had gone when they fled Jean's house. They don't stop, and they stay far away from the road. The hiking kills Akeno's calves, and he thinks he's sweat through at least one of his shirts underneath the hoodie. The cool December air blows gently on Akeno's face, which dries the sweat building up on his face and forehead. Sam seems to be enjoying herself.

She must have grown up around here, Akeno thinks. She decided to live on campus after the blackout. He wonders what her family's like. He won't ask.

By evening, just when the sun begins to dip low in the sky, they reach the intersection where they split with Jay and Amy. Akeno hopes they're alright, despite only knowing them for a short time. He thinks they must have found a place to crash. He bets they're drinking. He would after what they went through, the loss of a friend. He can't imagine what he'd do if he lost Sam.

Then, in the distance, he hears the hum of an engine and drops into a crouch.

"What are you—" Sam asks

"Listen," he whispers, pulling her down, pointing in the direction of the sound.

Sam kneels low too. "Where is it—"

The engine suddenly grows immense, and Akeno jumps up and grabs Sam's hand. He yanks her to her feet and shouts, "Run!"

As they push their way through the trees and slide downhill to the plateau of the fields below, the sound of tires rolling over mud and grass intensifies as they break through the tree's lining. They sprint through the fields and head for the other side. Off to their right, Oak Hills looms like a predator. Behind them, the engines grow louder.

Akeno glances back and sees it's a truck, though not the same one as Jean's. It's another truck, a gleaming black hulk, lifted from the ground, its exhaust billowing out black smoke, its floor lights glaring at them as it breaks from the road and dives into the field with them. As the truck speeds up and draws nearer, Akeno pulls the two of them into a hard left, back for the trees. With any luck, they'll spin out in the field and won't be able to follow them back into the woods. Akeno can't hope for either quickly enough.

"We can't outrun them," Sam shouts over the noise.

"I know," Akeno shouts back, running still faster, his hand clinging to Sam's.

"There's another truck!" Sam shouts and points to the road ahead of them.

"Shit," Akeno says under his breath. He stops running and backtracks, his feet coming to a halt. "Maybe we could make it back to the neighborhood," he offers, but then it's too late.

The first truck veers in front of them just as the other skids to a halt behind them. The second truck looks years older than the first truck, though it's the same color. It's beat up and has red paint scratched down the side of it like it had side-swiped another vehicle, probably where they ran someone off the road. They're tracking people, hunting them. Jean's words echo in his head. "There are crazies out there hunting kids."

Akeno and Sam are back-to-back, their hands still gripping one another's. The first truck rolls down its window. A man smoking a cigarette leans out the driver side. He has a hat on and sunglasses covering his face. "You were right, Al. The boy is a chink," he says. The driver's head leans over and smirks, spits into the grass.

"Told you," the other says, though Akeno doesn't take his eyes off the first man. "The slantier the eyes, the higher the price."

"The fuck do you want?" Sam shouts, asserting herself. Her fingers switch at her side, and Akeno sees the hilt of the hunting knife. He remembers the gun.

"Wait, I know that voice," the first man says. "Is that my little sister behind you, boy?"

Sam spins around, her eyes on the first man. Akeno glances at her, his head spinning. A look of dread washes over her face. The edges of her mouth twitch, like she's trying to say something, but nothing comes out.

"I thought you'd be dead by now," he says, waving. "So, you've turned to the Orient for help. What's she doing for you in return?" he shouts to Akeno, laughing.

"Is that little Samantha?" the second man behind them shouts. Akeno turns and faces him. He wears sunglasses and a hat too.

"Leave me alone, Rex," Sam says evenly, her eyes pointed at her brother. "Let us go. We're family."

"Family?" Rex shouts, laughing again. "You left your family, remember? You ran away, told us to rot. You don't remember all that?"

"I had no other choice!" she screams. "You made me do that!"

"I made you? And how can I make such a stupid choice for you?"

"You know what happened. You didn't do anything. You let it happen!" Her voice cracks.

"I don't know what you're talking about, you crazy bitch. Get in the truck. I'm taking you home. Tell your friend to hop in the back with the others. I don't feel like arguing today."

"I'm not going anywhere with you," she says. "I'd rather be dead."

"You'd rather be dead? Well, no use in you dead. You'll be sold like the rest. Mary Anne, get out there and fetch me my bitch!"

From the passenger side, a woman hops out the truck, a shotgun slung over her shoulder.

"You heard your brother. Now get in!" she shouts.

"Fuck you!" Sam yells and pulls her gun, aims it at the woman. Akeno grabs the hunting knife from Sam's side and faces the second trunk, who by now watches on with eager interest.

"Relax, sweetheart," Mary Anne says. "It'll be easier for you in the long run. Your friend, well, boys aren't used to the feeling, but they'll get there." She chuckles, and the driver laughs with her.

Sam doesn't hesitate. She shoots low, the gunfire echoing against the trees, and the woman crumples, her screams louder than the gun. Akeno turns and sees blood pouring from her knee, the shotgun now on the ground. Akeno runs forward, grabs the shotgun and pulls it back with him, back at Sam's side. He drops the knife and aims the gun behind them at the second driver. His hands are on the wheel, his eyes wide. He looks to Sam's brother, who remains expressionless. Sam's gun is pointed at him now, as the woman on the ground rolls back and forth in agony, bleed seeping into the dried grass.

"Get in the fucking truck, Sam, or I shoot you both here and now," Rex shouts.

She cocks the pistol and waits, her face just as expressionless. "Fuck you."

"Then shoot," Rex says. "Go ahead, shoot."

Sam waits. Akeno can feel her body shaking. He glances back. The gun's steady.

"You gotta be kidding me," Rex says and pushes open the door, steps out of the truck. "Come on, Sam. I'm sorry, okay? You're right. I should've done something. I should've said something. I just didn't. I just didn't know what to do. I just...I just got scared."

"You were scared?" she shouts, her voice breaking with tears. "I was pinned down in my own bed, endured *hell*, and you were in the next room, waiting till it was done. You don't know what fear is!" She steps closer, leaving Akeno's side. He doesn't break his stance. He keeps the gun on the driver, his eyes on her brother, his heart being torn to shreds. He feels several tears slide down his cheeks.

"We were drunk..." he begins.

"I don't care," she grits.

There's silence. The wind blows softly against Akeno's hair. His head is pounding, his chest heaving. He feels exhausted. He feels broken down. He wishes he could do something to make this feeling go away. He wishes he could hold Sam, rewrite her history, and pray she never has to go through something like that again. He wishes he could—

And then a loud crack.

Akeno falls, his head hitting the cold ground and bouncing before his eyes shut. He reopens them, his ears a dull ring. He watches as the second truck drives away, its tires spinning out in the grass, dirt, then mud. It sprays on Akeno's cheeks. He can't move to wipe it away. He feels something warm pouring down his left shoulder. Has he been shot? Or has his arm always felt like that? He tries to push himself up with his right arm, fails, tries again, fails.

From behind him, several shots ring out, the bullets ricocheting off the truck's side. He hears the clicking sound of a chamber gone empty. There's a sound of rushing feet, and Sam's on the ground beside him. There's a scuffle. Akeno turns, tries to push himself up right, fails again. He turns his head and sees Sam and Rex rolling around in the grass. Sam still has the empty gun in her hand. Rex manages to pin one arm, but Sam's quick. She uses the butt of the gun and slams it against his temple. There's a faint crack, and she does it again and again. Finally, he rolls off her, blood streaming down his face, in his ear, on the brown grass.

Sam grabs the shotgun lying at Akeno's feet, swings it around to face her brother just as he stands. His hands are in the air, his face ashen, enraged, bloodied. He's been bested by his little sister. His knuckles are bloody. Akeno looks up but can't make out Sam's face from the sun. Her feet are planted shoulder-length apart, the shotgun's butt resting against her left shoulder.

"It's over," she says, loading the chamber.

Rex's heavy breathing reaches Akeno's ear. "It ain't over. You know that."

"Are there others in your truck?"

"What?"

"Are there *others*?"

He doesn't say anything.

"Open the back. Let them out."

There's a pause and then the sound of crunching grass as he goes to the truck. Akeno sees his feet, Sam's feet as they shift to face her brother. Her face is turned away from Akeno now. The tailgate falls open. He steps back from the truck, his hands still raised above his shoulders. Akeno sees a shadow on the ground pull themselves out of the open tailgate, crawling so as not to hit their heads on the top cover.

First comes a woman, Akeno guesses her late twenties, then another woman the same age, then another and another. Then another. She's around Akeno's age. Another slides out, this time a boy, also about Akeno's age. He and the younger woman hug each other, both of them crying quietly in each other's arms. Then, from the very back, is a little girl, maybe fourteen at the oldest. And behind her, a little boy, still elementary school age. The kids huddle closest to the first woman, her hands on their shoulders as the group collectively hurries to get behind Sam.

"You're a fucking monster," Sam whispers, loud enough to carry. "You would've sold these people, fucking *children*." Sam shakes her head, her throat catching.

"Sam, I–'

A deafening sound explodes through the air. The group screams, and the children begin to cry. The woman shushes the kids, her arms pulling them close so their cries are muffled into her shoulder. The others simply stand there, unmoving. Akeno tries to push himself up, his one arm failing. Then someone lifts him up, and he winces at the pain from the wound in his shoulder.

"You're going to be okay," he hears a woman say.

Behind the truck, Rex's body lays immobile, blood blossoming on his shirt. He's passed out from the pain. Sam turns then, her face in shadows as she goes to Akeno. She bends, lays down the gun, and puts his head in her lap.

"I have bandages," she says to one of the women. "It's my bag." She points. "Please," she begs, and the woman hurries to get her bag.

Sam unzips the bag, pulls out the bandages, applies pressure on Akeno's wound. She pulls it away, douses him in alcohol. He doesn't even flinch. A few feet away, Rex coughs, spraying blood on the grass. He struggles to move and stops.

"Thank you," one of the women says to Sam. "I'm...I'm sorry too."

"Don't be," Sam says, wiping away the excess blood and alcohol. She grabs a small switchblade from the bag, cuts open the hoodie's shoulder, rips open the thin shirts underneath. "You can go," she says, gesturing to the truck. "Take it. Get yourselves somewhere safe and don't look back."

"What about you?" the woman asks.

"We'll be fine."

"And her?"

The woman, Mary Anne, lays passed out on the grass, blood still oozing from her knee.

"Leave her," Sam says. "Someone will find her. Or something."

The woman doesn't say anything. She goes to the truck and opens the back door. A slumped body spills out, a bullet hole in his chest, another that scraped his neck, where most of the blood is. The woman drags the body to the side, drops it.

"Come on," she says, motioning to the truck. "We can squeeze."

The teens file in the back. One woman takes the passenger side, the other in the backseat. The kids sit on the women's laps. The doors slam shut, and the driver gives a hard smile, waves, and drives off, the tires crunching through the field as they make back for the road.

Sam watches as they drive away, her eyes on the truck, then takes a glance at Oak Hill.

"I know you're in a lot of pain, but we have to get moving. I'm sure they heard everything. They'll be over to check things out pretty soon."

"Sam," Akeno whispers.

"Don't," she says, taping off the bandage. "It's fine. Come on, we have to get you on your feet."

She lifts him up and slings his good arm over his shoulder. He turns his chin down and inspects the wound. His legs buckle at the sight of fresh blood coming through the bandages.

"Let's just get through this field and into the trees. Once we're there, we can set up camp, but you have to help me this time. I can't carry you very far. Can you do that?"

Akeno nods, his shoulder throbbing.

"Did it go all the way through?" he asks, his eyes locked on the trees ahead.

"Yeah, it went through."

Akeno nods. "Thank you."

She doesn't respond.

When they get to the trees, Akeno almost passes out, but he urges himself on. They can't make camp on the edge of the woods. They need to get deeper in. They need to keep moving. Suddenly Sam lurches to the side, still holding on to Akeno, and vomits. Not much comes out. She vomits again, this time bile. She spits, wipes her mouth with her sleeve, coughs. She doesn't look at Akeno. Their feet crunch the dead leaves underfoot, his feet tripping on all the hidden roots and rocks. Sam doesn't miss a beat though. She has him tucked firmly by her side, the shotgun in the other hand. Her face is blank, her mouth a grim line, her eyes focused on something she can't see. Akeno wishes he could hug her.

135

From across the field, a truck's engine is heard storming down the road, making a hard turn onto the grass. It pulls up beside where Rex's body still lays. Two men dressed in camouflage get out and check the body. They both grab the body and lift him to walk. From this distance, Akeno can't see any movement from Rex, but he thinks he sees his head bob a couple times before the men ease him into the truck's backseat. He must be alive, or they'd put his body in the tailgate. The trunk drives off, leaving a fog of black smoke behind.

The sun dips below the treeline, casting them in a world of long shadows. When they can't see the field anymore over the rise of a gentle slope, they stop. Sam gently lowers Akeno to the ground, where he can put his back to a tree. She checks his bandages, doesn't make any sign of concern, and turns back in the direction they had come.

"They're there now, I think," Sam says. "Oak Hills."

"Can you see them?"

"Barely."

"What are they doing?"

"Probably taking that woman back with them."

"She's alive?"

"Most likely."

"Who was the third person?" Akeno asks.

"Don't know, some guy. He leaned over the driver's seat and took a shot at me. He missed." She pauses. "He hit you instead."

"I'm glad," Akeno says. "If he had hit you, you'd be dead. I couldn't--wouldn't--I don't know. I can't lose you."

Sam doesn't say anything. She turns away, finds that can of fruit Akeno brought, hands it to him. "We're out of water, so drink this, if you can."

Akeno takes it, holds it in his lap as he studies her. His skin burns,

136

and the back of his eyes fade in and out. He smells metal and knows it's him. He's sweating. He feels like he has to shit but can't.

"It's okay. We're okay," Sam says from a distance. She's giving him distance, but Akeno thinks she must be looking back towards the road, just in case the other truck decides to come back, in case Oak Hills wants to search the woods.

Sam doesn't say anything else. Akeno closes his eyes for just a moment and hears her receding footsteps. He waits a few minutes before opening his eyes. She's gone, but he knows she's not too far. His heart rate's still up, and his guts are telling him to keep moving, but he's just so tired. He needs a drink. He eyes the field, and it's as if everything has changed color. It's all grays and black now. He refocuses his gaze and sees Sam walking back toward him. She has something in her hand, the shotgun. The empty handgun is tucked in her waistband.

There's not much to say, and even if Akeno thinks of what to say, he doesn't. She takes a seat on the other side of the tree, so she's facing away from him. He turns his head, his face only inches from hers. He reaches out and grabs her hand, pulls to his lap, and squeezes tight, as tight as he can. She squeezes it back, and it's like a dam bursts. Her lower lip trembles, and her cheeks turn red. She opens her mouth, and a stifled cry escapes. Tears flow down her nose, over her mouth and onto the ground. She lets out a yell and then just screams into space, her chest tight, her eyes squeezed shut. He opens up his good arm, and she folds into his chest, her legs pulled up to her waist. He places his arm around her and holds her tight as his chin rests on top of her head. As they sit there together, her tears soaking into that gray hoodie, he thinks of where he'd be without her and shudders. It's cold out, but the two of them are so warm. It's time they rest.

CHAPTER 10

Akeno and Sam lay together in the sleeping bag, their bodies curled against the other. Once night had fallen, the temperature dropped dramatically. It began to snow in the middle of the night, leaving a thin layer of white all around them. Akeno lay awake through the snowfall, his hood tied firmly around his head. From under the tree, the snow seemed to be falling all around them, their little oasis of warmth untouched. Akeno's arms are firmly on his own side, one hand keeping the top of the sleeping bag pulled over his bad shoulder. He can't risk infection. He's running a fever, the pain in his shoulder throbbing. He needs to see a medic soon. Hopefully there will be one on campus.

They hadn't said much as they marched back through the woods. Akeno worried the trucks would return, or else Oak Hills would send out a search party, but all was quiet in the night. Sam was quiet. She didn't eat anything for dinner. They were out of water. She had half a Gatorade left, which she took one sip of before forfeiting the rest to Akeno. He took a long drink and saved the rest anyway.

Akeno knows Sam's awake on the other side of him, though she's facing away, intent on staring into the darkened distance of the thin forest spread out around them. He figures she must be exhausted, just as he is, but from the events of the day, there's no telling when either of them would find rest. Every image seems burned into his mind's eye, as if what he's seen will be with him for the rest of his life. Maybe they will be. He tells himself this is a good thing in case he forgets how many chances he's been given to live. He notes his good fortune is merely out of circumstance rather than by the choices he's made. It was owed to Sam that he was even alive. It was her choices that saved them both. He could never forget something like that, could never repay her. He owes his life to her.

"Are you up?" he asks, hesitantly.

She doesn't respond, but by the intake of her breath, he knows she's awake.

"Do you want to talk about it?" he asks, quieter.

She doesn't answer. He just lays there, waiting, listening to the rhythm of her breathing and thinks she finally fell asleep. He shuts his eyes, trying to imagine a world that's worth dreaming of. He imagines a place somewhere nice and cozy, maybe on the beach, a future when everything's gone back to normal, where his life is immensely boring and nothing happens at all. He's there, and Sam's there, and they have all that they need.

They lay there a while longer, both of them listening to the wind in the trees. Akeno hears the faint call of an owl in the distance. He doesn't hear any sticks breaking or branches snapping. He doesn't hear footsteps approaching or the cock of a barrel. He hears nothing at all, and that's as comforting as it can get.

The next morning, Akeno wakes to find Sam missing. At first he panics, rips the sleeping bag off him, and jumps up, his shoulder aching from the sudden movement. The snow around them has mostly melted. He can make out footsteps in the snow, but they don't lead anywhere.

"Sam?" he calls. "Sam! Sam, are you out there? Sam!"

"What?" she calls from behind him. He spins and sees she's holding something in her hand--a rabbit. Blood drips from its throat. She notices him staring and puts the rabbit down where she stands. "We needed something to eat." She pulls out the hunting knife and gingerly cuts into the animal. Akeno turns away.

"Thanks," he says. "Should I get a fire going?"

"That would be good."

Twenty minutes later, Akeno's gathered enough firewood to keep the flames going. With only one arm to bend and retrieve, the task takes him longer than he thought. By the time he returns with another load of firewood, Sam's already got a small flame licking up the wood.

"More smoke than fire," she says, watching as the flames grow. She stands and pulls sticks from the tree overhead. "The sticks on the ground are too wet," she explains. "Try reaching high. Not as much rain on the branches."

"Good thinking," he says and does as he's told. He hands her his findings, and she nods in thanks. She spears the rabbit and hangs it over the fire, watching as the flames dance at the edges of the pink meat.

"We probably could have found something to eat on campus," he says bashfully.

"Maybe. I doubt they're giving out free food ."

He nods. As the rabbit cooks, he tries to make small talk, but he doesn't know what to say. He wants to ask her a million questions, but he can't. Not yet, not now. She must have a lot to think about. She needs time. She needs some space. Whatever she's dealing with, it can't be easy.

"How's your shoulder?" she asks after a while.

"Uh, it's fine," he says. "Thank you again, for, you know, stitching me back together again. That's twice now that you've saved me. Probably would have died from exposure without your first aid kit."

She looks at him now, her doe-eyes big in the morning light. He chuckles to himself.

"I just feel so useless. You're like the hero in a storybook, and I'm the damsel in distress."

"That's not you," she says. "You're hurt because of me. Twice, because of me."

"What? No, that's not—"

"If you weren't mad at me, you wouldn't have taken a ride with Jean. If it weren't for my fucked-up family, you wouldn't have gotten shot."

"Sam, that's not—"

"It's all because of me that you're even here, one lame shoulder and a head injury to count. You could've died twice, and you're thanking me. What sense does that make?"

"You saved my life," Akeno says, his voice even. Is this what she's been feeling? "Sam, if it weren't for you, I'd be miles away from here. I'd be locked up with Jean, or I'd be in the back of a truck. If it weren't for you, those people *you* saved would be living a life not worth living. They'd be sold like cargo to God knows who and how many times."

Sam shakes her head, tears brimming in her eyes. "I shot my own brother. Don't you get it? I could've killed him. Hell, he might even be dead now!" The thought sinks in and she tilts her head back to keep the tears from falling. "I likely killed my own brother, and you're telling me I'm the hero."

"He kidnapped people for profit. He was going to keep doing it if you hadn't stopped him. Someone had to."

She shakes her head again. "You don't get it."

"I'm trying to—" He reaches out to her, but she pulls away. She wipes away her tears.

"I just need to be alone."

"Fine, take some space. I get it," he says.

"No, I mean alone for good."

"What?"

"We'd cover more ground on our way, and it'd be easier, draw less attention. You could, I don't know, you could find someone who..." She doesn't finish. "It's better this way."

Akeno blanches. "Wait, are you–" He chokes back a glob stuck in his throat. "You're not serious, are you?"

She doesn't say anything.

"Sam, I think we should stick together. We're better in numbers."

She shakes her head. "If you stay with me, you'll just get hurt again, and you can't afford it. They'll come looking for me. They'll be searching soon."

"They'll never find us. We'll find someplace to hide out. We can–"

"Don't you get it?" she shouts. "You have a concussion and a bullet hole in your shoulder! You can't go anywhere. You need medical attention. You *need* to go to campus."

"I took this bullet," Akeno says, his voice raised. "So I get to decide what I'm capable of. Don't you get it? If I didn't take this bullet, it would've been in your head. You'd be *dead*." He checks himself, his mind a chaotic mess of emotion and thought, his anger rising. "Granted, I haven't done anything at all to help you. You just went out and skinned a rabbit so we could eat, and I could barely collect enough sticks to start a fire. If taking a bullet is the one thing I could do to help, well, then I'll take the bullet. Literally."

She shakes her head. "Don't make this any harder than it has to be." She evens her voice. "I've made my decision."

"So that's it then? I'm just gone?"

"Yeah, that's it," she snaps.

"And what about you? Where are you going to go?"

"God, does it matter?" She shrugs, the anger building. "I don't know. There, I said it. I don't know what's after this. I don't really give a shit what happens after this!"

He's quiet. He exhales and looks away, his temper rising to the surface as her voice echoes through the woods.

"If you'd just let me help—"

"No, Akeno, I know you think you can help me, or save me, or whatever it is you're into, but I don't need saving, so you can go now. I'm not just some charity case."

"Charity? You want to talk about charity?" he shouts. "You don't know the shit I've seen under the face of charity!"

"And you don't know the shit I've been through! You don't know what it's like to be a woman here, of all places."

"You think being the only Asian guy for miles helps me?"

"So there it is."

"What?" he demands.

"We can't know anything about each other. We're two fucked up people thrown together, and you think we can help each other?"

"Yeah, I do," he says in earnest, in a final attempt to keep her there.

"And I'm telling you that you can't help me."

So that's it, he thinks. That's all there is to it. She's done. She doesn't need a good reason. She needs any reason to get out. Akeno squats and sits back on his heels, his eyes focused on the distant trees. It was just like everything else. He was always left behind.

Sam takes the rabbit off the stick and tears apart the meat. It's blackened on one side, burnt. He can feel her eyes on him, watching him, measuring him. She doesn't really care, he thinks. If she did, she would...

"I should get going," he says in a clipped tone.

She doesn't respond.

Akeno stops for a second, breathes. Just like the rest. It's his turn to take the initiative. He needs to leave. She's right. He doesn't need to make this any harder. He knows it's his pride. It's his pride, his fear, his anxiety, his doubt, but he convinces himself it's for the best, just as she's said.

He stands, but then he realizes he's got no plan. He has nowhere to go except for campus. He's not even sure what the plan is after that. He was hoping he could figure it out along the way, with Sam guiding him. It's like his mind has just suddenly been wiped out, turned off, blackout. He can feel his chest pounding.

Don't cry, he tells himself. *It's pointless.*

As darkness draws over Akeno's mind, he thinks life has always been full of too much noise. If the silence between them is what finally makes two people break, then it wasn't the blackout that's killed them. Their undoing was a false sense of security.

"It was nice traveling with you," he says. "I hope you figure everything out."

He doesn't have anything else to say, so he turns in the opposite direction and starts walking. That's all there is to it. He just has to walk away. There's an echo of tension that fades from the weight centered in his chest as his steps increase the distance between them . When he goes far enough, just over the hill and out of her sight, he drops to the ground, his chest heaving. Tears fall onto the leaves beneath him as he rakes his one good hand through his hair, his fingers pulling at the tangles. He can't breathe. He can't speak or move.

There, in the middle of the woods, on a cold November morning, he falls to one side and lays there, immobile, his mind racing, his heart pounding. When it's too much to bear, he opens his mouth and lets out a silent scream.

CHAPTER 11

He finally reaches the edge of the woods. The thin lining of trees separates him from campus, and he remains invisible among the woods. From his vantage point, he can see the outstretched roads and the crowds milling around the once abandoned residence halls. He views this place with a mix of mild curiosity and a sense of loathing. He hates himself for coming back. To him, his return proves how he has failed to survive in the real world. He hates himself for not being able to hold his own alongside Sam, and he hates himself more, knowing he has caused the derision between himself and the one person he considered a friend.

Akeno waits a few minutes, his eyes still red from crying. He stares at the campus roads, forming a map in his head. If he follows the road in front of him, he'll pass by the campus gym, wind through campus, past some of the dorms, though not the one he stayed in, and find himself at the edge of the crowd. Not a bad route to take. The alternative is veering off that road and coming in from the other side of campus, which doesn't seem to benefit him at all. He's looking for the familiar red cross that signals medical treatment, but from where he stands, he can't seem to find it. They may not even have any doctors or medicine. He's betting it all that they will though. If they don't, he can always leave, go back to the woods, and start his journey over. Maybe he'll find that cabin in the woods after all. He scoffs and starts his trek downhill.

The biting wind blows back his hair with a force that makes him stop. He glances up and sees clouds gathering. It could snow again, but the temperature's not quite low enough. He thinks it might rain, a freezing rain. He shudders and realizes all he has left is the clothes on his back. It's fitting. That's how it's always been.

Akeno reaches the road separating him from campus. He thinks of all its inconsistencies that lie there, the numerous people milling in crowds. After being alone for so long, being in public sounds claustrophobic. He hesitates for a moment and suddenly changes course.

He's tired of doing the predictable. Maybe that's been his whole problem. He marches alongside the road, his hands in his pockets. Nothing works out like it's planned, so maybe planning only complicates matters. As he nears a stop sign, Akeno slows and looks both ways before crossing the street, a habit he can't seem to shake. He stands on the other side, his back to campus, to society, to opportunity, to fear, to the unknown. He glances back, and seeing no one, crosses under the tracks and pauses in the archway. There's an echo from his footfalls. He takes a seat on the concrete and listens.

There isn't any sound around him or anything he can hear inside him. He lets that feeling of emptiness settle as he exhales. He's lost the only friend he's had, the only one who seemed to know what she was doing, and when it came down to it, she had to go her own way. Typical. He shouldn't be angry, but he is. He saw the look on her face, the insecurity of what she had just done, guilt most likely. It's all buried there and within him too. Doesn't she see that?

If she doesn't want his help, then there's nothing else he can do. If she must take time to sort herself out, then so be it. Who knows? Maybe they'll see each other again. He has no idea where he goes from here, but that's the point. Their entire realities have shifted. They only met a few days ago, but it was nice having someone to share the experience with.

He thinks back over the past few days and smiles. He can't believe he got caught up in so much shit. Frankly he thought that part of his life was over, and yet somehow the past seems to creep back into his life, just in another shape, taking form in someone else's life. He finds himself in these situations and asks himself why he finds himself alone. Maybe it's him. He's developed a type by now in temporary people. Whether by age, illness, neglect, or trust, he can't seem to land in a space where consistency matters.

A stick breaks off to his right, and he jumps up, his eyes searching the other side of the underpass for a shadow of a person. There's nobody there, and then he sees leaves falling from a nearby tree. He slowly takes a few steps in that direction so he can peer into the branches. Probably an animal, he thinks, as he steps out into the sun, the light blinding him as he glances high where the remaining leaves continue to flutter down.

Up in the tree is an elderly man. He's skinny, his arms thin as he hoists himself up on the branches, a pair of binoculars hanging from his neck. His coat is thin and worn in places around the elbows. His pants are torn as well. However he got here, it must have been a rough trip. The man's thin gray hair floats in the wind, about ear-length, as he balances himself and peers through the binoculars.

From this angle, Akeno thinks he can see onto campus from that high up. He wonders what he's searching for, or if he's just curious. He considers calling for him, but he doesn't want to frighten the old man either. He might fall out of the tree.

He doesn't need to decide. Akeno makes a movement to leave when the man's binoculars swerve to lock onto him.

"Who goes there?" he shouts. He removes the binoculars and looks down, his face a mixed expression of doubt and expressive irritation. "You like watching people, kid?"

"No, sir, just wondering what you were doing, but it's none of my business."

"You're damn right," the old man says, putting the binoculars back up to his face.

He doesn't say anything else, and Akeno makes to leave again, but the old man speaks up without taking his eyes off the distance.

"Them soldiers out there looking a little too uppity for me."

"Say again?" Akeno shouts.

"Why are you shouting?" the old man snaps and glares down at him. "You want to wake the whole neighborhood?"

Akeno glances around him, where no houses or apartments can be seen for a least a couple more blocks.

"You've got business just walking about?" the old man asks.

"No, sir."

"Good, climb on up then, and I'll give you a looksee."

Akeno hesitates, considering the intentions of the old man. They've been burned before, trusting people who seemed harmless, but then he thinks of Jay. In another reality, Akeno would've avoided Jay and Amy on the streets. He would've taken them for drug dealers, or addicts mostly likely, people who'd rob you in broad daylight. That wasn't them at all. They may have been on a party binge, but they were harmless in the end.

"Come on, kid. Quit lollygaggin'," he snapped.

Akeno climbs the trees, his arms straining to pull his weight. He was light now, but his strength had vanished over the last few days. He felt weak, numb, and underfed. He was better off on his steady diet of snacks and gas station food.

"Look through here," the old man said, pointing ahead. "Focus on that belltower there, then move your sight down. That's what you want to see."

The images crossing before Akeno's eyes looked like a swirl of colors and blurred trees blocking his view. The old man tilted the binoculars a few degrees to the right, and suddenly Akeno spotted the belltower. "I see the tower," he says, his mouth agape as he focuses.

"Good, now look at that green tent below that. There's people there checking in for something. What do you think that is?"

"Probably a registration tent," Akeno mutters. "Like signing in so they know who you are. ID and stuff."

"Sure, but what about them?" the old man tilts the scopes several more degrees to the left. "They're sure as hell not registering for nothin.'"

A few people are shoved on board a bus, their hands locked behind their backs.

"Trouble makers," Akeno suggests. "People caught trying to loot from the military. Only a dumbass would try it."

"Do they look like criminals to you?" the old man questions. "Even the kids?"

Akeno looks harder, searching for children but doesn't see any.

"I don't see any kids."

"That's cause you're a kid yourself."

The old man snatches the binoculars away and peers back through them.

"Name's Randy," he says, licking his chapped lips. "Yours?"

"Akeno."

"Funny name."

"It's Japanese."

"Good," he mutters. "Good. Well, it was nice to meet you, Akeno."
He climbs down and starts walking. Akeno jumps down, his ankles
weak from the shock of landing.

"Where do you live?"

"Oh, out there somewhere. Far away from this place anyway." He
turns and starts to walk. "Came to town for a little reconnaissance.
Need a better spot to check out more of the place. I'm thinking north,
above the campus for a bird's eye view."

Akeno follows after Randy, his pace matching his on the cracked
sidewalk as the old man leads the way up a side street.

"How did you get here? Do you have a car?"

"Hell no. It died months ago. Probably sitting on the highway
somewheres."

"You don't remember where you left it?"

"Oh, it's gone now. I left it there, and next time I came back, it was
gone."

"So how did you get here?"

"What kind of question is that?" Randy turns and stares Akeno in
the face.

Akeno can't tell if this man's crazy or just giving him the runaround.

"Look, you don't have to tell me anything. Just tell me what you've
seen on campus."

"Why? You goin' there?"

"I was thinking about it."

Randy gives him the onceover. "Don't. It's not a good place for a
fella like you."

"Meaning?"

Randy snorts.

"What have you seen? Are they helping?"

"Sure, they're helping someone."

"Are they giving out food? Blankets? Any supplies?"

"Sometimes."

Fine, the old man doesn't want to share what he knows. Then why did he invite him up in that tree, just to look?

"What can you tell me?"

"I can tell you that you shouldn't deal with those people over yonder. They're not looking for anything but what *they* want."

"Who's *they*?"

Randy shrugs. "The usual kind."

This is going nowhere, Akeno thinks. He should give in now. Then he sees something strapped to Randy's back, something under his shirt. A wire crosses up and attaches itself behind Randy's ear, just under his hair.

"What's that in your ear?" he asks.

"Radio telecommunications," Randy answers without turning around. He walks quicker, his scuffed shoes smacking against the pavement as they make their way uphill.

"What does it say?"

"Don't know. Can't get a good signal 'round here. I think them uniforms have blocked any incoming signals, so I haven't been able to pick up nothin.'"

"Can they do that?"

"Sure. Why couldn't they?"

Akeno rolls his eyes.

"What else have you heard on there, when you do get a signal?"

"Well, the reason I came here was 'cause some professor or whoever had sent an outgoing signal somewheres closeby. I asked him how many civilians were living down here, and he said at least a few students on campus. Looks like they've been evicted."

Akeno blushes but doesn't say anything.

"So's I come down here thinking I can find a few allies, but that signal went silent. Figured may as well try anyway and that was my first trip. Didn't find no one, so I left. Still had the truck then, but now it's just wherever my legs take me."

"You can't live far then."

"Says who?" Randy turns. "You tryna follow me home, boy?"

"No, no. Just curious how you got here is all. What else did you come for?"

Randy shakes his head. "Like I said, I've been listening to this radio. Got lots of folks sayin' them boys ain't up to no good. They ain't the government, or if they are, they aren't helping the people. That's plain as day."

"What makes you say that?"

"You saw with your own eyes."

Akeno couldn't understand.

"What else has the radio been saying? Any government officials on there?"

"Can't tell. Everyone claims to be someone of authority. Can't trust them all."

"Who do you trust?"

"A few people. Gotta' field the good ones from the bad."

"What are the good ones saying?"

"They're saying this whole blackout was staged. It was the government suits who decided to release all hell on the people. They say it was politics, but Lord knows politics would've destroyed this country long before, so what is it really then? Those answers, I'd love to know."

"What do you think it could've been, if it was the Feds?"

153

"Well my best guess would probably be taxes," Randy said, turning around, glancing over the hill they had just climbed. Akeno's out of breath, but Randy's breathing fine.

"Taxes?" Akeno asks. "That's your best guess."

Randy nods. "Rich folks love their money."

Akeno stops in place. "You're crazy."

He shrugs. "Believe what you want."

"Did you catch the name of the professor from campus?"

"Nope."

"Can you at least try?" Akeno snaps.

Randy's quiet for some time. Then, "Holden. That was his name. Like my cousin."

Akeno blanches. "So, he did make contact with the outside."

"You knew him?"

"He was my English professor," he mumbles. "He's a good guy." Randy grunts.

"I had been planning to get my own radio…"

"What you need a radio for?"

"What are you talking about?" Akeno nearly shouts. "To talk to people like you have, to know what's happening, to not feel so left in the dark."

"You're in the dark 'cause you don't see what's in front of you," Randy says. "From what I've gathered in the ten minutes I've met you, you only see what you want to see."

"I don't follow anything you're saying. It's like you've been talking in code!"

"Exactly."

"Listen, old man, I'm done playing your games. Go on ahead without me."

"Planned on it."

Akeno stops and watches as Randy tops the hill and heads straight into a cluster of trees. Crazy old man, he thinks. He doesn't know anything. So much for having a radio. He turns and heads back for campus, Randy's warning disappearing in the wind. If he wants answers, he needs to go looking for them.

CHAPTER 12

Akeno steps onto the road and doesn't stop until he finds himself in the thick of the crowds. He has his arms at his sides to appear as casually as possible, though at some point he crosses his good arm over his injured shoulder. Maybe if he looks really hurt, they'll rush him to the doctors, wherever they are. Akeno's stomach rumbles. He wishes he had eaten now. It's been over twelve hours since he last ate. Nobody seems to notice him. Everyone shuffles past him, either in a rush or otherwise just moving to keep warm. He soon realizes that not everyone is equipped for the winter. Some wear winter coats, and others wear thin windbreakers. Some don't even have shoes.

Just as he's passing the last of the dorms, he notices the university center just blocks away, the same building as the cafeteria. A mass of people are gathered outside the building's doors. They're all huddled together from the cold, their eyes peeking out of hats, scarves, hoods, and big jackets. Akeno makes his way to the crowd and looks around. They're all fairly hushed as they wait, though Akeno doesn't know what they're waiting for. The doors must be locked since no one's going inside. Akeno takes a chance and asks a nearby man what's going on, which the man doesn't seem to hear at first. Akeno asks louder.

"Food," the man snaps without looking at Akeno. "This is where all the food is. You have to take a number card to get in. If they call your number, you can eat."

"Why not just feed everyone?" Akeno asks the man.

The man barks out a laugh. "Are you stupid?"

"What?"

He shakes his head. "Your generation of people are next to worthless."

When he sees Akeno's blank face, the man rolls his eyes.

"They're running low on supplies, so they're rationing what they have, but in case you haven't noticed, some of these men look like they've been fed too well." The man glares at the doors, as if someone is standing on the other side of the glass, waving a loaf of bread at the hungry. Nobody's at the door, and it doesn't seem like the building itself is inhabited at all. "They're always so full and happy. I know they're hiding it somewhere."

"Who?" Akeno asks, confused.

"Them," he says, gesturing to the group of soldiers filing past, their guns held to their chests. They don't seem to notice the crowd as they round the corner of the history building.

"Where do you get the number cards?" Akeno asks.

"Other side of campus," the man says, pointing in a vague direction. "There's a line though. Doubt you'll get any good numbers."

"What's the calling number?"

"The last number they called yesterday was eighty-three."

"What's your card say?" He can't help but ask.

The man turns to Akeno and openly stares, a snide look Akeno's accustomed to receiving from men like this. He's about to give his retort when one of the doors finally opens, and the man rushes forward with the crowd, leaving Akeno unanswered. Everyone waves their paper numbers in the air, each crying out various numbers. Akeno can't hear above the din of the noise as he heads for the other side of campus.

157

What Akeno didn't realize was just how many people were on campus. While the east side of campus is almost entirely abandoned, the center to west side of campus is packed with tents, rows and rows of tents. He sees what looks like families, ashes from campfires, tons and tons of trash, and other odds and ends stacked up in piles like a hoarder's nest. Akeno expected a lot of people but not this many. Akeno can't see past the row of tents or through the heavy flow of traffic as people walk the center road running through campus. They seem to be bartering on both sides of the street, each person in search of something worth trading.

Akeno keeps his head down as he walks through the crowded campus streets. He doesn't have anything or anyone to protect him now. He thinks he should have taken Sam's gun, at least one of them, but he knows even if threatened, he would never be able to use it. He catches sideways looks from men standing on either side of the street, their arms crossed, their eyes sizing him up. He keeps pushing through the crowd, bustling against everyone going his way or in opposite directions. It's a maze of people, and Akeno can't help but feel flustered from all the bodies surrounding him. He still needs to find a doctor.

As he passes the geology building, he notices a woman and three kids sitting around a small fire, their hands outstretched to warm their gloveless fingers. Their round eyes stare up at him, and he realizes for the first time there are people already on the brink of starvation. The oldest of the three, maybe twelve, looks wary, even angry, like he might attack Akeno if he looks at them twice. He wonders if their father is around. He wonders if the men staring at him have tried approaching their family, asking for their mother, asking for the kids. Akeno shakes the thought away. He digs his nails in his palms and hurries past. He should consider himself lucky.

Metal and glass break against the pavement on the other side of the street, and a conflict breaks out. A man has another man pinned against the concrete, his fists beating into the side of the other man's face. There's blood, screaming, running, and then two soldiers rush up and grab the one man off the other. The other man lies unconscious on the ground, his head leaking an obscene amount of blood. A paramedic team runs up, lifts the man on a stretcher, and rushes off. Did someone call 911?

Akeno laughs to himself, and with horror, he stifles the sound with his hand. He hurries forward, leaving the crowd behind, all standing in a circle around the spot where the man had laid. He follows the rushing paramedics. There must be a medical tent up ahead. There must be some doctors and nurses stationed there. They should have some supplies, something for the pain at least. He wonders how many times they've heard that today.

Up ahead, Akeno sees the line for the food tickets. It stretches back into the crowd with no definitive end. The man was right. He would be lucky to get a good number. He should've eaten the rabbit Sam offered him. It was an easy meal, and he turned it away. For what? Pride? His nerves? Akeno berates himself for being so naive, so stupid.

The paramedics disappear inside one of many tents set up along the edge of campus, away from the crowds and noise. Akeno tries to follow them, but a woman stops him.

"Emergencies only," she says.

"That's fine. I, uh, I need something for..." He points to his shoulder, then at his head.

"What happened?" she asks, a little concerned. "Were you shot?"

"Yeah, but it went through, so I'm good, I think. I just need some medicine and maybe some ointment, bandages, whatever you have."

"We don't have much, sweetheart," she says and gestures for him to follow. She heads inside another tent next to the emergency tent. She nods at the man standing guard. The guard eyes Akeno, then lets him pass.

Once inside, Akeno takes in the scene. There's several boxes and containers with different supplies--needles, pill bottles, bandages, creams, medical equipment, and more. If this is scarcity, Akeno thinks. What are they missing?

"I'm Clara, by the way," she says. "You?"

"Akeno," he says. He could have said 'Lee' again, but what's the point?

"Alright, Akeno, let's take a look at the bullet hole. If you could take off your hoodie for me, I can apply some antibacterial *ointment* as you call it and assess any further damage."

Akeno nods and pulls his hoodie with one arm, fails to take it off, tries again. Clara watches from a distance, her eyes glowing with either pity or humor, Akeno can't tell anymore.

"There's a hole," Akeno says, pulling at the stitches Sam had sewn into his hoodie. She didn't bother stitching up the two shirts underneath though. He holds the layers back as Clara steps over to examine his shoulder.

"You seem like you're doing okay as far as infection is concerned. Have you applied anything to it since you were injured?"

"Uh, rubbing alcohol, I think. I was with a--uh--a friend when it happened, so she did whatever she could."

"She did a heck of a job," Clara says, turning to rummage in one of the containers. "It's probably what's helped stave off any infection, which is the good news. Bad news is that you'll have a lame shoulder for a while."

She takes out a swab cloth and alcohol, applies it to Akeno's shoulder, holds it there, and dabs at the dried blood as she works.

"I'd say you've got a pretty fair shot of survival, granted that you keep cleaning and rewrapping your wound, but as far as usage goes, you'll have to consider how much heavy lifting you do. Just because your wound heals doesn't mean your shoulder will be strong enough to use like you used to. Then again, nothing's like it used to be, so I don't know when or where you'd really need to do any heavy lifting. Do you hunt?"

Akeno shakes his head.

"Well, if you do, I would only hunt small game. Deer can be pretty heavy, and if you reopen this wound, even if it's partially healed, it'll cause more problems than you need. You'll have to start all the way back over and hope for the best. I don't wish that on you, so be careful."

"Thanks," Akeno says as she rewraps the wound in a fresh bandage over the ointment she applied. It stings like hell but knowing it's medicine eases Akeno's mind.

"You have any clean bandages or any more alcohol to keep that thing clean?" she asks.

Akeno shakes his head. "Ran out," he lies.

"Here, take some then. Limited supplies as they last." She hands him a small wrap for bandaging and a few small bottles of alcohol. They remind him of the airplane bottles he used to see kids buy at the gas station.

"Thank you, Clara," he says. "You don't know what I've been through today." He sniffles, catches himself, and smiles. "Anyway, thanks again." He quickly leaves the tent.

"Hey," Clara says, calling after him.

"Yeah?" he says and turns back around. He wishes he hadn't said anything.

"Take care," she says, offering a small smile.

He nods and hurries away.

The last of Akeno's energy finally runs out. He drags himself to the side of the road and drops down on the curb, his hands burying themselves in his pockets, wrapped firmly around the only things he now owns. As the wind blows past him, Akeno's hood flies off, revealing himself for just a split second before Akeno ties it back on.

"Hey," an almost inaudible voice says from behind him.

Akeno's ears perk up at the voice directing itself at him and hopes with everything he has that it's Sam. He almost smiles as he glances back over his shoulder, thinking she must have come back for him.

"Akeno," the voice says, now much closer.

Akeno's face drops into a frown. It couldn't be—

"Akeno, it's me, Kevin," a man with a thick beard says, bending down in front of him. He doesn't wait for a greeting back. He leans over and pulls him in for a tight embrace . At first Akeno is too stunned to speak, but then he leans into his old friend, feeling the warmth emanating from his burly body. "It's been a long time, bud," he says pulling back with a grin. " How's it been?"

CHAPTER 13

Akeno rests inside a supersize tent, his butt resting on the warmth of a sleeping bag. It smells faintly of corn chips in the tent. He wears a pair of bright blue women's gloves, a child's rainbow striped hat pulled over his ears, and an overused blanket around his shoulders. He munches on a snack pack size of trail mix, slowly but greedily, sucking the salt from the peanuts before chewing.

Kevin's family had been camping here for a couple nights. As soon as they got word that uniformed men had showed up on campus, they packed everything they had and started their journey here. They even drove the car until it ran out of gas. Luckily that was only about fifteen miles shy of campus, so the hike wasn't all that bad. Once they got here, everything was great. The soldiers have treated their family well and keep peace on the streets. There's plenty of food to eat, though Kevin's family doesn't advertise that they already brought enough for the family. His father's standing in line for another meal ticket. His mother should be back anytime with today's portion.

"I thought your parents were divorced?" Akeno asks, shoving the leftovers of his trail mix in his pocket.

"They are, but my parents think it's better to stick together as a family until things settle."

Akeno isn't sure things will settle, but he understands wanting to be together.

"And your sister?"

"Kayla's still annoying, but less so since the blackout. I don't know, it's like she's changed somehow. She doesn't complain as much as she used to, doesn't fight with me over stupid shit anymore." He pulls out a mini bag of chips and starts munching.

Akeno thinks everyone's changed, including Kevin. Well, not much has changed for Kevin, but he looks different. Akeno didn't even know Kevin could grow a beard. He was always soft around the edges, but it seems Kevin's body has toned itself into a sturdier, stronger looking version of the old Kevin. Akeno thinks the fifteen-mile hike could have done it, or the fact that there's less pizza to eat in the blackout, but either way, Kevin looks in much better shape than Akeno does. Now that he thinks about it, Akeno has lost weight too, but in a much more anti-climatic way. Kevin probably thinks Akeno looks like one of the starving people, and he supposes he is.

"So, what's the plan after this? Why are all these people here?" Akeno asks, now steering the conversation to what Akeno needs answers for. He needs to learn everything he can about this Sanctuary before making any decisions. If he can get everything he needs to know out of Kevin, he can hurry back to Sam and relay the information. That's if he finds her. That's if she'll bother to listen.

"So, here's the thing," Kevin whispers, leaning in close like others may overhear them. "Everyone's been hearing about this place somewhere off the grid. Nobody knows where it is exactly, but it has power and running water and all the regular things like before."

Akeno notices Kevin's inflection on "before." It's been almost two months. That's two months without power, two months in the dark, two months without anyone owning up to the blackout or otherwise explaining what happened. Does anyone know what happened? After all this time, can no one explain what caused the blackout?

"So, what caused the blackout?" Akeno asks. That should have been his first question. "Have the soldiers said anything about it?"

"They don't know either," Kevin says, his eyes big. "We've asked, believe me. Everyone has. They keep saying they don't know, but here's the thing: Someone has to know something."

"Exactly," Akeno says, bobbing his head up and down. "So?"

"Well, that's the thing. Nobody's talking. But if you think about it, why would they know? If it's some secret operation or say it's classified, then of course these soldiers wouldn't know. Why would they need to know? What if they tell everyone here?" Kevin says, gesturing all around them. "So, if they don't know, then who would know?"

Akeno pauses and smiles, one he hopes emulates innocence.

"Anyway, just a thought. I don't know who would know, but someone has to, and when we find them, they'll have all the answers." Kevin sits back and smiles. "I'm ready for that day to come, when finally the truth comes out."

They sit there together for a moment, Kevin basking in a remote future and Akeno watching on with a feeling like pity washing over him.

"It just feels like such a short time for the government to have been able to build something so large so soon," Akeno says, more to himself than to Kevin.

"Yeah, well, the government keeps things in line," Kevin says, sitting back up. "I'm sure they've pulled all their resources together after the Cold War. There's bound to be some hidden files that have detailed what to do in case of a national emergency. You never know who could have attacked us."

"Attacked?" Akeno asks, Kevin doesn't seem to hear him as he continues.

"I'm just glad they're here now to get us. This place must be kept somewhere in the Midwest. Can't imagine it'd be close by and us not knowing where it is."

Akeno shakes his previous question. "I met a woman who talked about this place. She called it Sanctuary."

"There's loads of names for it, but yeah, that's the one I've heard the most," Kevin says. "I've heard names like Babylon, Atlantis, Garden of Eden and hell, I've heard Purgatory, but I think my favorite has to be the Garden of Eden."

Akeno doesn't respond, doesn't know how.

"You know, cause like the Garden of Eden is where humanity first began, and like, you know, now it's where humanity is restarting."

"What do you mean by 'restarting?' Humanity hasn't died off."

"Not yet," Kevin mumbles.

"Look all around you," Akeno says, his voice rising. "This is humanity, and they're starving. They're dying."

"Yeah, I know, and it sucks, but like, you know…"

Akeno doesn't know, but he drops the subject. Kevin leans back and rests his hands behind his head. He almost looks at home here in this tent, like he's done this his whole life. He looks well rested too. Then Akeno remembers the last time he saw Kevin. He just disappeared, no goodbye, no note. Akeno refuses to bring it up, more so out of pride, mainly because he doesn't have time to listen to anymore excuses.

Akeno and Kevin immediately fall back into their old habit of conversation. Kevin plows on without noticing Akeno's inexpressiveness.

"I hear this Sanctuary place is really selective, though," Kevin says. "Like only the chosen ones can enter." Kevin snickers, probably remembering the same Garden of Eden reference.

"What do you mean?" Akeno asks.

"Families are first priority, of course, and kids. Then single, young women. Then single, young men." Akeno notes the emphasis on age. "Everyone else just sort of gets picked over."

"Who does the picking?"

Kevin shrugs. "I mean, I get it. A small, functioning society like this one doesn't have the room for the sick and elderly. Everyone has to work to get a meal. It's a fair trade."

Akeno doesn't say anything, his jaw locking down on his teeth.

"It just seems so weird. It's almost too good to be true. Had I known that the military would come here, I could have just stayed on campus. It seems like the safest place to be. Did you ever leave?"

Akeno shakes his head.

"You must have hit the jackpot living in the dorms. What kind of goodies did you find?"

Akeno shakes his head. "I ran weeks ago," he lies. He doesn't want to reveal he had run from the military. Kevin's an okay guy, but he's a staunch supporter of the government.

"What happened to all your stuff? Didn't you bring anything?"

"Storm blew it away," Akeno says, staring down into his hands. He wonders how Sam's doing in this crowd. Is she safe?

"That sucks, man. Well, hey, before you go, we can raid the market, see what we can pick up. There's loads of goods out there."

Akeno doesn't like the way Kevin says "raid" or "goods," but he doesn't comment.

Just then, a middle-aged woman steps into the tent, carrying a wide box, at first confused when she sees Akeno. Then, she grows angry, glares at her son, but her face quickly softens. "I didn't realize we were going to have any guests. You've made a friend?"

"No, Mom, this is my roommate, Akeno."

Akeno notes that he said "is," as if this statement is still true, as if it hasn't been weeks since they've seen each other. Akeno reaches out to shake her hand, but she turns her back without noticing Akeno's gesture. He pulls it back slowly and watches as Kevin's mother places a load of food onto the tent floor. It looks like enough to feed five.

Kevin stands, along with Akeno, and takes a small bag from the corner of the tent. Akeno assumes it contains something to bargain with. They step out of the tent and onto the streets, which instantly becomes a crowd of flowing people in a busy marketplace. Akeno and Kevin take the streets slowly, checking out the tents with mats in front of them, little trinkets or accessories laid on some, clothes on others. Some have jewelry laid out; others have pairs of glasses. Other mats hold regular household items like toothpaste, floss, combs, hair bands, forks, spoons, scissors, and coup syrup. Anything or anyone, as Akeno noticed, was viable for trade. In some of the larger tents, men and women wearing makeup stand outside, their eyes beckoning, their smiles flirtatious. Several men stand with them, whispering in their ears, offering whatever it is they are willing to trade. There's nothing here that meets Akeno's needs, but Kevin seeks to find entertainment bartering and haggling for useless things.

They pass a woman wearing a long skirt sitting on top of a thin mat, her legs crossed underneath her, her hands facing palm up on her knees. She seems to be meditating. From the way the thin material of her clothes rest on her limbs, Akeno thinks she must be starving. Kevin doesn't give her a second glance.

Kids run through the streets, and Kevin brushes past them as they run by. Akeno watches as the kids head to the outskirts of the market, where they run past a group of kids in their early teens standing by a tree, their eyes picking over the crowd.

Kevin stops next to an old man and asks to barter a robot toy for one of his cheap gold necklaces. The man's white strands of hair blow in the wind, his jacket filled with holes, his hands thin and pale, his veins purple. The man grumbles and takes the toy, exchanging it for the jewelry. Kevin turns with a triumphant smile, pockets the jewelry, and walks to the next booth. Akeno follows. He glances behind him to see the old man peek his head inside the tent behind him and hand a smiling toddler the robot toy. The old man slumps over, his head dangling on his hunched shoulders, smiling as the boy flies the robot through the air. Akeno smiles too.

As they walk back to Kevin's tent, Akeno searches for a way out. He's done hanging out with Kevin all day. He doesn't know anything. Then again, it wouldn't be Kevin who knew the details of his family's migration. His parents would know though. Considering Akeno doesn't have a tent, and all that he's wearing is what he has, he doesn't see a better chance of making it through the night. The temperature's already dropping, and it's not even sunset yet. He needs to learn more about Sanctuary, or the Garden of Eden, as Kevin prefers to call it.

Kevin doesn't speak for the first time, and Akeno's grateful. Then he wonders what changed for Kevin by the time he left campus and now. His parents were divorced, and now they're together. That must be strange. He lost a lot of weight too. Kevin showed Akeno that they have plenty of food, but even so, losing that much weight that fast can take its toll, not to mention the several miles he's traveled to get back here. Akeno thinks he should ask Kevin about any number of these things, but he doesn't. They're not friends, and Akeno shouldn't pretend that Kevin gave a shit about him when he up and left.

Akeno thinks it's time to just turn around and get lost in the crowd, but he knows Kevin would find him. It was easy to find Akeno's face in the crowd, especially in a place like Johnsville. Come to think of it, Akeno hasn't seen any other Asian person. He's seen a few black people and the one Hispanic couple. As Akeno looks around, he realizes the crowd is almost entirely white. He wonders if he's made a mistake coming here.

From the corner of his eye, Akeno gets the feeling that Kevin has been watching him all day, despite the constant chattering. Akeno can only guess why Kevin would be glancing over his shoulder so often, but when it comes to Kevin, sometimes there's not a reason for what he does. He's just in a constant state of existence. On the other side of the street, Akeno catches a girl looking at him. Her hair is tied back and hidden under her hood, but Akeno recognizes Sam immediately. She turns suddenly and heads in the opposite direction. He watches as she disappears into the crowd without even a chance to pursue after her.

That night, Kevin's family shares their dinner boxes with him-- beans, rice, and unsalted boiled carrots. His father, mother, and sister all sit in a circle inside the tent, their eyes casting uncertain glances at Akeno. The family introduced themselves, and Akeno shook Mr. Howard's hand, greeted Ms. Howard with a nod. He doesn't know what else to call her. She still hasn't spoken to him, barely looks at him. Kevin doesn't seem to notice the tension and continues rambling about his days in college, as if they were old graduate buddies, as if they weren't living together just a couple months ago, eating pizza and playing video games.

Akeno thinks that time is long past and doesn't see a future where normalities like those will happen again. Whatever becomes normal won't include the technology they've had. No more gaming systems, no more wifi, no more television. Despite the blackout, electricity is a novelty invention that's here to stay. Humanity couldn't return to the Dark Ages, not after being spoiled for so long. That was why everyone was gathered here now. Nobody understood survival, not the real meaning of it.

"Akeno's really smart," Kevin says then, mouth full of beans. "He was always reading some book and had a stack of them on his nightstand. First guy I met that actually read anything he was assigned too."

"I'm not surprised," Mr. Howard says. "Your family must be strict on academics." He looks up at Akeno, forces a thin-lipped smile.

Akeno makes the conscious effort not to roll his eyes. "Yes, sir" is all he says. Better to be a "yes man" when it comes to dealing with people like the Howards.

Akeno never told Kevin about his familial situation or lack thereof. He pauses and thinks of Sam, then continues before anyone notices his mental lapse. His food tray is nearly finished, but there's still a few bites left. Somehow, it's become difficult for Akeno to eat anything else. His stomach feels full, but he knows that's not true. He needs to eat all he can, but he just can't. He hands his tray off to Kevin, says he's finished. Kevin shrugs and devours the rest.

"Well let's hope your street smart too," Howard continues. "Better to see reality for what it is, not just what you've read about in books."

Akeno isn't sure what he means by that, but he doesn't elaborate. Ms. Howard seems intent on staring into her lap. He can't help but feel she didn't want to share their food, despite the excess. She must have lied and said they have one more kid than they actually do. He wonders why the soldiers didn't fact check that source of information.

Ms. Howard is well-dressed and traditionally pretty for a middle-aged woman, and she still wears a trace of mascara. The appeal of a woman like her is enough. She's someone people can easily trust, and maybe she even reminds them of their own mother. She's got the charm, but she doesn't use it now. She's silent, solemn, and looks to be considering her options.

Akeno notes Kevin's sister, Kayla, and her natural beauty too. They're almost too similar looking. Had he not known any better, Kayla could easily pass for eighteen or nineteen years old, which must have its own perks. Her large, blue eyes feel ice cold when they land on Akeno. She must feel the same way as her mother does about Akeno.

"What degree were you pursuing?" Howard asks abruptly. "One of the STEM degrees?"

"Um, no. I was undeclared," Akeno replies, clearing his throat.

He gives a curt nod and finishes his dinner box. Howard goes on to say, "We've been thinking…"

Akeno thinks this is where he'll be dismissed. He thinks they'll let him keep the free meal, but in exchange, they never want to see him again. They'll demand payment for the meal, or they'll want it back. Nevermind if he freezes outside or if he starves to death, but this isn't a charity; this is reality. They must insist he leave now.

"If you're willing, we'd like you to join us to the Garden of Eden. I'm sure Kevin's filled you in with the details," Howard says.

Akeno feels his heart rate suddenly spike and then slow back down. He feels a sense of a relief and then a sense of danger. Why did they want him? They didn't seem to like him at all.

"We are a family of three," Howard continues. "With a daughter of fifteen. Kevin's eighteen, which makes him too old. Kevin's considered a legal adult for the workplace and won't count as the family."

"I, uh, I don't know what that has to do with me," Akeno says uncertainly. "And I'm not actually trying too--Did Kevin say something? Because I don't–"

The tent grows quiet, and all eyes are on Akeno. The noises from the street filter into Akeno's mind. He wonders how long he'd have to sleep on the hard concrete before he agrees to follow this family across the country to an unknown place run by the government. Not too long. He'll freeze. Winter's setting in. If he doesn't go now, he won't make it to spring.

"Can you give me a little more detail?" Akeno asks.

Howard grins. "Atta boy. It's simple. We'll have you, say you're our adopted son, and Kevin can come with us as a single adult."

"Oh, I see where this is headed, uh...Why couldn't you just lie about Kevin's age?"

"Does Kevin look like he can pass as sixteen to you? I mean, look at him," Howard says and laughs.

Kevin's cheeks turn a bright red, and he puts down his two empty trays. Kevin's long, unruly beard and dirtied face couldn't possibly pass for anything under twenty-five, but he doesn't say this. Then Akeno realizes what this must mean for him. He'll be twenty in under a month, but thanks to his smooth, Japanese face, he can easily be mistaken for a younger teen. Akeno takes a deep breath, considers his options. He knows that when the Howards get there with Akeno in tow, they'll just switch Kevin and Akeno. Kevin will stay with the family, and Akeno goes wherever they tell him to. It's pretty simple, but there's so much that could go wrong, especially within a militarized government facility.

Akeno thinks he understands how this will go but is still hesitant. What about Sam? They never made a decision about going to Sanctuary. They're supposed to be getting information, not agree to go with another family. If Akeno goes, he wants to go with Sam.

Howard flashes a thin-lipped smile, like he's expecting a certain answer. Akeno glances at Ms. Howard. She must think he'll refuse her offer, but Akeno couldn't imagine any other alternative except living on the streets, homeless and freezing, without anyone else. He thinks Sam must be negotiating a similar deal. It's her only chance to get into Sanctuary, unless she doesn't see the offer as appealing, unless she'd rather head for the mountains and make the best of it there. That was always her plan. Maybe she only came down here to accompany him, gather some supplies, and head out without a second goodbye.

"I'll do it," Akeno says. "Just tell me what I need to do."

CHAPTER 14

Akeno doesn't sleep that night. This would be the last time he was adopted, he thinks. The irony of the situation doesn't escape him, but he doesn't feel like laughing. Maybe Sam would laugh if she heard the news.

Throughout the night, he wakes up in a sweat, his heartbeat accelerated, his stomach in knots. He doesn't remember the last time he's experienced such increased anxiety. This isn't the first time he's slept in a close space with a family he doesn't know. He gives up on sleeping and thinks of the woods, of the stars, of what he can't see anymore under the tent. He's thankful, yet resentful. He's sold himself out.

He slides out from underneath the heavy comforter the Howards had given him and suddenly feels the hardness of the cold ground beneath him. He can just barely make out Howard's body in front of him in the dark, lying restless and immobile on his back, his arms tucked in his extra-large sleeping bag. He's even larger and taller than Kevin, which makes him somewhere between 6'3" and 6'4." He wonders what kind of power Howard must feel around people like Akeno, small in stature and lightweight.

On the other side of her ex-husband is Ms. Howard, her head cradled in the crook of her elbow. Next to her is Kayla. Her breathing is steady, her hands are clasped just below where her breasts would be under the sleeping bag. Akeno is immediately reminded of Sleeping

Beauty. She looks asleep, but the way her fingers move in circles tells Akeno that she's awake.

Akeno watches Kayla twiddle her thumbs until he finally falls asleep, only to wake to the rising dawn and Howard's heavy movements as he packs everything up. Akeno quickly stands and hurries to put his stuff away, but Ms. Howard has already done that. When the family has everything accounted for, it's the early morning after dawn, and Akeno stands carrying one of the larger packs on his back.

As they start making their way across campus, the cool air freezing on Akeno's cheeks, his senses finally kick in, and he realizes why they've packed their camp up. He glances behind them and sees the empty square where they had once been. He knows it'll be filled before noon, where someone else will see the open spot and make their claim.

Up ahead, Howard leads the way, his son behind him, and Kayla behind her. She walks alongside her mother, their voices low as they exchange conversation. Akeno can't hear. He's a few paces behind them, his joints and muscles stiff from the night before. Kayla glances sideways and covers her mouth with her hand. The two share a look before catching Akeno's eye. He quickly turns away.

Despite where they slept last night, Ms. Howard's hair seems to be brushed neatly back into a thick ponytail. Kayla's is the same. There aren't many tangles in either of their hair, and Akeno wishes he had asked Sam for his brush before they parted ways. He's had it up this whole time, and Akeno can only wonder what he smells like.

Suddenly Ms. Howard drops back to be in time with Akeno. Kayla plows forward, as they fall behind. She offers a smile, but Akeno doesn't look her in the face.

"Did you sleep well?" she asks, her voice soft and low. Akeno glances up at Howard, who doesn't seem to notice they've fallen behind.

"Not really," Akeno says.

"Sorry it was so early. I was actually surprised you had slept through the night at all. I was thinking you'd have left."

"No," Akeno says, his eyes darting sideways. She's smiling. What does he say to that? "Why would I do that?"

"I was thinking you might have come with others, maybe you wanted to say goodbye to them one last time."

"No, I came alone."

"Really? Kevin says you recognized someone at the market."

Kevin must have seen Akeno's face when he saw Sam in the crowd. Akeno has to admit he was surprised himself. He didn't think Sam would find him on campus. He figured she would be there for fifteen minutes tops and leave. He can't believe Kevin noticed. Did he see her too? No, he couldn't have. He was facing the wrong direction. But he knows she exists.

"Uh, no, I mean. Yeah, I did see someone, but it was someone I had class with. It's, uh, yeah, it wasn't anyone important."

Ms. Howard nods.

"By the way," she says, reaching her hand out. "I'm Joanna. I didn't get a chance to introduce myself last night. My husband likes to do all the talking. Be careful not to listen to too much of his nonsense."

She's still smiling at him, pleasant almost. So it's like that, Akeno thinks.

"It's alright. He's fine."

"Oh, he's a fine man, but still. He likes to tell his stories." She laughs softly. Akeno glances up and catches Howard's eye. He stopped to wait for Akeno and Ms. Howard.

"Having a good time back there?" he calls, his face blocked from shadow. The rising sun is just over the top of this hill. Must be a pretty view.

"Yeah, we're keeping up," Ms. Howard says with a gentle wave. "You go ahead."

Howard looks on, his body tense. He turns and walks down the hill. Kevin waits for his sister and mother. When Akeno and Ms. Howard reach the top, they all start down the hill together.

The five of them approach the building where families register and apply for Sanctuary. Howard turns to Akeno. "Take off your bandages. They don't need to know you're hurt."

Akeno blushes and carefully undoes the bandage. Joanna attempts to help him, but Akeno's already finished by the time her fingers reach for his hair.

"Do you need a brush?" she asks with uncertainty.

Akeno thinks yes but doesn't ask for any favors. He shakes his head, ties his hair back to cover the bruise. With his fingers, he gently feels where a bump has formed. Akeno tentatively feels at his shoulder, the bandages hidden underneath his clothes. He can't really take that one off. He can't risk infection. He needs to apply some medicine on it once they make camp again. He wonders how he'll find the privacy to do that.

As they enter the old, brick building, Akeno recognizes it immediately as the history building. It looks so different coming in from the back, Akeno thinks. The soldiers are standing by the entrance, their guns held at their side. The soldiers don't move as they enter into the front lobby. A man sits at a desk. All over the room are pictures of happy families. There's signs and insignias all over the walls with the word "Amity" written inside a logo. The logo pictures several hands holding one another in a circle. The hands are all different shades, but mostly they're white. It's supposed to symbolize peace, Akeno thinks. Already they have ads for this place. Amity, he whispers to himself. Kevin glances over at him and smiles.

The man at the desk wears a blue uniform with a couple pins on his jacket. This man isn't with the military, Akeno thinks. The soldiers outside wear standard edition uniforms. This man seems to be wearing a uniform of a different kind. The man smiles and greets them.

"Good morning. How many I help you today?" he asks.

Howard steps forward, skips small talk, and explains what they need to apply for. The man at the desk doesn't seem bothered by Howard's abrupt rudeness. He's too pleasant, Akeno thinks. Nobody's been that happy in months. It's strange to see someone exuding the soft joy that comes with customer service.

"Should I fill anything out?" Akeno whispers.

"No, we've got it," Joanna says quietly. "They'll ask you a series of questions, and you'll need to answer them as best as you can."

"What questions?"

"Just listen." There's a spark in her eye, but then she turns, and the feeling's gone. She was practically mute last night, and now she's hovering around him. Was she trying to threaten him? No, needless to say, Akeno's already nervous enough. Was she trying to tell him something?

Akeno doesn't like the condescension he hears in Howard's tone while standing at the desk, but he lets it slide as he, Kevin, and Kayla sit back and stare blankly at the walls. Howard hands the desk clerk a stack of papers and whispers something low. The man politely nods, forcing that same sickly grin. When Howard and the clerk are through, Howard returns with information.

"We wait here for the interviews and physicals," he says.

Physicals? Akeno thinks. Why do they need to have one of those? He remembers what Kevin said about the selection process. It's specific and unforgiving in expectations. He wonders if he'll be allowed in with a head injury and a lame shoulder. The bruise on his head is fine, Akeno thinks. But the shoulder could be an issue. They might deny him access to Amity.

The five of them sit close to another as they wait. From a glance, it looks like the five of them are lined up to take their annual family photos. Akeno notes the camera in the corner of the room and smirks as something clicks behind the glass.

When the family starts to get called back by an attendant, Akeno is last to be interviewed. The attendant is a woman in a plain blue uniform, like the one the clerk was wearing, and she wears plain, clear framed glasses. She holds a clipboard and pen. Beside her is another woman who types away on a silver laptop, wearing the same uniform, glasses and all. Neither of them glance up when he enters the room.

"Stand in the center of the room," the woman with the clipboard says, pointing at a red X on the floor. He does.

The other woman's typing fills the silence of the room as the interviewer starts asking Akeno several detailed questions: Is he a citizen? Where is he from? When was he born? Do they have any records of his adoption? Does he have a birth certificate? Did they come with anyone other than family? Do they know anyone here?

Then they measured his height, weight, chest, and arms, and they took blood to test for disease and illness. All of this was explained as they went, though it was all said too quickly. When they get to the physical portion of the exam, they ask him to strip down to his underwear. Akeno sits quietly at first, waiting for the attendants to leave so he can change. That's the usual procedure, Akeno thinks. After a few seconds, though, the woman asking all the questions looks up from her chart and raises her eyebrows.

"Is there an issue?" she asks.

"Uh, do I change right now?"

"Yes," she says. "And with haste. We have other applicants waiting."

Akeno does as he's told and takes off layer after layer. The two women don't seem to notice or care as he undresses. In the corner of the room, Akeno notes a camera and immediately feels bashful. He crosses his good arm over his chest, holding fast to his hurt shoulder, the bandages now in clear view.

The women both look up at the same time and note the bandage. The woman with the laptop sits back, air hissing through her teeth. She glances to the other woman, who simply shrugs. She checks something off on her clipboard and slams it down.

"How did you hurt your shoulder?" she asks, her tone now showing irritation.

"I, uh, fell and landed on it wrong. It's just a sprain," he lies, making sure to keep eye contact. He smiles. They don't.

"Can you achieve full mobility?"

"Yes," he answers plainly.

She eyes him warily, seemingly searching for an excuse to deny his account. She shrugs again. "We'll have that checked out more thoroughly if or when your application is approved."

The woman scribbles something at the bottom of the clipboard. She rips off a ticket and hands it to him.

"Give it to the front desk," she says. "Good luck." She waves him away, and he leaves the room. When he returns to the lobby, the Howards are waiting for him.

They allow the Howard family and Akeno to camp nearby until

their reports come back. Howard takes this as a good sign, boasting about their family's good genes and great prowess as survivors of the land. Nobody responds to his assurances. Instead, Joanna insists they go to the market and trade whatever they don't need. If they're approved, they won't be able to carry much of anything. Best to stock up on snacks and clothes before they make the long trip to Amity.

Joanna's sure they'll get in too, Akeno thinks. At first, he wasn't sure if she ever wanted to go to Amity, but now he realizes this must have been her plan from the start. While she doesn't show any affection at all for her ex-husband, she does keep a steady eye on her kids, always smiling when they look at her. She must care for them, he thinks. Amity's the best place for her kids to be, so that's where she'll go.

As the adults pack up a couple packs of nonessential items, they leave for the market. Kevin and Kayla sit across from Akeno as they share a small lunch. They each get one apple with bruises on them, a handful of nuts, a spoon of peanut butter, and one water bottle. Akeno thinks this is a luxury and devours it all in no time. Finally, he's got his appetite back.

The three eat together within their tent, and Akeno realizes just how much space they have for people to fit comfortably inside. Granted, Kevin's the tallest of them, but even when he stretches his legs, his toes don't reach the other side. It's only when they're all packed in there does it suddenly feel cramped. The warmth from their bodies and breath makes the tent feel warm after a while, and Akeno can't help but feel grateful that he no longer has to bear the cold nights in just one sleeping bag.

Kayla looks up with her eyes, her gaze on Kevin and then Akeno. She has a blanket wrapped around her shoulders, her heavier coat off to one side. It's a parka with a faux fur hood. It's cute, but it can't be comfortable while they're just sitting there.

"So why are you here?" Kayla asks. She picks at the nuts in her hands, either because she doesn't like nuts, or because she wants to look like she's taking her time.

"Kayla," Kevin snaps.

"No, it's fine," Akeno says. He pulls his legs in closer together. "I don't understand your question. You already know why I'm here."

"Because Kevin looks like he's forty? No. That's not it."

"What do you mean?" Akeno asks with a nervous laugh. "That's all there is to it."

"It doesn't make any sense," she mumbles.

"I'm there with you," Akeno replies, offering a smile. "I don't get it either."

Kayla looks up at him and then her brother.

"We just have to trust Mom and Dad," Kevin says under his breath.

"We have to trust *Mom*," she says.

Kevin shrugs. "Dad knows what he's doing."

"He's on the shit again," Kayla says, staring down into her lap.

"What?" Kevin asks, looking up. "No, he's not."

"Yes he is. I saw him."

"Saw him do what?"

"Swallow some pills."

"When?"

"Last night. I stepped out to use the bathroom and saw him."

"Did he see you?" Kevin asks, his eyes searching. He almost looks worried.

"No," she mumbles. "He took a piss after that."

The two don't say anything after that. Akeno sits uncomfortably in the silence with them. He'd leave, but there's nowhere else to go.

"Your mom's cool," Akeno speaks up, quietly. "She seems...nice."

Kayla nods. "She's the only one who knows what the hell's going on."

"Don't say that."

"It's true."

Kevin turns away, grabs his backpack, and stands. "I'm going to the market."

"Mom said we should stay put."

Kevin doesn't answer. He leaves. His footsteps crunch against the brittle grass and piles of leaves. His footsteps recede, and Kayla looks up at Akeno.

"Look, I didn't mean to sound like a bitch. I'm just saying, it's not all adding up."

"It's alright. I get it," Akeno says, his eyes turning downcast. "I meant what I said about your mom. I'm sure she just wants the best for you and Kevin, even if that means dragging me along on your family road trip." He smiles. "I can see that you and Kevin butt heads sometimes."

"He's an idiot," she says, pulling her legs to her chin and resting her head there. "He doesn't get it. He wasn't there for the divorce. It was... bad."

Akeno nods, as if he understands, which he supposes he does. Family trauma comes in all forms, he thinks.

"So your dad's got a problem?" he asks gently. "It can be a hard habit to break."

She nods. "He's not himself." Her eyes tear up. "But what do I know? He's always been an asshole. He's always yelling at Mom, at me, at Kevin. I'd rather him rot here than come with us to Amity. He was never supposed to come with us in the first place."

"What do you mean?" Akeno asks, his attention again refocused.

"Why not?"

"The divorce was finalized a few months ago, like in March. He didn't even pack the rest of his shit, and he was already living with some other woman. So, like, he showed up the day after the blackout, saying how he's sorry and all this other bullshit about how he loves my mom and me and Kevin, and how he wants to be with us." A tear drops from the corner of her eyes. She brushes it away, her cheeks turning a pale pink. "I just wish he meant half of what he said."

Akeno nods. He should say something, do something, maybe rub her back. He's not used to all this sharing, Akeno thinks. He should try comforting her. He decides against it, in case he says the wrong thing. He doesn't know what to say. He doesn't know what to do.

More feet crunch outside, and the front flap of the tent opens. Howard peeks his head in, sees the two of them together and frowns. "What's going on here? Where's Kevin?" he asks.

"Where's Mom?" Kayla asks.

"Don't get smart with me," he says, glaring at her. "I asked you a question."

"I don't know the answer."

He shifts his gaze onto Akeno. "Where's Kevin?"

"He said he went to the market," Akeno replies.

"Why?"

Akeno shrugs. Kayla won't look at her father.

"So what have you two been doing in here, huh? How long has Kevin been gone?"

"God, Dad, can't we just sit here and talk without Kevin breathing down our necks?" she snaps. "Why don't you go find him if you're so concerned?"

"What did you say to me?" he barks. "You can't talk to your father that way."

"You don't talk to anyone else any other way."

"What are you talking about?" he says, stepping fully into the tent. "What are you trying to say?"

"I'm telling you that you're a fucking asshole," she says, standing up to meet his eyes.

"Say that one more time, little girl," he sneers. "One more time."

"Or what? You'll hit me? Come on, do it. Go ahead and do it. Go ahead and–"

There's a quick reaction and a sharp slap. Akeno's on his feet, his fists clenched, but Howard shoves him back down with his forearm. Kayla's head is turned to one side, then she shifts back to face her father. "You didn't hit me hard enough," she says and spits at his feet, smearing blood on his worn boots.

"Both of you, out," he growls.

"Why?" Kayla snaps. "So you can swallow more of your pills?"

"Out!"

"Swallow the whole fucking bottle while you're at it," she mumbles.

She leaves the tent, Akeno right behind her. He reaches out to stop her, wants to say something, but she pulls out of reach, her body facing away from him. He doesn't pursue her. She stands there for a moment, the edges of her lips working fervently as she turns to face the tent, like she might say something. She turns to Akeno, who stands to one side, waiting for her comeback. She just looks at him, her eyes boring into Akeno's, a knowing look. She decides against whatever she was about to say and stalks off in the direction of her mother.

Joanna's standing on the sidewalk closeby, her eyes focused on something in the distance. Her arms are folded around her chest. They must have gotten into a fight, Akeno thinks. Maybe she found the pills.

When Kayla reaches the sidewalk, Joanna turns and opens her arms, where Kayla melts into the crook of her mother's shoulder, Kayla's body shaking. The two stand there together as the noon sun shines through a thin layer of clouds. Akeno looks on for a moment, glances back at the tent, and heads in the opposite direction.

Later that afternoon, just before the sun begins to sink in the sky, Akeno sits outside the tent, his back against a tree. He doesn't keep track of time anymore. He just watches the sky. On days like these, he can tell it's the afternoon, somewhere between two and three-thirty, he thinks. It would be something like six when it got dark on these winter evenings. He hasn't taken the time to watch a sunset in a while, he thinks. He likes the way the soft orange mixes with pink. Sometimes there's a purple and indigo hue on the far horizon, but it hasn't gotten to that point yet. Right now, it's just a cool sun on a chilly day. Akeno thinks it's a little warmer than yesterday. The sun sinks slowly, soft yellow. Off in the distance are some growing clouds, stark and gray against the pale blue sky. He thinks it might rain tonight. Better to be on high ground for that. Their tent is on flat ground, blocked from sight by a few ridges, which is usually good for cover, but tonight they should consider moving the tent. It might flood.

"How's it going?"

Akeno glances beside him and sees Ms. Howard, or Joanna, approaching. He almost lets out a sigh but decides against it. He wonders what she wants from him. Despite what Kayla said, he doesn't buy Joanna's nice mom act. She didn't act this way on the first night, so what changed?

Akeno nods as a way of response, but he doesn't make eye contact.

"You've got a nice view," she says. "May I join you?"

He's surprised that she asked. He wants to say no, but he nods anyway.

"Thanks," she says, taking a seat next to him.

Akeno takes her in. She's wearing a plain long sleeve shirt underneath a heavy coat. She wears gloves too and a pair of worn brown boots, a pair of boots he wouldn't see Joanna wearing in a normal setting. She looks like someone who would be comfortable wearing business casual slacks and blouse. She looks warm but not altogether flashy. She's pretty, he thinks. She has a nice face. The crow's feet at her soft eyes appear maternal, yet appealing. The frown from last night is gone, replaced with a kind of sincerity. The tension's gone. She's out of sight from her family, he thinks.

"I want to apologize about earlier," she says, and Akeno flinches. "Kayla told me what happened."

He doesn't say anything, but he looks at her.

"I can't imagine what you think of us."

He shrugs. "It's none of my business."

She nods. There's a long pause.

"Listen," she says. "I want to be even with you."

"Yeah, that would be good," he interjects and immediately regrets snapping at her.

Her expression doesn't change. She clasps her hands in her lap, her eyes steady. It's then that he realizes she's not the doting wife and mother. She's a woman with a plan, someone who adheres to caution and patiently waits for an opportunity. He feels like he's shrinking, being this close to her. He'd hadn't realized before, but they're about the same height, which makes her taller than most women. She's not intimidating, not in the generic way. She's calm, level-headed, and he can see how she would unsettle many other men, her ex-husband included. He waits.

"Michael isn't a good man," she says, evenly and without any intonation. "We divorced for several reasons, but that's the short end to a long story. There's a lot Kevin and Kayla don't know about their father." She closes her eyes, but only momentarily. "I won't get into details, but know that he is a terrible, horrible human being. He's never cared for anyone but himself and that's including how he treats Kevin and Kayla. He lies constantly, oftentimes fluidly, and what he says can sound convincing if he has the right motive."

"What are you trying to say?" Akeno asks, turning to her. "Why are you telling me this?"

"Because I don't trust my husband, or ex-husband," she says with clarity. "You shouldn't trust him either. Whatever he's promised you—"

"So his reasoning for bringing me along, it's not true? All that he said about Kevin's age, the family…"

She shakes her head. "No. He made it all up."

Akeno blanches, snorts, and lets out a short laugh. "So what am I doing here then?" Akeno pushes himself off the cold, hard ground. Suddenly he's warm, hot even, as the adrenaline races through his body. He can feel his heartbeat pick up as he realizes his mistake. He should never have trusted this family. He should never have trusted Kevin. He left. He never said goodbye, and he left. They were never friends. How could Akeno have thought any differently?

"You know Kayla asked me the same question, asked me why I'm here, and now I don't know the answer." He shakes his head. "I'm such an idiot." He barks out a laugh, and he notices that his eyes are watering. Probably from the cold, he tells himself.

"No, you're not. You heard what you needed to hear. Let me be clear. Amity is a golden opportunity for a lot of people, but it's not for everyone. There's a lot you don't know."

Akeno runs his hands through his hair. "Okay, so tell me. Tell me what's going on here. Why am I here?"

She shakes her head. "I don't know for sure. I don't know what deal Michael's made with the officials. I just know it's a chance that's not worth taking. There's too much at risk."

"What are you talking about?" he shouts. "You're saying I shouldn't trust your husband, who recruited me to do this. Actually, Kevin's the one who found me and brought me back, so am I not supposed to trust him either?"

Joanna shakes her head, her eyes filling with tears. Akeno feels his own face and swipes a tear away.

"Kevin trusts his father. He thinks the world of Michael, but..." Joanna stifles a sob. "I don't know what he's told Kevin, but whatever it was, I don't think Kevin ever intended you harm. He was just doing what his father told him to do. It was never intentional."

Kevin sits back down, his back leaning heavily against the tree. He thinks of Sam. What would she do in this situation? Probably walk away. She'd get up right now and start walking. She'd never look back. Akeno can't do that, not yet anyway.

"So your family," he says. "You're worried Kevin and Kayla won't be able to get in. That's why you let me fill out all the paperwork, get the physical, answer those questions."

Joanna nods. "I wanted to wait it out, see if I could learn anything before coming to you. If I had told you to leave last night, you would've thought I was crazy. You might have stayed. You might have told Kevin, who would have told Michael. I needed proof. I needed some confirmation, and I got that today."

Akeno waits, his eyes boring into Joanna's, studying her face as she stares into the distance. She glances at him with a grim smile.

"I overheard them discussing you, your physical. They said you were a good match, except for the shoulder wound. They were talking about your options in Amity, something about needing more labor." She shakes her head, as if she's trying to clear the thoughts in her head, as if she's trying to organize what she means to say. "They were careful not to say anything too specific, but they mentioned Michael by name," she says, now with more urgency.

Akeno crosses his legs, the wrinkles between his eyes deepening as he tries to find the pattern in what she's saying.

"They talked about Michael's records, his *first* application and the results. He was initially denied access to Amity. He was deemed unqualified and inadequate. They noted his alcoholism, drug abuse, his potential for bipolar personality disorder, which was news to me though not shocking. He would need to be medicated, which they can't afford to risk, not on him. They needed someone healthier, someone who could in the labor force."

"So he picked me," Akeno murmurs.

Joanna nods, reaches out to take Akeno's hand. "I'm so sorry for dragging you into all this, Akeno. I really am. I wish I had known sooner."

"He's going to trade me in." Akeno blanches. "I have to go," he says, quickly standing once again, his hands running through his hair, over his face, back through his hair. "I have to leave now."

"Not yet," she says, hurriedly, standing with Akeno. "Wait until it's dark. If they see you leaving campus now, if Michael notices you're gone, they'll come looking for you, and you're—"

"Easy to spot, I know." Akeno shakes his head. "I can't believe this is happening. Again." He strains out a dry laugh. "Fine, I'll leave tonight." He stops and considers. "What are you going to do? What are you going to say when *he* comes asking questions?"

"I don't owe him anything," she says with a wry grin. "Meet me back here after the sun sets. I'll get you out."

CHAPTER 15

In a few short minutes, Joanna tells him what he needs to do. She leaves first, then Akeno ten minutes later. He needs to pack. That was her first instruction. Granted, he doesn't own anything, but Joanna said she'd help him find some extra supplies. She wouldn't mind if he took a few things from their store--some food, maybe an extra pair of socks and gloves, a backpack. He'll be running far away from campus, again. He should've trusted his gut. He shouldn't have come back. This time he won't chance the woods. He'll take the streets, find an abandoned storage unit or apartment. He'll hide out there and move locations frequently. If he can find a bike, he can trek out of the city and into the next town over, taking the backroads all the way. He'll do this until he reaches the East Coast. That's the dream anyway. He'll make camp on the beach and stick it out there. He'll become a fisherman, live in those tiny beach homes, and make due there.

He shakes the thought. He's thinking too far ahead. He's daydreaming. He needs to focus. He needs to face Kevin and Kayla. They sit by the tent, each of them facing the opposite direction. They don't seem to be on speaking terms. Akeno doesn't say anything as he approaches, slowly and timidly, hoping for what comes across as a casual walk and not a hurried rush. Kayla glances at him first, gives a wan smile, and turns away. Kevin doesn't bother to look as Akeno gets closer to the tent. His eyes seem to be focused on something far in the distance.

He steps inside the tent and sees Michael Howard lounging one top of his sleeping bag. His eyes are shut, his breathing slow, but he doesn't actually seem to be sleeping. Akeno's halfway in the tent, allowing a slant of sunshine in the tent, its diagonal glow grazing the top of Howard's head. Akeno means to make his quiet exit when one of Howard's eyes shoots open. Akeno catches that eye and flinches, feeling exposed.

"What do you want?" Howard asks.

"I was just coming in for some water, but it looks like you're sleeping, so I'll just—"

"I ain't sleeping. Here." Howard hands Akeno an unopened water bottle. "Take it," he says, Akeno still standing in the entrance. "You said you were thirsty."

"Thanks," Akeno says quietly, accepting the bottle. He tries to leave again, but now Howard's sitting up, his back resting against his oversized backpack.

"I've been meaning to talk to you," Howard says, waving his hand in, gesturing for Akeno to come inside. He hesitates at first but decides it would be better to indulge Howard's wishes. He wouldn't have to put up with him for long. "Look," he finally says, as Akeno lets the tent flutter close. "I think you and I got off on the wrong start, you know? Our family, you know, we have our issues, but we love each other. We rely on each other in ways you can't know, being an orphan and all."

Akeno feels heat rise to his cheeks. He tells himself this is what Howard wants, to get a rise from Akeno. He won't cave.

"I mean you've only seen how we act around each other during this crisis. This isn't us when things were normal, you know? We were happy. We loved each other right. We ate meals together, you know, the whole family values thing. I hope you don't see us as nasty people because sometimes we get a little stressed."

"I understand," Akeno says, making to leave.

"Hold on a minute," Howard says. "I'm trying to talk to you."

Akeno turns, eyes the man. "I'm listening."

"My point being, we're sticking together no matter what. That's just how things are. Family sticks together. So, whatever it is that you think you know, or think you should do, or what my kids should think, it's not any of your business, alright? Whatever Kim says to you, most of it's a bunch of lies. She tries to turn everyone against me, even my own kids. You see how they are. Kim's done that to them, their minds. They know in their hearts I'm a good man. I'm a good dad."

Akeno homes in on Howard's face, his eyes, his cheeks. He's flushed. His eyes are red at the rims, bags under his eyes, his head bobbing from side to side. He's on the shit again.

"I know, Mr. Howard. You're doing your best."

"That's right. I'm doing my best here. I'm trying. It's tough, though, you know? It's hard keeping your family together. It's hard when your wife's a lying bitch."

"Stop," Akeno snaps.

Howard grins. "What's the matter? I'm like a ref, call it as you see it, and Kim, well, she's a lying bitch."

"Happy men don't call their wives a 'lying bitch.'"

"What do you know? You don't know who she is. I do. I know exactly what she's capable of. She says all these things about me that ain't true. She makes them up in her head, and my children, *my* children, believe it all. Don't you see how that makes her a liar?"

"You're wrong about her." Akeno makes to leave when he feels a vice grip on his wrist. He turns and Howard's standing, his eyes boring down into Akeno's. His eyes flash.

"I don't like your tone."

"I don't like the way you treat your family." Akeno yanks his wrist away, much to Howard's surprise. "You should consider yourself lucky you even have a family, considering what a *great* job you've done so far."

Akeno leaves the tent, heading toward the market. Howard doesn't follow. Akeno will need to gather what he can there. If all goes well, he should have what he needs to last him a couple days. That's all he needs. He just needs a couple days.

CHAPTER 16

Back on the streets, Akeno manages to trade one of his lighter coats for a small backpack. He trades his gloves for food, not something he was willing to do, but at least he'll be able to eat. The rest he manages to pick out of the overflowing Dumpsters on the edge of campus. There isn't a lot to find there, but he manages to find a few stained clothes, some ripped but not too badly. It's not ideal, but he needs everything he can get. He even manages to find a compass. The glass is cracked, but it still works.

The sun's setting now, but it's dulled by the clouds growing overhead. When he makes it back to the Howard camp, it begins to rain, a soft and steady, cold rain. Everyone seems to be inside the tent. From the gas lantern on the inside, he can vaguely make out the shadows of bodies. What a heartfelt sight, Akeno thinks. It's not quite after sunset, but with the sky as dark as it is, it's close enough. He heads back to the tree, the meeting spot where Joanna told him she'd be waiting for him.

He passes the tent and thinks surely it'll flood on flat ground. He turns away and rounds the corner to one of the buildings. He spots the tree in the distance. Joanna's not there yet. She's probably making an excuse to leave the tent, bathroom break or something. Or else she's coming back from the market like he is. She traded a few things just to bring something home. He waits a while longer, his body flush against the building, the awning overhead keeping him dry. He thinks this is where he usually sees a crowd of students waiting for the bus after their classes. He thinks now it serves the same purpose. Now he waits on Joanna.

He shuffles his feet against the cold, his uncovered hands buried in his coat pockets. He can feel a hole forming there too, letting in the cold. He ducks his head close to the jacket in attempts to break the wind beating against the building, raindrops whipping against his face. He pulls the hood around his face closer to his skin. Getting wet on a December day without the luxury of a hot shower poses a threat to his health, he knows that, but like Joanna said, he has to leave tonight, or there may not be another chance. He might come down with the flu tonight, but he's strong. He'll survive it, even if it nearly kills him.

When the sun finally sets, and the rain starts to beat down harder, Akeno decides it's time. He doesn't see Kimberly. She must not have been able to get away. It's alright, he thinks. He didn't ask for her help. It's up to him now.

He steps outside the security of the awning and rounds the corner. He makes to break past the tree, just to see if she left anything there for him. Nothing. He shakes his head and dips his chin low as he walks with the direction of the rain. His back is soaked, his body shivering. His eyes make sight of the road ahead. If he follows that road to its end, it's a straight shot into downtown once he crosses the street. It's his path to freedom.

Through the deafening wind, Akeno makes out footfalls behind him. He hears someone slip in the mud behind him, and he quickly turns to see Howard barreling straight for Akeno, his hands outstretched, his balance off center. Akeno shifts his weight and slides out of the way of Howard's running fall. Howard slides again as he tries to stop his momentum, falls and hits the ground with one elbow, all his

198

weight leaning on one arm and one leg. He pushes himself back up, his feet sliding into the mud. Akeno doesn't wait. He takes off at a hard run away from Howard and towards the street, his feet sliding down the hill.

"Stop!" Howard shouts. "I said stop!"

Akeno doesn't bother looking back. He's got a headstart on Howard. Once he hits pavement, it'll be impossible for Howard to catch him. It's almost pathetic to know a drunk like Howard thinks he can catch Akeno in a race. He laughs out loud, his voice lost in the wind and rain. He's nearly to the end of the road. He can no longer hear Howard chasing him from behind. He starts to slow, glances behind his shoulder, his breath catching in his chest.

Howard has been replaced with several others dressed in black gear. In front of them and coming close to Akeno are four black dogs on his heels. Akeno picks up his pace, knowing that he won't be able to outrun the dogs. If he climbs a tree, he's trapped by the men. If he veers off onto another street, it's unlikely he'll be able to hide from the dogs. It's his only chance though.

When he reaches the end of the street, instead of crossing the street for downtown, he enters into one of the nearby neighborhoods. It's the same one where college students would go to parties and get drunk, do things they won't regret, and live together in tandem. It used to be a lively street, but now it's mostly flooded, the water building up in the overflowing gutters blocked by leaves. The houses are boarded up by the windows and doors. Akeno races through backyards and hops a short, chain link fence.

When he does, he cuts through his clothes to the skin under his thigh. When he lands, he wavers and lands sloppily on one knee. He reaches back with one hand and pulls away, the blood on his fingers and palm. It's not a minor cut. Akeno can feel it throb as he pushes himself back into a sprint across the yard. The dogs hit the fence behind him, their barking close enough now for Akeno to hear. He glances back and sees the gnashing of the dogs' teeth, their noses pushing through the gaps in the fence. It looks like they're trying to break it down, and given the state of the flimsy fence, they were bound to slip underneath it.

He cuts back onto the street and takes a left turn back toward downtown. If he can get close enough, he might be able to hide in one of the local shops until the storm passes and his pursuers are gone. Lightning cracks in the distance, and thunder crashes overhead. He covers his head with his hands, as if this act would save him. He runs faster, the thunder shaking him as his feet pound against concrete. The rain pours harder, like tiny spikes puncturing his exposed face. It stings, and Akeno can feel his face go numb from the cold and pain.

Akeno nears the intersection leading directly on the main street. He pushes himself to reach this point, knowing he'll have to go farther, but he pushes himself as if this is the finish line to a long distance race. If he can just make it there…

At the stop sign, a black van skids around the corner and veers onto the same street Akeno runs down. There's only one second for Akeno to switch directions. He skids to a halt, his heart giving out, his adrenaline jumping through his veins. Somewhere in the back of his mind, he knows this is it. He slips and falls to one knee. His feet slip against the rain as he bursts into a short sprint back the way he came. There, at the end of the street, his pursuers round the corner, their dogs in tow. Akeno looks side to side, searching for a way out, looking for a narrow alley, an open window, any way out.

Suddenly Akeno is weeping, his breath coming in ragged takes, his chest heaving, his lungs burning, his throat dry despite the rain. He wants to scream but he can't. Nothing comes out of him. He sinks to the ground, his clothes completely soaked through, his body shaking and shivering from the effort. He knows he's sick. He knows he's beat. He puts his hands up over his head to show he has no weapons. It's a familiar sight, something he's seen friends do, friends he never saw again. Where will they take him?

Someone from the van shoves Akeno's face to the ground, his skin rubbing against the concrete, forming road rash on his cheek. He's still crying, his lips forming an ugly shape. Snot pours from his nose, washed away by the rain. Akeno's body is pulled up to face someone striding towards him. The figures pull something from a pocket. As the masked person nears him, Akeno lets out a desperate wail. A needle slides into Akeno's neck, and the world fades as another crack of lightning streaks through the night sky. Gunshots ring, then thunder.

Akeno wakes with a start. He raises up and hits his head on something soft. His eyesight's blurry. All he can make out are shapes, colors, and other bodies. Akeno pieces together where he is, or at least where he thinks he is. He knows he's in a moving vehicle. That much is obvious by the rumble of the engine, his seat's shakiness, and the flashing colors passing by the window on his right. He blinks and lifts his hands to rub his eyes, only to realize his hands are bound behind his back. Metal clinks against metal, and Akeno's vision clears.

He's on a commercial bus. The gray seats in front and behind him are marked with the familiar blue and red shapes and squiggles. On the other side of the aisle is another person, a male it seems. He's lying on his side, his body slouched to one side, his feet dangling into the aisle. He's fast asleep or otherwise knocked out from the drugs they gave him too.

Akeno remembers it all, the needle, the lightning, the gunshots. He remembers gunshots, but he doesn't seem to be shot. He doesn't feel any pain, doesn't see any bandages. Somebody else must have gotten hit. Who else was there? Howard maybe, trying to kill Akeno even at his capture. Where is Howard now?

Akeno glances around the bus, his head peeking over the seats in front of him. There are several armed men sitting at the front of the bus. Their eyes are on the road ahead or else looking at one another as several men crack jokes, the others laughing like chaperones on an uneventful school field trip. Akeno glances behind him too, sees another body lying on the seats. He must be the first person to wake from his long sleep.

He faces the window, tries to figure out where they are. They're on the Interstate. Signs pass too fast for Akeno to read them. His vision's still shaky, and his head throbs from any mental effort. He lays back down on the seats, his head resting smoothly against the soft cushion of the seats. He watches the world pass by him until he falls back into a fitful sleep.

When he wakes up for the second time, the evening sun shines through the windshield of the bus, the light resting on Akeno's eyes, his head on the edge of the seat closest to the aisle. His eyes flutter open, and he meets the face of another man, his eyes blank and unblinking as Akeno flinches. The man lays limply on one side, his eyes focused on Akeno, drool spilling from his mouth. He's not come down from the drugs, Akeno thinks. The man blinks, and Akeno forces a smile as he turns away.

It seems like the other passengers have woken up by now. Akeno peers in front of him and sees their heads rest against the seats. When he looks behind him, he sees several women. Their faces are battered and bruised, tears dried to their cheeks. Akeno doesn't want to think about what they've faced. He doesn't speak to anyone. He leans his head back against the seat and tries not to think of what's ahead of him, but it's hard not to picture the worst.

Joanna said there would be labor forces, or labor camps, as Akeno knows now, something like internment camps or concentration camps. They wouldn't kill them all. No, death seems to be wishful thinking.

This is what Joanna was warning Akeno about. She told him this would happen, in not so many words. She said she would help get him out. She never showed. Howard was there instead. Akeno replays the scene back, but everything seems hazy now that the drugs have run their course. He remembers running, the pursuers, the dogs, the black van, the thunder, the gunshots. Howard must have found out about Joanna's rendezvous point and beat her there. Akeno wonders what Howard must have said to her to keep her from stopping him. He must have threatened her or their kids. He thinks Howard must have tied them all up and left them in the flooded tent.

Whatever the case, Akeno is here now, a traded body so Howard could live the life he imagines with his family. He hates to think Joanna, Kevin, and Kayla are trapped living with a psychopath for a father and husband. There's another part of him that doesn't care either. He doesn't care for the family that tricked him in being here in the first place. He doesn't care if he lives or dies, yet a part of him desperately wants to live. It would just be easier to die, Akeno thinks. It would be so easy.

He watches the bus drive into the sunset and knows they're headed west. He glances over at the man beside him. His eyes are glazed over, and Akeno knows he's dead.

The bus sits idling, and Akeno wakes up with another start. His eyes rapidly adjust to the blurry images of dawn. His face and neck are drenched in sweat, his breathing erratic. He puts his face to the window and sees they're waiting in line with tens of other buses. He can see little hands and tiny heads sticking themselves out the windows of the other buses. They look excited, awestruck. Children, Akeno thinks. Even children have been taken. Then he sees women's scarves and other pieces of clothing being stretched out the window in greeting. The other bus passengers wave gleefully behind them at their comrades. There's all whoops and hollers, and Akeno can even hear laughter. The soldiers at the front of the bus grin in turn. They must have arrived. This must be Amity, Sanctuary, the Garden of Eden, Akeno's personal Hell.

Looming up from one side is a concrete wall hundreds of feet high that round on either side, but he can't see where the walls turn. On top of the walls are sentry houses and armed soldiers walking along the top. A helicopter flies above them and into the city, where it disappears out of sight. At the entrance gates, one bus enters the city, and the gates shut again. soldiers approach the next bus, and the line creeps forward.

A weight of dread drops into the pit of Akeno's stomach. Everyone said this city is their best chance at surviving, but Akeno thinks there must be a catch, a secret clause to being admitted into this closely guarded city, even for the people who willingly came here. He wishes he had listened to Sam and stayed with her. He wishes she were here with him now.

All around them is desert. It doesn't seem like there's anything for miles. They could be in Arizona, or Death Valley, or they could be in

South Dakota for all Akeno knows about the American West. There's no telling what direction they've been driving, and Akeno hadn't kept track. Mostly he's slept. Mostly he's tried to pretend he was anywhere but here. He's surprised they've already arrived and can't decide if he's ready to leave the bus. Getting off the bus now means the inevitable is here, a fate he has been dreading for several days.

When their bus reaches the entrance to the gates, the soldiers motion the driver forward. The driver pulls up to the line of soldiers and opens the door. One guard steps up, and the driver hands him a badge. The guard barely glances at it and nods. He welcomes the driver back and eyes the bus full of passengers. The guard's face falls for a brief second as he hands the driver back his badge. He mumbles what looks like an apology and exits the bus. The entrance gates swing open, and the bus lurches back into motion.

As they pass under the concrete arch leading into the city, Akeno cranes his neck back to get a full picture. There's an inscription just above the arch, Akeno notes. It's in Latin, which means nothing for Akeno. The walls, he notices, are several feet thick. If he thought escaping was an option, he was sadly mistaken. His heart falls. There aren't any buses leaving the city. It's a one-way ticket in, no way out. Once they enter the city, there's no turning back. This is it. This is where they live now. This is their new home. This is their new normal.

The entrance beyond the gates doubles as an unloading zone, parking lot, and what appears to be a welcome center. To the left are all the buses that had entered before them. There's too many buses to count, but he guesses there must be somewhere close to a hundred. He imagines they travel all across the country, bringing people here, with or without their consent. To the right is a large glass building with big, open windows. Akeno thinks it's supposed to appear transparently

welcoming, but all that glass is simply bound to break. The dingy gray
of the concrete walls make the glass building seem like an out-of-place
tuft of grass in the crack of a sidewalk. In front of the welcome center
are several men and women dressed in a blue and white uniform. They
smile jovially and wave at the passing bus.

The driver pulls the bus to the curb and opens the door. He doesn't
say anything, nor does he stand as he gestures with one hand for the
passengers to exit the bus. The soldiers bark an order, but Akeno can't
hear anything anymore. All he can do is follow the shuffle of feet off the
bus. He glances at the man on the other side of the aisle. Someone has
shut his eyes, but they've left his body. Nobody mourns him. Nobody
knew him. They exit the bus, the hot desert air washing over them like
a dry shower.

The driver doesn't make eye contact with anyone as they leave the
bus, nor does he bid them farewell. As Akeno passes the man, he sees
the lines at the edge of the driver's face and takes notice of the man's
apparent age. He must be in his sixties at least. Why he drives this bus
from state to state, picking up and delivering passengers, is lost on Akeno. He can't imagine this man chose this job. It must be grueling, sat-
isfying, a tear on the soul. Akeno can see the abject hurt on the driver's
face as they file off the bus. He wonders if the driver, like his passengers,
were forced to come here, too. Maybe he had a family once, a wife and
kids, maybe even grandkids. Now he's here, solemn and quiet, his eyes
shifting uneasily to the soldiers holding their guns aloft as they point
the passengers in the direction they should be going.

Those who were standing by the welcome doors now quickly and
happily escort the other bus' passengers into the glass building. The bus
drives off, leaving a cloud of smoke streaming behind it. Akeno follows
closely behind the person in front of him. They don't enter the wide

206

open doors like the other bus passengers. They're not grouped in with the families and children, mothers holding babies, fathers carrying toddlers. They're escorted into a side door, a metal door that squeaks when someone opens it from the inside. When they all enter into the glass building, there's a cramped room with scattered food and room temperature water. The passengers hurry to it, guzzling the styrofoam cups of water, cramming the food in their mouth. Leftovers, Akeno thinks. At least that's what it seems like from the soft cheese, the stale crackers, and the browning fruit. Akeno shoves his face full, his first taste of food or water in days.

From the other side of the wall, Akeno can hear the noise from the main room. There's a booming effect that echoes off high ceilings. From the range of noise, there must be at least a hundred people moving around in the next room, reminding Akeno of the same urgency and bodies of an airport. With all those bodies packed into one space, Akeno feels an immense wave of heat wash over him. Suddenly he feels cramped, claustrophobic, his breath catching.

Several minutes pass and all the food and water is gone. Akeno barely got anything to eat. He managed to get two cups of water to drink. From the ceiling, a crackling static sound came from an unseen speaker, a woman's voice calling over the intercom.

"Welcome to Amity," the voice echoes. It sounds like a recording. Her voice is too plain, too neutral, too happy. "Here in Amity, you will find the peace and tranquility you have been searching for. In Amity, we ensure that all our citizens maintain a positive balance between family and community. If you are a member of a family unit, please make your way to the left side of the room, where you will be led by our family coordinators to the family planning center. If you are a single-person community member, please make your way to the right side of the room, where you will be assisted in choosing your community. If you have any questions, please ask any of our welcoming guides, who will be more than happy to help in any way they can. Thank you."

A burst of energy fills the next room and the deafening noise that accompanies so many people's movement. People talk loudly to one another so as to be heard over the din of others. Akeno imagines all those people asking the welcoming guides their questions, and the guides pleasantly smile, their answers rehearsed, their reactions to difficult questions in feigned ignorance. People will start to wonder where their relatives are, the friends they know have come to Amity before them. They will know someone like Akeno, who suddenly disappeared one night. All the while, Akeno and the others are packed into this room, their shuffling quiet, the soldiers tense, their guns still raised to ensure silence. It's the only means of enforcement that keeps this crowd of people from forming into a mob.

It's evident nobody has bathed in days, if not weeks. The stench builds until Akeno feels like he's going to be sick, but that would only make the smell worse in the room. He hopes they are able to bathe soon, for the sake of everyone. Nobody asks when this will happen. Nobody says anything. He is smashed between several people--one young woman with dark hair, dark skin, a man who looks like a mix between white and Indigenous , a Hispanic woman, an Asian woman, and then a petite black girl who looks young enough to be in high school. They really were stealing children, Akeno thinks.

Akeno's ears perk up as someone dares to whisper a question to the soldiers.

"You will wait to be directed," the guard shouts, cocking his gun, spit flying from his mouth. He shoves a man back, and the crowd shifts from his weight. There's mild grumbling and then more silence as they listen to the people in the next room file to their rooms.

Overhead, the static drones on and then the same woman's voice.

"At Amity, we want all our citizens to feel eager about their new home, but patience is another quality we cherish. Please, wait patiently until the bell sounds. Then you may enter your new forever home."

Forever home, Akeno thinks. So he was right. There was no leaving Amity. Once they were here, they were here forever.

A guard from the other side of the room opens a door just as a bell rings in the distance. He motions for them to enter, and the crowd moves forward, slowly at first, then quickly when the soldiers start shoving people in the next room.

They enter into a brightly lit room, and Akeno has to blink back the blinding white lights overhead. There are several backless benches positioned in the room. There are two guides and several more soldiers in the room. The guides stand at the front of the room in front of a projector screen. They smile and greet those entering through the door. The guides gesture at the empty seats as they file in with curious eyes and quick glances around the room. The walls are bare except for a few posters that seem to advertise the amenities within the city--a park, a museum, a cafe, a fancy restaurant, a spa. There's also posters of hard-working people, many of them people of color, Akeno notes. They're smiling in the posters, their faces fresh and proud as they till land, work in factories, mass sew clothing. As the door closes behind the last person, the room falls into an uneasy quietude. The guides' forced smiles puts Akeno more on edge. He wonders if they're forced to do this like the driver is forced to be an accessory to kidnapping. He wonders if anyone here has a choice in what they do for Amity.

Akeno shifts in his seat in the second row, now feeling both uncomfortable and unsettled by their gazes. In unison, the guides launch into their speech.

"Hello and welcome to Amity. Here in Amity, we want all of our citizens to explore the benefits of living in our single-person community. Here, we strive to make the lives of our citizens simpler and easier as they work hard to contribute to our newfound society."

The synchronicity of the guides unsettles Akeno. He thinks it must be a cute trick for the audience in the next room, similar to how theme park productions carry that same tone of geniality and quirky humor. These two guides, though, look like they have a metal rod clamping them into place from the neck down. They're too stiff, too automatic. When someone hesitantly raises their hand, one of their heads snaps to attention and says, "Please, hold all questions until the end."

The person's hand lowers, and people start whispering among themselves. One of the soldiers shouts for attention, and everyone shuts up. The guides take no notice and launch back into their regime.

"For those of you within the family unit, you will be escorted to your neighborhood," one guide says. "Here, you will meet like-minded people who will be your community members. Within your community, you can relax in your home, take a stroll through the neighborhood, or engage in group activities, such as group fitness, book clubs, sewing circles, and other personal favorites."

For how generic the pitch sounds, Akeno thinks none of this must actually exist. It's all just a diversion, a hopeful distraction, something to occupy the mind of what could be rather than what is. The posters on the wall show pictures of the park, the neighborhood homes, and so on, but they look staged, like plastic. It's all too new, too strange. Similar to how quaint the 1950s feel to the 21st century, the posters' modern, solar-paneled homes feel ancient, both known and unknown.

"Your homes will be selected based on your occupation," the other guide says. "Homes will be placed near your selected or provided occupation path. Transportation is limited to walking and occasional biking. There are no automobiles here. Here in Amity, we want to promote environmental awareness as well as physical wellness. Communities have been compacted in size to accommodate short travel distances."

"Amity provides all that was lost during the blackout," the first guide says. "Amity provides clean, running water from local streams, and all homes are powered by the sun. When the sun is hot, the homes are cool. When the sun sets, the homes are warm. When all is provided, courtesy of Amity, our citizens can feel more at ease knowing that Amity will care for its people."

People's heads perk up at the sound of running water.

"Within your new homes, natural sunlight will be your greatest ally," the other guide says. "Stoves will operate on natural gas, and fireplaces, which are only to be used in the winter months, will be fueled by gas as well. Running water will be available at all hours but in limited supply."

"Are there any questions?" they ask in unison.

There's no time to ask any questions. A buzzer sounds at the door, and the guides continue smiling. In unison, they announce the session has ended and to exit the room on the left. There will be no further questions. Everyone stands and shuffles to the other side, where the soldiers escort them out into the open once again, back into another parking lot, where several white trolleys await them. The door closes behind the last person with a click and the sound of another buzzer. The next group must be filing in now.

Akeno turns around and sees the blank white walls of the building. There are several more guides who usher people onto the vehicles, their faces cracking under the hot, morning sun. They don't frown, but the tips of their lips are falling. They're stressed, Akeno notes. He can see the sweat running during the women's legs, the pit stains on the soldiers. Everyone's on edge out here. The soldiers snap at the slow-moving passengers. Hurry, hurry, hurry, they shout. They don't want the families to see prisoners being loaded onto a trolley. That wouldn't fit with the narrative. Akeno packs himself on the edge of a seat designed for two as two women press themselves farther away from him.

Two trolleys are loaded full of people, and quietly, they follow one after the other without preamble. Despite the guides having said there is no automotive transportation, there is one road, albeit a narrow one, designed specifically for these trolleys. Akeno looks to the left side of the road, where straight ahead he sees a much larger building than the one where they were just previously held. It's a large, concrete building with several small windows on one side. It reminds him of the dorms from campus. That must be one means of housing. It didn't look anything like the glass homes from the posters.

As they approach the building, a guide stands at the front of the trolley, her manicured fingers holding a thin microphone. Her uniform, like all the rest, is pressed to perfection. She wears a white collared shirt and blue jacket with an ascot tied round her neck. She wears a pretty navy coat over the jacket in light of the cold weather, but as for her legs, she wears a knee-length skirt and nude-colored pantyhose, coupled with a pair of modest, navy-colored heels. She looks nervous to be speaking to the likes of them. They must look like criminals, Akeno thinks. They're handcuffed, many of them beaten, all of them wearing the same expression of hate and sorrow. Akeno would be nervous too.

"Hello and welcome to Amity," she says in a tiny voice. "We'll be taking a short tour of the city as we introduce our new citizens to their designated living communities." She braves a stronger voice. "To your left is Amity's military institution. It houses two thousand, five hundred armed soldiers. These soldiers help keep the peace within Amity's walls. They are also deployed beyond the walls to recruit new citizens for Amity. We are grateful to our soldiers for bringing back citizens like you to help Amity grow as a community."

So that's it, their confession. Amity willingly acknowledges that their military personnel brings people to the city. They're sent far and wide to save people from their destitute situations, from poverty, from starvation, from suffering. If Akeno came here as a husband and father, if he was sitting beside his wife and holding his children, he would think Amity were the good guys too. Amity saved them. The military is here for protection, as any family would think. In reality, the soldiers are here to ensure obedience, to protect the same world order that has been dated back to history's beginning.

Akeno scoffs, and the women beside him shoot him a dark glare.

The trolley edges around a corner, and a small city forms all around them. To the right and across the narrow street from the military's institution is a small park. There's long patches of grass, or what looks like grass, and a few benches along what appears to be a walking path. There are great, tall cacti all along the walking path, along with some shrubbery and trees. There's an open field, a small playground, and a basketball court. These images are ones he forgot existed. Without anybody in the park, though, these images represent what life has become for everyone: lifeless. He wonders where the children are.

When the trolley ahead of them comes to a stop, Akeno looks around. They are on the outskirts of a neighborhood. All around them are unlabeled, brick buildings with windows peering out at the narrow road. There's a walking path leading to the squat buildings, where a small, empty courtyard can be seen through a tall iron gate. The guides begin calling out several names, and many people depart the trolley, a few soldiers included. Those left standing on the dirt path seem confused, but they nevertheless edge forward when the trolleys leave them. The guide waves amicably from the trolleys, but those walking towards their new homes don't look back.

As they pass through the living communities, other buildings rise up around them. Smokestacks line the roofs, and Akeno covers his nose from the putrid smell of the white fog that escapes the tops of them. Tall, spiked fences surround factories, and as they pass by them, Akeno can make out a few figures standing within a small, square courtyard. Their faces follow the trolley down the path, their faces patched in dirt and grime. soldiers patrol these courtyards with bats in hand. They do not look at the trolleys as they pass.

Akeno's face starts to sweat. He feels nauseous despite not having eaten much in the past few days. He wishes he was back in his dorm, where he was safe, decently fed, and had everything he needed to survive until the spring. Was that only a few days ago? Akeno thinks. When he was resting in his dorm bed, he found Sam. That was only last week. Now the weather has changed from frigid December to the dry desert sun.

They pass building after building, and suddenly Akeno is acutely aware of how small this place feels. There is order and structure; there is modernity and normalcy. Chaos does not exist here. There is no room for chaos when all the details have been mapped out for them. There is a pattern to all of this, a routine. Should everyone follow this pattern of normalcy and order, there should be no cause for question. They will know when they will be fed, when they will sleep, when they will wake, when they will work. There is nowhere and nothing else. This is all that is offered; it's their best chance, their only chance. Akeno knows his fate before it's dealt.

As they pass alongside the rest of the unlabeled brick buildings, where they drop more people off and leave them behind, the factories continue down the line and increase in number. Akeno looks out over the tops of the buildings and can barely make out a white pinnacle cresting over the skyline. As the trolley nears closer, there's a thick, white wall surrounding what looks like a miniature of the Washington Monument. There's a pretty mural along the side of the wall that depicts all types of people holding hands, people of all color, sizes, and ages. It's meant to represent unity along with amity, but its clear-cut lines, too sharp features, and lack of color blending all comprise an image of an altered reality.

"Here, to your right, we have the Capitol of Amity," the guide says. "Its white walls represent the purity of Amity and the peace in which unity brings when we work together in complete harmony. Behind those walls are those who have designed Amity and those who ensure Amity continues to uphold its values of integrity and prosperity."

As they pass by it, Akeno can make out the roofs of other buildings. They're covered in solar panels, the blue of the panels contrasting sweetly with the pale reds, greens, and blues of what appears to be residential housing. The guide rambles on about luxury, the amount of space allotted for each family--a central living room, a full kitchen, three bedrooms, two bathrooms, a small garage between units as the laundry room and storage unit. There are several community centers accessible to all families, local grocery stores to select which foods the family will have for the week, a central school for children of all ages, and family planning centers for young couples wishing to have more children within Amity.

They turn a corner, and the white walls grow smaller in the dis-

215

tance. They've circled back around now as they approach another set of short, brick buildings. The guide continues to smile as she calls off the last of the names. Akeno hears his name, and he weakly stands, following the remaining few off the trolley. With his hands still bound behind him, he watches as the trolley pulls off, leaving Akeno and the others standing there, dust in their eyes and dirt layering their skin. As the small pack walks desolately to their new living quarters, Akeno takes one final look back at the white walls just down the narrow road and wishes more than anything he could find himself on the other side.

PART II: AMITY

CHAPTER 17

Five seasons later—when the flowers start to bloom, the sparse patches of grass turn a shade greener, when the rain comes again—Akeno wears a thin, long-sleeved tunic and a pair of patched pants to the factory four blocks down the narrow road. He carries a brown paper bag in his hand. Inside it is his lunch for the day: an apple, two pieces of bread sandwiching three thin slices of what appears to be ham. In his back pocket is his sweat rag, a pair of safety glasses, his work gloves, and a large stick. These essentials are all standard protocol, except for the stick, but Akeno will need that in time.

He walks along with a group of men--their backs broader, their heads taller, and their voices deeper than Akeno's own. Their conversations are cruder than what Akeno's used to, but he doesn't mind. Sometimes he laughs at their jokes, but altogether he simply enjoys their company. He has to, at least to some degree. This is his team, the men he works, sleeps, eats, and showers with every day for the past year. If he didn't like them, his situation would be harder to tolerate. Besides, they like Akeno, or so he thinks. They pick on him in the usual way they pick on each other. Akeno never refutes their jokes, only nods and smiles, and they like that best about him. He doesn't fight back, never raises his voice, never accuses anyone of stealing, cheating, or lying like many of them do. And they do steal, cheat, and lie, but nobody likes to be singled out for what everyone else already does. Those who are not stealing, cheating, or lying (at the moment) are being stolen from, cheated, or lied to. The trick was to know the balance of when to steal, cheat, and lie, and accept fate as it was dealt.

The men jostle one another as they walk the path to the factory. The sky is the dark indigo of early dawn. This color had soon become Akeno's favorite color because it was the same consistent color that told Akeno he was alive, that he had survived another day and night in Amity. It's the little things, Akeno reminds himself.

When they reach the factory's door, one of the men pushes forward and sounds the buzzer, the voices and laughter of the men echoing off the brick walls surrounding them on three sides. They wait a few minutes longer, and one of the men presses the buzzer again.

"Come on, you filthy pigs, open the fuckin' door," the man says, pressing the buzzer again and again and again. The speaker on the buzzer was busted when Akeno arrived on his first day. The soldiers still hadn't fixed it.

"It's a hard job in there, Heinz," another man says. "It's hard to get out of that chair when you've been sittin' in it for so long. You know that feeling, seeing as you are."

"Shut the hell up, Gabrio, or I'll put you out like an old dog," Heinz says.

Akeno can't help but smile. It was ridiculous, coming from Heinz, who liked to play the bad guy. He was a 6'2" 250 lb. white guy, but he was soft at the heart. He was older than the rest of them, his hair fading to the sides of his head. Heinz sleeps in the bed next to Akeno's. On sleepless nights, he can hear Heinz cry as he repeats the names of people he loves. Family, he thinks, maybe even a girlfriend. It's usually the same three names: Penny, Tammy, and Georgia. He's never worked up the courage to ask about those names. It feels too private, and the last privilege they get is any privacy.

"See, even Pancake thinks it was funny," Gabrio says with a wink at Akeno.

Gabrio is the same height as Akeno, maybe an inch taller or shorter depending on who they ask. His olive skin is flawless, beautiful even. He has dark brown eyes that shine close to black. His defining features are his sharp, dark eyebrows that furrow when he's thinking. He's certainly the most educated of them all, though he won't reveal much of his backstory. He changes the tale every so often, to keep people on their toes, he claims.

"I'm just saying you could teach us a few tricks on how to maintain some weight since you seem to be the champion of it," Gabrio says with a wink at Akeno. "We're basically starving, Heinz."

"Try eating shit," Heinz says and chuckles.

A chorus of laughter bubbles up from the group of men as the buzzer sounds from the other side, and the gates open. Heinz leads them, Gabrio and Akeno behind him, and the rest following. From the back, Akeno feels a shove and stumbles forward. He glances back with a face of contempt and sees Church's wide smile and suddenly an arm wraps itself around Akeno's shoulders.

Church has the darkest complexion, his eyes a deep amber brown. The muscles under his shirt are light and limber. He's average height, a few inches taller than Akeno and Gabrio, but shorter than Heinz. He claims 6'1 but Akeno thinks he's closer to 5'11. He used to play basketball in college, not on the team but with his crew, he said. He's several years older than Akeno, but like Akeno, he was never able to get his degree. Although Church's demeanor is generally lightweight and carefree, when Church talks about something serious, he tightens his lips and looks the other way, as if he doesn't find the topic all that interesting. Church squeezes Akeno tight, smashing his face into Church's armpit, which reeks already from the morning workout he squeezed in before they left their living quarters.

"Ready to be on dry end today, Pancake? Think you'll be able to reach the ropes this time, or are you gonna need some of papa's help?"

"Don't call yourself 'papa,' Church. Makes you come off as a pedophile," Gabrio says from the front.

"'Papa' is for Pancake. Gabrio, you can call me 'Daddy,'" Church says to Gabrio, and gives a wink and an air kiss. "But for real, we can't be covering for you every time, Pancake, and you know the boss man's a real dickhead when it comes to pacing. Just holler if you need anything, okay? We don't all need to get in trouble cause you're too damn short to reach the ropes. Hell, if Gabrio can do it, so can you."

They enter the building, a blast of cool air washing over them in a wave of fresh air. It almost makes Akeno shiver in the early dawn, but he knows that the same blast of air will hit him when he leaves after the shift. It's that single moment that Akeno looks forward to every evening. The air flows into the front room, and the men pass through the metal detectors one-by-one, the soldiers lounging in the break room intended only for them. The two soldiers on shift hold a cup of coffee and a bagel. Their eyes lazily glaze over the machine's lights as one hand waves them through to the factory floor. When Akeno passes through undetected, he knows with certainty that the machine doesn't work at all. He hides a lopsided grin as he carries on.

"I've got that figured out," Akeno says to Church. "I found something in the park the other day."

"What did you find? Recruitment forms?" Church laughs with a snide look back at the soldiers. "Don't take their word for it. You'll never know where you're sent."

"No, not that," Akeno says as the large doors to the factory doors open.

A group of men flood out, their faces covered in sweat, the night shift. Only the worst of the worst are sent on night shift, or at least that's what someone told Akeno. Better that they're not seen, someone used to say. They're convicted felons--rapists, murderers, child molesters. Akeno wonders if they were felons from before or if they became felons when they arrived in Amity. Akeno didn't even know there was a judicial system here, but he supposes if there was a judge and jury, the outcome was clear. Akeno tries to avoid eye contact as they pass, but he can't help but look. They pass the night shift, wordless, as Gabrio shakes hands with a few of them.

"Why does he do that if they're all rapists and murderers?" Akeno asks, eyeing some of the men Gabrio claps on the back, out of the sight from the guards lazing by the door.

"Hell if I know. I guess they're not all bad."

Gabrio catches Akeno's eye, finishes up his conversation, and returns to the pack.

"What's the issue, boys?"

"Akeno asks why you talk to guys like that," Church says with a look of contempt.

"Don't believe everything you hear, Church. It's unbecoming of you," Gabrio says with a flick of his wrist.

Church scoffs, and Akeno pulls back, determined not to find himself in between anyone.

The incoming shift files into place. There's a few minutes between shifts, and the men take this time to put on their gloves, safety glasses, and other necessities.

Gabrio doesn't miss a beat with Akeno.

"Some of them, yeah, they're as bad as they say," he says under his breath. "But some of them are the good guys. War criminals, if you will. Got caught doing some Robin Hood shit for the people."

Akeno nods, doesn't question him. He can feel Gabrio's eyes on him as he laces up his shoes, which came loose during the walk over here.

Gabrio then joins the group as they make their way onto the factory floor. It's always steaming inside, despite the cool air Akeno felt walking in. The heat from the machines fills the room, stifling the air so the heat feels close to the skin. On Akeno's first day, it was Gabrio who gave him the crash course. It's too loud to hear much of anything, so all the men scream at one another. Akeno has gotten better at reading lips. He also learned to cut slits just under the armpit of his shirt so there's more ventilation for his torso and back. That trick he stole from Church.

Church sets his stuff down at the station next to Akeno's, which is only twenty feet away. Akeno pulls out a long stick, and at the end of that stick is a metal hook he unhinged from the living quarters' supply closet. He did it quickly one night when the janitor left the supply closet unlocked, something he has a habit of doing.

"No way, that's where that went," Church says with a laugh, pointing at the hook. "You know Steve's been going on and on about that for days."

Akeno nods and laughs.

With the whirring of the machines and the engine belt revving back up for production, Akeno can't make out what Church says next, but Church is shaking his head with a nod at one of the soldiers standing on the walkway hanging over the floor. He's watching Akeno handle this shit, his eyebrows raised more out of curiosity. Another guard sees Akeno holding the stick and stands alongside the other, watching with their arms casually slung over the bannister.

The machine whirs to life, and the assembly begins. What they make at this factory are a variety of mechanical parts. These parts fit into the daily appliances, features, amenities, and basic construction of Amity's foundations. The procession starts with the usual slow-moving tendency, but after a few minutes, the belt starts to pick up, and Akeno's side of the line approaches with speed. Akeno's gloved hands work deftly to ensure all parts of his assembly are accounted for and adequately dried before moving to Church's side.

What Akeno must do is allocate several bits of hot metal into a steam-pressed drying machine. He must pull this skinny lever to bring down the lid of the machine, pull a separate lever that heats the steam, and another lever that releases the moisture onto the metal parts. These metal parts cannot be adequately assembled in another factory without first being properly dried.

To do his job effectively, though, he needs to be several inches taller. Akeno has tried switching with his fellow team members, but the soldiers wouldn't allow it. Rotation is rotation, and nobody likes doing this job, mainly because it's the hottest machine in the factory. They hate the steamer, and they hate the boss. If Akeno's too short to reach the lever, it means there's less production. If there's less production, there's less benefit for the boss. When production resulted in low numbers because of Akeno's height, the soldiers brought him a step stool to reach the levers. It was not only degrading to Akeno's dignity, it was degrading because his fellow men ensured this would be degrading. They called him "Short Stack" at first, a name that bothered Akeno, at least to some degree. He's certainly heard worse. Then they started calling him "Pancake," deriving it from "Short Stack." He hasn't heard anyone call him by his given name in months, but he has to admit that "Pancake" has grown on him.

The stool is there again, waiting for him like always. He glances back up at the soldiers, who smile and point at the stool with a cheap thumbs up. Since Akeno's putting on a show now, he kicks the stool over beside Church, whose eyes raise in apprehension at such a bold move. He watches with amusement as Akeno reaches for his stick with the hook stuck to the top. The hook catches on the tied end of the rope lever, and Akeno yanks it down. The metal lid closes on the mechanical bits inside. Akeno takes the stick and pulls the second lever, which allows the steam to filter through the vents in the metal cube. Akeno times it perfectly. He reaches back up, pulls down on the first lever and releases the latch. Akeno presses the button for the conveyor belt to continue its path, and with a self-congratulatory smile, he looks at Church with satisfaction.

Church isn't smiling, though. His head is bent, and Akeno's face slackens. Church's eyes glance up at the walkway above the factory floor, and Akeno turns to see several soldiers pointing down at Akeno and his tool. The boss leans heavily against the railings, his beady eyes and tight lips discerning Akeno's station and the apparatus he's constructed. Akeno stands his ground and pulls his invention closer to him. It's a small gesture, but Akeno stands with his face turned up at the boss, his stick appearing more like a staff.

The boss eyes Akeno for a while, the man's button up shirt and slacks looking freshly pressed and cleaned. Akeno refuses to let go of his makeshift tool or drop his gaze from his superior. The boss says something indiscernible to the soldiers and walks away, leaving the pair to glare down at Akeno as they follow after him. Akeno waits a few moments before releasing the breath he was holding, his heart pounding as he continues to work his shift without any disturbances and successfully navigates the machine that had previously given Akeno so much grief.

By the time the lunch bell rings, Akeno's starving. The floor isn't given a lunch break, but the men have timed their meals with their machines. Akeno finishes up the last set before reaching behind him for his sack lunch. He pulls out the messy sandwich he had brought early that morning and the apple he had intended to eat earlier for breakfast. He quickly takes a few bites of the sandwich before the next set comes down the belt.

He pulls down the levers with easier succession than he had earlier in the shift, now that he's used to the feel of the rope connecting with the hook. He performs his job quicker than he would using the step stool, since sometimes he has to rearrange the parts to fit inside the metal bin or the lid won't close. Sometimes there's too many pieces in at the same time, which requires Akeno to take them off the belt, walk back around the machine, lay them down on the conveyor belt, walk back to his side of the machine, etc. The process is altogether a tedious one, though not a difficult or laboring one.

The only downside is the burns Akeno suffers. Sometimes his sleeves snag on the mechanical parts, raising his shirt, and thus burning the inside of his wrists. Sometimes Akeno forgets the pain of the burns and pulls up his sleeves because of the heat. This usually results in a burn. Sometimes his too-bulky gloves can't grab the tinier mechanical pieces, and Akeno has to take his gloves off and use his fingers. This always results in a burn. These things happen at least once a shift. He was given burn cream by one of the floor managers when he first began his job, but they only give one tube. The rest must be bought at the local drug store within their living communities. Their local drug store does not carry burn cream.

Akeno finishes his lunch and wipes the sweat from his face with his damp rag. He puts his hands on his hips and looks to Church, who's kneeling along the conveyor belt. There are no chairs to rest in throughout the shift.

"Tired, Church?" Akeno goads.

"You know I'm tired, man," he says with a smile. "You ain't tired yet?"

"Me? Never tired."

"So he says," Church says when he sees the soldiers eyeing him from the walkway. He stands and shakes out his legs. "What's for dinner, Pancake? You makin' us anything tonight?"

The men can eat within the community dining halls, though for a price. At least they have a choice to have a hot meal. When it was much colder, on those cold February nights after work, a hot bowl of soup and semi-fresh baked bread shipped from the other living communities was a treasure. When they had nights like those, it was always worth the dining hall's expenses, but usually the dining hall offered the same meals every day. Akeno grew tired of beans, meat, and greens, so he cooked.

It turns out that Akeno's not such a bad cook after all. There's a local grocery store in their living community. It doesn't offer much, but it's enough to get crafty with. When his team found out Akeno was a decent cook, they wanted what he was having, but as Akeno pointed out, he couldn't afford to feed them all on his budget alone. Rather than bully him to make their food anyway, they pitched in their currency's worth for a plate, which was cheaper to do than go to the dining hall. Not all his recipes turned out great, but if it meant trying something new, the men would place their bets on Akeno over the dining hall.

He had never really tried cooking before. He never felt he had the chance to, or any reason to. He used to live off fast food and campus dining, but he remembers the old recipes Hugh and Sandy used to make for him. It was their hobby to try out new dishes all the time, and they taught Akeno how to make the ones they knew by heart. Akeno loved to eat and enjoyed the company they provided. Even when he messed up the recipe, they said anything could be fixed with a little extra spice, or a little sugar, depending on the error. Something he remembers fondly is the way they sang together when they cooked, even if they were offkey. That's why Church has become a favorite companion in the small, worn-down kitchen in the community building. Church loves to sing, used to be a choirboy. That's how his name stuck.

"I'm thinking of an old-fashioned chicken and gravy recipe. It's easy to make," Akeno says. He pulls on a few levers and waits for the steamer to start. He watches it closely as he continues laying out the night's menu. "Then we can steam those peas, slice up a few potatoes, and I think we're set."

Akeno releases the steamer lid that allows the rest of the mechanical parts to move down the machine. He leans against his staff, thinking how Sandy used to love feeding people. He wishes more than anything he could go back to that old farm house and cook with them again.

"Eyes up!" one of the soldiers yells from the walkway. "I said eyes up!"

Akeno snaps out of his trance as several soldiers form a line on the walkway. They sneer once they catch Akeno's eye. The boss strides out of the upstairs office, his face slack. He hops down the narrow stairway, where a guard unlocks the downstairs gate door to the factory floor. He makes directly for Akeno, his eyes on fire.

"Hand it over," he snaps at Akno. The boss has never been on the factory floor before. He usually delegates the soldiers to dole out pun-

229

ishment. "Your weapon will be detained in the office and furthermore destroyed after your shift is complete."

Akeno hands over the staff, and the boss snatches it quickly away. "It's not a weapon," Akeno begins. "I was just–"

The boss takes the staff and whips it around. There's a sharp crack, and Akeno falls. The concrete floor wavers underneath him, and Akeno feels a sharp pain on his head. Then there's a foot kicking him once, twice, three times. He coughs and wheezes, spit spilling from the corner of his lips. Feet move all around him, but the boss shouts something over the din of the noise, the only voice that can be heard over the sound of the machinery.

"Bringing in a weapon like this is considered an act of subterfuge and is grounds for punishment. Bringing a weapon onto the factory floor is prohibited by machinery operators. If you cannot abide by these rules, you will be punished and tried in Amity's court of law."

The boss snaps the staff over his knee, but Akeno keeps his head down as he lays on the floor. The broken mess lands in front of Akeno, his hands still placed over his head, expecting more punishment.

"This is your final warning," the boss shouts. "Any more slip ups and you'll be leaving in handcuffs, understood?"

Nobody says anything for a moment.

"I said, is that understood?"

"Yes, sir!" the factory floor shouts, including Akeno.

The boss stands in front of Akeno a moment longer, then hobbles back up the stairs and into the office, where the door slams shut. The soldiers return to their positions, and the only sound that's heard are the machines cranking and whirring. As the soldiers retreat into an interior hallway, Akeno could hear their faint laughter. Several feet come running to Akeno's side to lift him up. Akeno stands, coughs again, and feels for any broken ribs. He's fine, he thinks. He can take a few blows.

"Are you alright?" Gabrio asks, lowering his face to Akeno's so they make eye contact. "Hey, are you alright?"

"Yeah, I'm fine," Akeno says, brushing them off. Church comes around from behind him, his eyes full of concern and pity. Akeno wishes he would stop looking at him like that. "I'm fine, really. He barely touched me."

"It's 'cause the main man is here," Heinz says, coming around from the side. "Look up."

The four of them glance at the office, where a man in a suit stands within the small office, his silhouette barely noticeable from the small window that overlooks the factory floor.

They get Akeno to his feet and brush the dust and grime off his permanently dirty clothes. The office door opens, and the man in the suit and the boss walk out together, grinning as if they shared an inside joke, without glancing at the factory floor.

"If it weren't for him, the boss wouldn't have cared, so long as the numbers look good," Heinz says. "If beating you up is what the main man wants, it's what the boss will do."

"I'm surprised he ain't got bruises on his knees from all the dick sucking he does for that guy," Gabrio says, and they laugh, or rather, Akeno wheezes at the tail end of his laugh. Gabrio smacks him on the back, but not too hard. "You're gonna be alright, Pancake. Just take it easy the rest of the shift, alright? Church will help you through the last of it, right Church?"

"Yeah, no problem," Church says gleefully. "We're nearly halfway done now."

"Five more hours," Akeno grumbles, standing upright. "Yeah, I can do five more."

"That's the spirit, kid," Gabrio says and flashes a bright smile. "Let's get back to it, boys. We got time to kill."

Once the shift was over, Akeno nearly fell over on the streets. Church had caught him before he fell, and Heinz carried him the rest of the way to the living quarters.

Akeno lied to himself when he said he was okay. He went to the bathroom just after the bell rang for the shift's end. He raised his shirt and saw just how badly bruised he was. His ribs are an ugly purple and blue, but he still doesn't think any of them are cracked. He would know if they were cracked. When he coughs, he has a coughing fit. He worries there's blood in his lungs, but he hasn't coughed anything red up. That's a good sign. It was just a few kicks, Akeno thinks. Just three, plus the head injury.

He thought he was finished with the head injuries. The one from last year had healed well, and now this one was basically on top of the original. Akeno touched it gingerly with one finger, and he flinched from the pain. His head was pounding. Now that he was away from all the noise of the factory floor, he realized how badly he needed a drink of water.

He's exhausted, but he smiles at his team surrounding him in the community center. He still insisted on cooking, though he let Heinz carry the groceries in for him. Church offered to be his sous chef, but Akeno preferred to work alone while he was in the kitchen. Plus, he couldn't handle another look of pity from them. He knows parts of their stories, and they know parts of his. This wasn't the worst that's happened to any of them.

232

He rests on a stool by the stove as the food crackles and pops, his flimsy seat beneath him wobbling back and forth on a crooked leg. The others sit at the white card table. They laugh and carry on as they slam down their hands. They don't bet on anything other than the last baked roll. It was a delicacy to have in the dining hall, so they ran to grab a few before they ran out. This time Heinz takes the last roll.

"As if you need another roll," Gabrio says under his breath.

"Jealousy looks good on you," Heinz says with a wink.

Gabrio laughs.

"Believe it or not, I used to be sixty pounds heavier," Heinz announces through a full mouth. "God, I miss those days."

"Didn't you say you boxed, Heinz?" Church asks, leaning his head on his hand, as he watches Heinz finish the last of the last roll.

Heinz nods. "Sure did, but it was more of a backwater thing. Used to make a lot of money that way."

"I'd put my bet on you," Church says with a smile.

When Akeno announces the food is ready, they all hop to their feet and push their way to the kitchen. As they get a whiff of the finished food, they all visibly melt.

"Smells like home," Heinz says.

As they sit around and enjoy their meal together, Akeno is the last to finish his plate. He watches as the others pat their stomachs with satisfaction. Heinz groans in agreement; Gabrio closes his eyes, and Church mimics a marriage proposal on Gabrio's right.

"Best meal I've had in ages," Church says.

Akeno smiles, nodding in agreement.

"Ah, wait till you have Papi's tortilla pollo soup, do you, Church?" Gabrio says with a teasing, self-satisfied grin, his eyes still closed as he leans farther back in his chair.

"Oh, it's Papi now, is it?" Church laughs. "Alright, Papi, you win this round."

"Finally, I get the recognition I deserve," Gabrio says, placing his hands behind his head. "What'd you think, Pancake? Pretty good stuff, right?"

Akeno nods. "Yes, I think I managed the gravy better than before."

"I see your strength, Pancake," Gabrio says, peeking an eye open at Akeno. "You don't have to prove anything to me."

Akeno smiles.

"So, Pancake, can you make anything else other than the classic white man's food?" Gabrio asks. "You know, being ethnic and all."

"Sure, I can make a few other dishes," Akeno replies as Church clears away the table and carries them to the kitchen to wash in the tiny sink.

The community center only restocks supplies once a month, if they remember, so sometimes soap isn't as much a necessity as hot water. Thankfully, the hot water works here, most times. Sometimes they boil enough water to soak the dishes in when they don't have soap. Akeno glances at Church, one towel slung over his shoulder as he whistles while he works.

"Anything authentic?" Gabrio asks, bringing Akeno's focus back to the table.

"I can make one really good Thai stir-fry, a bratwurst plate, a variety of pastas, and I can make some mean tacos." He smiles. "Any of those sound interesting?"

"You said you're Japanese, right?" Church calls from the kitchen.

"I am," Akeno replies, loud enough for Church to hear.

"Can you make anything like that?" Heinz asks.

"I can definitely try, but I never learned a recipe from anyone. My mother passed before I was old enough to cook."

The room pauses a beat but presses forward.

"So tacos, huh?" Gabrio asks. "You have to elaborate. Tacos like real tacos, or like Taco Bell tacos?"

Akeno laughs. "I can't even remember what Taco Bell tastes like anymore."

"That's something I don't miss," Heinz said, his arms crossed, his head tipped back. "Taco Bell used to give me the shits."

The room erupts in laughter, Gabrio's hands clapping in applause. "Amen," he says.

"Mexican tacos are best though," Gabrio says with authority. "I mean the other tacos, they're good too, but I wouldn't recommend anything except Mexican tacos."

"You'll have to teach me how to make Mexican tacos then," Akeno says with a smile.

"My vote's on the Bratwurst," Heinz says. "Gramps used to put away a plate of Brats, and Gram had the best homemade kraut."

"Do you remember the recipe?" Akeno asks.

"We should have Heinz whip something up next," Church calls from the kitchen.

"Yeah, if you want food poisoning," Gabrio says with a chuckle.

Heinz ignores Gabrio and looks to Akeno. "I'll teach you what I remember someday."

Then Heinz smacks his hands on the table and stands. "Thanks again, Pancake. You need more currency for the next meal?"

"You actually gave me more than enough last time. I'll use the rest of it," Akeno says.

Heinz nods and puts his hand up in a wave. "See you fellas later."

He leaves the community center, the door slamming shut behind him.

Gabrio pulls out a half-used cigarette and lights it with the spare matches he keeps in his pockets. Cigarettes aren't sold at the community store; they're a banned item, along with the other vices. Amity has instilled a sense of morality and virtue in its people by forcing them to give up anything that would steal from the balanced life Amity has advertised.

They sit for a long time, each of them quietly thinking, quietly resting, as Church dries the old plates carefully. There's a couple cracks in each of them, but they've been glued together by someone in times past. Akeno's had to glue one back together a few months ago. It's become a tradition it seems.

"Gabrio, what did you say to me earlier today?" Church called from the other room. Hearing *Gabrio's* given name sounds strange, since only Church is allowed to say it, but he never does around the others. Akeno prefers *Gabrio*, a name that rolls off the tongue.

"Oh, right," Church says, peeking his head around the corner of the kitchen. "Something about a clever mouse sticking to the cracks in the wall."

Gabrio exhaled and considered this for a moment.

"Pretty smart thing you did with that stick and hook," Gabrio says and takes another drag. "Clever stuff but not too smart."

"What do you mean?" Akeno asks, his brows knitting together.

"I'm just saying, I wouldn't do something like that again," Gabrio puts out the remaining bit of his cigarette out on the bottom end of his chair. "People out here don't like smart people. That's why there's so many dummies out here."

Church leans against the sink, watching the two of them. "Gotta say I agree, Pancake. You didn't deserve what happened, and it probably wouldn't have happened if the main man wasn't there today, but they get buggy about shit like that, you know?"

Akeno feels a rush of heat hit his cheeks. He feels both outraged and embarrassed. He should've come to them first with his idea, but he didn't because he already knew their answer. He knew they'd be like this. He hates that they're right. He doesn't know what he was hoping for when he pulled the big reveal. Applause, maybe, for finding a way to make work easier? He mentally berates himself. Who's he kidding? They were right. They don't want to make life easier for people like Akeno. They don't care if the work is hard to do and it slows production. It's not about production anymore. It's not about the bottom line.

"Now don't go lookin' like that," Gabrio says, leaning over the table. "I'm just tryin' to protect you, you know?" He lowers his voice, his eyes glancing to the door. "They're watching you now, kid, and that ain't a good sign. I've seen them watch people before. Weird shit happens. People disappear."

"Weird shit always happens 'round here," Church says. "People go in and out all the time. They transfer factories, transfer living quarters, transfer to the military. It's all based on what you can do, what you know, who you know."

"Some people disappear and nobody knows where they go after that." Gabrio says, glancing back over his shoulder.

Church looks from Akeno to Gabrio, his shoulder shrugging up and down in a slow and languid way, as if he's stretching muscles buried deep down. He drops the towel on the edge of the sink and takes a seat at the table.

"That's not what they said–" Akeno starts.

"Forget what they've said," Gabrio interrupts. "You weren't here when all this shit started. Nobody started going missing when it was

237

just a few of us, but then they started shipping in people from all over, and it's them who get to thinking we have a chance and we don't. Not like this, not here," he says, jabbing a finger at the table.

"Then how else—" Akeno begins to ask, but he's suddenly cut off.

"There's more to it," Gabrio snaps.

Akeno and Church are quiet for a moment as Gabrio's nostrils flare, his brows furrowing. He notices the shock on their faces, and he sits back in his chair again. He closes his eyes, smoothes back his hair, refocuses himself.

"One night you start talking with someone about this and that, and *they* overhear all that shit." Gabrio eyes Akeno and Church and leans forward onto the table. "Don't ever think they're not paying attention. They're always listening, always got someone lookin' out for people who get big ideas." Gabrio points at Akeno. "Pancake's a bright kid. He's young and educated. He's still fresh with ideas. He's not used to how things are and how things have always been. If they can't break him, they take him out. You understand?"

Neither of them responds, and Gabrio exhales a long sigh. He stands and pushes in his chair. "I'm hitting the showers," he announces. "Let me know when you need more currency," he says to Akeno and heads for the door. With one hand on the handle, he stops. He makes as if he's going to say something more, then he leaves.

A few days go by, and Akeno continues to work as he had been. He thinks of Gabrio's warning. It's not that Akeno doesn't trust Gabrio, but Church made a good point: He had never seen or heard of anyone disappearing. Men got transferred all the time from one factory to another. He had seen at least a dozen faces before they were moved off the floor and to another factory. It was commonplace. It's not like they chose to work in the factories to begin with. For all they knew, Amity needed more help on the farms outside the walls. Crops had to grow somewhere, and someone had to farm the land. It made sense. Gabrio might just be paranoid. Who knows how long he's been here? Years, it seems. He never talks about it, even when asked, though he constantly reminds people he was here in Amity's beginning.

When Akeno had first arrived at the living community, Gabrio had been the quietest of them all when they met. The three of them were already well acquainted with one another by the time Akeno had shown up at their door, so it made sense that he was the odd one out. Akeno, as passive as he is, didn't have any issue melting into the mold of the men's routines. He remembers the terror. Despite all its illusions, he knew Amity wasn't a place of goodwill. He would never forget the feeling of being chased down like a criminal and transported here. He was a slave to their society, regardless of its benefits. He followed them around like a newborn pup. After a while, Akeno lost the impression that Amity was an evil place. It felt almost normal.

When it was clear he was there to stay, Gabrio made sure to fill him in one every little thing as they went. Heinz made sure to counter whatever Gabrio said, just for good measure, and Church made sure to play neutral, a recommendation he made to Akeno on his first week. Eventually Akeno learned just how these men operated on their own.

Akeno hates to disappoint any of them. He still remembers Gabrio's words echoing in the back of his mind. *They're watching you.* All the other references of "big ideas," or what could otherwise hint at an ideological revolution was unheard of, especially in Amity, where information was closely monitored. They are only allowed the books available in their local library, which Akeno has yet to find. The media they watch is called Amity TV, written and produced by Amity's only official media station. There's a TV in the main room of the living quarters, but it's kept on mute. Nobody wants to watch the news. They mostly ignore whatever happens on screen. There's a printed edition of the news too, *Amity Times*. They don't even get a daily copy of the paper. Mostly Akeno finds them in the trash, leftover by the soldiers from their shifts patrolling the community. There's nothing interesting on the news or in the paper. There's no real news, only announcements and commendations for Amity's progress: a new park that Akeno has never seen, a new school he will never go to, adult education courses, which he will never be able to afford. Sometimes they drop a few "elected" officials' names to promote their campaign for a "better tomorrow." It's all the same to Akeno. They'll never reap the benefits.

If there ever is a revolution, it's certainly not in Akeno's better interests to be the leader of one. It was clear he wasn't the one to lead the charge, especially after being kicked to shit in front of his own team. If anyone was going to lead an uprising, it would have been Sam.

Thinking about her now feels like a cold shock of water. He hadn't really thought about her all that much, not that he has time to think about much of anything really. Since the first day, he's been working nonstop. They work six days a week—twelve hour shifts for each working day—but in accordance with the weekend (which can fall on any given two days), they only have to work six hours for two days, and on the third day, they're off.

In the few moments when he's alone with his thoughts, he thinks of Sam and hopes she's safe, wherever she is. She's probably back in the mountains by now. She would have found a nice cabin to settle herself in. She would have put gas in an old truck found abandoned on the road so she could go back and forth from the cabin to town. She'd survive off the game she'd hunt. She'd be safe and comfortable. She wouldn't be caught dead in a place like this. She's too smart for that.

Akeno sits up in bed, rubs at his eyes. It's nearly bedtime. There's a single clock in the room. It's digital numbers read out the time by the door: nearly nine-thirty. Heinz has been out all night, probably getting into some old fashioned gambling. Alcohol is illegal, but on nights like these, Heinz always comes home drunk. Akeno doesn't know where he gets the liquor, but his breath always smells like moonshine or rum. He imagines the only way for people like them to get the stuff is through the soldiers. Since the soldiers are associated members of the military, and the military are the only ones allowed to leave Amity, that's the only way a black market can flourish as it has.

Gabrio says he wouldn't drink what the soldiers gave him. Instead, he opts for the marijuana grown inside and around the living quarters, in secret spots all around Amity apparently. How they began growing there isn't a question Akeno asks. Better to mind his own business. Akeno doesn't partake in much of either, though he doesn't turn down a swig of liquor or a hit from one of Gabrio's joints when they offer.

As for Church, he spends his days in the community worship house. The center doesn't ascribe to any particular religion, so it's a place for anyone to go and worship. Church says not many people go. It's just him most nights, he says.

Akeno doesn't have any particular routine for his off-days, but he thinks tomorrow he'll take a walk, get some fresh air, maybe read a book. He never found a library, but he has found a few books lying around here and there. Sometimes the soldiers leave them lying around. Other times, charity presents itself in its usual form: a white woman from another community, whose guilty conscience offers her solace when she donates used books to the lower statuses. She always wears white and makes sure to step carefully around the building to ensure she doesn't get herself dirty. Sometimes she brings cleaning supplies and drops them off with the books. Nobody likes her but Akeno. He appreciates the books she brings, even if she is uptight.

From the small nightstand between his bed and Church's, he eyes the short stack of books. A couple of them are Church's, one being a Bible and one being a nonfiction story about someone he's never heard of before. The other books on the table he's already read, and while they were okay, they weren't exactly thrilling. He guessed the ending of one novel from the start, didn't quite understand the point of the second, and the last one's characters were so flat, he didn't even feel like finishing.

He takes one of the books at random and begins to read one of them again. The lights will be shut off soon, but it doesn't take long for his eyes to slip close. He falls into a restless slumber, where factory floors and angry machines don't exist. He thinks back to one of his happier memories, the ones he can paint vividly in his mind. He remembers open fields and sunsets. He remembers the cows grazing miles away. He remembers the smell of home cooking.

Then he hears a thump in the background and remembers a heavy fist hitting a wall. He remembers the smell of scorched skin and the taste of blood behind his teeth. He remembers the muffled grunts down the hall, the noise breaking between the hands placed over his ears. He remembers crying once. He remembers there are worse places to be than Amity.

The door opens, and Akeno quickly sits up in bed, sweat running down his face, the book he was reading now on the floor. Heinz steps into the room. The lights are off. The clock reads nearly midnight. Akeno can sense that Heinz is drunk from the way he stumbles around the room, feeling for his bed. He's the first to come back, Akeno realizes, as he squints through the dark at the other beds opposite him. Not even Church is back yet.

"Hey, you up?" Heinz whispers.

"Yeah, I'm up," Akeno says groggily.

"How was your night?" Heinz slurs. "I won a couple...a couple, nothing."

"You won a couple nothing?" Akeno asks and snickers.

"I won a round and then lost, then lost again, then won, then lost." Heinz falls on his bed, the springs protesting loudly from the weight as they throw him back up. Akeno can hear the thin blankets on the bed being untucked and moved around. "I won some."

"Good," Akeno says. "Glad to hear it."

He waits a few moments and hears the rumble of Heinz's deep centered snores. He only snores like that after he drank, which was most nights, but the sound has become a comfort to Akeno in the pitch black of night. It reminds him he's not alone after all, that there are others here with him, going through the same motions as he is to survive.

The door opens again, about twenty minutes later, shedding a dim light from the hall into the room. Though they shut off the power, they keep the halls dimly lit for the soldiers to monitor through the night. Gabrio turns and catches sight of Akeno sitting up in bed. Their eyes lock together, and Gabrio jumps.

"Hey, man, you tryin' to kill me?" he whispers. He pats at his heart to mimic how fast it's beating. "It's alright. I think I'll live."

There's a click as the door shuts. Akeno can hear Gabrio rustle his own sheets as he climbs into bed. Akeno lays down in his own bed, his head resting on the thin pillow. The paper thin sheets cover Akeno, the heavier blanket, though not much thicker than the sheet, rests on top of that one. It's chilly in the room, since they keep the air off, despite the cool nights.

"Is Church back yet?" Gabrio asks softly in the dark. Akeno knows Gabrio's usually the last to come into the room each night. Akeno can always hear him shuffling around in the dark, even after he closes his eyes and drifts off to sleep.

"Not yet," Akeno whispers, loud enough for Gabrio to hear him from the other side of the room. Gabrio's bed is across from Heinz. Church's bed is across from Akeno's. Heinz is the heaviest sleeper, though, so whispering was hardly necessary. Heinz would be out for the night.

Gabrio grunts to acknowledge he heard Akeno. They lay there in a solemn quiet as they hear others in the hall make their way back to their appropriate rooms. Curfew is set for lights out at ten, but the soldiers stay downstairs in the main lobby, their drinks much more potent than the stuff Heinz manages to find. They mainly monitor the buildings' doors to ensure nobody is coming or going in the dead of night. The doors are supposed to be locked after curfew anyway, but Akeno guesses that's not exactly the case, since Gabrio seems to come and go at all hours of the night. Last night he slipped in the room around two in the morning. He never had the guts to ask Gabrio where he went so late. It was rich that Gabrio would give Akeno the riot act when he couldn't even follow the rules himself.

"You don't think Church is stuck outside?" Akeno asks quietly. "Should we check?"

"Nah, Church is fine. He knows what he's doing."

"What *is* he doing?"

Gabrio chuckles to himself. "You'll have to ask him that. It's top secret."

"Top secret? Like what?"

"Like I said, you'll have to ask Church yourself."

They wait a while. The clock ticks past a half hour, and Akeno still remains wide awake. He can hear Gabrio from across the room and knows he's still awake too. Akeno thinks he shouldn't have gone to sleep so early. He knows better. He's a light sleeper. It's easy to go to sleep the first time, but it's harder to go *back* to sleep the second time.

The knob turns in the door, and the dim light fills the room. Akeno peeks one eye open and sees Church slipping in the room, a towel wrapped around his waist. The showers weren't supposed to be used past ten either, but as stated before, the soldiers stayed downstairs and wouldn't notice a man taking a last minute shower.

"Good evening, moonlighter," Gabrio jeers in a whisper. "Where you been? We've stayed up all night worried sick about you."

"Shut up," Church snaps. "Been a long night."

He closes the door and slides over to the bed, slowly, delicately.

"Everything alright over there, Church?" Gabrio asks, a note of concern in his voice.

"Fine," Church mumbles again. "Just tired."

There's a pause, then the striking of a match. Gabrio slips out of bed and goes to Church's bedside, the match's tiny fire wavering from the movement.

"Dios mío," Gabrio exhales. "What happened?"

Akeno slips out of bed and goes to Church's side.

"Who did this?" Gabrio demands. "Who did this to you?"

The match goes out, and Gabrio strikes another. Akeno peers into Church's face and sees he has a busted lip, a black eye, and several other cuts along his face and neck. His hands are also scratched up, like road rash. Church shallows back a cry, pouts his lip in an act of defiance.

Akeno's never seen Church cry.

"Where'd they get you?" Gabrio asks.

"Outside the church," he says, exhaling slowly. "They were waiting for us there. Me and my...my friend, we ran, or tried to, but they blocked us off. There were so many."

Akeno didn't know Church went to church with anyone.

"How many of them were there?"

Church shakes his head. "Five, maybe six. I don't really know. I didn't get a chance to...I just..." He lets out a stifled sob, and Gabrio lets the match go out.

There's a shuffle of bodies on the bed as Gabrio takes a seat next to Church.

"It's gonna be alright, Justin," Akeno hears Gabrio whisper, using Church's real name, which Akeno truthfully forgot. When Church hears his own name, he lets out a defeated sob.

"I don't know what I've done to deserve this," he chokes. "I didn't, we didn't, we were just...I'm just–"

"I know," Gabrio whispers. "It's gonna be okay. Everything's gonna be okay. Your friend, did he get back safe?"

"Yeah," Church says, spit clogging his mouth. "Yeah, he's back home. He's...He's..."

"He's gonna be okay too. You're both gonna be okay."

"I can't see him again. I can't, not after..."

"Shh, quiet now. We'll figure this out in the morning. Just sleep now. We'll deal with this in the morning."

Akeno imagines Gabrio reaching out in the dark to pull Church in close. There's a gentle rocking of the bed, and Akeno reaches out in the dark, his hand finding someone's leg. Then there's a hand on his hand, as they sit together, the three of them. Church quietly weeps, and Gabrio's rocking puts them all to sleep in the same bed.

A few more days pass, and Church's face looks much better than it did. There was no way to cover up what had happened to him the next morning, and Heinz was in disbelief.

"He don't mess with nobody," Heinz said to Akeno on their walk to the factory that next morning. "Who done it? Why would anyone want to hurt Church?"

By then, Church didn't want to talk about it anymore. He shut up, kept his head down, his eyes on the ground as they walked to work that morning. When they entered the factory in the early dawn hours, a few of the soldiers jeered at Church and made a passing comment about losing a fight.

Gabrio was outraged, his body tense from the anger building inside him. Every time he passed a guard, he'd throw a dark glare at them, as if assessing what they knew. Church had asked them to leave it alone. He just wanted to move on from it all. Akeno knew the feeling, but he didn't feel right just letting things happen as they did. He asked Church if he could accompany him to the worship center in the evenings, just to be safe, but Church said he no longer wanted to go anymore, that he needed a break. Prayer could be held anywhere, he said with a broken smile.

Now it's evening again, and the four of them sit on their respective beds. Church reads Scripture. Heinz picks at his bitten nails. Gabrio rests his back against his pillow, his eyes closed, his breathing even. Akeno wonders if he meditates or if he just sits there, brooding. The single window in their room is a slit just above eye level to show when it's light or dark outside. Right now it's dark. The clock reads nine-twenty-nine.

They've already showered for the night. Heinz doesn't have any money to gamble, and Gabrio says his guy is dry, so that leaves them all together in the same room, an oddity.

There's a swift knock on the door. Heinz looks to Gabrio, but Gabrio doesn't make to answer it. Heinz groans and gets out of bed, goes to open the door that doesn't lock. It's courtesy to wait for the door to be answered when people go knocking. They know it isn't the soldiers, because the soldiers don't bother to wait.

"What's up, Steve?" Heinz says in greeting.

The janitor, Akeno thinks. What's the janitor want? Probably looking for that hook Akeno nicked from the supply closet to make his staff. He was weird like that, always noting missing items weeks after it went missing.

"Say again," Heinz says, leaning closer to the doorway.

From this angle, Akeno can't see Steve, but it must be something important for the janitor to come knocking. He's not a social guy, usually just mumbles under his breath when people pass. He sees a lot, though, that guy. The janitor knows a lot more than anyone would think.

"No kidding. Okay, well, thanks for the intel. See you 'round." Heinz closes the door and faces the room, a grin spreading on his face. "Guess what Steve just heard."

"What? What's going on?" Akeno asks, trying to disguise his excitement as concern.

Not a lot happens in Amity, not around here anyway. Sometimes the men hold street fights behind the building. Anyone can place bets. The soldiers know about it, and they place their own bets, out of sight from the fight itself. Lots of currency can be won or lost in a single night, and that can set off other fights.

"Some soldiers got sent to the hospital," Heinz said with a grin. "Steve says they were jumped during the shift change. He was the one who had to call the officials. Says one guy had several broken bones, couldn't even stand. Isn't that something?"

Church's head pops up from his reading, his eyes on Heinz, then on Gabrio.

"What's going on?" Church asks.

"Sounds like some no good soldiers got what they deserved," Gabrio says with a devilish grin. "Can't say I feel sorry for 'em."

"Gabrio, what did you do?" Church demands, shutting the Bible. "I said to leave it alone, didn't I?"

"You did," Gabrio says with a nod. "I remember that. But I haven't done anything. I've been here all night. You can attest to that." He settles deeper into his pillow, his self-satisfied grin giving him away. "Sounds like karma came back around."

Heinz snickers and flops back on his bed.

Gabrio opens his eyes a slit, smiles, and closes them again. "Turns out the soldiers talk as much as the girls across the way, and the girls know all the sordid stories. They spread it like wildfire over there. Can't miss a thing when you talk to the ladies."

"How'd you find them?" Church asks.

"Like I said, it wasn't very hard when they run their mouths. They like to brag." Gabrio's face darkens. "They brag about the other shit they do too. It ain't right."

The minute the clock switches to ten, the lights power down with a flicker and then a sharp click. It's dark in the room, very dark. Still no full moon, not yet. Sometimes when it's full, Akeno sits under the window just to get a peek at it.

Akeno leans back on his flat pillow and exhales. He feels the air

249

seep in and out of his lungs, the heat from his body dissipating, and he leans back, his head softening into exhaustion. Gabrio's an interesting guy, he thinks.

From across the room, Akeno hears Church's whispered gratitude. "Thanks," he says.

"Anytime," Gabrio whispers back.

Akeno doesn't remember what he dreams about that night. He prefers it that way.

CHAPTER 18

Several weeks pass uneventfully. Church was able to walk a little more freely after the news came that those soldiers would be hospitalized for months and transferred upon their recovery. He didn't stay out late anymore. He came home just before lights out every night. Akeno continued to struggle with the dry end levers, his eyes glancing up at the office door every time it opened, just so he could look at the boss every day, just to remind himself there's a distinct line between him and Akeno. His team, they were all he had now. Over the past year, he had come to rely on these three men, all very different from the next.

Every night, Akeno and Church had developed a makeshift workout routine, one that Church made up himself. There were three sets of pushups, three sets of squats, core exercises from the edge of the bed. One person would grab the other's legs as they lay on their bed horizontally, pushing out fifty sit ups. Akeno used to think he knew what exhaustion felt like, but after those workouts, he never had any trouble sleeping through the night. Granted, he was sore every morning for the first week, but then he started to notice a chance in his body. His muscles got bigger. He was able to move around more flexibly, especially at work. It was fulfilling to know he could improve himself, despite not having any means to a gym.

Just thinking about what a gym looks like is foreign to Akeno now. It seems like forever since he's seen the inside of any other building besides their living quarters, the community center, and the factory. That's all he knows. That's all he'll ever know if he can keep his head down long enough to survive through this. He doesn't know what the future holds, but he doesn't care. He doesn't think about it, doesn't dwell on it like he used to. He used to wonder how he was going to survive the winter in his cramped dorm room with no heat, no food, no water, but those essentials are covered now. A small part of him is grateful for Amity, but then he remembers where he is and what he and his team endures day in and day out, and he's no longer grateful, only resentful. He tries to let those feelings of resentment go, but it's hard, especially when there doesn't feel like there's a way out. So he doesn't think, or tries not to. He simply exists.

He heads out the door and starts walking. He isn't sure where he's going today, but he thinks if he keeps walking, he'll find something to do or a place to sit and rest. His one day off feels gratifying. As he's walking, he passes by several other living communities exactly the same as his own: long brick buildings, windows lining the sides, knowing there's four people per room. He knows there's an all-female living community designed to suit the needs of the individual women who came seeking a better life in Amity, though they're a far walk from his own community. Akeno imagines how co-ed living communities could lead to trouble. From what Akeno has learned, the single, working men are on one side, and the women and working families are on the other.

Yes, families. Akeno didn't know some people brought their kids along. They attend Amity School every day, their minds soaking up the knowledge Amity provides in their classrooms. The women's line of duty typically includes works within the domestic. They sew clothes, crochet blankets, aid in childcare, teach in the schools, etc. If there's a father in the family, they live separately from the women and children. They can visit on their days off, if they want. That's what a line of men are doing now, heading to spend time with their wife and kids. There's no such thing as female contraception here in Amity. Condoms can be bought at the store, if anyone can afford them. He imagines all the bursting bellies of the pregnant women as they have one child after another, each of them growing up to be a naturalized Amity citizen.

Once Akeno passes the living communities, the factories start rising up all around him. At first, he's locked in a row upon row of factories and smokestacks. He thinks this must be the biggest factory complex he's seen and wonders what each one produces inside. If Akeno's job is to aid in creating the mechanical parts for a machine, he thinks this must be the factory that puts all the pieces together. What could be big enough for Amity to need? He thinks of cars, airplanes, and helicopters, but considering he hasn't seen any of those things come off the finished line, he isn't sure that's what they've got stored down here in this sect.

Akeno navigates his way through the beaten walking roads. He steers clear of the main road that the trolleys use. The trolleys usually cart Amity officials back and forth between the military institution and beyond the wall. Other times, soldiers are carted in to and from the wall. Akeno doesn't like seeing them, nor do they like seeing Akeno walk doggedly along the street, his dirty clothes yet another reminder of the squalor the workers live in. It's not their fault, Akeno thinks darkly. If they provided any regular form of laundry service, they wouldn't have to hand wash their clothes, which quite frankly, can smell worse after a cleanse.

Once he's out on the other side of it all, he doesn't glance over his shoulder as he leaves it all behind and faces the white stucco wall at the end of the road. It's the same wall, the mural of people holding hands. It's been added to, it seems. There are children depicted in the mural now, their tiny holds enfolded into one another's.

He thinks for a half second that he should break down this wall, let the people on the other side see exactly what goes on here, and suddenly the thought's gone. He knows the rules. Working hard and living day-to-day is all that Amity means. Everything else is moot.

He passes by the white wall and hears the faint sound of children playing on the other side, their voices ringing from a higher point. They must be inside a building, more likely their two-story home, the windows thrown open to allow the cool breeze to refresh the stale rooms after a long winter. There's a faint shriek and a chorus of giggles. Akeno misses the sound of children's laughter. It's pure and sweet, and from children, there's an essence of innocence Akeno hasn't experienced in a long time. He never thought that was a sound he would miss, considering he never hung out with too many children to begin with, but it reminds him of his childhood, when everything was much simpler. Everything he knows now is crude and repulsive humor, a brand of comedy Akeno never truly enjoyed until recently.

When he's past the wall, suddenly he hears a woman's scream from behind him. Akeno jumps from the sound and spins around. There's another scream, a blood curdling, frightened scream. It's not the children, Akeno thinks. It's coming from down the wall, down a short road where the trolleys sometimes park.

He immediately runs to the side of the wall and peeks around the corner. He looks down the path he had just walked and sees nobody. He hears faint talking, a man's voice, and thinks there must be someone approaching from the other side. He puts his ear to the wall and listens. He hears another scream, though this time muffled, closer this time to where Akeno is. Whoever was screaming must have been running. Akeno's hair stands up on the back of his neck, and the pit of his stomach drops from a keen sense of anxiety.

He doesn't see anybody within the vicinity, nor does he hear footsteps or the sound of an oncoming trolley. Don't the soldiers usually rotate around the compound? Where are they now? He's completely alone on this side of the wall, and all that can be heard is a faint scuffling and another muffled cry as Akeno panics. He doesn't think. He jumps for the top of the wall, missing the edge by mere inches and tries again and again. His fingers brush the top of the wall and slide off, no grip. Akeno thinks about crying out for help himself, not for him, but for whoever is on the other side. He knows that wouldn't work. If anything, he'd be arrested.

Farther along the wall, Akeno sees a parked trolley. It must be for the soldiers entering the living communities. There must be a shift change. He doesn't think. He breaks for the trolley. He climbs up the back and stands on the handrails to reach the roof of the vehicle. He pulls himself on top of the hard plastic and stands unevenly on the slick roof. His legs shake as he looks at the wall in front of him. It's only a few feet away. He's eye level with the wall now. If he jumps, he'll be able to grab hold of the edge and haul himself over.

He takes a hesitant step forward and leaps with both feet, grabs hold of the wall's edge, and feels his shoulders nearly give way as his body slams into the concrete. His arms shake as his weight drags him down. A couple weeks ago, Akeno would have flopped on the ground in a miserable state of helplessness, but since working out with Church every night, he manages to struggle and pull his way onto the wall, his feet kicking against the slick concrete. He straddles the wall with his legs, and suddenly he's reminded of jumping the fence at Oak Hills with Sam.

Ahead of him is a looming brick building with a sparse number of

255

windows on the backside. He looks to the corner where he heard the cry for help. He looks down and sees at least a twelve foot drop. There's nobody around that he can see, no wandering eyes from the street. He thinks if nobody can see him atop the wall, then certainly nobody can hear the screams.

He slides his other leg over the wall until both feet are dangling. He takes a deep breath and drops down. He lands unceremoniously hard on the grass, where his legs collapse beneath him. He hits the ground with both elbows and pushes himself upright, his body feeling like a pulsing bruise. With the adrenaline still coursing through his veins, he springs up and makes quick, quiet steps to the corner of the wall.

He peeks around the side of the building and sees a man straddling a woman, his back turned to Akeno. He's leaning close to the woman's face, despite her gasps for breath between sobs and pleading.

"You and your kind always think you can just come and go whenever you want," he says.

"Please, please, let me go," the girl whimpers.

"Not until you've learned something here."

Akeno doesn't have a weapon for attack. He's completely defenseless. The man could have a gun, could shoot Akeno and get away with it. He's supposed to be here. This is not his side of the wall. But he can't leave. Not now. It's too late. He tries not to think as he pushes himself forward into a forceful run. Midway through, he lets out a deafening cry he'd been holding in for months, a shout that alerts the two on the ground. The man turns with an expression of rage and fear. With what little speed Akeno was building up, Akeno tackles the man off the woman, the force of the blow slamming the man heavy on his back. They turn and twist, and the woman's feet kick against them both as she rips herself from beneath their weight. Akeno finds his elbow wrapping around the man's neck. It was something he'd seen in a movie once, saw someone use on the streets, and now he tries it on a predator.

The man wiggles and turns, his body weight crushing Akeno's small frame, though he refuses to let go of his grip around the man's throat. The woman kicks at the ground, pulling her legs out from under the man. She pushes herself up against the wall and watches as the man thrashes, his fingers clawing at Akeno's arm. The man's breathing starts to fade, and Akeno knows he's about to pass out. When the man finally stops moving, Akeno slowly releases him, the man's body slack, his pants still undone. Akeno knows from experience that the man will be stunned long enough for him to get away, but once air flow comes back, he'll wake up and realize what happened. He saw Akeno's face too. He'll know the woman got away. He'll come looking for them both.

At first the two of them stand there for a second, Akeno's back against the wall, his chest heaving from the struggle. He chokes something up, swallows it, and looks to the woman standing a few feet away. She looks unbelievably scared, confused, and then something like gratitude when she meets Akeno's eyes.

"Who are you? Where did you come from?" she asks, taking in his clothes. "How did you get here?"

"I heard you scream," he says. "I was walking on the other side of the wall, and I heard you scream."

"You heard me?"

Akeno nods.

They stand there a moment, and then the woman's face shifts into anger. "Low life piece of shit," she spits. She steps forward, her eyes on the man on the ground. She careens her foot back and kicks the man's limp body hard in the stomach, then the chest, then the groin. There's a heave as the man's body takes each blow, and Akeno doesn't stop her.

She raises her foot up and stomps on the man's nose. There's a swift crack, and they both know it's broken. She spits on the ground next to the man and turns to face Akeno.

"Come on," she says. "We have to get out of here."

Akeno doesn't make any movement as she glances around the corner.

"Come on," she repeats, when Akeno still doesn't move. She keeps staring at the man before her with equal parts fear and hate. "He'll wake up eventually. You're safer with us."

Akeno takes her appearance in. She's wearing a long, dark blue fabric skirt down to her knees, where it brushes faintly in the breeze. She's wearing a white blouse, now stained green and brown from the struggle. Her shirt contrasts with her skin, which is darker than Akeno's. Her long dark hair has fallen around her face in several strands, bringing out the sharp features of her cheekbones and nose, her face red.

"Who was he?" he asks suddenly.

"What?"

"The guy, who is he?"

"He's an Amity official, one of the soldiers' superiors." She shakes her head. "I can explain everything later. Right now, just follow me. Unless you want to hop the wall again and get arrested for something you didn't do." She points at the man on the ground. "He'll say you did this. He'll say you jumped the wall, raped me, and that you knocked him out when he tried to save me. It's the same bullshit narrative from time's beginning. You won't be the hero of this story."

Akeno nods, trying to process all that's happened. He should just go. He should leave right now and get back to the living quarters. His team would vouch for him being there. He would never be tied with what happened here. He tells himself these safeties, but he knows what she's saying is right. They'll come for him. They'll know exactly where to look for a dirtied, brown, Asian boy with long, dark hair. It won't be hard. He'll face a mock trial, and then he'll be found guilty, tried for sexual assault, and probably lynched by the end of the day.

The woman takes Akeno's hand, and the two of them run across the street. She dips behind the buildings and Akeno follows. They race across the grass, their footfalls muffled, until they reach a three-way intersection and a dead end. From around the corner, Akeno can see the soldiers on the street, their weapons passively at their sides. The woman's breathing is low and quiet, and Akeno is surprised at how collected she seems. She points across the street and motions to the left. That's the direction they're heading, but he doesn't think they can both cross without attracting attention from the soldiers. The intersection is completely empty, and they're the only two people outside, other than the soldiers. Akeno doesn't know the routines of this living community, but it's clear they're not supposed to be out on their own right now.

Akeno starts to panic again, because regardless of who the woman is, she undoubtedly lives here in the community. He, on the other hand, just snuck over the wall and looks the part of a runaway. He must look deranged.

Somewhere above them, a soothing chime rings out. It's loud and scratchy from the static in the speakers, but the woman looks relieved.

"Quiet Time is over," she explains quietly. She points to the streets, where people suddenly pour from the buildings. On the other side of the intersection is what appears to be a neighborhood with small homes in a variety of pastel colors: blue, pink, green, yellow, and white. They have a bit of yard space and a white fence to separate the homes. People spill out of the doors, children running from the short walks from their doorsteps to the street. As everyone begins to mill into the intersection, the soldiers start to break up and filter themselves throughout the crowd.

The woman makes a break for it, and with a sudden dash, Akeno follows after her again. When she reaches the street, she slows to a slow gait and motions for Akeno to walk ahead of her. He does so with some hesitation, his head glancing over his shoulder. She snaps at him from her waist, and he doesn't look back again until he hears a man's voice behind them.

"Hey, excuse me," the man's voice calls. "Excuse me!"

The woman turns and so does Akeno, with as much courage as he can muster. He can't see the woman, but from the sound of her voice, he can picture her elusive smile as the guard visibly softens when she faces him.

"Hi, officer, is everything all right?" she asks.

"Yes ma'am, everything is in order. I was concerned about the grass stains on your shirt."

"Oh, this?" She brushes a hand aside. "I apologize sincerely, sir. I must look foolish walking around like this. See, this is our new gardener, and he was just tending the landscape behind my mother's cafe. I was gardening alongside him, to show where the flowers should be planted, how to uproot the weeds, and how much water to give each plant, because as you know, certain flowers require certain amounts of water, and I must have mindlessly wiped my hands across my shirt."

"Yes ma'am," the guard says, his tone bored. "I was just checking in. Would you like an escort back to the house, ma'am? I would be more than obliged considering your company." The guard glares at Akeno standing behind her, but the woman gives a courteous laugh.

"I appreciate it, sir. Our house is just on the next corner. You've been so helpful already. Thank you so much for your kindness and ensuring our community's safety."

"Yes, ma'am, always obliged to do so. Have a good rest of your day."

The guard walks off, and the woman turns with a snarl and motions Akeno forward. She was telling the truth when she said her home was on the next corner. They took a left at the intersection, where they crossed the street amid hundreds of other people, and surely enough, the fourth house down was hers, and she let herself in, her hands gesturing for Akeno to enter.

Once inside the house, the woman locks the door behind her and leans heavily against the white-painted wood. Her face contorts into something like relief, then concern once again. She pushes herself from the door and goes into the kitchen, where she splashes her face with water and dries herself with a towel.

All the while, Akeno stands at the doorway of the house, which also serves as the main living space. There's a white couch, a glass coffee table in between the couch and the TV mounted on the wall. There's a vase of flowers in the center of the coffee table, but they look like they're well past their expiration. White curtains are tethered to either side of the wide windows beside the door, with blinds that shades the room in shadow. There's an intricate green and gray rug under the coffee table to make the space look more inviting. What a waste, he thinks. He compares the small room he shares with his team to this oversized, unused space.

His eyes frequently glance up the staircase and into the hall above. Then he goes to the window and peeks out the blinds. It's strange being inside a home again with actual windows. It's a foreign feeling now. He watches the people outside mill about the streets. It's only for walking, he thinks. No bikes. Everyone's dressed in the same colors as the houses, the women wearing the same style as the woman in the kitchen.

It's all too...familiar.

Akeno glances back over his shoulder at the landing upstairs. He feels like somebody's watching him. He turns to face the kitchen and realizes it's her who's watching him.

"Nobody's home," she says, her arms crossed. She doesn't say anything for a moment. She just stands there, taking him in with the towel still in her hand. He doesn't think she knows what to make of him, and he doesn't blame her.

"Who are you?" she finally asks.

Akeno wrings his hands together, his shoulders tense up from all the anxiety of the last twenty minutes.

"My name's Akeno," he says. "Yours?"

"I'll ask the questions," she says. "Here, sit down."

She pulls a chair from the table and sits down herself. She puts her hands to her face and massages the base of her hairline. Her eyes are closed at first, but then her dark eyes gaze into Akeno's own.

"I'm not going to hurt you," she says with a tone of frustration. "Please sit. You're making me nervous."

Akeno takes a seat at the opposite end of the table, closet to the door. He holds his bag in his lap, his eyes taking in the room. It's a medium-sized kitchen with a round dining table for four. The cabinets are painted white like the door, and the countertops are a black and gray granite. The pots and pans hanging above the sink are stainless silver and black. There's a few household appliances like a toaster but not a microwave. Akeno doesn't immediately see any kitchen knives or utensils that could be used as a weapon. He remembers the last time he was in a stranger's kitchen and feels his stomach turn at the thought.

He can't imagine what she must be going through, much less what she's thinking. After what just happened, he's not sure he'd trust anyone again.

"Your name's Akeno?" she asks. "What ethnicity?"

"I'm half Japanese," he says. "And you?"

She smiles. "I said I'd be asking the questions." She rolls her eyes. "I'm Cheyenne." She adds the last part as if to clarify. "It's weird seeing another person of color inside these walls. We don't have a lot of them. The only Asian people I've seen have been white, never brown toned."

"It's not weird outside these walls," he says. "I work with plenty of skin tones."

She almost laughs but stops herself. "I guess I should introduce myself. It's the least I can do since you risked your life helping me." She clears her throat, reaches her hand out across the table for a handshake. "My name's Neha, for the rain."

He gently shakes her hand, their hands retreating back to their laps, a sudden quiet falling over the room.

"And thank you. For helping me. Saving me actually," she says, a little timidly, as if she's embarrassed.

She has no reason to be embarrassed, Akeno thinks. It wasn't her fault.

"There's no guessing what would have happened had you not stepped in," she says. "He probably would have killed me honestly, or worse." She stares down at her hands, the towel working its way through her fingers.

"You don't have to thank me. It shouldn't have happened to begin with. Did you know who he was?"

"Yes," she says. She looks away, her eyes fresh with tears. "I shouldn't have trusted him, and it was my fault for being so naive. He said he was going to help me, help me find a way out of here. It was all just...It was all just so stupid. I shouldn't have gone."

263

"Please don't say that," Akeno says quickly.

Her eyes dart to Akeno over the table, water building at the corners. "Please don't blame yourself. It isn't your fault."

She looks at him with newfound gratitude and sniffs. "That's nice of you to say. I'm not sure others would agree, but thank you."

Akeno sits for a moment as the room settles. He leans forward, his hands on the table. "Okay, Neha, so you've brought me here. What happens now?"

She mulls the question over for a moment, thinking. Her brows furrow the same way Gabrio's does, he notices. Her nose scrunches up too, the lines in her forehead following. She lets the tension break and sighs. "I'm not sure. We have to wait till my friend gets home. She's better at planning these things than I am. We'll be safe here, at least for now."

Akeno isn't positive about what that means, but he could probably guess. If she knows he is, then he must know who she is and where she lives. People will want answers when the man wakes up. Someone's probably found him by now, lying motionless on the edge of the community, beaten and unconscious. It doesn't look good for the two of them. He'll say they jumped him, that he was attacked first, and then they ran.

"We have to get out of here," she says. "That's certain. We have to get past the walls." She massages her temples again. "Do you know another way out? How did you get in?"

"I climbed on top of a trolley and jumped over the wall."

She looks up, her face stricken and confused.

"It wasn't exactly well thought out," he says. "I panicked. There could be another trolley still there, but—"

"A chance like that won't happen twice," she says. She pauses for another moment and looks at Akeno. "I said you were the hired help. You must have gotten in here somehow. The hired help don't stay here; they have to leave eventually. Where are the entry points? Where do they bring you all in here without everyone noticing?"

She's thinking to herself now, though out loud. Akeno doesn't have the answers to these questions. He wishes he did. He wishes he knew anything at all about these white walls surrounding them, closing them in. Akeno wishes he was on the other side now.

He blanches and lets slip a concealed laugh. He stops short when her eyes focus on him again. "Is there something funny?" she asks.

He shakes his head. "No, I was just thinking is all."

"Of what?"

"I just..." He takes a moment to collect his thoughts. "I always wondered what was on the other side of these walls. Life on the other side... It's...Well it sucks. But this doesn't seem any different. It's all the same in the end." He crosses his arms, his eyes wandering over the kitchen. "It really is all the same."

She shakes her head. "I don't think you realize the gravity of our situation," she says, a hard edge to her voice. "Let's focus, okay? We have to find a way out of here. We *have* to leave. Nobody is going to help us. Nobody here gives a single fuck about everyone else."

"You're right," he says. "I'm sorry. What other ways are there to get hired help? You said gardeners, but who else comes in these walls?"

The woman thinks and slams her hand down. "The restaurants," she says. "Of course, it's the restaurants. The back of the house is always made up of the hired help."

Akeno's head reels from the old terminologies--people of color, back of house, restaurants. Akeno had nearly forgotten about restaurants and customer service. She had a point though. Old habits die hard. If

265

the cooks and dishwashers are coming over to work in these communities, there was to be a clear way in, even if discrete. They probably don't take the trolleys; they'll walk to work like everyone else. There must be an entrance that's hidden from view of the homes.

Neha starts rummaging through cabinets and drawers, evidently searching for something. She mumbles something about a map, and Akeno thinks that's a good start. They'll need a map to find their way around the community, or at least he will, in the event that they get separated, which seems likely as the minutes tick past.

There's a clicking sound as the door's lock turns in the door. Neha jumps up and pulls Akeno out of the chair and points to a doorway off from the kitchen. Akeno hurries inside just as the door opens, and he softly closes the door. He takes a small step back and hits something: a toilet. The bathroom, he thinks, and a small one at that. There's not even a window in here, just a toilet and a sink.

He hears Neha's voice on the other side of the door. "You're home early," Neha says. "Thank God. Thank God you're here."

"What? I'm not early," another woman's voice says, muffled through the bathroom door. "Quiet Time ended like ten minutes ago. Where have you been? You weren't here for breakfast. Did you get the stuff we needed?" She lowers her voice, says something inaudible from the bathroom, even as Akeno's ear is on the door, intently listening.

"About that," Neha says. "There's a lot I have to tell you."

"Can it wait? I have to eat and change before work. My shift starts at fifteen till."

"No," Neha says. "We have to leave. We have to leave like right now."

There's a quiet tension in the air. Akeno can hear the kitchen chairs scrape against the floor as one of them takes a seat at the table. "What's going on?"

266

Neha explains what happened, starting from the beginning. Akeno gleams details he didn't know. When Neha and the man planned to meet, he was supposed to have a trolley and several others waiting for them so as not to look suspicious on the drive through the communities. He was going to show her where the exits are, how to get over the massive walls that contain Amity. When she got there, though, he was completely alone, and the rest followed suit. She knew something was wrong, and then he attacked her.

"Fuck, Neha, are you okay?" the woman asks, pushing the chair aside. "I should've been there. I should've gone with you." She curses herself under her breath. "I'm such an idiot. I knew I should've gone with you this morning."

"Don't say that. I'm fine, really, I am. Everything's okay. Well…"

Neha had left out the part where Akeno had saved her.

"I have something else to tell me," she says, hesitantly. "Someone heard me scream and came to help me. He saved me, so I brought him back here…"

"Neha, tell me you didn't."

"Just wait," she says, gently rapping on the bathroom door.

Akeno twists the knob and gently pushes open the door, stepping out of the bathroom slowly and turning suddenly very pale. It's like he has tunnel vision, as if his ears have stopped working. He shakes his head clear.

"Sam?" he says.

"Akeno? What the hell?" Sam says, turning sheet white. "Oh my god, Akeno."

Sam's wearing the same long, blue skirt and blouse that Neha wears. It's almost unsettling to see Sam look so feminine. She doesn't look comfortable, and she's cut her hair since he's last seen her. She's chopped

267

what used to be kept in a ponytail. All her hair now rests above the base of her shoulders.

"Wait, you two know each other?" Neha asks, now visibly frustrated.

Sam runs to Akeno and presses him into a hug. "Where have you been?" Sam demands. "Oh my god, I can't believe you're here. You're *alive*."

"Yeah, I'm alive," he says, sheepishly.

"Where have you been?" she asks, taking him in. "You're labor, aren't you?"

"How do you two know each other?" Neha asks louder. "I need answers before we move on. What the hell's going on?"

"We left campus when Amity showed up," Sam explains. "We went back for, well, hell I don't know. We weren't doing too well on our own so…" Sam trails off and shrugs. "We separated, and it's a long story."

She shakes her head, her head tilting up to the ceiling to keep the tears at bay.

"I was keeping tabs on you, you know? I was following you around, making sure you were safe. After what happened, I felt…I just felt so awful. I didn't know how to process. I thought I did the right thing, telling you to go on your own, and…like now, clearly I've made a mistake." Tears swell up and spill over the edges of Sam's eyes. "I'm sorry, Akeno. I really am. I shouldn't have left you."

Akeno nods, swiping at the tears building in his own eyes as she plows on.

"I saw them take you. I saw them take you that night in the rain. I tried to save, tried to…I don't know." She took a deep breath, casting her eyes at Neha and back to Akeno. "I took a few shots at the soldiers, missed them all. I just felt like I needed to do something."

268

"So you were behind the gunshots," Akeno says, a short laugh breaking through the tension. "I didn't know where those came from. I thought I had been shot." He laughs again, then turns serious, his eyes on Sam. "Did they take you too? Did they hurt you?"

"No, I got away, barely," Sam says. "I came here on my own. After I saw them take you, I started asking around. Everyone already knew. People had been disappearing for days, even before Amity soldiers came to campus. Once I knew where they were taking you, and hoping that you were still alive, I came here for myself."

She sighs, takes a seat again at the table. Akeno joins her, Neha standing behind Sam, her eyes flicking back and forth between the two of them.

"They stuck me in this house, in these clothes. I tried finding you for weeks after I got here. Neha remembers." She smiles. "I was going crazy, asking people all these questions, getting weird looks, until eventually I was avoided on the streets." She bubbles out a soft laugh. "People here don't want you asking questions. I learned that pretty quickly." She holds up her hand, revealing a missing pinky on her left hand. "It's a sign," she explains. "It says I'm no good, that nobody should talk to me if they know what's good for them. I'm sort of a pariah out here."

There's a brief pause as Akeno digests the information. Sam closes her eyes, her hands shaking, and Neha takes one in her own, rubs it gently with her forefinger. Sam smiles, and Akeno can't help but blush.

"Small world," Neha says.

Sam smiles.

"I'm glad it was Akeno who found you. He's a good one." Sam reaches out to Akeno, who hesitates before stepping closer, slipping his hand in her own. She squeezes. "Let's stick together from here on," she says.

Akeno nods.

Neha steps back and goes to the window, peering out onto the streets.

"We've gotta move," she says, letting the curtains fall shut. "They'll be here any minute. We have to find a place to go."

Sam brushes the hair out of her eyes, tucking one piece behind her ear. She stands, an eagerness overcoming her. "We've still got the original plan," she says to Neha, who glances upstairs to the landing.

"Will it work?" she asks. "I thought we agreed we needed more time."

"That was before," Sam says. "It's not a perfect plan, but it's bound to work. It has to."

There's a rap on the door, and everyone freezes. Neha looks to the door, and Sam steps behind one of the kitchen chairs to put space between her and the entrance, her hand sliding down, pulling her skirt up. There's a holster strapped to her thigh, and out comes a knife. It's no ordinary kitchen knife either. Akeno wonders where she could get something like that. It's bound to be a banned item in Amity. No weapons allowed.

"Hey, it's me! I live just next door," an older woman's voice sounds from the other side of the door. "I left my key inside my house. Could you let me in until housing services arrive?"

Neha shakes her head at Sam and puts a finger to her lips.

The woman pounds against the door again. "Hello, girls, is anyone home?" the woman says more fervently. "It'll only be a few minutes. It's hot outside, and I just need to take a seat where it's cool."

Akeno glances at Sam, but she doesn't move any closer. Neha tiptoes around the table and gestures for both of them to follow her up the stairs. They do, as quietly as they can, as the woman still pounds against the door. At the top of the landing, Neha and Sam break for their respective rooms, leaving Akeno in the hall. When the pounding stops, Akeno pauses and turns back. It's unusually silent, and Akeno can hear the woman mumbling on the other side of the door. Through the window, Akeno can just make out the visible outline of several shadows by the door.

"We gotta go," Akeno says, scrambling into one of the doorways, Sam's room, a plain and functionless box with nothing for decoration or design. "That woman, she's not alone. They're gonna—"

Suddenly there's an explosion of wood splintering from the frame.

"Check everywhere!" a man's voice calls. "I want all of the contraband found and the criminals apprehended."

Akeno turns back to face the hall and sees the same man that had attacked Neha. His face is badly beaten, where Neha broke her nose, his lips busted, though his midsection seems fine.

"There, upstairs!" he calls, pointing to the landing. Neha runs in from the other side of the hall and slams Sam's bedroom door behind her. She quickly locks it and shoves a tall bureau in front of it.

"That's not going to hold," Sam says, glancing over her shoulder.

"It will for a moment."

Sam has a backpack hanging over her shoulders and stuffs something metallic inside her waistband. Her blouse has come untucked, and it looks like she's wearing pants underneath the skirt. She reaches inside a drawer and tosses Neha something Akeno can't quite make out.

"We're going to have to go in pairs," Neha says to Akeno. "How much do you weigh?"

"I don't know, maybe one-forty-five. Why?"

She doesn't answer him, but she weighs the odds, shrugs, and nods.

Akeno turns back to the window and sees Sam's body hanging halfway outside as she slings a metal piece over a thick coiled wire suspended above her windowsill. She grabs onto the rope knotted on either side of the metal piece and pushes from the ledge. She leaps into the air and glides down the wire. Akeno can see sparks flying above her hands as she ziplines across a large wooden fence and into the park behind their house. There's a playground in the center of the park, and Sam lands on the highest of the park's platforms, where a plastic slide juts out from the landing. There are a few kids on the playground, and they scatter back to their parents as frightened screams reach Akeno's ears.

Akeno hears the sound of the wood door splintering behind them and the bureau sliding, its feet scraping against the floor. Neha pushes past Akeno and slings her own backpack across her stomach. She slings her own metal piece across it, her hands gripping onto the rope ends.

"You'll have to hold on to me," Neha says, her hand outstretched. "Come on!" she shouts, noting his hesitation, reading the doubt on his face.

The door behind him breaks completely. He glances behind him to see someone's hand forcing its way through the middle of the door. Neha pulls both of his hands around her neck and tells him to hold on. His ears fill with compressed air as Neha jumps, and vertigo takes over. Suddenly he's screaming, Neha's grip slipping from their combined weight.

Their weight carries them halfway, but then they start to slow when they pass the fence. They're still twenty feet up when Neha starts swinging her legs to edge them closer to the ground. They manage to slide their way as far as they can go before they come to a dead stop, and Neha cries out as both her and Akeno's dead weight forces them to fall. They both land on the park grass, and Akeno tumbles to the ground, his knees bending. He rolls to stop, his legs on fire from the effort. Neha lands in a crouch and shakes out her hands as she stands, the palms red from rope burn. She reaches a hand down for Akeno and lifts him up, her eyes looking past his shoulder and back to the house they just fled.

Akeno turns and makes eye contact with the same man he had tackled, his eyes, even from this distance, filled with fury and rage. He shouts something from the window, pointing back to his men, who file out of the room. For the first time in a long time, Akeno feels like they've won something, and he laughs, turning to Neha in triumph.

"This isn't over yet," Neha says. "We need to hide. Where do we go from here?" She turns and faces Sam, who's already climbed down from the playground.

"The cafe," Sam says, striding down the sidewalk, Akeno and Neha keeping stride. "Kay will hide us."

"You mean your boss?" Neha asks, incredulously. "Will she hide us?"

"She's already made it clear that she should come to her if there's trouble. I knew there'd be trouble, so I added her as the Plan B, in case our first plan didn't work out, which it didn't."

"Won't they go looking there first?" Neha asks.

"Who goes to their job when they're on the run? They'll check the exits before they think to check the cafe."

Neha nods as they begin to blend with the crowd on the streets. The soldiers haven't notified the public of a disturbance, at least not yet. The alarm is sure to come. Neha brushes her hair behind her ears and pulls her skirt down. Sam tucks her shirt back in, her eyes darting to both sides of the streets. She glances behind her shoulder and motions for Akeno to walk ahead of them. He quickly trots in front of them, and Sam slaps something over his head. It feels like a bonnet, with the way the flaps come over the sides of his face, but then he realizes it's an outdoor hat. The string flops lazily on the sides as he pulls the brim lower over his eyes.

"You're the gardener, remember?" Neha whispers. "Just keep your head down and your eyes forward."

"There'll be a cafe on the right," Sam whispers. "It's between a clothing store and a pet shop. Don't go in the front door. Meet us round back."

Akeno's nerves jump and tingle, and he feels like he might be sick. Maybe it's the adrenaline, or maybe it's his nerves. Then Akeno thinks, maybe it's the thrill.

As they make their way through the street, Akeno sees lines on the road intended for the biking paths. Families and young adults ride on pink, blue, and yellow bikes with baskets on the front, a bell at the top. Those on bikes honk playfully at some of the people they pass by. The people on the street give a friendly wave, especially from the young women to the young men. Akeno catches Neha doing the same, her bright white teeth glinting in the sunlight. He can tell Sam's making an effort not to roll her eyes, though she keeps an even stride with Neha's gait.

"You don't have to act the part," Sam grits through her teeth.

"If we don't wave, we'll look more suspicious than we already do," Neha says through her forced smile.

The shops all around them are painted bright pastel colors, just like the homes, to mask the cheap plaster underneath. Every shop looks almost identical, and the only things telling them apart are the pictures plastered all over the storefront. They pass boutique after boutique, each featuring some new accessory for their outfits or new item for their homes.

Though every woman wears the same skirt and blouse, he can tell now that some women wear necklaces, bracelets, rings, and earrings, and some of them wear bright colored bandanas, headbands, and bows to match. The men wear white or blue buttoned shirts and khaki shorts, with colorful bow ties or hats to match their clothes. Everyone looks comfortable and relaxed as they pass by the shops, their attention focused less on the objects and more on the people around them. Everyone knows everybody else. That must be how social class is determined in the walls, Akeno thinks. How many people do you know? How many friends do you have?

Several children filter in and around the pet shop up ahead. This pet shop holds cats, dogs, small birds, rabbits, hamsters, etc. There's definitely not anything like a pet shop in his living community, he thinks. It would be good if his team was able to keep a dog, but he knows this is impossible from the long shifts they work.

Was impossible, he realizes then. He'll never be able to go back to his team now. He can't, not anymore. It'll be worse for them if they find him there. He'll never get a chance to say goodbye. The thought crushes him.

Sam taps Akeno on his shoulder as she passes by him. He notices the cafe just past the pet shop and the small alleyway between the pet shop and the cafe. He dips around the corner. He walks like he has a purpose to be back there. There's another man loading animal feed through the side door of the pet shop, paying Akeno no attention at all. He reaches the end of the building and waits by the back door of the cafe. There's a small plaza between the cafe, the pet shop, a clothing boutique, and a bakery.

As he leans against the wall of the building, he can hear the faint roar of the people on the street--their voices chattering amongst each other, their bubbly laughter, their cries of joy when one of the small dogs barks playfully at the children. This living community teems with life and comfort, and Akeno accosts himself for ever thinking he would be able to live here. He wonders where the Howards are within these walls, if they're even here. He pictures Kayla shopping, Kevin watching an old show on the TV in the main room, Joanna cooking dinner in the kitchen. He doesn't want to think of their father. He doubts they're any happier, but he hopes they've found some peace here.

The back door to the cafe opens and Sam motions Akeno inside. He does so and enters the back of the cafe where all the supplies are stored. It's not a very large room, but it's large enough for three people to stand in together.

"K's still out front," Sam explains. "She's handling some business right now." She catches the look on his face and frowns. "She's someone we can trust. You just have to trust me on that one."

"I don't know, Sam. If the soldiers come knocking on her door, do you think she'll lie for us? She could be arrested if they know she's lying. She'll lose everything."

"Trust me," Sam says.

They wait several minutes together in the back. Neha enters the back, pushing through the door separating the rooms. She's wearing a black apron. When the door swings shut behind her, she's noticeably more tense than Sam, who sits on a crate of oranges and pulls out a half-smoked doobie. She lights it and takes a deep inhale, the smoke billowing up in translucent waves to the ceiling.

"Really, you're doing that now?" Neha says.

Sam shrugs. She takes another drag. "It calms my nerves, helps me think."

Neha shakes her head and watches the entrance of the stock room. She keeps eyeing the back door too. She must feel trapped, Akeno thinks. Sam's mild manner doesn't seem to be helping. In fact, it seems to make Neha feel more anxious.

The door to the supply room opens and a girl walks in. Her platinum blonde hair is tied high in a ponytail with a blue ribbon. She wears the same outfit as Sam and Neha, blue skirt and white shirt with the black apron to signal she's working. She's also accessorized her outfit with more personalizations. She wears a blue bandana around her ankle.

"What's going on?" she asks Sam. "It's rush hour."

"Good, that'll give us plenty of cover."

"What are you on about?"

"Oh, don't worry, he's with us," Sam says, gesturing over her shoulder at Akeno.

The girl had walked in and barely looked at Akeno, but now that she does, her eyes wide with shock. "Oh my god, Akeno?" she asks. "You're...Wait. What're you doing here?"

"Do you know everyone?" Neha asks pointedly at Akeno.

"Kayla?" he says, standing up. "You've colored your hair."

She waves the detail away. "Hold on." She disappears back out into the cafe and returns minutes later. "I can't believe you're here," she says, flopping down on one of the crates. "Where did you go? You disappeared."

"Your father chased me down," Akeno says with a soft smile.

She shakes her head. "I'm so sorry, Akeno. He's...Well, frankly, he's a piece of shit."

Akeno nods.

"I always wondered what had happened that night. You never came back to the tent, and when it started raining, you still didn't show."

"I was waiting on your mom. She was supposed to get me out. You know your dad sent a pack of trained dogs and a group of men to take me captive?"

Kayla sits a moment, mulling the thought over, her head bobbing up and down.

"I knew something had happened. I just knew it." She exhales, tightening her bow at the back of her head, a mindless habit. "Dad got pissed off that night, said you had run away. Mom said she'd go looking, but then Dad started yelling. And...Well, things got worse. He hit her, and then he pulled a gun, said that we needed to stay in the tent. So we did. When he came back, he was soaking wet and covered in mud. We didn't ask what happened, and Mom never told us."

Akeno nods. He had replayed that night over and over in his mind when he laid down for sleep. He never knew what had kept Joanna from meeting him there, but he figured it was her husband that kept her. It wasn't her fault. At least she tried to help Akeno, even if it all ended the same. He's about to ask where the rest of the family is when a woman steps through the door, her back to them.

"Let me see if I can find any extras in the back," she calls and turns, her dark brown hair swinging in a short ponytail. She turns and faces them, a smile playing at the edges of her lips. She steps in through the door as it swings close behind her.

Akeno recognizes Joanna then, though not immediately. Like Kayla, she had dyed her hair, though several shades darker. What was once cut to her shoulder now extends past her collarbones. Just like her daughter, she had altered her appearance. Akeno thinks she's prettier with dark hair and looks much cleaner than he had last seen her. Unlike the three other women, Joanna wears a navy blouse with her blue skirt. She smoothes down her apron, and Akeno recognizes what's different about her: She's much more confident, more in control.

"I'm glad you've come, Akeno," she says gently. "It's good to see you."

"It's, uh, good to see you too. And Kayla. And Sam." He laughs awkwardly, now extremely confused. How long had they known each other? Was he the boss that Sam had mentioned? Were they working together? "I didn't know you guys knew each other."

Joanna smiles. "I understand how confused you must be, but right now, we don't have time to talk. The soldiers are outside asking questions on the streets. We need to get you somewhere safer than here." She turns to Sam. "Where are you headed?"

"Our plan's been pushed up, and none of it's going the way we wanted. It's all falling apart." Sam's eyes look pleading, pained even. Joanna gives her a sympathetic look and glances at Kayla.

"They'll be at every exit," Joanna says. She thinks for a moment. "You'll need to head back to my place," she says. "At least for the time being. Once they've realized you're not going for the exits, they'll come asking questions here. They'll want to know everyone you've been in contact with. Have you tied up loose ends?"

Sam and Neha both nod.

"Good. We don't want anyone else getting more involved than they need to." She looks at Kayla. "Take them to the house and then come straight back here. I'll come by in the evening to collect you three, but until then, don't leave the house and don't answer the door, not for anyone. As far as anyone knows, nobody's home. Our schedules say that everyone's at work."

"What about the rest of your family?" Akeno asks in a small voice.

"They...won't be an issue," Joanna says, eyeing Kayla. "Someone can fill you in later. I'll see you all tonight."

She leaves the stock room and returns to the bustling sounds of the cafe. Kayla removes the apron she's wearing and tosses it to the side.

"We've got to hurry," Kayla says. "Our house isn't far from here." She goes to one of the supply room's corners and reaches into a small box. She pulls out a couple of men's and women's accessories. "Here, put these on," she says.

"Why so many bows and ribbons?" Sam asks with a hint of disgust.

"It's just for protection," Kayla says.

Sam ties a bandana around her neck, and Kayla fixes the knot to look more appealing. "If it looks messy, they're going to notice," she says.

"Always the perfectionist," Sam says with the roll of her eyes, fixing a sun hat on her head, the bow at the top wobbling from the movement.

Neha brushes out her long hair and puts it back up in a ponytail. She ties a pink ribbon at the top and ties another ribbon around her neck.

"They're not very good disguises," Sam says. "Our faces are still showing."

"The idea is to blend in with the rest," Kayla replies in a monotone.

Akeno still wears the gardener's hat.

Kayla leads them out the back door and into the alley. They cross to the other side of the street and enter into a packed street. Akeno notes there are more restaurants and bistros on this side. It must be the lunch hour. They melt into the crowd with ease and follow a short distance behind Kayla, who leads the pack. Akeno walks on his own, Neha and Sam walking together behind him.

Up ahead, several soldiers push through the streets, their eyes up, scanning the faces of people as they part the crowd. Some of the citizens throw nasty looks at the soldiers as they hurry past. So the soldiers aren't a fan favorite here either, Akeno thinks. Nobody likes to be told what to do, where to go, how to look. Yet it feels natural here. The soldiers are just a stark reminder that what they do isn't their choice, that enforcement of the rules stands outside their doors.

Akeno picks up his pace to catch up with Kayla. Then he hears men's voices calling out from his left. He turns and sees they've got their eyes on him, their bodies forcibly waking their way to him. He tries to turn away, but they're calling to him, shouting, drawing attention in his direction. Behind him, Sam and Neha are panicking. This time he doesn't hesitate. He panics, and then he runs.

As he pushes his way through the crowd, the people he passes grunt in disbelief, many of them outraged. They call out to him, tell him to slow down, and point him out to the soldiers hurrying after him. He should have probably made a better exit, because now the whole street knows who he is, but if it means he can lead the soldiers away from Neha, Sam, and Kayla, then at least they're safe, even if he gets taken. He passes Kayla with a soft push and glances back with an expressive eye. He's telling her to run, to forget about him, to make it back to the house with the others.

He faces front again and dips down an alleyway, the sound of pounding feet just behind him. He breaks into a dead sprint, his arms pumping as fast as his legs will move. The hat falls off his head and into the gutter, exposing his black hair trailing behind him. He rounds a corner and slows his pace as he steps back into the crowd. He walks briskly through the streets and immediately ties his hair back into a bun, his eyes searching for a way to disguise himself any better. He pulls a soft yellow bandana from a mannequin and ties it around his head.

He crosses the street again, speeds down the alley, and turns a different corner. He does this several times, each time reversing his direction and taking different streets. He's hoping he can find the wall soon, and with any luck, maybe he can climb back over it. Just as he's walking down another street, this time past several craft shops, he feels someone grip his arm. It's Sam, and Akeno quickly falls into line with her pace. He keeps his head down, his face forward. He thinks if he doesn't look guilty, he'll be glanced over.

"You're stupid to have run off like that," she grits under her breath. "You could have been killed." She throws him a white button up, and he quickly slips it on. "What makes you think you should do something so stupid, dangerous actually?"

When he's buttoned up the shirt and tucked it into his dirtied pants, she eyes the bandana and smiles, despite herself.

"It was bold, but it was good work. You helped Neha and Kayla get back to the house without anyone noticing. They're waiting for us there now." She gives him a light punch. "I didn't realize you could run like that. I never thought you were the, uh, athletic type," she says.

He nods, grinning. "I had it all planned out," he says with mock confidence, his lungs still gasping for air, his legs shaking.

Sam laughs. "It's good to have you back." Then she grows serious. "You've changed."

Akeno nods. "For the better."

CHAPTER 19

When they reach the house, which looks identical to the ones around it, he notices this one is much larger than the one Sam and Neha lived in. It's a two-story home too, but it's much wider and appears more updated, as if recently installed. Akeno wonders how much of this was rebuilt after the initial blackout, or if this neighborhood once belonged to a community before the government intervened.

Akeno quickly follows Sam up the road, coming up on the house from the front, though Sam already made it clear they needed to enter the back entrance. As they walk past the house, Akeno notes the winding sidewalk to the front door, a superfluous detail that was supposed to enchant the guest with the cute shrubs lining the small garden that made up the front yard. Akeno notices the flowers have bloomed under the front windows, which reflect a vibrant myriad of colors off the glass windows of the house. To the right, there's a small garage off to the side that's only wide enough to hold the bikes. As they reach the back of the house, Sam takes a sharp left turn and unlatches the back yard's painted gate.

Sam knocks on the door, drumming out a quick beat--three fast knocks, a pause, one knock, a pause, and then two slow knocks. The door immediately opens, and Neha's hands pull Sam into an embrace. The two hold each other for a moment as Akeno slips in the door and locks it behind him. He finds himself in a narrow hallway leading to the kitchen.

"Stupid, you're so stupid," Neha says and kisses Sam fast on her lips. "Let me go next time. I'm faster than you."

"But not as nimble as I am," Sam says with a smile and returns the affection. "I'm so thirsty," she says, falling back into her usual flippant tone. "Kayla, can I have a glass?" she calls to the kitchen.

"Kayla had to go back to the cafe," Neha says. "If she's not there, they'll suspect something's wrong, that she's involved."

"Right," Sam says and takes a seat at the kitchen table.

Neha and Akeno follow behind her. Neha stands in the kitchen, as Akeno steps into the living room, his eyes scouring the place of its size and grace. There are small antiques resting on the mantelpiece. There's no pictures of the family, since it's doubtful that they had any pictures with them when they arrived at Amity's gates over a year ago. There's a few pieces of artwork hanging on the walls. They're rather plain and noncontroversial, a feature of Amity in all its uniformity.

"So we just wait here until Joanna comes and gets us?" Sam asks.

"I guess that's the plan," Neha says, taking a glass out of the cabinet. She fills it with water and hands it to Sam.

"Well, it's not a very reliable one," Sam says. "What if they do take them in for questioning? Are we just supposed to wait here until more soldiers come busting down the door?"

"No, we won't wait that long. She said she'd be here before the cafe closes."

Akeno waits near the front door and takes a seat on the same white couch Neha and Sam have at their house. The glass coffee table in front of him is scattered with weekly magazine editions, *Amity Fair*. Akeno rolls his eyes. All they can do now is wait.

Sam and Neha find a seat in the living room. There's a brief silence as the three of them rest their feet in the living room. Sam takes the lone chair on one side of the couch. Neha takes the other. The two share a few awkward glances until Akeno finds himself staring at the wall. He blinks and sees Sam's watching him.

"Can I help you with something?" he asks her, in what he hopes comes off as playful.

She shrugs. "I've just got so many questions."

"Me too."

"Shoot then."

Akeno pauses. He does have several questions. He can't picture what his life could have been like if he had stayed in this house for the past year and a half. In a house like this, he wouldn't have any problems. He wouldn't have to work long hours in an un-air conditioned factory in the hot summers, and even if he did, coming back to a place like this would have made it worth the labor. He could have his own room, his own space, maybe even his own bathroom. He could lock the doors. He could have a sense of privacy again.

"Do you know what it's like on the other side of these walls?" Akeno asks. "The inner walls, not the outer ones."

"I know. At least I've heard stories," Sam answers. "It's not fair, the way people on the other side are treated." She pauses. "I've never actually been on the other side. We aren't allowed to leave, the same way you aren't allowed to see what's over here."

"We know what's over here," Akeno says. "We can see the rooftops from our cells." He chuckles. "That's basically what they are: prison cells. There's four men to a room. No locks, no space. The stories, whatever you've heard, they're probably true."

Neha brings her knees close to her chest, her chin resting on top. Her eyes flick back and forth between Akeno and Sam, and Akeno can guess what she's thinking. It's not any easier for women like her on this side of the wall. They might have the nice houses and the pretty clothes, but after what happened today, what Akeno had seen, he couldn't convince himself that was what they wanted.

They're quiet for another moment.

"How did you find Joanna?" Akeno asks. "It can't be coincidence."

"It is, and it isn't," Sam says, leaning back in her chair. "After they cut off my pinky," she says, showing them the stub again. "Kay heard about it. Everybody knew about it by then." She takes a deep breath. "Something you have to know is that this place might look big at first, but it's a small community. There's only a few thousand people living here, so information spreads fast." She pauses, takes a deep breath, and takes a sip of water.

"I guess it started when Joanna offered me a job," she continues. "My last boss was an idiot. He fired me before I could quit, said he couldn't have a delinquent in his shop." She rolls her eyes. " So, Joanna hired me at the cafe. She was kind, and she actually listened to me when I spoke." She smiles. "She was the first person I told about me and Neha."

Akeno glances at Neha, who blushes a pale pink.

"For people like us, we aren't allowed to be together. We hold hands in public, and nobody bats an eye, but if someone sees us kiss, well, the officers are at our doors and ready to commit us." She grimaces. "I don't say that lightly. I knew someone who was taken away. He's...Actually, I don't know where he is now. They only let you out after you've signed a contract and a liability waiver, or so I've heard. I don't know if they ever come back. I don't know where they end up going."

She pauses, and Neha continues.

"Sam introduced me to Joanna. I've lived here a few months longer than Sam, and before we met, I was virtually alone. It's hard to...

286

get along without your friends." She swallows back tears and continues, "She asked questions about my heritage, about the Cheyenne people and our customs." She smiles too. "When Joanna asked if we'd be interested in doing some charity work, we both agreed. We just didn't know how far she'd take us."

"When she said charity work, we were thinking like baked goods and clothing drives," Sam continues. "All the charities and fundraisers are usually held for the labor force, you know, as a way of 'thanks.' That's what the brochures say anyway. It's really just to make white women feel good about themselves since they don't have to work in the factories or the fields."

Neha nods.

"And that's what we did, at least that's what we thought we were doing. We packaged the clothes and meals, but what we didn't know was that there were some underlying supplies at the bottom of the boxes: things like books, pamphlets, essays, sometimes weapons. They were essentials to something bigger than us." She pauses, takes another sip of water. "I didn't mean to find anything when I was packing boxes one night. I confronted Joanna about what I found, and the rest is history." She grins. "That's how I joined the movement."

"What boxes?" Akeno asks.

"Just ordinary boxes. We have certain people drop them off at specific locations."

"Like the living quarters on the other side?" he asks, impatiently.

"Yeah, like the living quarters. Like I said, they're just filled with a bunch of junk except for what's in the bottom."

"Nobody ever checks those boxes," Akeno says dully, remembering the boxes the women would drop off in the lobby. "I was the only one who ever looked through them. I never found much of anything."

"That you know of," Sam says. "There were specific items in these boxes. The drops are specifically coordinated because of a contact we have in that building. You wouldn't know what to look for unless you already knew."

"Someone in my building must have been in league with you guys," Akeno says.

Sam nods. "It wouldn't be unlikely. We have hundreds of contacts."

"Do you know any names?"

Sam shakes her head. "I can't remember them all, and besides, they all go by an alias."

"Nicknames," Akeno says, taking a moment to process. He runs his hands through his hair. There's an underground movement, he thinks. There are people trying to bust out of here. Neha is one of them. Sam is one of them. Who else does he know that could have been involved? Why didn't he ever notice? Why had no one told him before? How did he miss the clues in the box?

"What's the overall goal here? I mean, what's the point of all these missions?"

"Isn't it obvious? To bring the system down, to take back the power," Sam says. "Maybe then we can figure out what the hell is going on."

Akeno pauses.

"Her husband, Michael Howard, where is he now? Where's Kevin?" Akeno asks.

Sam and Neha share a look. "We don't actually know where her husband is," Sam says. "She's mentioned him a few times, but we've never met him. They don't live together, that much I do know. She says they were divorced before they came to Amity, and I guess the same principle applied when they got here."

"And Kevin? Kayla's working at the cafe. Where's he?"

"From what she says, as soon as he got here, he signed up for the military," Sam says. "There's a four-year contract. He won't be out for another few years."

"Do they get to see him?"

"Never. Military personnel aren't allowed familial contact." Sam shakes her head. "It's honestly more like a gang. The soldiers here, they don't keep people safe. They incite fear. I mean, they walk around with guns strapped to their chests. How could anyone feel safe like that?"

"The soldiers at our place don't give a shit," Akeno says. "I mean they're locked and loaded, sure, but they don't enforce any of the rules. Except..."

Akeno trails off, remembering what happened to Church.

"You're right, though. It isn't safe," he says.

"That's why there needs to be change," Sam says. "That's what the movement's for." Sam shrugs. "There's so much happening all the time."

"Tell me more," Akeno says. "I can't believe I've missed out. What else about the missions you run?"

"I don't run them myself. I assist, as most everyone does. There's never really one leader. There's a select few who always head the missions, but there's never just one face to the operation. It takes a whole team usually."

"What else do missions include, besides charity?"

"Missions vary in size," Sam says, leaning back, settling into the couch. "Some take as little as a few weeks to enact. Others take months, sometimes years. Sometimes we destroy property, vandalize buildings, steal some supplies, and the like. There are a few rescue missions where we relocate people from bad situations and get them out of Amity. I don't know where they go after that, but at least they're out." She sighs.

"That was our plan," she continues. "I just...I had the wrong con-

289

tacts, trusted the wrong people. I take responsibility for that." Neha opens her mouth to protest, but Sam holds up a hand. "The higher standing officers, they know what's going on. They know there's an underground movement working against them. It's why the soldiers are armed and why everyone's on edge."

As the sun starts to sink below the sky, the three of them take the time in between to rest. Akeno has no further questions. He needs time to think.

Sam leans her cheek against her hand, and then her eyes close, her mouth partially open. Neha lays awake, her eyes focused on something on the floor, her body curled inside the chair, her feet dangling off the ends. Eventually her eyes close too, and Akeno's does the same.

It's nearly sunset when there's a sudden knock on the door. It's the same knock Sam had used. Akeno jumps from his spot at the sound but relaxes when he sees Sam open the door and Joanna steps through the door.

"Sorry, I'm late," Joanna says, bustling inside. "Some soldiers came through the cafe. One of them stopped to interview us. Kayla's there now. She's cleaning up before the truck comes in with more supplies. I imagine they'll be checking the trucks now before they leave the community." She says all this in a rush and unbuttons the top three buttons on her neck-high blouse. Her cleavage peeps through the shirt, and Akeno politely averts his gaze away as she takes off her shoes and ties her hair back behind her shoulders.

"What happened? Did they suspect anything?" Neha asks.

"No, I don't think so. Kayla performed beautifully, cried even. I don't know where she learned that, but…"

Neha's awake too, looking amused, but Sam brushes the theatrics aside. "What did you say to the soldiers? What did they ask?"

"Just asked if you were scheduled to work today, which they knew you were. We said that you hadn't shown up, that it was unlike you to miss a day of work." She sits down at one of the dining table chairs and faces the living room. "We said we were worried. They asked if we knew where you might be if you were to have a day off. We said probably the park or the theater, both of which are pretty common places to be on anyone's day off, but we figured we should act like we don't know you very much."

"Do you think they're still watching the cafe?" Sam asks.

Joanna shakes her head. "They might have one guard posted on our corner, but they didn't stay long. If they knew anything else, they would've asked to check the back room more thoroughly. They walked in, glanced around, and left."

Sam's eyes glance at the window as she tries to mask the evident doubt on her face. She goes to the living room and sits by Akeno at the door. She looks agitated as she bites at her nails and continues to keep her eyes on the window.

"What's the plan then?" Neha asks. "If you say the trucks are going to be watched and inspected, do you think it's still safe to use that route?"

"I doubt any escape plan is safe, but at this point, we have to try something. You can't stay here. They'll make a visit tonight or maybe tomorrow morning. I'd say we have until then to get you out of the house."

"What do you think we should do?" Neha asks Sam quietly.

"I think we should be asking Akeno that," she replies, eyeing Akeno. "You got in, didn't you? You can get out."

"It was an accident. I wasn't really—" Akeno starts.

Sam cuts in. "It doesn't matter what your intentions were. It matters how you did it. How'd you do it?"

"I climbed, but that way of escape relies on the chance that nobody's watching."

"They're always watching the walls. It's a shock they didn't see you then," Joanna says with uncertainty. "Where were you?"

"Down by the main road," Neha answers. "We—Wait," Neha says, interrupting herself. Suddenly her eyes glow with inspiration. "It isn't the where; it's the when. He came at the start of Quiet Time. Everyone's inside, so there doesn't need to be as many soldiers on patrol. The ones we came up on were all collected in the middle of an intersection. I think they were—"

"Switching shifts," Joanna finishes. "They were away from their posts just long enough for Akeno to sneak over the wall."

"How long did it take you to climb the wall?" Neha asks Akeno.

"A couple of minutes maybe. I had a leg up, though. There was this trolley--"

"There's rooflines we can get to," Sam interjects, looking at Neha.

"The next switch must be at curfew," Joanna says, standing now. "If we can get to the edge of the community right before the switch starts, we can get you three over the wall."

"But where do we go from there? They'll have realized we got out. Someone's bound to see us," Neha says.

"It'll be dark," Sam points out.

"Until dawn," Neha says. "We don't have anywhere else to go. We can't leave Amity in that short of a time. We'll be arrested before then."

"They'll have patrols out looking for any escapees, I'm sure," Joanna says as she stands, now pacing the floor.

"We can go back to my community," Akeno says. "I mean, they don't know who I am. They don't even know how I'm involved. They think I'm a gardener who doesn't exist."

Joanna turns to Akeno. "Which community are you from?"

"Our gates are labelled number eighteen," he says.

Joanna's eyes glow. She takes an indulgent breath and exhales with a smile.

"Do you know Gabrio?"

As dusk approaches, Mrs. Howard had just finished explaining what's to happen next. When she has to return to the cafe, she stands and brushes down her long skirt. Akeno sits processing all that's about to happen, should they get so far to worry about what comes tomorrow. As Neha walks her to the door, Mrs. Howard bends her head and says something in a hushed tone, her eyes firmly on Neha as Sam runs water in the kitchen. Neha bobs her head up and down. Mrs. Howard grips Neha's hands, her lips set in a grim line, though she forces herself to smile. She says something else in an even lower voice, glances at Akeno, who sits quietly listening, his eyes pretending to be focused on the ground. Neha nods again, and Mrs. Howard leaves.

Out of the corner of his eye, Akeno sees Neha brace herself for tonight. She paces the floor, her hands wringing themselves together as she mumbles something under her breath. She glances at Akeno, and by chance, their eyes meet. Akeno smiles in spite of himself. Sam was still in the kitchen, busying herself by checking the cabinets for anything to eat. It would be a long night, and Akeno knew he should eat, but the anxiety building inside him wouldn't allow him to hold anything down.

"Sam told me some about you, before we met anyway. You two sounded like a good team. I envy that."

"I think you and Sam make a great team yourselves. You've made it this far." Akeno says, gesturing to the house.

"That's true," Neha says. "Truthfully, this is the nicest house I've ever been in myself. I can't believe how big it is for one person."

"Nice houses make nice prisons," Akeno says, eyeing the stairs. He remembers tumbling down a flight of stairs similar to those, carpeted but still just as painful to hit all the way down.

"Did your family stay in a house like this?" she asks.

"A couple of them did. There was just as much violence in those homes as there were anywhere else I'd been, though."

"So you're from the city? Foster care, right?" Neha asks.

He nods.

"Me too, well kinda. I was technically put in the system. My mother died when I was fourteen." She shifts in her seat, her eyes briefly avoiding his gaze.

"I never knew my parents," Akeno says. "I think that makes it easier. You didn't have any other family?"

"Not any that was a good family." She smiles. "I couch surfed for a while. Luckily, I found a decent family to stay with until I was eighteen. They were alcoholics, but they were good people. Fed us, clothed us, didn't try to molest us. We were fortunate."

"And now? How'd you get here?"

"Same as anyone else. When the blackout started, we heard of a place called heaven, so we came here looking for food."

"We?"

"A few of my friends. They...didn't make it," she says with some hesitation. "We ran into a bad group. Things got out of hand."

"I'm sorry to hear that," Akeno says, his brows furrowing together. He couldn't imagine how he'd have felt if he had to watch Sam die. There were numerous chances for that to happen. Yet they were lucky.

She clears her throat. "What about you? How'd you get here?"

"The Howards," Akeno says with an ironic smile. "Kevin and I were roommates. He was at the refugee camp on campus, and he introduced me to the family. It was thanks to Kim I got away, but not quick enough, I guess."

A profound silence filled the space between them.

"We deserve better than this. We all do," Neha says.

"What is it about this place?" Akeno finally asks. "I've been trying to work that out in my head for as long as I've been here, and I can't understand it." He rises to his feet, his blood pumping through him now as he works himself into a state of frustration. "I mean, there's this blackout, and then everything goes to shit. There's this place, and I think it might be all right. It's better than starving or freezing to death, but it turns out to be another rouse for safety. Now I'm here, and suddenly I'm caught up in a lot of other shit."

Neha doesn't immediately reply, and Akeno flops back down on the chair. "It's been a lot to take in. I'm just...trying to figure out what's going on," he says.

"We should start from the beginning," Sam says, evidently overhearing their conversation. "You're clearly stressed. You don't know who to trust, and I get it. You didn't ask for this, but here you are now. What other questions are floating around in that thick head of yours?" Sam falls back down on the couch.

"I want to know everything about the Howards. I want to know why they chose me to kidnap and sell to this place. Why me?"

"Isn't that the question we've all been asking ourselves?" Sam retorts, taking a huge bite out of the wrapped granola bar in her hand. She tosses one to Akeno and hands one to Neha. Neha puts hers aside as Akeno quickly unwraps his own and swallows it nearly whole.

"I don't know this to be true, but this is what I've learned over the months working with Joanna." She clears her throat. "The Howards helped form this place, among thousands of others."

Akeno's eyes meet Sam's.

"Okay, so what does that mean?"

"It means this place was under design years and years before the blackout. Joanna was one of the lead designers of the homes. They didn't tell her what the homes would be used for, only that it was a new development project for middle-class families. That's all she knew. Michael Howard, on the other hand, knew what was happening and kept mum about it. He helped design the infrastructure of the communities."

Akeno nearly blanches. An idiot like Howard helped design the framework for this place.

"I know what you're thinking. Howard's a drunk now, but a few years ago, he was mostly sober and decent at his job."

"So when did Joanna find out about all this?" Akeno asks, his heart picking up speed. Had she known all along? Didn't she know the first day that this was the system he'd be confined to? Why didn't she say anything? "She never said anything to me about this," Akeno says.

"She couldn't have known Howard would do this. I don't think she realized the scope of it all until it was too late. Unlike Joanna, Howard's been involved in Amity for some time. After he finished his work on the landscaping, he wanted more work, so they gave him more. He finished the designs they had for the housing projects, an artillery space, and the wall, of course.

He knew something was taking place, but now even he knew the extent of it. He never told Joanna. By then, she was working on some of Amity's other minor assignments, ones that involved the community and didn't have a lot of classified files. It was by accident that she found out about Amity's intentions.

"It was enough to make Joanna's stomach turn, from what she said about the documents she found in his office," Sam says, her feet shifting. "That's when she filed for divorce."

"That wasn't too long before I met Kevin," Akeno says, biting back the gnawing anxiety in his stomach. He feels like he's going to be sick. All of this could've been prevented.

"I don't think Kevin knew," Sam says softly. "If that helps."

Akeno shakes his head. "He found out later."

"I'm sure he did. He and his father were close. He signed up for the military as soon as he got here. His father didn't want him to do it, which was shocking. Howard must know something Kevin doesn't. Even so, Kevin left the following morning. From what I heard, Kevin doesn't speak to his father anymore. I wonder if he finally figured it out."

Akeno nods. "So if Howard's a key designer, then why isn't he living high on the hill?"

"He was fired," Sam says with a satisfied smile. "He took to drinking after the divorce was filed, and they let him go. They didn't care if he was in the club or not. He had loose lips when he drank." She shrugs. "He was a liability. I'm surprised he isn't dead yet. Amity doesn't have time for liabilities."

"Did either of them say anything to anyone?" Akeno asks, feeling the bile build in his throat. He swallowed it and closed his eyes for a moment.

"Of course," Sam says. "Joanna spoke out with good intentions, but nobody believed her. It's hard to believe something like this could happen. Michael told others out of spite. Who would believe a raving drunk?"

"Kim stayed on the job, despite what she knew," Sam continues.

297

"She played along and didn't say anything to anyone else after that. She kept her head down and her ears to the wall. When asked about her husband, she played it up like the drinking was the reason for their divorce, not his affiliation with Amity."

"So, she's staying here under the guise of normality?"

"Exactly. She wasn't high enough on the ladder for them to ship her out here directly, but they told her she and her family would have a place here waiting for them. When the blackout started, she was just as shocked as anyone else. She knew the big picture but never knew the method. She put two-and-two together and sped up her agenda. She pulled Kevin from campus the day after the blackout."

Akeno sits up as blood rushes through his head and down his arms, his chest, his legs. "Joanna got Kevin out?"

"Of course, that's her kid, for better or worse. Kevin couldn't have known what was going on beforehand. She must have filled him in, or their father did before she could."

"He was the one to ask me to join the family."

"That doesn't shock me. Joanna mentioned how close the two of them were. At least it was that way until he enlisted. Joanna thinks the boys must have had a falling out, or Kevin finally came to his senses. Either way, he left the family high and dry."

"Poor Joanna," Neha says. "Her own son left her."

"She doesn't mention his name anymore. I'm not sure if they've talked since he left, but I'm sure she keeps her own tabs on him."

Akeno soaks it all in, his heart starting to slow now that he's been given the time to process. They wait as he finds the words to speak again. There's the one question that's been itching at him this whole time.

"Why didn't Kim tell me earlier? When Kevin brought me to their tent at the camp, why didn't she say something to me then?"

Sam sighs. "She didn't know there was a merit system. Like I said, she got the big picture but never any of the details. She didn't realize Howard could trade you in. She figured it out after the interviews. Amity needed labor, and they didn't care how they found it."

Akeno nods, trying to find space to understand. She wasn't the enemy. She was trying to do what was right. She *is* doing what's right. It must have been difficult to pretend something inhumane wasn't happening in hopes of figuring it out in the end. If she could come this far with a plan in mind, it was time Akeno played his role too.

An abrupt knock sounds on the door. They fall silent. There's another rapid knock and a man's voice.

"Kim, please answer the door."

Akeno's ears perk up at the sound of his voice. The knocking continues.

"Kim, please, Kevin's worried about you. I'm worried about you. Please, just answer the door. I know you don't want to see me, but let your son know you're alright."

The knocking continues. "Kim!"

Neha, Akeno, and Sam stand in the kitchen as the knocking goes undisturbed. After a few minutes of quiet, the knocking stops. Akeno gestures to the door and begins to open his mouth, but Neha shakes her head and holds up a hand for silence. They wait a few more minutes, and finally there's a jingle at the lock, and the knob turns.

Sam moves first. Just as the door opens and Howard enters the foyer, Sam kicks the door hard, slamming it back against Howard's head. He yells out in pain and takes a step back from the doorway. Another man shoves his way past Howard and enters the living room. He's massive, 6'2" and at least 260 lbs. He turns and sees Akeno, Neha, and Sam, who pulls back her fist and lands the first hit.

The man staggers back, his face barely scratched from where Sam connected. Howard's face is red and blotchy as he moves into the room. He pulls his hand back on Sam, but she doesn't flinch. Neha moves in front of her and grabs the arm as it swings. She yanks him forward, and he falls off-balance. He trips over the ugly rug in the room, and Sam moves out of the way so his momentum carries him head-first into the wall separating the kitchen and the main room.

Akeno makes his way to the kitchen, his body between the table and the chair, his eyes on the counter for a knife. He sees Howard right himself and turns to the women. Sam faces Howard, and Neha faces the other man, who corners himself between the couch and the wall. Howard makes a move forward, and Akeno picks the chair up and throws it. It doesn't hurt Howard as much as it distracts him. He turns to face Akeno and grins a crooked smile.

"You're back," he says playfully. "Like a stray dog coming home. Has she been keeping you here all this time?"

"You stay the hell away from me," he says angrily. He finds a knife and pulls it from the set on the counter. "You sold me."

Howard laughs. "What are you going to do with that knife?" He drops his gaze and smirks at Akeno's shaking hands. "You couldn't kill me if you wanted to, and I know you must want to." His speech slurs, and Akeno feels something inside him release. He's been drinking.

"You don't know me."

"I know enough. When Kevin said you were smart, but he's easily impressed. You never knew a thing." Howard shook his head, his hand sliding across the countertop as he made his way closer to Akeno. "You know, I thought maybe you were some kind of retard. I couldn't believe how easy it was to convince you to go with us. All I had to say was where we were going, and you jumped on board faster than anyone I'd ever seen. Hell, I thought maybe you were some queer with a crush on my boy."

"I never trusted you, and I never trusted Kevin."

"And you never said anything either," Howard said with a grin. "Never fought back, never defended yourself. Look at you now, kid. You're hiding in the corner of my wife's kitchen, letting two girls defend the house. Do you know what we're going to do to them once I beat the shit of you? It'll be fun, and I'll let you watch."

Howard kicks the upturned chair out of his way and makes his move toward Akeno. Akeno backs up, pushing the table askew and putting another chair between him and Howard. He clutches behind him at the counter and feels the cold surface. He's reaching for anything and nothing at all, his eyes wide and focused on the man coming for him. The knife is still in his hand, a loose grip.

"It's time you learned your place," Howard seethes.

Howard reaches out, and Akeno lunges with the knife. Howard turns to the side and grabs Akeno's wrist. He's faster than Akeno thought. Howard yanks the knife from Akeno's loose grip and throws it on the floor. Then he arches his fist back, his knuckles connecting with Akeno's jaw. Akeno can't recover before he feels another blow and then another. He feels dizzy, swollen, and watches as blood drips from his mouth. He leans heavily against the counter and waits for another blow. Howard smiles and he hits him again and again. Akeno slides against the counter, his arms barely holding him up.

"How many times has someone beat the shit out of you?" Howard laughs and pulls Akeno close. "It's all you seem to know."

Akeno leans his head back and spits blood into Howard's face. He doesn't even flinch. He puts his mouth closer to Akeno's ear and says, "

Don't worry. You'll live through this. Just barely."

Howard arches his bloodied fist back again, but suddenly Howard's body is pulled off Akeno. Akeno's eyes glance up, his vision blurred, and sees Sam on Howard's back, one of her elbows locked around his throat, the other pulling on his hair.

Howard cries out in pain and reaches his arms up to grab hold of Sam. He has a hold on her hair, but she keeps steadfast and pulls him back until they've slammed against the wall. His hands grip her arm. He's much stronger than her, though he gasps for air, his face reddening. Sam leans down and bites his ear until there's blood. Howard lets go of her arm and puts one hand on his ear. Suddenly they lose balance, and Howard falls on the kitchen tile with Sam still on his back. There's a loud crack, and Howard lays unmoving on the floor, his head leaking blood.

They all wait motionless, and there's a deafening silence ringing in the room. Neha enters the kitchen, blood spotting her clothes. There's a bruise forming on the side of her face. She eyes Howard's body on the floor and Akeno's swelling face.

"He's dead," Akeno breathes.

"He's not dead, at least not yet," Sam says. She pulls herself off the man quickly and moves out of the way to examine the body.

"Soldiers will be coming soon. We have to leave," Neha says. She runs to Akeno. "Are you okay? Can you move?"

"I'm fine," he mumbles. He spits a glob of blood on the floor.

In truth, Akeno is fine. He thinks he might have a broken nose and a broken blood vessel in his eye, but he's taken worse beatings.

"Can you hand me a towel?" he asks.

Neha runs back to grab a towel from down the hall. When she returns, he places the wet cloth against his face and wipes the blood from his mouth and eye. Sam doesn't say anything as she throws her bag over her shoulder and eyes Howard's body on the floor.

"Let's move," she says.

As they move through the main room, the house now eerily quiet, Akeno spots the other man lying motionless on the floor. There's a ribbon around his neck.

"Let's go. He'll live," Neha says to Akeno.

Sam throws open the door and lets the other two leave before her. She glances back at the two bodies and shuts the door behind them as they round the corner of the house. It's nearly dusk now. There's a siren ringing down the street, and Akeno knows it's for them. He can hear foot falls beating against pavement as they run from the house. Neha and Sam pick up their pace, and Akeno's feet move as quickly as they can to keep up with the blurred figures moving before him. His eye swells up, but Akeno doesn't stop moving. They round a corner, and Neha points to the end of a street. Sam makes a break for it, and Neha pulls Akeno's arm over her shoulder. "Open your eyes, Akeno. You've got to see to run. Don't let them get you now."

Akeno wipes the blood from his left eye and staggers forward, his eye straining to see. Sam's up at the corner, her hands waving them forward as she disappears. They go down a couple of back alleys behind shops and stores, their footsteps sounding like thunderstorms as they race down the abandoned walkways. They see nobody in the meantime, and Akeno realizes where they are. They're back at the corner where Akeno had first found Neha. It's all come full circle now, Akeno thinks, but he isn't hopeful they'll get out the same way he came in. He's not sure if any of this will work out in their favor.

Neha pulls him to the side of the wall and gestures for him to follow after Sam. He does so willingly, his hands covered in blood from the amount of times he's wiped his face from the blood still pouring from his nose. He wipes it on his shirt now and thinks if anyone sees him, they'll assume he's a murderer, probably Mr. Howard's murderer. Akeno assumes him dead now and feels better for it. He still feels dizzy.

Sam suddenly stops at the corner of a shop and retraces her steps back, gesturing for Akeno and Neha to go back the other way. Akeno skids to a halt and bumps into Neha as she and Sam turn around and head the other way. They push him forward when Akeno hears the sound of soldiers' feet. Sam breaks ahead of them both and runs around several buildings, corner after corner. The soldiers' pounding footsteps follow quickly after them, and Akeno thinks this must be it. He remembers all the movies he's seen before and knows what's coming for them. Nothing is ever based on the absence of truth. They'll be tortured for answers, and he'll willingly give everything they want to know. Akeno thinks they'll all submit themselves to the system eventually; everyone always does.

He feels the sweat pouring down his back as adrenaline takes over his body. He feels like he's having an anxiety attack as he runs after the two women he follows. Just when he thinks he's about to vomit from the race, Sam stops short and opens up a cellar door. She points inside, and Neha jumps in, then Akeno, then Sam. She closes the door and listens quietly for the soldiers' footsteps. Akeno doesn't have time to breathe. He holds his breath inside his hands and closes his eyes, waiting for the soldiers to fling open the doors any minute now. He hears their footsteps coming closer and waits in heavy anticipation. He hears their pace come to a gradual halt at the intersection above them. Their voices call codes and street names, their voices sounding just a few feet away from where they hide. He can't make out much of what they're saying, but then he hears a man's voice plain and clear above them.

"We've lost their direction. The cameras aren't picking up their movement. Something's gone wrong with the system. Check diagnostics and run the program again. See if there's anything—"

The man's voice trails off as he walks away. Sam waits for a long time, much longer than he would imagine. She's thinking of waiting it out, or if they should take the chance and leave now. From the crack in the cellar doors, there's just enough light to see Sam's face lost in thought and Neha's hand resting on Sam's shoulder. Akeno releases the breath he was holding and leans back against the metal wall of the cramped cellar, his knees bent to conserve room for Sam and Neha. Akeno didn't move anything within the cellar, lest they should make a sound.

Neha sits on the two steps leading into the cellar, her head leaning against the wall, her knees to her chest. She glances at Akeno, and in that moment, they both realize they're just as lost as the other. Their only choice is to follow Sam's lead. They're both relying on her now. Whatever the plan was, it's over. It's evident on the look of Sam's face. This was improvised. Whatever Mrs. Howard said to Neha earlier, Akeno can't ask and won't know until nightfall.

Once the light filtering in from the crack disappears completely, Akeno knows their time is running short. They hadn't anticipated this delay. Mrs. Howard wouldn't have anticipated this delay, or maybe she did. None of them have spoken to each other, but from each of the women's body language, Akeno can guess what the plan was and what it is now: survival. He can tell from the anxiety on Neha's face that she doubts they'll make it out of this. Whatever window of opportunity they had before, she thinks it must be gone now. Sam, though inexpressive, continues to look outside the crack in the cellar, her eyes staring off from a remote and distant place. He knows she must be planning for their escape routes, the alternative routes, the backup plans, the worst-case scenarios, and the what-ifs.

Sam pats Neha on the leg and gestures to Akeno. Neha lays a gentle hand on Akeno's shoulder and wakes him from his reverie. He can't see her, but he feels the comfort of her touch and gives her hand a squeeze to acknowledge that he's ready. He shifts his feet under him and makes for a standing crouch. He waits for the light to sting his eyes, but when Sam slowly opens the cellar door, there's no light outside at all. The moon is covered by a thin shadow of clouds that shift in the sky, and Akeno gives thanks.

They creep out of the cellar one by one, and Sam shuts the door behind them. She motions for them to follow her, but Neha grabs a hold of Sam's arm and gestures in the opposite direction. Sam shakes her head, but Neha insists.

Sam hesitates and looks to Akeno. He nods and gestures to follow Neha. They keep to a standing crouch as they run up the walls of the streets and check rooftops for shadows. It's hard to see directly in front of them, much less at a distance, but as their eyes grow accustomed to the profound darkness, Akeno thinks he can't see anything.

They make their way across a large plaza under the guise of darkness. They move along the walls, Neha leading the way, her head poking around each corner as they go in a direction unfamiliar to Akeno and Sam. They finally reach a large building. Considering how far they've come, Akeno thinks they must be near the wall. Akeno can't make out much more than a looming shadow behind the building they've come to. Neha skimps alongside the side of the building and stops at what seems to be a door. She knocks light and firm, the same knock Akeno had heard Mrs. Howard use before.

There's a reply knock, and Neha slips inside. Akeno and Sam, with some surprise, follow after her. The three of them stand in a small foyer inside what appears to be a restaurant. Tables sit all around the room with their chairs turned up on the tops. The tables are covered in long, white linen cloth. They almost look like ghosts within the darkness of the room. Along the far wall is an empty fireplace, the chimney going up along the wall and through the ceiling.

The door closes gently behind them, and a shadow of a figure comes around and leads them into the next room. Neha follows closely behind the figure, past a grand staircase that leads up to the next landing. Akeno peers up and sees the second landing, alongside a looming, glass chandelier. Akeno looks down and realizes their steps are muffled by a soft carpet. There are several more tables within the next room, with more space for a number of guests.

As they round the corner, there's a long hallway leading to the back of the restaurant. Along the hall are candles lit within the ancient candelabras hanging on the walls. They file individually through the passage, and Akeno can't help but peer at the portraits hanging in gilded frames down the expanse of the hallway. Men and women donned in traditional, royal garb with sullen expressions of seriousness and contempt stare down at them all. Just below one of the candles, there's an oil painting of what appears to be a woman from the Victorian era. She leans against a chaise, her dress plain in contrast to the golden palace surrounding her figure. Her face was made up, the red blush highlighting her plump cheeks, her eyes wide and doe-shaped to express a sense of innocence, her eyes as stale as the painting itself.

When they come to the end of the hall, the door hangs slightly ajar. Akeno can hear voices from the other side, all of them in a hushed whisper. The tone within seems to be a quiet argument. The shadow figure who has led them through the rooms knocks softly, his back turned to them. The door swings open, and the three of them are ushered inside.

The small crowd turns their heads and eyes upon them standing lamely in the doorway, waiting for someone to invite them to the large table they're crowded around.

In the midst of them all, a familiar face sticks out, like a warm spot in the depths of cold water. A brown man steps forward, his hair combed back behind his head, showcasing his modest forehead and arched eyebrows. He wears a long, red coat with several gold buttons and two gleaming cufflinks. He appears to be dressed for a role which does not suit him, though he plays the part naturally. His eyes are on Akeno, and a grin stretches across his face. He and Akeno suddenly move and go toward each other, and to Akeno's surprise, he is greeted with a strong embrace.

"I knew it would be you," Gabrio says to Akeno. "I'll admit I'm a little surprised at hearing all the heroism, but I knew if it would be anyone, it would be you. Didn't I warn you not to go drawing attention to yourself?"

Akeno can feel himself blush and looks away.

"Sam, always a pleasure to see you again," Gabrio says, extending a hand, which Sam accepts with a firm grip. "This must be Neha, the wonderful woman Sam cannot stop raving about. It's a pleasure to meet you officially. We've corresponded a few times before, if you recall, the boxes of toys."

"I do," Neha says, her eyes darting a quick glance at Sam. "It's nice to meet you in person. Joanna has always mentioned the mysterious man beyond the wall, and you've got the charm she always described."

"Kim tends to exaggerate my good character," Gabrio says as an aside to Joanna. She profers a warm smile and gestures to the table. "But we're in the middle of business, so we'll have to catch up another time." He turns to address the party now gathered in clusters around the table. "Now that our comrades are here, we can finally get started."

"Care to introduce us?" a dark-skinned man says, eyeing Gabrio with an intense gaze.

"Gladly," Gabrio says. "You know Sam and Neha, both of whom work with Joanna at the cafe. This here is Akeno, who seems to have teamed up with our fellow comrades, which makes him a comrade by principle. He's one of my fellow teammates back in the labor camps. He's the kid I was telling you about, the one who got remonished for the stick incident."

The man who spoke the first time nods and averts his attention to Joanna, who has her eyes on Sam and Neha, trying to read the expressions on their faces. She couldn't have known that Howard had come to the house, or maybe she did. Akeno felt the pinch of anxiety hit his stomach, and he forced himself to smile as he was introduced to the room.

"Now that the formalities are out of the way, I'd like to remind everyone that we haven't agreed on the particulars yet," a light-skinned woman says.

She wears the same formal dress as Gabrio does, coattails and all. She and Gabrio stand at the same height and stare one another down as Gabrio crosses the room to point at a map spread all along the table. Neither of them breaks eye contact when Gabrio explains again the details of a plan unfamiliar to Akeno. Sam and Neha appear to be interested, but he can't tell if they know the specifics. If they do, nobody fills him in.

"Mikal is right," the dark-skinned man says on one side of the table. "There isn't enough time to make it through that route. We need to cross at the intersection and go underground."

"And if the alarms sound, then we're trapped, Adisa," Gabrio says in reply to the man. "We don't want our backs against any walls."

"And we don't want to be caught in the open where we could be surrounded anyway," Mikal says. She slams her finger at a point on the map. "We have an opening here with minutes to spare. That's all we need to execute this plan."

Gabrio throws his hands in the air, and Adisa turns away with aggravation.

"If we cannot agree on the route we take, can we agree this is worth the risk?" Adisa asks. "Because if we cannot do the latter, then we bother too much with the former."

"Of course this is worth the risk," Gabrio says. "We can't just let this get postponed again. We need more resources. We need more allies!"

"What allies are you referencing? Surely not the ones you search for in the wrong corners?"

"And which corners would that include, Adisa?"

"You know where I am concerned."

"Addiction doesn't preclude someone as an ally."

"Neither does it ease my doubts."

"I've told you I have a hold on the situation."

"Your results are slow to show."

"While you continue to vote against my plans, you complain of slow results!" Gabrio says with an exasperated expression.

"I will continue to vote against risky endeavors that jeopardize the security of our operations, yes!"

Gabrio slams his flat palm against the table and seats himself in one of the plush, velvet chairs encircling the table. The room grows quiet. His outrage burns behind his eyes as he stares at a distant point on the wall. Mikal rolls her eyes, and Adisa brings his fingers to his temples, his body turned away from Gabrio as the room settles.

Sam, Akeno, and Neha stand flush against the wall, their eyes glancing from one person to the other. There are several within the room who do not intervene in the heated debate. They watch as closely as the three newcomers do.

"There seems to be many opinions at the table today," Joanna says, her voice steady, calm, and absolute.

"We're lost for what to do," Gabrio says, raking his fingers through his slick hair. "We can't seem to agree on our target."

"I can see that," Joanna says, glancing over the map and seeing where each person had marked their individual trail. "We can discuss further details later. What we must do is move. We have an opening, and we must take it here."

She points to a spot on the map. Akeno gauges the reaction of the others in the room. Some have resigned themselves to her decision and begin to move accordingly--shuffling papers, handing specific documents to individuals around the room, their whispers growing in earnest. Akeno nods, digesting her decision, though he seems disappointed as Joanna continues to explain the plan to specific people around the table, as the others seem to be reacting to her instructions. When she's finished, she glances up at the others with a challenge in her eyes. From the sound of it, Akeno thinks it's a sound plan. The others agree with affirmation.

"I'll gather my men," Mikal says and exits the room, a couple of people following hurriedly after her.

Joanna smiles in her direction and looks to Adisa. "Please, Adisa, if you would spread the word to the others, we can make sure our countermeasures move as fast as we do."

Adisa gives a polite bow from the shoulders and exits along with the rest.

"Gabrio, we can discuss your other concerns later, but right now we have three people who need to get beyond these walls before the officers break down every door in the community."

"Of course," he says with a polite nod. "What would we do without you?"

"Rip each other's heads off, it seems," she says with an affectionate laugh.

Gabrio smiles and agrees. As the two talk in quiet conversation, Akeno notices the way Gabrio seems so relaxed here, as opposed to the Gabrio he worked with in what he called a "labor camp." Akeno thinks it's a fitting term now that hindsight has provided him with a better conception of Amity's hierarchical structure. He also senses a deep-rooted friendship and trust between Gabrio and Joanna. It's in the way he says her name. The man Akeno's accustomed to was never as careful when speaking to their factory fellows.

"The sewers under the compound are the only paths that intersect all sectors other than the roads," Gabrio says, gesturing at the map. "Our decoy for the roads has worked well enough. When everyone's looking up at the walls and along the streets, they won't be looking at their feet."

Sam smiles at Gabrio's rhyme.

"We've drawn several routes along the sewers," Gabrio adds. "In case one exit is blocked."

"Don't want to risk a cave-in," Joanna says thoughtfully. "Good plan. And the others?"

"Already setting up."

Akeno doesn't understand what they mean by this, but Joanna gives her nod of approval. "You amaze me every day," she says, and Gabrio takes the compliment in great stride, his confidence increasing as he rolls up the map and hands it to her. "Have everyone meet us at the

312

rendezvous point at oh-five-hundred."

"Yes, ma'am," Gabrio says with a salute.

Joanna's eyes turn to Akeno, and she steps over to the three still along the wall, waiting their turn as the others finish their meeting. Everyone left in the room exits, leaving the five of them alone. At her height, which is a few inches taller than Akeno, she seems more domineering in this lighting, more than Akeno previously had in mind before. She tilts her chin down so she can look Akeno in his eyes.

"Thank you for saving our best girl," she says and smiles at Neha. "I'm sorry we've caused you this much trouble. It probably wasn't in your plans today to get wrapped up in the middle of all this."

"No, it wasn't in my plans, but I'm glad to be here anyway." Akeno attempts at a smile as humility and doubt alike both creep in. He feels out of place, like an observer in a game he's not sure how to play.

"We're glad that you're here, Akeno," Joanna says, and Akeno feels Sam's rough calluses as she squeezes his hand. "Listen to Gabrio. He knows what he's doing."

"Thanks for keeping us safe," he says.

She shakes her head. "Don't thank me. It's your right to exist."

Gabrio turns to face Akeno, Sam, and Neha, who are the only four left standing in the room as Joanna makes her exit. When the door shuts behind her, Gabrio leans against the wall and sighs. "I hate wearing all this shit," he says and rips off the decorative collar on his shirt and the other buttons and pins holding his costume neatly in place. "I feel like some kind of colonizer with bad taste."

Something rises up out of Akeno's chest, at first a bubble of warmth which suddenly turns into a fit of laughter. The others watch on in disbelief for a brief second as Akeno points to the ruffles on the white shirt Gabrio wears. His trousers are likewise in the same traditional style as

313

the British redcoat from America's colonial period. Gabrio can't help but chuckle to himself as he rips off the theatrical clothes and throws it against the wall.

"You wouldn't believe what we have to wear to get a little attention around here," Gabrio says, facing the corner, looking at what appears to be several boxes of clothes. His shoulders flex under his thin undershirt, his hands on his hips as he selects a few articles of clothing from the boxes. "Here, change into these." He tosses Sam and Neha each a fresh set of clothes, something seemingly more comfortable than the long skirts and blouses they're wearing.

"Why are you wearing clothes from the American Revolution?" Akeno asks. "Auditioning for a play or something?"

"As a matter of fact, yes, it is for a play. I was cast as one of the secondary actors but for good reason. I could've been the star, but Joanna felt that learning my lines would have distracted me from the mission."

"What was the mission?"

Gabrio merely winks back in response. "That's confidential, comrade."

He tosses a black shirt at Akeno. The girls go to a separate corner and face the wall as their shirts start to come off. Akeno quickly turns away and changes into his own set of new plain, black clothes. Gabrio faces the table, his finger tracing something along another smaller map he has spread out before him. When Akeno's finished changing, he tentatively glances behind him to ensure Sam and Neha are also finished. As he waits, he hears Gabrio mumble something under his breath, and for a second, it seems that despite all of Gabrio's bravado, he seems doubtful in the plan they have prepared.

"Everything okay?" Sam asks, and Akeno catches sight of the two women, now fully dressed.

"Everything's perfect," Gabrio declares, slamming his flat palm against the table. "First things first, let's get you three to the other side of paradise. Our mission begins now."

CHAPTER 20

Akeno can't see much of anything. The light attached to his forehead dimly shines on Neha, who's in front of him, her back hunched, her steps slow, careful, and deliberate. Akeno brings up the rear of the single-file train running along the sewers beneath the middle sector. Gabrio briefly explained the plan, but through it all, Akeno could hardly keep his eyes open. He had been up since early that morning with no chance to rest. He guesses it must be the middle of the night by now. It's all he can do to stay awake. He doesn't dare pull off his gas mask, not even for a moment, despite its awkward fit around his head, his hair pulled under the tight rubber. Though to Akeno's surprise, it's remarkably dry in the sewers, except for the thin stream of water flowing smoothly beneath their feet. Akeno's grateful for the thick soled boots Gabrio supplied to the three of them.

Akeno wasn't usually averse to cramped spaces. In fact, sometimes small spaces felt comforting to him, but these cramped quarters were slim, even for Akeno. He pushed out all thoughts away of being buried alive, of a cave-in, of suffocating to death, of passing out and being eaten alive by the rats, of drowning in sewage, or of losing their way in such an intricate maze of underground sewers.

Akeno's seen all the movies where those things happened, except those movies feel like a forgotten dream, as if they never existed. Akeno couldn't remember the last movie he'd seen, much less the last time he'd be in a theater. Everything seemed so normal, or at least sorta, but Amity doesn't have those luxuries here. There is no Hollywood. There is only Amity TV. He wonders if there are cameras planted in the sewage system. Akeno quickly stores the thought away. They wouldn't have come down this way if there were cameras. Joanna and Gabrio were far too informed to let a major facet like that escape them. He needed to trust them and trust in the plan, even though it sounded a bit vague and contained plenty of margins of error.

It seems like hours pass by before the procession stops. Akeno looks around wildly, straining his ears to listen to any noise from above, when a sliver of light nearly blinds him and forces him to shield his eyes from the incoming draft. He feels someone's hands pull him forward and up from the sewer. He can barely see, can hardly stand on his own two feet from the exhaustion of his cramped legs that are now able to stretch themselves to their full length. He feels dizzy at first and finally he realizes where they are: a back alley, behind a tall stucco building with a hand painted sign in what appears to be Italian.

"We're at another restaurant?" Akeno asks.

"Quiet," Gabrio snaps. "Follow me."

The four of them rush through the alley and into an open backdoor. As one butler shuts the door, several maids hurry forward and begin throwing more clothes at them and demanding their old ones. The maids' faces screw up in disgust, and Akeno realizes they must smell like death and dysentery. A few maids take a wet sponge to their faces, underarms, and backs as the four turn away from each other, their old clothes coming off and the new ones being tugged on. Then the maids nearly drown them all in perfume, which forces half the room to violently cough. The maids and butlers hurrying to and fro suddenly vanish, and the four of them are left standing well-groomed and fitted for an event.

"What are we wearing?" Akeno asks, his hands tentatively sliding through his hair, his fingers wet from the unknown gel styling his hair back behind his ears. It's tied elegantly back in a low ponytail at the nape of his neck, a small black ribbon tied for adornment. He wears a white shirt cuffed at the wrists with gold buttons and black pants that fit tight in the waist and around the legs. The pants cut off at the ankles, revealing a pair of black suede shoes, which were surprisingly comfortable.

Sam and Neha exchanged pants for yet another skirt, this time high above their knees, with white stockings that stop above the knee, an abundance of lace around their sleeves and collars. Akeno can see the appeal, and Neha blushes when she catches Sam's lingering eye.

"We're servants now," Gabrio says as he checks a hall mirror to closely examine the details of the maids' work. He seems nearly impressed as he slides a stray hair back into place. "There's a midnight dinner we're about to attend and after that, there's a banquet. We'll need to look the part."

"And what's our part exactly?" Akeno asks.

"Entertainment," Gabrio says with a tentative smile. "It's not ideal, but we'll need to be on high guard. This is a burly crowd of men, for the most part."

"Do we know if our target's on site?" Sam asks.

Gabrio nods. "Our informant says everyone is here and in their usual rooms. Sam, if you'll remember the names of the men and share them with Neha. Akeno, things are about to get shifty real fast, but as long as you stick close, we'll lead you through."

"Gabrio, I just...I'm not sure I can do this. I don't think I can fake it. They'll know I'm a fraud."

"Kid," Gabrio says, clapping both hands on Akeno's shoulders. "You've got the brains, the skills, and the heart. There's nothing that you can't beat out there. You just need the confidence to do it." He squeezes hard on Akeno's shoulders. "Find your conviction, Pancake. Use it."

Akeno nods, and Gabrio takes a step back.

"You've got me and Sam to lead this thing. If she tells you to go, it's on my word too. If we split up, we have our rendezvous point." He looks to Sam and then back to Akeno. "Any other concerns before we go?"

A nervous tension hangs in the air. Akeno realizes then that Gabrio must be as exhausted as Akeno is, as they all must be, but none of them show it. For a second, Akeno feels his eyes water at the life they used to have, before the blackout, before he and Sam agreed to come here, before he left the regular schedule the factory afforded him. He's here now, and it's up to him to do his part of the act.

"Good. Now keep your heads down and look like you're busy."

Gabrio hands them all a few miscellaneous items: a tray, an empty glass, a couple wine bottles, a bottle of champagne, clean tumblers. He straightens his shoulders and breathes out a short, fast breath, as if he's preparing for a showcase debut. He walks to the end of the hall, the other three following closely after, and they enter into the hustle of the main foyer, where all numbers of staff slide up and down the main staircase as guests filter through the room.

If Akeno thought the last building they were in was nice, this building is like a castle. The walls are painted a neutral creme to offset the inlaid gold all along the white marble staircase. A deep burgundy rug with intricate patterns of gold and blue run up the stairs. In the center of the room, which everyone carefully avoids stepping on, is what looks like a family crest. There's a large golden eagle in the center of the design, along with a large crown, a scepter, and a Latin insignia scrolled along the circular frame.

"What's the Latin mean?" Akeno whispers under his breath to Sam. She shrugs.

"Something about inherent power," Neha whispers.

Akeno glances back at her.

"I studied Latin for a year in college," she says with a shrug of her own.

Akeno bites back a smile and hurries after Gabrio, the din of the crowd overtaking them all, who now strides as he inspects the room. Everyone is dressed in their finest evening wear. Women don the fine feathers, silks, and lace, and the men all wear black suits of different name brands. Akeno eyes the watches and the shoes. He knows nothing about fashion, but he can instantly recognize the familiar names and styles. So, fashion wasn't dead after all.

The crowd doesn't seem to notice the four of them as they weave their way through the pairs and groups. Everyone is absorbed in the roar of private conversations, of music spilling in from the other rooms. Gabrio takes a right at the stairs and guides them into a crevice beside a massive pillar designed after the Greeks.

"Sam and Neha, keep to the second floor and help with whatever the staff appears to need. Try to stay out of sight and in the background. Comrades will find you. Otherwise just look preoccupied." He leans in close and whispers, "Don't let them get to you."

The two nod, and Gabrio leaves them there. Akeno follows after him, leaving Sam and Neha in the room, lost among all the other faces. Neha gives a short wave goodbye as they disappear in the masses. Gabrio hurries up another, narrower staircase, his eyes never leaving the floor. Akeno breaks his eyes from the carpet and chances a glance down.

The other butlers and maids glide through the crowd, their fashion

320

of clothes distinctly more provocative than the guests' choice. Some of the patrons brush shoulders or force their way through tight spaces to gather around a central seating area. In large armchairs and long sectional couches are large men in suits, ties loosened. Women sit on the men's laps, their tight lips painfully twisted into what appears to be a smile as they listen to the men's stories. Fat cigars rest on the thin lips of these aged men, their widow's peaks unmasked for all to see, the tumblers along the tables numerous and empty. All of the men are white, but the servants appear to be a mixed range of skin tones, including the women on the men's laps.

They stop on the landing above the din of noise. It's relatively quiet up here. There's only a couple standing around, and they leave upon their arrival.

"Remember the plan and stick with it. Don't let anything else distract you tonight."

"When do we meet up? You never said—"

"When the time's right. You'll know it when it comes. Good luck. Stay sharp."

And with that, he disappears into the throng of others down below, leaving Akeno stranded on the landing. Without much else to do, and before he catches the wandering eye of the other staff members, he quickly assesses the room. The target he's looking for is a white man, 6'2" in height, weighing about 280 lbs. He has dark hair parted to the side, a gold Armani watch clipped to his left wrist.

"What do you think you're doing up here?" someone asks him.

Akeno jumps at someone's presence and notices it's one of the staff. He's wearing something similar to what Akeno does, only more personalized, a flash of sapphire blue tucked in his shirt pocket, his shoes a blue suede. Likely he's a staff leader.

"You don't seem to be finding any luck. You look new, but shyness doesn't excuse you from engaging with our patrons," he drawls, scanning the crowd. "What about that gentlemen in the far corner, the bald one. He seems in need of company from a young man like yourself."

Akeno glances in the direction he was gesturing towards and nearly blanches. He's an ugly man with beady eyes and a bumpy head. His hunched back asserts no dominance but rather a submissive judgmental undertone to his nonverbal gesticulations as he took a seat in the corner.

"Yes, sir. I'll see to him," Akeno says.

"Since you're new, I'll give you some advice. Don't look so nervous. These people can smell it from across the room. They'll request you first if you're not careful to remain unnoticed."

Akeno nods and leaves. The servant watches Akeno disappear down the stairs. Once Akeno's halfway across the room, he glances back over his shoulder to catch sight of the landing. The other servant is already gone.

Akeno doesn't dare ask questions; he's learned better than that by now. He tries to blend in with everyone else by walking a little taller, holding his chin a little higher. He has to pass for sophisticated obedience. He bypasses the bald man and exits the room, his eyes glancing over his shoulder once more. He needs to find the target he's after. He could be in a number of rooms. If Sam and Neha are on the second floor, then Akeno will move through the bottom floors.

He passes back through the large foyer, now clear of incoming patrons. A few servants loiter around the door, their conversation muted as a late arrival makes their entrance. One servant takes the men's coat, who already appear drunk, as they throw their coats at the servants. They give a raucous laugh and move in the drawing room. Akeno follows, hoping to blend in with the small group. As they enter the room, he breaks away and follows along one wall, his eyes searching this room for a large man with black hair.

There's quite a few men in this room, though some younger and skinnier. His target was somewhere in his late 50s. He still dyed his hair in hopes for youth's effect, but Gabrio described the job as greasy and unkempt. A few of the female servants caught Akeno's eyes, their quick glances scanning him up and down. He thinks they don't recognize him and are probably questioning who he is. They don't seem to care too much though. They look away when the men make a point in their story and everyone forces themselves to laugh.

The servant beside Akeno nudges his elbow and gestures him aside. He barely nods in one direction until Akeno can make out Neha standing on the other side of the room, her eyes large and luminous as she takes in the crowd. She spots Akeno and gives a small smile. They meet each other in the west corner of the room, slowly but determinedly so as not to draw attention. Neha motions for him to follow her when she passes by him.

"Why are you on the ground floor?" Akeno asks.

"Sam and I had to split up. Something came up, but he's not on the second floor. Sam's moved to the third, where the bedrooms are, and then she'll make her way back down to the second and then the first."

"That sounds like it's off script," he says. "Gabrio said—"

"We know what Gabrio said. Remember, Sam has a hold on this, too."

Akeno leans against the wall. "He's not in the parlor, and he doesn't seem to be in the drawing room. What if he is preoccupied? Do we just wait?"

"Yes, that's generally the plan. We need to catch him unawares. It

323

would be better if he was intoxicated and recently...satisfied."

"We shouldn't be here, Neha. It wasn't our plan to be here. I don't think it was Sam's either, considering her past."

"You know about that?"

Akeno nods, forcing the memory of Sam holding a gun out of his mind. "We need to get out of here."

"Then just follow our lead," she says.

"Where did Gabrio go?"

"I don't know. Just stay out of the way and hope for the best. See you soon."

Neha heads back into the drawing room. Akeno hesitates and turns the other direction, his mind swirling with the unexpected. He feels like things could go sideways at any time, like something drastic might happen. He can feel the sweat rising on the back of his neck and on his palms. He rubs them against his pants, his eyes darting in every direction. He can't be spotted, he thinks. He needs to remain unnoticed. The least he can do is trust that everything will fall into place. All he needs to do is wait. Akeno enters back into the main hall, finds a place on the wall, and watches as more guests are escorted through the doors.

He watches the other male servants take coats and hats. Akeno sees as one servant disappears into another hall. Akeno acts and fills the position of greeter with a slight bow of his head at the guests passing by him, his eyes downcast like the others are doing. The other servants at the door don't seem to notice him. They work silently organizing the coat closet and checking names off a long list. As a woman steps through the door, Akeno hesitates. He wasn't sure if women partook in this evening event, but she seemed delighted to see him. He helps her take off her mink fur coat, which Akeno guesses is real mink, and gently slips it off her shoulders. She slides out of the coat with ease and eyes Akeno with a smirk, her dark red lipstick drawing attention to her face: her small lips, her high cheekbones, her strong nose, the wrinkles ornately covered by the layers of makeup. She tests out a smile and turns to the man coming in behind her, whose robust face gives off an impression of steel and apathy.

"They are adding some exotic new tastes to the mix, aren't they, dear?" she says, resting her hand softly on the man's arm.

The man hands his coat to Akeno, along with a card with their names on it. The man she's with eyes him disdainfully. "If that's what you like."

"You can never tell with this one," she says to Akeno with a wink. They walk off together into the drawing room, their arms interlinked. Akeno doesn't say anything, doesn't make any gesture, his stomach churning with nausea as he puts away the coat in a side room. This process continues for at least another half hour before all the guests have been accounted for.

A woman walks briskly to the coat room and snaps her thin fingers. "Let's move, people. We need more bodies in the drawing room. It's full capacity in there."

Her face is pulled tight at the cheeks, her blush applied too heavily, her big hair teased out to appear like a hood angling her face. She looks frightening, like a cobra. Her eyebrows are painted on thin, giving her a wistful impression, but when he looks at her eyes, he sees only resentment. Perhaps this resentment is for the guests that enter into the house, those that bind her to her position, or maybe the resentment is at her young staff, all of whom Akeno realizes don't seem to exceed their mid-thirties. The woman is the only one who doesn't match this sense of youth and beauty, and maybe that's why she's in charge.

Once the front doors are officially closed, the woman enters back into the main hall. With a wave of her hands, the other servants immediately turn and head off in different directions. Akeno hesitates, not understanding where to go next, and she catches his eye. By the time he turns and follows the other servants en masse, he feels a hand on his shoulder. He stops momentarily and feels her pulling him back toward her.

"What's your name?" she asks without the preamble of grace or formality.

"Ken," he says quickly. He regrets using a name so close to his own, but he hopes this is enough and that she doesn't really care.

"Ken," she says, mulling it over, as if she's tasting it in her mouth. "Like the doll."

"Yes, ma'am," Akeno says. He doesn't really think he looks anything like the Ken doll, but maybe it's her way of selling the appeal.

"Good cover," she says, and Akeno nearly blanches. He remains emotionless though and gives a curt nod, a safe move. "You're new, aren't you?"

"Yes ma'am." Probably best not to lie.

"I don't think I've seen you before. Who recommended you?"

"I can't be sure, ma'am. They brought me here after registration. I met with many people before being assigned here." Akeno hopes this is the best answer he can provide. It's vague enough to give some semblance of an answer.

"Yes, of course," she says with a nod. "You've got a unique face. I suppose that calls for an immediate assignment." She considers this for a moment. "Hurry along now. There are guests waiting. I imagine you'll be requested by many tonight. Be sure to use your manners. Never decline an invitation. That will be all."

The woman turns and walks away, her short heels clicking along the white tile of the floor. She enters a side door and vanishes. Akeno exhales a sigh of relief and heads back for the drawing room. Several of the servants are lined against the wall, their hands behind their backs. Some circle the room holding trays of drinks or food. Akeno immediately picks out Neha and Sam, both of whom are holding trays and serving them to guests quietly and with a small, encouraging smile.

This all feels like a game, Akeno thinks. There's nothing here but niceties and desire. He can feel the tension in the room as the guests eye the servants along the wall and throughout the room, as if they're sizing them up. The men comment on the sizes and shapes of the women, and Akeno feels sick, knowing the women can hear them. They keep a passive face, however, and when one girl is selected for the men's company, the other girl seems to be relieved.

Neha catches Akeno's eye and heads to the same side room to refill her empty silver tray. Akeno waits a beat before casually crossing the room to the same door. He stands beside the wall, waiting for Neha to re-enter the room. Sam passes him with a half-empty tray of drinks. She gives him a wink only he's able to see, and it almost makes him smile. She gives the room another turn before her tray is emptied. Sam approaches Akeno slowly and leaves through the side door with an imperceptive nod in her direction. He waits a moment before following after her.

"We've found the guy," she whispers as the two of them stand at a mini bar stuffed with appetizers and mixed drinks. He glances around the room, but Neha's already vanished. There are several bartenders fervently mixing drinks, and the sound of sloshing ice and liquid reminds Akeno just now parched he is. He notices a glass container filled with a clear liquid. He grabs an empty glass on the counter, not caring who used it last, and attempts to fill it when Sam smacks his wrist.

"It's vodka," she says. "I wouldn't."

"Isn't there anything for the servants?" Akeno whispers.

"You can steal a few edibles from the counter there. It's all botched material. It's been laying out a while, so avoid the perishables."

They make their way over and Sam slips what looks like a burnt piece of pie crust in her mouth. Akeno picks through the leftovers and finds an oversaturated sandwich quarter that he chews twice before forcing himself to swallow.

"So now what do we do? What's your plan?" Akeno asks, his mouth now craving something to drink to wash the foul taste away. "What is it that we're looking for again?"

"He has a key card to the control room. It's what we need to escape. It opens the outer gates. He's the man in there by the east corner. He's with a few other men right now. He doesn't seem to want much company right now, but that can change."

"Won't he notice the card's gone before we reach the other side of the city? He'll alert the soldiers. They'll have the whole place locked down before we reach the city's center."

"Ordinarily, yes, but we have a plan for that too. This was actually designed for escape. Should Amity find itself compromised, there's always an emergency exit for the important people. That's where we are now, and that's where we're headed."

"All right, so we know who has what we need, but how exactly do you plan on getting the card? What if there's a password once we get to where we're going? What if he notices before we can even get out of this house? Say if something happens--"

"Don't worry about any of that," Sam says, cutting him off. "We've got it all worked out. You just have to be ready when it happens."

"Who's 'we'? Nobody's told me anything, Sam," he says with a rising pitch in his voice.

She shushes him and hurries him away from the table and back to the bar.

"Everything will make sense when it happens. Dinner's about to start, so just pay attention and stay close."

She shoves an empty tray in his hand and hurries him out the door. When they re-enter the drawing room, an unseen bell chimes in a low, resonating vibrato. The guests slowly pull themselves out of their seats and make their way to the dining room. Once the guests have cleared the room, the servants begin to clean up after the guests and return their dishes to the kitchen. Sam and Akeno line up with the other servants before they file away to join the guests at the feast.

The grand dining room doors are opened with a flourish. Akeno marvels at the scene around them. White draperies are hung on either end of the doorway and white marble pillars are positioned in the entryway to give the impression of an ancient paradise lost. At the back of the room is an imported marble fountain that lightly sprays water from the top and cascades down into the multilayered pools below. Statues of baby angels playing harps hang around the naked female statues sitting at the water's edge.

The servants line the walls, their hands behind their backs. Some stand at attention with drink pitchers and wine bottles, but Akeno is not one of the few trusted with this laborious task. Instead, he stands with the others, his eyes fixed ahead, staring at nothing, but all the while paying close attention to those seated around the magnificent, mahogany table laid with dishes upon dishes of food.

Sam is only a few people down from him. Finally, he spots Neha out of the corner of his eye on the other side of the room. He thinks she sees him too and feels a sense of relief but also a tinge of nervousness at what's to come. He doesn't understand why they're all collected around the room like this, especially since some aren't holding anything of importance. Perhaps it's the principle of the matter. Servants must watch the masters eat first.

On the table are delectable items Akeno wishes he could have the chance to taste: roasted duck, quail, a full ham, baked apples, leafy greens, squash, and other items he either couldn't name or could barely see. The guests' plates are already filled and placed according to the name cards along the table. They barely pick at their meal, though, their aging bellies already full from just a few bites of everything.

He hasn't eaten most of the day, having had a meager lunch and missing dinner altogether, not that they had time to eat before. He had eaten his shared allotment of oatmeal-gruel from the workers' cafe. If he had known he wouldn't be coming back, he would have spent all his credit on the biscuits and meat provided at the cafe for an extra cost. Since he left the compound, Akeno's appetite had been silent, at least until now.

The guests talk amongst themselves, their voices maintaining an even volume in the spacious room. Akeno pretends not to pay attention as he listens to the clipped conversations the guests are having. Nothing they speak about seems to be of any relevance. They discuss the mundane--the routines they fulfill every day in their glorious homes, the quality of their own staff, the food they've been served, the hobbies they've attempted, the love affairs and scandals between families and couples.

Akeno could have screamed. Maybe he should have. He wished he were anywhere else but here. It was yet another reminder of how much he's never had and never will have. There are those seated at the table, and there are those standing along the wall. From one perspective, it may seem that those standing are waiting to take their turn at the table, but anyone who understands the complexities of class and structure knows that those standing will never receive an offer at the table.

As the guests finish their consorting and laughing, their plates still mostly full, an hour passes before the guests tire of looking at their food and begin to stand. As one person stands, the rest begin to follow, and soon all of them have left the room, leaving the feast grossly unfinished. Once the last guest has left the room, the servants dive at the plates, their hands grabbing plate after plate of food before hurrying off back to the kitchen.

Akeno does the same with an automatic fear that if he doesn't, something will happen to him. His hands grab plate after plate, his fingers stretching to hold three, though the plates he grabs are emptier than the plates the other servants have. When he returns to the kitchen, he enters a scene of near chaos. All of the servants--no matter their age, size, or gender--scarf down whatever is left on the plates. Akeno, upon seeing this, takes a step back at the ravenous destruction taking place in suits and dresses. The servants with the fullest plates eat quickly and without delay, their hands tearing at the meat from the bones and shoving it in their mouths. Not a single person has a fork, spoon or knife in their hands as they devour what's in front of them. Food is laying everywhere, falling on the counters and onto the floor. Some even stoop down to pick what's dropped on the white tile and shove it into their mouths, more food slipping out from their stained lips.

Akeno, shocked and horrified by the sight before him, forgets his appetite. He lays the plates on the counter beside him, which is quickly snatched from the corner and devoured like the rest. He leaves the room before the bell chimes. He's only a few steps from the door, when the other servants shove past him, their faces freshly wiped, their hands cleaned of any spit or stain. It's as if nothing has happened, and all is well. Akeno has the sudden urge to vomit at what he had just witnessed. The woman from before rushes into the kitchen and sees everyone leaving, the plates left on the counters, the kitchen staff already clearing away the mess.

She seems satisfied at the urgency of the servants' movements to get out of the kitchen. She smirks at the sight of the dirty plates and the food that had fallen on the floor.

"Like a pack of wolves," she sneers. "The night's not over yet, people! I want to see everyone's best performance!" She exits the room from the opposite door from which she came, leaving Akeno at the back of the line leading back into the drawing room.

He feels a hand tug at his elbow, and it's Neha, her hand grasping his arm tightly, her eyes swollen with tears. She walks slower than the others, and Akeno falls into step beside her. He reaches over and gently squeezes the fingers holding onto him. She releases her grip, and he slips into the room with the crowd, Neha following closely after him.

They enter the drawing room, but Akeno doesn't see the target.

"He's in the parlor," Neha whispers. "Only the gentlemen are allowed in there, no wives or mistresses allowed."

A few male servants filter through the crowd in the drawing room, which is filled with couples and a few ladies. They flirt and tease and court as they are expected to with the older women. The few men who walk among the crowd do it slowly and silently, waiting to catch the eye of a woman seated nearby. The women laugh among themselves, the male servants pretending to enjoy the attention, and perhaps they do. Akeno is curious to know what the women in this room want from the male servants. He wonders if the outcome is any different in the rooms upstairs.

In the parlor, it's a different scene. Male and female servants walk the room. The male servants are generally less reserved as the female servants. They keep to themselves, separate from the other male servants in the room. They eye the crowd, waiting to be approached rather than approach anyone, less they offend. It doesn't take long before Akeno is stopped by two men, and Neha quickly hurries off to the other side of the parlor. Akeno keeps his one eye on Neha and the other on Sam, who he notices is also watching Neha too, both of them keeping a protective watch.

"You must be new," the shorter man says in a sweet voice, his eyes taking in Akeno's figure. "We'd remember you anywhere, surely."

"I am new," Akeno says with a bashful smile. He isn't sure if the gesture is playacting or if he's actually blushing. Either way, the men are pleased by it.

"Please, take a seat with us," the taller one says, leading the way to the center of the room. "We'd love to hear all about you."

Even seated, both are taller than Akeno by a head. Ironically enough, the men carry similar features: dark eyes, dark hair, light complexion, mid-forties if he had to guess, but they could easily pass for ten years younger. All eyes were on them. Some of the male guests turned their gaze when Akeno caught them staring, and some of the female servants turned their heads away in jealous disgust at their choice in Akeno. They were handsome after all, the cleanest and youngest couple in the room of old men. The two men seemed unperturbed by all the eyes on them, almost as if they enjoyed basking in the attention, but Akeno felt uneasy. He tried finding Neha and Sam in the crowd, but since he couldn't see either, he assumed they were behind him.

"What's your name?" the taller one asks.

"Ken," Akeno replies. "Like the doll."

Both of the men heartily laugh. "You're a riot," the shorter one says. "I like that. I'm Charles. This one here's Dominic. He refuses to be called Dominic except in formal settings, so you may call him Dom."

Dom smiles mischievously but says nothing as he finishes his drink. He calls for another, and one appears in his hand immediately. He offers Akeno a taste. It looks like scotch on ice. Akeno never really liked drinking.

"No, thank you," Akeno says politely. "You're our patrons. The drinks are for you."

"Oh, come on. I know you're not supposed to, but I insist," Dom says. "We can break a few rules." He winks as Charles' lips curve into a predatory grin. "Just a sip. If you don't like it, I won't make you finish it."

Akeno suspects he means more than he's saying, and he eyes him warily. He reaches out his hand for the glass, takes a sip, and chokes down the smooth liquid. He nearly coughs, but he holds back, more out of pride than anything else. The liquid eases its way down his throat and into his chest, where it warmly rests.

"Good stuff," Akeno says. "Best I've had."

"Oh, I can imagine," Dom says. "Only the best for us here."

Akeno nods, though he isn't amused. He glances around at the layout of the room, something he's finally been able to notice now that he's seated. All the chairs and couches are facing in to provide more intimacy among the patrons. There are card tables situated throughout the room, though only a few seem to be playing, uninterested in the people around them. There are women standing close to the men at the table, their hands resting lightly on the backs of the men they're with, but even that small touch seems to be taken for granted. The furniture is soft but mostly uncomfortable. It's like these couches aren't used often. It doesn't feel like a home as much as it feels like a hotel. That's the better word for it, Akeno thinks. A seedy hotel for guests with ill-intentions in mind.

"Tell us about yourself," Charles says, leaning forward. "What were you like *before?*" He says it with a smile, and Akeno is obliged to return the favor.

"When you say 'before,' do you mean before the blackout?"

"We all used to be somebody else back then," Charles says with a playful glance at Dom, who doesn't seem to notice. His eyes are fixed on Akeno.

"Somebody else?" Akeno asks. "I don't know what you mean."

"He means to say we were all different people with different goals," Dom intercedes. "I mean, my father used to be majority whip, but now that that's over, he's either dead or likely hiding in a secret bunker."

"You're telling me you don't know where your parents are?" Akeno asks.

"I know where my mother is. She's dead in the ground and burning in hell, and as for my father, I'd rather him be dead too. It'd make my life a lot easier." The two laugh.

Akeno gives another nod, forcing a smile, and Charles looks squeamish. "Ken, I love that name. Did you pick it for yourself, or were you actually birthed into that name?"

"I chose it," Akeno says with truth. "I wanted to be someone...different." Akeno eases back into flirtation. He side- eyes Dom, who's just downed his second drink and gestures for one of the servants carrying trays to bring him yet another.

"And what about you, Ken? What's different from before and now?" Dom asks, taking another drink without thanks. Akeno glances up at the servant who brought the glass, and it's Sam. She gives him a warning glance and turns away.

"Well, I've never been able to stay in as nice a place as this before," Akeno says. "I was in school, but that's pointless now."

"What were you studying?" Charles asks eagerly. "I have a degree in marketing. It didn't go too far in this economy, but it was fun while it lasted." He lightheartedly laughs, but nobody joins him.

"I hadn't actually decided," Akeno says. "I wasn't in school very long."

"The education system is a scam," Dom says. "You've saved yourself thousands of dollars of debt. Congratulations," he finishes, toasting Akeno before starting his third drink, though it may have been his fourth or fifth. Charles doesn't even look at Dom; he has his eyes glued to Akeno.

"You're still young," Charles says. "You'll have your whole life to do what you want," Charles says.

"I'm not sure there's much else to do," Akeno says with an awkward laugh, and Dom smirks, nudging Charles a little too hard in the arm.

"He got you," he says. "There's nothing to do in Amity but eat, drink, and fuck."

"That's everywhere," Charles says with a bite to his tone. "And regardless, it's not stopping you to partake in it now."

"I'd rather be here than bored. At least before the blackout, there was society and the public. Now there's neither society nor a public. We're left to slave labor and old, outdated whoremongers as company."

"You're a charm, you know that?" Charles snaps at Dom.

"I'm speaking what's on Ken's mind. Look at him! He's pale as the nymphs. It's because what I've said is honest."

"What you've said is disturbing," Charles exclaims as he examines his partner's face. "My god, you haven't even the decency to clean yourself," he grits, throwing a cocktail napkin on Dom's lap. "You've got *powder* on your collar."

"It's for show," Dom says with a snicker.

For a moment, it's quiet, but Dom continues, sullenly but with earnestness.

"Has anyone told you about the blackout?" Dom asks. "Has anyone revealed their part in all this fabricated paradise?" Dom quickly starts pointing at people in the room with the tip of his glass still in hand. "She manages the funds for this house. He helped design the pleasure garden out back. He financed the privacy wall separating us from the rest, a magnificent gate too, as I'm sure you noticed on your arrival."

Akeno hadn't but nodded, listening intently. He didn't need to feign interest in them now.

"She's overseer of new arrivals. He oversees the helipad operations and all its flights. Did you know about that one? There's a helipad on top of the wall!"

"Lower your face," Charles seethes. "You're drunk."

"I'm not finished," Dom says, emphasizing his words, turning a pointed glare that threatens consequence based on Charles' reaction. He sits back and avoids eye contact with either of them now.

"Do you know why the blackout happened?" Akeno asks, tentatively.

Dom smiles. "Taxes," he says.

There's a quietude around Akeno's ears as he processes the one word. He blanches, and it shows, because Dom laughs.

"Work it out in your head," Dom says insistently. "Come on, you're a smart kid."

"They raised the taxes?" Akeno proffers.

"Dom, stop," Charles pleads. Dom holds up a hand for silence.

Akeno ignores Charles and keeps his gaze on Dom. "Tell me."

"Because the public was on the verge of a civil war. The civil and political unrest in this country was leading up to it all. After the riots in Chicago, New York, Seattle, and LA. People were clearly unhappy. And then on the other hand, there were the counter protestors, who only made matters worse. The government knew they weren't going to be able to control the public or the outcome, so they did what they thought best: They got ahead of the inevitable and created their own chaos."

Akeno feels the edges of his eyes shift out of focus as the impossible worked its way through his mind. He had always considered the idea, had almost believed it, but he tossed the thought aside. It took all he could have to survive. There was such a heavy burden weighing on his shoulders that he couldn't face the reality in front of him.

"You're telling me all of this was staged?" he whispers, his eyes refocusing on Dom. "That the government started the blackout, that they did it not just to create chaos?"

"Not just chaos. Her sister too."

"Chaos and order," Akeno says to himself. Dom sees his lips move and smiles, crossing one leg over the other, his drink now empty once again. "They advertised this place as a city of order, as a safe haven, a refuge. Like heaven when you're living out there like it is now."

"It's hell out there," Dom says. "But it's not just the government to blame. It is the people, too. Nobody commanded them to act this way. Nobody told them to loot the stores, to purchase their rifles, and guard their wealth like they have. I'm sure you've seen it all out there."

Akeno nods, remembering the armed soldiers at the grocery store, at Callahan's neighborhood behind the fence, the military arriving on campus, which effectively evicted him from his only home. He remembers the trucks and the children being kept in the back like animals. He remembers the woman willing to kidnap him and Sam, if it meant she could trade them for her own safety. It was just like the Howards, like

Kevin..

"How else do you think this place got here?" Dom asks. "It hasn't always existed. What do you think these walls do? It's an illusion, Ken. Break out of it. Get out of here if you can. This is not a place of angels." Ken stands abruptly, nearly knocking the ottoman in front of him over. The people around him turn their heads and eyes, but they only seem half-interested. If any overheard what Dom was saying, nobody contradicted him. Nobody argued or denied. It was simply a series of facts, a reality that they all partake in.

"I have to go," Ken stammers. "I need to freshen up." He hurries off, embarrassed at the excuse and ashamed that he still has to pretend to be someone he's not. Or maybe this is him. Maybe he is everyone that these people despise. He's the servants, the entertainment, the Asian one, the spy, the criminal, the hero, the pretender.

Over his shoulder he sees Charles stand from the couch and leave from the opposite side of the room. Dom remains where he is, his face stoic but angry. He sets his glass down and follows after Charles, his long strides feigning confidence as he staggers through the crowd.

On the other side of the room, Akeno spots Neha. She's seated on the arm of a chair, next to a man whose hand is resting on her thigh. She catches his eye, and before he can move, she shakes her head. The man beside her is a large man spilling from the armchair, a red tip of a cigar visible behind Neha's shoulders, which blocks him from Akeno's view, but he sees a patch of black hair on the back of his neck. She's made contact with the target.

Akeno feels overwhelmed by his rising anxiety, his heart pounding to an incessant countdown. He leans against the wall, his chest gasping in the stale air of liquor and smoke in the parlor. He looks for a window or a balcony, but there is none. He begins sliding to the floor when a strong hand grips his shoulder. His eyes register the person in shock, thinking he's been found out; it was only a matter of time.

"Get up," the man whispers next to him. "Keep moving, or they'll take you out of the room." Akeno stands, squinting at the man's face. He leans close. "It's me."

Akeno stands peers into the man's face, which is partially masked by makeup and the shadow of his hair, now tousled and curling over his temples. He recognizes the playful glint in the sea of the man's golden-brown eyes. For the first time Akeno realizes that Gabrio may not be as old as he initially thought. He couldn't have been any older than thirty.

"Where have you been?" Akeno asks.

"Consorting, my friend," he says. "Glad to see we've made contact with our target."

"Neha's there, but I haven't seen Sam."

"Look to the other side of the room," Gabrio says.

Akeno glances up and sees her instantly, though he had missed her before. She's holding two drinks in her hands as she crosses the room. "See that man?" Gabrio asks, gesturing to the man beside Neha. "Sam's going to take him upstairs. Then you and Neha need to be there in ten minutes. We're nearly there."

"I've got to tell you something," Akeno says, recalling Dom's outburst.

"There's no time," he says. "Keep an eye on them." He saunters away, a close-lipped smile playing at his lips as he greets a female patron.

Akeno turns back to Sam, who is on the other side of the man's chair and hands him a drink. He takes it with delight, and they clink glasses together. He pulls Neha closer as he drinks the whole thing.

Akeno sucks in a deep breath and makes his way to the corner of the room, his eyes on Sam and Neha. Sam doesn't sip at the drink in her hand. She flirts carelessly with the man, her breasts leaning close to his face. He seems to be paying only half attention to her, his hand still pulling Neha closer, who looks uncomfortable as she watches Sam shamelessly play her part. Sam bends low and whispers something in the target's ear, but he only smirks and looks away. He's not interested.

Sam smiles with grace and leaves his side, her face neutral but her eyes on fire. She sees Akeno and passes off her drink to him. She doesn't pause to talk and instead stalks to the other side of the room. Akeno takes the drink and swishes it around. It smells of tequila. He swallows it quickly and makes his way across the room to where Neha and the target are.

Neha catches his eye and shakes her head at him again. Don't approach, she's saying. Don't blow our cover.

But he's tired of taking orders. It's time he does something.

"I see you've made a friend," Akeno says playfully, his hands slipping over her shoulders and interlocking over her torso. He leans his face in close to hers, their skin gliding together.

"I have," she says. "Mr. Du Pont, I'd like to introduce you to my friend."

"It's a pleasure," Akeno says, keeping his eyes on Neha.

"And you are?" Du Pont asks, though less with antagonism and more with interest. "You must be new."

"I am. She's helped break me in too. I didn't know there were so many rules and customs of the house. She's been a real delight."

Akeno's soft voice slides through Neha's hair, and Du Pont's eyes grow wild. Akeno can feel Neha blush beneath his touch but follows through with the act.

"He's been nothing but fun to have around," she says, bringing him around to sit on the other arm of the chair.

"I've found that she has rather good...taste," he says, remembering the word used to describe himself, and moving to the other side of the chair.

The man gives a brief laugh and waves the others around him away. A few of his friends leave, and the space becomes more private.

"How have you liked your stay so far?" Du Pont asks Akeno. "You know I helped design this house and all its grandeur."

"It's impeccable," Akeno says with an accentuated air. "The art, the style, it has so much grace. I always imagined the person who designed it must have been a genius."

"Class and talent are both something that's inherited. Either someone has it or they don't. I must have been born with a keen desire for the finer things." He eyes Neha and then Akeno. "Would you oblige me by fulfilling those desires?"

Akeno glances at Neha and then at Du Pont. "We'd be honored."

The man takes his hand off Neha as he forces himself to stand and steady himself. He grabs hold of Akeno's arm, and the two interlock. He holds Neha close on the other side of him, and it feels more like the two of them are holding this man up rather than leading him away. Akeno turns his head and catches Sam's eyes. She looks surprised and clearly impressed. She gives him a curt nod and turns the other direction. Ten minutes. They have ten minutes to get what they need. It's just a matter of how.

Thankfully there's an elevator, because Akeno wasn't sure they were going to be able to get this man up a flight of stairs. When the elevator opens, there's an elevator attendant.

Easy job, Akeno thinks.

Du Pont fishes a card out of his pocket and hands it to the attendant. He doesn't have to glance at it to know who he is. Two other couples and another throuple step inside with Du Pont, Akeno and Neha. The elevator is wide enough to fit more people, the mirrored wall on one side giving the impression that the elevator is even larger. When they reach the second landing, one couple gets off. When they reach the third landing, the others exit. The elevator attendant puts a key in the metal siding where the buttons have stopped glowing. He touches one of the top buttons, and the elevator begins to rise again. When it stops, they exit into a penthouse, the foyer enclosed by a metal gate, which the attendant unlocks for them again.

Akeno worries how Sam will reach them.

"You've never been to the top floor before, have you?" Du Pont asks the both of them.

"Can't say I knew it was here," Akeno remarks truthfully. "I suppose that's the privilege of being with the man who owns the place."

Du Pont grins hungrily, but it's hard to see anything attractive about a man that has to lean so heavily on his escorts to get into his room. Akeno would rather push the man down, take his key, and run, but somehow that doesn't feel right. If they're going to do this, they need to do it as planned, or at least as planned as Sam had it marked out to be. They couldn't leave the attendant as a witness. That then begs the question of how they'll be able to escape the penthouse. He wonders if Neha has any ideas about how this is all going to happen. He tries to catch her eye, but the man's too wide and on his side for Akeno to see over Du Pont's shoulder.

When they reach a room at the end of a hall, Akeno realizes there are multiple rooms with shut doors, all likely locked. There was security detail here, even if they were not in the room. There were no visible cameras in the room, but it was wishful thinking to believe they were truly alone.

Where's the bedroom? That's where they'll head first, Akeno thinks. He wonders if there's anything inside that he can use as a weapon or as a restraint. They'll need something to take this guy down. He might be top heavy, but he's still large enough to pummel Neha or Akeno. Akeno weighs only about one-sixty, and if he had to guess, Neha probably weighs less. It wouldn't take much to keep either of them down on the floor or on the bed. Akeno can feel the heat rising in his face as they enter the master bedroom suite.

Whatever Akeno thought they'd find inside is different than what he expected. Though the hotel is all gilded in white and gold, this room is all dark colors: black, gray, and deep purple. It looks like a fantasy room more than anything else, and Akeno can already guess what sort of acts Du Pont has in mind.

Akeno and Neha lead DuPont to a seat along the side of the room, where he falls back onto a loveseat. There's not anywhere else to sit except here. The rest of the space is open floor. There's an iron bar attached to the wall on the right and a concrete wall on the left with manacles hanging from chains.

"I didn't realize we were playing," Akeno says with a soft smile, trying to remain in character. He checked around the room, pretending to admire its contents, all the while looking for a safe. If the keycard wasn't in the man's clothes, it would be locked away somewhere private to access when he's ready to leave this place behind.

He picks up a cat-o-nine tails hanging from a wall, though without the barbs. Akeno had never seen anything like this before, and quite frankly, it made him squeamish thinking about what happened in here. How much blood would they find on the floor and walls if they shined a blacklight over the whole apartment? He imagines bodies being carted out of here, half alive and weeping for what was lost.

"I'm glad you recognize a few of my toys," the man says with relish. "Entertain me."

With the wide open spaces and all the toys spread throughout the room, it seems it's up to Akeno to create some fantasy.

"We have our lone princess here," Akeno says, taking Neha by the shoulders and leading her to the center of the room. "She's lost in the deep woods, her clothes partially torn from the brambles of the forest and her hair disheveled from the humidity." He rubs her hair and tangles it. She's tense, but she falls into character immediately.

"I've run away from home," she says with despair.

"She's scared and desperate." Akeno rubs his hands up her arms and over her shoulders. He can feel her skin tingle and can smell the sweat on her back. She's nervous, he can tell. "Play along, little princess." He drops his voice to a whisper. "Trust me."

He hopes this is enough to soothe her anxiety. She lets out a breath and relaxes her shoulders. "Please don't hurt me," she says in mock begging.

"You're in no place to be begging," Akeno shouts. He glances at Du Pont to see how he's taking it. The man's already unbuttoned his pants and has his hands down the front. Akeno quickly glances away and forces himself to retain his composure. He feels like he's going to be sick, but if he stops now, they're both ruined. If Du Pont's enjoying it, maybe he'll play along with anything.

"Take off your clothes," Akeno says, pointing at Du Pont.

Du Pont nods with enthusiasm, though he takes his time. Neha actually looks frightened when she looks at Akeno. He adjusts his gaze from her to him and stares at Du Pont. "Do as you're told. Quickly."

Du Pont falters for a moment but tentatively smiles with curiosity. He doesn't say anything, but he strips himself of his shirt and pants.

He's left wearing a thin undershirt, his underwear, and his socks. Akeno steps forward and places his hands on the man's knees. It's taking everything in him to keep from coughing. The stench rising from Du Pont's exposed body makes Akeno's stomach churn. He's glad that he didn't eat before.

"Are you ready to see what happens to the lost princess?" Akeno whispers.

"Yes, take her," Du Pont says back in earnest.

"Not yet, my lord," Akeno says with a hint of approbation. "Patience is what drives our pleasure. We must wait. We must watch her first."

Akeno tosses Du Pont's clothes over the couch, closer to the wall with the iron bar. "Walk," Akeno says, returning to Neha. He pushes her roughly to the iron bar. She stumbles and falls, and Akeno hopes it was on purpose. "Keep going!" Akeno shouts at Neha on the floor. She scurries across the ground and edges to Du Pont's clothes.

"My turn," Akeno says, bringing the focus back to himself. Akeno needs to improvise. Du Pont watches Akeno eagerly, his attention diverted from Neha. From where Du Pont's sitting on the sofa, he can't see much of her on the ground. He'll want her standing soon.

Akeno takes off his own shirt, exposing his skinny body underneath. If he was honest with himself, he lacked the confidence and the mind to do this outside of this room. He had only been with a handful of girls before this, so he lacked the experience entirely. He hated himself for being so frail, for losing what muscle he used to have before the blackout. Frankly he missed normality. Du Pont closes his eyes for a moment, relishing in the moment.

"We'll need something to chain you down," Akeno calls from across the room. "Can't have you squirming around," Akeno says, searching the room for restraints.

"Yes, tie her up," Du Pont encourages.

Akeno finds a long, thick rope curled up on a side table, along with a few crude metallic tools. He leaves those there and walks back across the room, his hands twisting the rope. "You're next, my lord. Now you are a prisoner, thrown into the same cell as our princess. There are no soldiers to keep watch. What happens in this cell is open game."

"Take me as your prisoner if you must," Du Pont says, reaching both hands out. Akeno can see the erection in his underwear and glances at Du Pont's hands. He tries not to touch them as he binds Du Pont's wrists together. Akeno ties them tight and watches as Du Pont finds pleasure in this small pain.

"Have you ever played prisoner before, my lord?" Akeno asks.

"If it means I get to spoil the princess, I'll do anything."

Akeno forces a smile. It's almost been ten minutes. As Akeno leads Du Pont to the iron bar, Neha stands and leans against the wall. She gives Akeno a look and he understands. "Come, prisoner. Your fate awaits you."

"Shouldn't the princess be tied to the bar?" Du Pont asks.

"The princess cannot escape a place she does not know. She is trapped here."

"Please, sire, please help me out of this cell," Neha interjects. "A gentleman like you can save me from this prison." Neha gets on her knees, imposing an idea into Du Pont's head.

"All right, I'll play," he says with a devilish grin. "As long as she remains on her knees."

Akeno loops the rope around the iron bar and secures it.

"Come, princess, and surely I can help you," Du Pont says.

"Can't help anyone while you're tied up," Neha says stoutly. She stands and kicks Du Pont in the groin. "Eat shit."

Du Pont cries out in pain, and Neha grabs Akeno's hand. "Let's go," she says.

Akeno grabs his clothes and Neha's. They race to the front door of the penthouse, leaving Du Pont in the bedroom. Neha pulls on the handle of the door, but it's locked from the outside. She starts to beat on the door mercilessly, but Akeno expected this. How many others have tried to escape this room and failed? Neha screams for help, but Akeno knows it's just as useless. The room is probably sound proofed too.

"Stupid, imbecilic children," Du Pont spits as he staggers into the main room. "You thought you could get away that easily?"

He laughs with derision, his voice echoing out across the room.

"After all this dramatic theatre, you actually thought you could just walk out the door?" Du Pont holds the rope binding his wrists. "Poor knot tying skills by the way. I wasn't going to say anything, but you looked so sure of yourself, I couldn't help but pity your attempt."

He laughs again, a sense of mania spilling into his voice. "Playtime is over. It's time we get to the real fun."

Du Pont grabs a long whip from a side table and turns the handle over and over in his hand, feeling for the strength that will come with the first lash. Akeno steps in front of Neha, his body entirely covering her own. "You can't take us both," Akeno says.

"I've taken more bodies than you can count, boy. You're nobody else." Du Pont reaches his arm back to crack the first lash. Akeno flinches his face away, preparing himself for the first blow when a shot rings out in the room. Akeno opens his eyes, expecting to find himself shot, or worse, that Neha had been shot. Instead, in front of him lay the crumbled body of Du Pont, his hand still gripping the whip, blood soaking into the rug beneath his still corpse. From the other side of the room, Sam stands with her arm still raised, a gun in her hands. Her whole body is trembling, but her face shows nothing but innate rage and hate. She lowers the gun and looks to Akeno and Neha, who stand motionless by the door, Akeno's body still shielding Neha from the room.

Sam doesn't say anything. She just turns and leaves the room. Akeno and Neha gather themselves and hurry after her. Akeno has Neha's hand in his own. He glances over his shoulder as they leave the penthouse through a narrow stairwell. Tears flow down her cheeks, but she doesn't say anything. She squeezes Akeno's hand as they take the hidden passage down. Quickly and quietly, the three of them half-run down the servants' hall. When they reach the steps, Sam leads the way. She exits on the first floor, and they slip into the kitchen. There's nobody in the room, and they make their way to the back door of the house, the same way they came in.

"He should be here," Sam says as she paces the floor. "He should be here, so where is he?" She nearly shouts, and Akeno can see that she's still shaking. She works her hands through her hair, the same way he does.

Neha sees her agitation and comes from behind Akeno and goes to Sam. Neha wraps her arms around her, pulling her head down to her shoulder and holding her there. Sam's arms wrap around Neha, and the two women hold each other for an unknown amount of time. Eventually Sam breaks into muffled sobs, her chest heaving. Neha doesn't say anything. She just holds her as tears stream down her face.

Akeno thinks back to that day in the field, her face after she shot her brother, her only choice in the wake of evil. He wishes he could have been there for her then, so he's glad to see she has someone now. He knows she'll remember this night for the rest of her life. They all will.

CHAPTER 21

A couple minutes later, Gabrio comes flying into the room, his fingers working off the tie he has on. Sam is pissed.

"Where have you been?" she demands.

"Never mind that," Gabrio says, gesturing to the door.

A car pulls up outside, its lights flashing twice in the darkness. Akeno's surprised to see an armored car with black windows waiting idly by the back exit. Gabrio breaks out the door to the alley, and the three of them follow. He opens the car door and gestures them inside. They get in the back as he moves to the front seat. In the driver's seat is Joanna, something serious weighing heavily on her expression, something she picked up as soon as Neha and Sam entered the vehicle. She doesn't ask any questions as she puts the car in drive.

They're all silent for a few minutes. Gabrio flips through something he's holding. It looks like a tablet, but it's encased in a hard black shell. Akeno wonders where he got it and where Kim got the car. He doesn't ask, though. It doesn't matter. They're here now.

"When we reach the dropoff point, all of you need to dive into the sewers," Joanna says, her voice even. "You'll cross the inner wall, and from there it's a straight shot to the outer wall. There will be others waiting for you when you get to the other side."

"What about you?" Akeno asks when nobody responds.

"I'll be doing my part on this end. Don't you worry about me." She gives a small smile, something that's meant to encourage Akeno and the others, but all he sees is doubt. "It's going to be fine, Akeno. We've already planned it all out."

Right, Akeno thinks. All of these plans he's supposed to trust.

As they cross a small bridge, Akeno makes out the towering gates at the end of the road, the golden arches intricately weaving a pattern. It's the only monument lit up at this time of night. Shadows move across the privacy wall, the lights blazing. Despite the beautiful design of the stone archway draping the gate, the decor feels fraudulent, a beacon of hypocrisy within Amity's walls.

Something in the car clicks and then suddenly stops.

"What's going on?" Gabrio asks.

"I don't know. I'm hitting the gas," Joanna says, panic rising in her voice. "The car isn't moving." Tires screech against the pavement, but the car is stuck in place.

"Everyone out!" Gabrio yells.

All four doors are flung open wide, and everybody spills out of the car. Akeno trips getting out. His face hits the pavement below, and he feels like he can hear something, a faint noise coming from below the bridge.

"Run!" Gabrio shouts, waving her arms wildly. "Everybody run!"

All of Akeno's adrenaline forces him up on his feet as they break from the car. Something metal clicks, and an explosion rings out from behind them. The impact sends Akeno flying. His body scrapes against the concrete. His flesh rips along with his clothes, his scorched back singing from the heat. He feels like he's on fire.

In a confused daze, he looks behind him to see the car engulfed in flames, the wave of heat crashing over him wave after wave. He feels the back of his neck, his fingers in his hair. Patches of his hair have been burnt to the scalp, and it hurts to touch. He can't grasp what's happening in the moment.

"Come on," someone yells from above him, but it sounds distant. He squints up into the darkness of the night. "Come on!" they shout even louder. It's Gabrio. His hands lift Akeno up, and he looks around. Sam and Neha have already crossed the bridge, their eyes focused on the sky above, at all the fire and smoke that towers above them.

They look so small from here, Akeno thinks.

Akeno looks behind them and sees Joanna's body on the ground. At first Akeno thinks she's dead, but then her head lifts up, and she sees Neha and Sam on the other side of the bridge. Then she sees Akeno and Gabrio on the other side of the bridge, adjacent to where they stand. She's able to push herself up on her knees, her back facing the edge of the bridge.

From behind them, hundreds of feet pound across the bridge, guns at the ready. Several people in black firebombing jackets come rushing through the flames. They're too close.

"Joanna!" Akeno shouts, tearing away from Gabrio and immediately falling. "Joanna, they're coming!"

She glances down at her legs, which Akeno realizes no longer exist. Everything from the calves down are gone, blown off her body. Akeno sees the expression on her face, a mark of sadness but with a touch of acceptance. She pulls a gun from her hip's holster and puts it to her head. She closes her eyes and turns the other way. Before Akeno can scream, she pulls the trigger, and her body collapses.

Through the ringing sound in his ears, he hears nothing at all. There's a silence that permeates his thoughts. He can feel his throat burning from his own screaming. His weight pulls him down. He can no longer see from the number of tears blinding his sight. He tries to make it back to her, just to hold her in her final moments, just so he could say goodbye, to thank her, but he can't.

He feels Gabrio lifting him up from the shoulders and pulling him across the bridge. It's easy for Gabrio to carry Akeno across the bridge. Akeno is so light. He's lost so much weight since coming to Amity. He's lost so much of everything.

When they reach the end of the bridge, Sam and Neha are already hurrying down the street. Sam pulls a crowbar from across her back and wedges it between the lip and the metal. Together they're able to prop the sewer lid up to slide it across the pavement and slip inside. They climb down the hole and disappear from sight.

Akeno can't feel anything. It's like something inside him has turned off. Everything he does is by his own memory of the motions. Gabrio urges him to climb down. He does, and Gabrio jumps in after them, pulling a flashlight from his belt. He flips it on and tells them to run, so Akeno runs. They're all moving away from death, away from the gate-keepers. They're heading for a life outside the walls. They're heading for safety.

Inside the back of Akeno's mind, he knows this isn't true.

They weren't in the sewers long, just long enough to get to the other side of the privacy wall. As they climb the ladder to the surface, there's a faint echo heard behind. The authorities coming for them, coming to finish the job. Akeno won't let that happen; he can't lose everyone tonight. He and Gabrio push the sewer lid back over its hole.

Sam and Neha stand off to the side, their bodies shaking from the shock and fear of tonight. Sam wails into Neha's shoulder, her body shaking. Neha cries too, though softly as she holds Sam. "She's gone," Sam repeats over and over again. "She's gone, just gone. She's just—"

Akeno doesn't know what to say or how to feel. He looks idly on, his rage burning within him. It shouldn't have happened like this. They shouldn't have lost anyone. His chest is heaving as he recalls what happened only moments ago, how they're standing here now, one less person with them.

"How did this happen?" Akeno shouts at Gabrio, turning on him. "I thought you had everything planned out, every little detail, remember?"

"I just...didn't know," Gabrio says, his voice sounding hurt, remorseful. "I wish I had known. If I had, she would have – There was no discussion of a bomb on the bridge. It must have been a last ditch effort, a fluke..."

Gabrio stares off into the distance, his hands on his hips, his voice breaking as grief overtakes him too. He turns away from them all. Akeno's lower lip trembles, like a child, his emotions carrying him further than they have in years. All his pain returns, suddenly and overwhelmingly, his fists shaking as his chest racks itself with grief. He conjures up the faces of Sandy and Hugh, his memories of them resurfacing. He locks Joanna's face away -- her kindness, her stability, her reassurance in the face of trouble. For the sake of justice, she never waivered.

"Why did she kill herself?" Akeno asks, his voice speaking for them all. Sam and Neha look away, their eyes downcast.

"She wouldn't have made it," Gabrio says, turning back to face them, his eyes and voice even. "She was losing a lot of blood, and there was no one around to save her. If the soldiers had managed to save her life, they would have only made her pay that mercy back with more blood. They wouldn't have let her go, not with everything she knows."

"She'd have gotten away."

Gabrio shakes his head. "You don't know how many people we've seen taken and returned back to us–" He chokes back another sob. "They come back in pieces, as a threat to us. She knew what the stakes were."

"It wouldn't have been the ending she deserved," Sam says.

A brief silence follows. Akeno feels the burning in his lungs, his eyes sore, his body aching all over. Everything hurt, but this wasn't the end. Not yet.

"Gabrio, look--" Neha's voice trails off as people's heads poke out from upper-level windows, their eyes upon them. .

The four of them tentatively walk further down the open street and away from the sewer, the golden gate dividing them now behind them, a faint glow in the dark. Gabrio leads the way, but it's obvious where they're going next. Straight ahead is the concrete monolith that keeps everyone in, the great outer wall.

The wall is much larger than he remembers some fifteen months ago. He remembers the way he saw it the first time. He came here unwillingly, forced here by others wanting to keep him in. At first he felt fear. Now all he feels is resentment. He gazes upon the great wall once again, his imagination soaring beyond its height, its imprisonment from the open fields beyond. The sprawling desert, the sunrise over the horizon, the sound of running water in a nearby creek. It was all he longed for. That fantasy seemed far away, though, like a forgotten memory. He urged that feeling to take hold again, but as lightly as a butterfly's wings, the memory vanished. In its stead was the bite of doubt, insecurity, and instability. He wanted nothing more than to exist and want only what he needs, but how could he accomplish such a feat on his own? Where could he go? Who lay await out there to attack him when he grew weak? Could mere routine, a gruesome and back-breaking routine, distract him from the reality of it all?

He is not free, nor is he imprisoned. He is not bound to these walls, yet he longs to stay within their confines. He is bound to himself, the only body he has and the only life he leads. How much could he handle before he breaks?

At the end of the street, Gabrio stops and lets out a low whistle. The others stop short behind Gabrio and wait. They peer up at the wide, flat-topped buildings around them. Faces of all shapes, sizes, and colors peer out from the windows on the buildings. Another low whistle answers him back. Slowly, a few people come out of the buildings one by one, some of them armed, to ensure that it's safe. Gabrio replies to the call, and the people facing him break out in smiles. They whistle again, this one a collective, high-pitched eighth beat that came across as a victory cry, its resonance striking at Akeno's heart as the cheer continues.

People begin to flood the streets, some of them carrying small bags, others not carrying anything at all. From a distance, they look like short people, but then he realizes who they are: children. They're all children except for a few adults scattered between, some of them holding hands and one carrying a baby not much older than two-years-old.

"Why are there so many kids?" Sam asks.

"They're leaving this place with you guys," Gabrio says, eyeing the street behind them.

The edge of the wall is not far from where they stand. Gabrio hurries over and taps a space set into the concrete wall. There's a handle connecting to a metal door that blended in with the concrete surrounding it. Gabrio wonders where the soldiers are amid all these people. He wonders if there were any bodies. They may be hidden in a shallow grave behind the buildings. Akeno sees a toddler staring in his direction. The child's black curls don't grow past his forehead, his thumb in mouth, staring back at Akeno with one blackened eye.

Sam and Neha hurry behind Gabrio. Neha pulls a card from her

356

pocket, the one prize that nearly cost them dearly, and slides it across an electronic box by the door. Its electronic face barely glows through the mass of gray. A heavy lock clicks, and the seal of the door breaks with a hiss. Gabrio slips inside. Sam and Neha slide in after him, leaving Akeno standing in the cold of the night.

He glances around and sees the others are waiting for him to enter first. Despite their desperate need to escape, they expect him to lead the way. He is their guide to their freedom. He hurries inside, where there's an interior room inset with another, second-defense door. There's a keypad that keeps glowing red as Gabrio fervently types a variety of codes. Akeno sees the screen flash red with each incorrect answer. The other adults on the outside, likely comrades of Gabrio's, usher in the children as quickly as they can. One of them speaks in several languages, her voice calling out the same phrase to the multiethnic kids pushing each other to get inside: Hurry, *prisa, Isoide, Cōngmáng, jaldee keejiye,* 𝕏𝕏𝕏𝕏 𝕏𝕏𝕏.

"You don't know the passcode?" Sam shouts impatiently.

Akeno turns to face the situation at hand.

"If I didn't know the passcode, I wouldn't have brought you all this way," Gabrio grits through his teeth.

From behind them, gunshots ring out, and the children scream.

"Shit," Gabrio mutters, whirling around. "Get everyone inside!"

It was a very small space, one that would not fit everyone else, but Gabrio would make everyone fit in the box if he could. Someone shuts the door most of the way as someone else ushers more and more children inside, shielding the children from injury. Gabrio types out a few codes more tries as children swarm into the small space, pressing Akeno back against Neha and Sam. More gunshots ring out on the other side of the exterior wall, and the children scream again, the terror palpable at such a close proximity. Gabrio swipes the card again just as the screen flashes red. It beeps, pauses, something clicks, and the light turns green.

Gabrio pushes the door wide open and draws his weapon. From its shape, Akeno thinks it must be a standard semi-automatic handgun, the same gun that all the soldiers carry in their holsters. Gabrio enters the room first. Sam draws her own and enters next, right behind him at a diagonal cross to cover the other half of the room. From the momentum of Gabrio's push, the door swings back, almost closing them off entirely from the interior room.

The exterior door slams shut at the same time, the metal clicking in place, locking them in. More bullets ring out against the metal door. Flashes of light and sound burst from the darkness in the interior room. The noise combined deafens Akeno and the kids too, whose wailing can't be heard above the din.

Neha draws close to Akeno, waiting expectedly for someone to appear in the doorframe. They don't have any weapons to guard themselves, nothing they could use to shield their bodies. They're completely defenseless, left to the mercy of God or fate. What happens now?

In a moment of held breath, Sam reappears from around the side of the door, her face ashen but determined. "Let's go," she says. "We're almost there."

Akeno brushes his way past Sam and into the larger room as the kids flood inside. Most of them are young, but he sees the faces of some kids who have already hit puberty. One of them carries the 2-year-old that the woman had been holding. The baby is wailing, but Akeno can barely hear it.

There's a metal staircase that leads up the wall. Akeno watches as the many footsteps climb the looming shadow that leads to the top. There's a slam of the inner door, closing them off to the outside. Gabrio hurries to the keypad on this side of the door and quickly types in a four digit code. There's another click and a green light. Gabrio sighs with relief.

"They changed the codes. I can't believe they could do it that quickly. But they didn't change their algorithm." He winks at Akeno and gestures to the stairs. Leading at the top is Sam, her ponytail bobbing up and down as she hurries the fastest kids along after her.

Gunshots ricochet off the interior metal door and echo inside the large room. Some of the kids stop to look down at the door, but they resume when they see the door is still locked, for now. To Akeno's right, bodies lay scattered, but it's too dark to make out if they're dead or alive.

Gabrio leans heavily against the wall, his hand clutching his leg.

"You're bleeding," Akeno says, immediately crouching down on one knee. Akeno glances down and sees Gabrio's hand is covered in blood.

"No shit," Gabrio says with a clipped laugh. "I'll be okay. It's just skin deep, no biggie. Nothing some quick salve, a bandage, and a beautiful nurse can't fix."

"I'm no beautiful nurse," Akeno says as he quickly pulls off the grimy, white button up shirt he was wearing for the party. He wears a mostly clean, black undershirt. He rips off a sleeve and wraps it tight around Gabrio's leg, just above the wound in his thigh. Akeno takes the second sleeve and repeats. He reaches behind Gabrio's thigh, and Gabrio stifles a groan and a laugh.

"Not too frisky now," he says.

"The bullet is still in your leg," he says in a clipped tone. "There's no exit wound."

"Go," Gabrio says. "I'm fine. I can stay here. I still have bullets."

Akeno looks at Gabrio, his face a blend of emotions. Tears build in Akeno's eyes, but Gabrio is stone-faced. "Go. Don't let all this be for nothing. Get these kids out of here."

Akeno can't stand the idea of abandoning him, not like this, not after all that he'd done for them. He can't go, not him and Joanna too.

There's a tight clench in his chest as he stands, looking at the stairwell. From the other side of the interior door is a loud banging. They're trying to breach the door. He understands what needs to be done.

Gabrio reaches out his hand, and Akeno grasps it. He clasps his free hand around his own and Gabrio's bloody one. Akeno lifts Gabrio to a standing position and hauls one arm around his shoulder. Gabrio motions to the other side of the room. They cross the space between the walls, hollow, Akeno realizes, despite its image of solidity. Akeno supports Gabrio as he limps across the room, his leg dragging feebly behind him. Gabrio stretches out and flips himself against the wall, his back leaning firmly against it. He faces the doorway, his angle a direct shot at anyone who enters.

"Take this," Gabrio says, pulling a spare handgun from his belt. "It might save your life, so here, take it."

Akeno holds it gently, then with a firm grip as he tucks it firmly along his back.

"Don't die on me," Akeno says. "See you soon."

"Yeah, see you soon," Gabrio shouts after Akeno, who takes the stairs two at a time up twenty-five flights of stairs.

Most of the others are closer to the top, but a few straggle far behind Sam and the other kids. Akeno rushes to catch up.

He feels claustrophobic inside this metal hole in the wall. When he looks up, it feels like the walls are falling inward, as if they might crash on top of him and everyone else at any moment. His head spins. For a moment, he thinks of all the bodies within these walls, all of them forming a mass grave. The thought jars him awake. He pushes himself to go faster.

He approaches the first fallen kid. Malnourishment and neglects wrecks her skinny frames and thin wrists. She clutches at the stairway's bars, willing herself to keep going, but she's unable to continue on their own. Akeno kneels beside the child and takes her hand in his. She clutches his fingers, her half-lidded eyes on Akeno's face.

"I'm here to help you," he says. "We're getting you out of here."

She smiles and closes her eyes. Akeno lifts her gently into his arms, his one hand bigger than her both her thighs combined. He sees another girl slow down significantly further ahead.

"I'm coming!" Akeno calls after her. She looks down and waits for him. He adjusts the other girl as he kneels down. "Can you climb on my back?" he asks.

The girl gently climbs on his back, keeping her head protectively against his shoulder as he bounces her up and locks one arm, then the another, around the krooks of her knees.

From down below, the pounding against the inner door commences. They're getting closer to breaking through. They need to get to the top. The faster Akeno goes, the faster they're safe. Akeno pushes the thought of Gabrio from his mind. His focus right now is getting these kids to the top of the wall. From there, he isn't sure what will happen next.

Up ahead, there's a loud clatter as metal slides open and slams against the ceiling of the room, the top of the wall. Moonlight spills onto the stairway, clearing up the dimly lit space. From six flights down, he can see Sam moving through the latch first. Neha is behind her, and the two help each other lift the kids through the hole in the ceiling.

If Akeno could capture this moment, from a different vantage point, it would appear as if the hands of God were giving her children over to the woman in the wall, an evil caricature of the feminine divine. Nevertheless, from six flights down, he merely saw two women delivering the next generation to the open world, their careful hands hosting them up into the boundless sky.

A line starts to form, and Akeno urges the crowd to keep moving, despite how exhausted the last half of the kids look. He sees a little boy leaning his head against the stairway, and he takes hold of his hand.

"Come on, kiddo. You're almost there," Akeno says.

"I don't know where my daddy is," he says with a whimper. "He's not here."

"It's gonna be okay," he says, adjusting the first child in one arm and lifting the third child in his free arm. The little girl in his right arm peers over at the boy, her thumb in her mouth. The two of them look at each other a long time before the boy finally lets his head drop against Akeno's shoulder too, listening to his beating heart race as he climbs the last steps.

When they reach the top, Akeno hands the girl over to Neha first, who clings mercilessly to her. "Come on, babe, we have to get you up to the top. They're waiting for you."

She starts to cry as the others from above pull the girl through the top. Akeno hands the little boy to Neha, who doesn't say anything as he's lifted into Sam's arms. The last one offers to jump in order to help Neha lift her. Neha smiles through closed lips and consents to her plan. She jumps high, and Neha lifts her the rest of the way, as Sam takes hold of both her hands. She screams in delight, for a moment forgetting all that is happening to her.

Sam peers down at the two of them, her hands at the ready to help pull Neha up. She jumps once, then twice. Sam grabs Neha at her forearms, and Akeno hurries to stabilize Neha's feet, which hang limply.

They make contact with Akeno's hands, and she jumps off them, his fingers pushing her to the stretch of his height. She doesn't scrape the edge of the opening as she climbs out.

Akeno follows after with as much grace as he can muster, his whole body aching as he grabs onto Sam and Neha's reach. They pull him to the surface, his feet kicking at air as he sees the helmets of military men on the stairs. He didn't even notice the breach in the interior door. As his knees make contact to the lip of the opening, he pushes off and slams the metal door shut behind him. Sam kicks the door's latch until it bends at a sharp angle.

His ears finally tune in as the engine of a helicopter whirs to life behind him. Suddenly there's a gust, then a flash of hot air. Akeno shields his eyes from dust as debris flies everywhere in a swirling flume. "What the hell?" Akeno shouts through the noise.

"Look," Sam shouts back, pointing behind him.

Akeno manages to look and peers through his windblown hair with one hand still guarding his eyes. Hovering before him some sixty yards away are two helicopters. The first has its engines on, and the other is starting to rev itself down as it turns off its blades. Akeno finally manages to look around and sees the group of kids standing around people dressed in black, their faces mixed shades of brown. Akeno grins and can't help but laugh.

Ingenious, he thinks. He didn't know what to expect when he got to the top of the wall. Gabrio had explained the highlights, but he never thought it could actually happen. He thought by now he'd be dead or arrested. He expected something to go wrong, for something to end their journey short, but here was now: a witness to the escape from the city of Amity.

There's a call to the wind, a sound indistinguishable to Akeno's un-

363

trained ears, but Neha hears it. She turns, and the wind blows back her long, dark hair, which she has tied low at the nape of her neck. She grins, cups both hands around her mouth and returns the call. Akeno turns, searching for the person she's called to.

Sam ushers the rest of the kids off to the vehicles waiting to fly them out of here. The people in black are placing helmets on the kids' heads. Many of them are excited by the helicopters, but so many of them are terrified. Akeno wonders where their parents are, if any of them are still within the walls, or if they're kids just like him, wandering the world alone. And yet, they're not alone, he thinks. They have people who care about them, who are willing to sacrifice their lives for the lives of these kids, all the people here now.

A few people in black ask Sam questions, but she just shakes her head, her eyes glancing over her shoulder as a woman runs across the wall, past Sam, dressed in dark clothes like the others. Sam makes a motion like she'll step between the woman and Neha, but Neha gives her no chance. Neha runs past Akeno and throws her arms around the unknown woman, their lips kissing each other multiple times on the same cheek. They pull back and take each other in. They're speaking to each other quickly and without pause. The woman's hair is long and dark like Neha's, though it's braided down the length of her back and past her waist. Akeno notices the high cheekbones, the strong jawline, the circular shape of the woman's face, and the angle of her nose. She's several inches shorter than Neha, but their eyes are on each other.

Akeno smiles. Despite everything, this is what Neha looks like when she's happy. There's a flash of jealousy in Sam's eyes as she comes to Akeno's side, and the two stand awkwardly together. The wind blows loudly on top of the wall, and it's hard to make out anything the two women are saying. Neha glances back at Akeno and Sam. She says something quick to the woman, and the two of them run over, their voices shouting against the wind.

The woman gives no preamble as she locks her arms around both Sam's and Akeno's necks at the same time. Akeno and Sam both have to crouch down for the hug to work.

"You have saved my sister, and for that I am grateful," she shouts in their ears.

She takes a step back, releasing them, and grins. She says something quick to Neha before she runs to the helicopter to help load the last of the kids into the carrier.

"Who is that?" Sam asks.

"That's Waynoka," Neha says breathlessly. "She's from my sister tribe. They were the ones who took me in," Neha replies. "That's my best friend. She and I were inseparable before I had to leave the camp."

Sam nods, understanding and smiles. "It was nice to finally meet her."

"Wait, so these are your friends?" Akeno shouts.

"Yeah, they're with me," she says. "They're why I came here."

"I never knew," Akeno says.

"We just met!" she says with a laugh he had never heard before. It was all-encompassing, and Akeno wishes he only had more time to learn more about her. He smiles, and she says, "I'm glad we met. You've really proved yourself in ways I never thought people could. Thank you." She grips Akeno's hands. "I wish you'd come with us. We could use you on our team."

"Time to go," Sam says, nodding to the far side of the wall. Each section of the wall is separated by command towers. Both towers are dark, but from the curve of the wall beyond the west tower, dark figures move through the night, on their way to where the helicopters landed.

She's not saying what's on his mind. She doesn't ask where Gabrio is or what happened to him. She knows she won't make it on the helicopters. Then again, Gabrio never said he'd be someone leaving. He didn't speak for anyone else.

"You've got to go," Akeno says to Sam and Neha. "Get to safety and take care of yourselves." He rushes forward and takes them both in for a hug, like Waynoka. "Hurry, before they take off."

The blades of the helicopter begin to pick up speed again, the wind picking up rhythm as the vehicles prepare for flight.

"Wait, what are you saying?" Sam shouts over the din of the noise. "You're not coming?"

"No, I can't. I have to stay here."

"No, you don't," Sam shouts over the din of the helicopter's heavy blades whipping through the air, creating another windstorm. "Leave with us!"

Akeno shakes his head. "There's no time for this! You need to get on those planes now!"

"So that's it then? You're just leaving us?" Sam shouts.

"Never." He takes hold of Sam and Neha's hands. "It's been the best time of my life, but I have to go back. I have to help Gabrio, or at least finish what he started here. I have to help the others, our friends." He turns his head down against the wind as tears sting his eyes. When he looks back up, Neha and Sam have the same looks on their faces. "I just know it's what I have to do. I can't just leave these people here."

"What about us?" Sam shouts. "We need you too."

He smiles, a true and humble smile at the sound of those words. "It's not that either," he says. "I've spent my whole life just taking what life gave me. I can't just sit back anymore and do nothing. I have to do something, *anything*. I have to fight. I have to help."

366

"You just helped save all these kids, all these people," Sam says, the tears streaming down her cheeks. "Who else are you wanting to save?"

"Everyone," he says with a smirk. "Now go! Before it's too late." He pulls them both in for a longer hug, Akeno's face pressed between both of their shoulders. "Please, take care of yourselves and each other. Make sure the kids get to where they're going, and if you can, be happy, for me." He pulls away, tears brimming his eyes. He wipes them impatiently away.

"Akeno," Neha says. There's a tinge of pain in her voice, but also of pride. She smiles. "This isn't the end."

"No, it's not," Sam says, pulling Akeno in for one final hug. She plants a kiss on his cheek, short and quick. "We'll come back for you. Stay alive in the meantime."

He smiles and hugs her one last time. "Thank you for pulling me after you. I didn't know I needed it at the time, but I did. You helped save me."

"You've found redemption in Hell?" Sam shakes her head, a laugh playing in her eyes. "We'll be back for you. Go find Gabrio, and if you can, tell him we'll be in touch."

The first helicopter starts its takeoff, its wheels rolling along the wall's paved ground, dust from the desert parting as the blades spin faster and faster. Sam and Neha run to the last helicopter just as the first begins to rise into the air. Two hands grab Neha, then Sam, and they're both lifted on board. The black doors close behind them as they rise into the air.

Akeno waves frantically from the ground, his arms swinging wide. He sees two shadows peer through the passenger windows, and then they're gone. He watches as the noise and sensation of a chopper pass over the vast expanse of sand, headed for the mountains he can't see.

There's not much light coming from the moon, but the clouds are thin. There's a moment of silence, and then the quick sound of gunfire as soldiers from the other side of the command towers start shooting into the sky. He finally brings his arm down and comes to a crouch. After a moment, the vehicle disappears from sight altogether, the blades' sound dimming.

The air stops churning; the night falls quiet. The wall stretches all around him. There's a brief static moment around him as the moment settles. He feels oddly out of place, alone. For the first time in over a year, he finally takes the time to feel the wind through his hair. No longer does the wind break itself against the walls, shielding him from its cool touch. He breathes in its scent, knowing he'll miss this feeling of euphoria. Gabrio said there would be this moment of pure relief. He's glad he could be here to take it all in, a feeling becoming a memory he'll only cling to later.

A loud crash echoes behind him, and his abused nerves jump at the sound. The soldiers continue to beat on the doors leading down to the stairwell. There are more soldiers trying to break into the command towers from further down the wall on either side. He doesn't know what the resistance had done to curtail the soldiers, but he hopes their methods were sound, otherwise they were going to break through both towers and leave him surrounded. He feels the panic rising inside him, but as quickly as it comes, he drives the feeling away and replaces it with a sense of purpose. He backs against one of several cement barricades on top of the wall. He slips behind one, so he remains unseen from either command tower, should the soldiers come spilling out at any moment. He keeps his eyes on the closest command tower before finally turning to look out over the city.

Just for a moment, there's a slight catch in his chest as he lets out a small exclamation at the sight before him. He takes in an immense spread of lights twinkling over the darkness below. The lights along the wall are dim, but they're clear enough for aircraft to see – an ironic aide to the mission – forming an oval-shaped bowl around the city of Amity. From this height, he would think Amity is a magical city shining bright in the midst of an abandoned desert, the chosen people living within the promised land. And yet it was divided into uneven pieces, a jigsaw puzzle designed to feel ungratifying when the whole picture comes together. There's a sense of failure here; there's no pride in unproportionate division. These dividers separate the people, alienating whole populations.

To the right was where they had come, where the lights shone the brightest, the party ongoing at the mansion. There was no sleep tonight. Surely, they must have heard about tonight, and yet they continued to drink, eat, fuck, and rest peacefully, knowing they'll never be held accountable in a city like this. To the left, where the lights were dimmer but numerous together. This was where Sam, Neha, and Joanna had spent their lives over the past year. He didn't realize how large their portion of the city is until he looked out at it from this angle. There were so many people crammed together in that place, hiding behind the interior walls that divide the lights in clear sections. Large sections of Amity were dark, the vastness of the night stretching out to the wall's end, which he could not clearly see. By now it was lights out for everyone in his block, soldiers included. They were told it must be completely dark to preserve the energy of the commonwealth. What a scam that was, he thinks. Then, his friends. Church and Heinz are likely asleep, wondering where he and Gabrio are. A missing persons report was probably filed on Akeno, considering he never checked back in with his block. Gabrio was always missing, but he never got marked for it. Now he knows why. He got away with everything. He planned it all. Time was almost up. It's the middle of the night, but he isn't tired. Not here.

He glances back at the command towers, the pounding increasing as the soldiers attempt to break down the doors from the other side. He can hear their shouting as they call commands to ram the doors at once. They must be locked tight. Good. That would hold for now.

He checks his surroundings, searching for the escape route Gabrio had described, but he can't make it out, at least it isn't evident.

That's the point, he thinks, hearing Gabrio's voice in his head.

Akeno rushes between concrete block after block, his eyes frantically searching for the one thing he needs to see tomorrow.

Then he sees what he didn't expect: bodies. There's a pile of them off to one side of the block facing the nearest command tower. They're unmoving, and he sees what appears to be dried blood on their uniforms. He thinks of Neha's friend, Waynoka, a short girl full of smiles and love for her returned friend. Did she help drag these bodies here? Had she helped hide the evidence of what their unit had done, to save the scene from the kids? Had she taken one or several of their lives? He wants to puke, but he can't. He hasn't eaten anything most of the day. He gags and turns away, his heart rate increasing by the second. He needs to get out of here.

He turns to go when a hand reaches out and grabs his ankle. Akeno muffles a scream, jumping back in abject horror, his ankle shaking free of the hand's grip. He peers down at the bloody hand reaching out to him from the pile of bodies. He follows the hand up the arm, his eyes treading the path where blood had flowed down his skin. He reaches the source -- a large cut on the underside of the arm. It looks like the attacker was aiming for an artery and missed. Above the cut is a shoulder buried beneath someone's leg, the face of the hand propped up on someone's stomach. Akeno nearly falls backward when he recognizes the fallen soldier's face. Kevin pleads with him, his eyes barely open as he moans something Akeno can't hear.

"Help me," he whispers.

Akeno hesitates. All his memories come rushing back from the year before. He remembers who he encountered tonight, the whole family, each with different purposes. He remembers why he was in Amity, who had left him alone the first week of the blackout and who had recruited him into his father's trafficking ring. Michael Howard had attacked him earlier that day, his fate left unknown after Sam saved his life. Joanna Howard had saved everyone tonight, her fate decided by nobody but herself. Kayla Howard was home safe, according to Gabrio, a precautionary detail he had taken to prevent Kayla from following us into the heat of tonight. Then there's Kevin, half-alive and begging for help.

He gulps down bile and makes a split-second decision. Who is he going to be? If he doesn't know now, he'll never find out.

He kneels down and takes Kevin's hand as he pulls him out from under the first body. He's heavy, though, and Akeno is exhausted from the last twenty-four hours. He grits his teeth and pulls harder on Kevin's arm.

Kevin groans as his body shifts to expose the upper half of his body. There's a long cut in his side, another wound that's dried, a good sign that he isn't bleeding out. He finds Kevin's other hand and takes it, dragging half of his body out from underneath the others. Akeno couldn't bring himself to touch the dead, a lost sacrament of respect for the fallen, but one he'll keep nonetheless.

"Come on, big guy. You've got to push yourself out," Akeno groans.

Kevin's feet find traction as he presses against the flesh of his fallen comrades.

So much for respect, Akeno thinks, pulling Kevin off the side to another concrete block, resting his back against it.

As soon as he leaves Kevin sitting upright, his good arm moves swiftly to his side and pulls a gun, its barrel aimed directly in front of him.

Akeno blanches and immediately throws both hands up. He looks over Kevin's body, which is in worse shape than he initially thought. He's beat up pretty badly, and it looks like an ankle is twisted by the angle that it's laying. Akeno helped him, but Kevin's fatigues clearly represent which side of this fight he's chosen. Akeno berates himself. This might be it. Then he notices the shaking gun. He might still have a chance to get himself out of this.

"Come on, Kevin. Don't do this."

"Shut up!" Kevin shouts. "Shut up!" He points the gun at Akeno, his arm shaking from the effort it takes for him to shout. "You don't get to--You don't get to tell me what happens next. You don't get to talk your way out of this."

"So what happens next then?" Akeno asks, his confidence returning like an ebbing tide.

"You're going to shoot me?"

"They're coming," Kevin grins, a maniacal look gleaming in his eyes, and his teeth are caked in fresh blood. His face is a dark mess of dried blood. "Once they come, they get to choose what happens to you."

There's a quiet moment.

"Kevin, you're the one holding the gun. Right now you get the choice."

He clenches it tighter, shifting it uneasily in his hand.

"Why are you doing this?" Akeno asks. "What about where we began? We were *roommates* before all this shit. What happened to that?"

"Don't pretend. We were never just roommates, at least not to you." Kevin spits. "I saw the way you looked at me. You must think I'm an idiot. Anyone could have seen it. I ignored it, though, to keep the peace.""

"Whose peace?"

Kevin clenches his teeth. "I don't care," he grits through his teeth. "It's over now. They'll be here to take you away, and it won't matter at all."

"What doesn't matter?"

"You, you won't matter."

"Is that what you think of me?" Akeno asks. "Or is that what you're telling yourself?"

Kevin's hand shakes harder.

"You don't have to do this."

"It's my orders," he snaps. "And it's personal now."

"Why?"

"I heard what you did to my dad," he says. "I got the call right before your *friends* killed my friends."

"Did you hear the part about your dad threatening to rape and murder two women as soon as he was done killing me? Was that a part of the memo?"

"Shut up!"

"Your father was a monster," Akeno shouts. "I know it because I was forced to come here, and you know it too 'cause you helped him!" He sees Kevin's shaking harder now, though the anger begins to shift, and Akeno takes the leap. "I thought we were friends, man."

Kevin's body racks itself with convulsions as he coughs up a fresh spurt of blood in his mouth. He spits it out, and Akeno knows the damage is great. Internal bleeding, likely in the stomach or maybe in the lungs.

"Why'd you do it? Why'd you sell me out?" Akeno shouts.

Kevin shakes his head, tipping it back against the wall, as he steadies the aim of his gun. Then he shrugs. "It was you or the family."

"No, it was him or me," Akeno says. "Your mother told me everything."

"You're lying. You don't know my mother."

"I've known her all along. That night, before I was chased in the rain by your father, your mother told me there was space for you, Kayla, and her. He was the only one going to be left behind. He didn't want that to happen, so he went to the extreme."

"You don't know—"

"She knew what he was, what he knew, and what he planned to do with me, and she didn't want him around her kids."

"Stop!"

"She loved you, Kevin, and you broke her heart."

Kevin releases a shot, and Akeno's eyes close for a moment, the sound reverberating through his ears, down his spine, and into his toes. For a moment, he thinks he's in shock, that he can't feel the bullet because his body doesn't know how to respond. He slowly peers down at himself, his eyes scanning his body for blood, his own limbs shaking.

Then he sees Kevin's gun pointed at the sky, tears streaming down his grimy face. He drops the gun at his side. Akeno feels overwhelmed as he kicks the gun away and kneels down close to Kevin. All the sounds die away, and Kevin's eyes open to face Akeno.

"I'm sorry," he says. "I didn't--My mother. Where is she? Is she okay?"

Akeno chokes back a sound. He merely shakes his head as tears splash on the concrete. "She, uh, fought up until the very end. She fought defending others." He wipes his tears and smiles. "She saved so

374

many lives tonight. So many lives."

Kevin doesn't say anything, doesn't move. He drops his chin to his chest as he stares listlessly at the ground. "And Kayla?"

"Safe," Akeno says. "She's home, safe."

Kevin doesn't move his gaze from the ground. "I can't die here, Akeno."

"I know, and you're not going to."

"I've got to get home to my sister."

"Yeah, you do."

"She needs me."

"Yes, she does."

"Help me see her again," he pleads.

"Help me get off this wall, and I can."

He shakes his head. "I don't know any other way."

"Where's the air vent?"

He looks puzzled but points behind him. "They're on the south side of every command tower. They're bolted shut, though. You'll need tools...or a gun." He glances at the gun on the ground, out of reach from either of them. "I can't go in there with you."

"I know, but once I'm in, your friends will come to save you."

He shakes his head. "They're not my friends."

"They'll save one of their own."

"They won't reach me in time."

"Yes, they will. Just trust me."

"If that's all it takes..."

"That's all it takes."

Akeno suddenly jumps up and grabs Kevin's gun. He runs to the farthest command tower. There's pounding coming from within the tower's walls. They're close to breaking it down. He can see the exterior giving way as they beat it down. As he comes closer to the tower, he can make out the thin steam the vent leaks out into the cool night sky. He glances back at the exterior doors leading inside the command tower. There's a keypad next to it, not unlike the one they used to get inside the wall. He pulls out the gun Gabrio had handed him and turns his attention away from the keypad. He takes a firm stance and concentrates, his eyes focusing in on the corners of the vent. Gabrio knew he'd be a bad shot, but it was the only way out. It was nearly fool-proof, Gabrio explained. His voice echoes in his mind again. He unloads the chamber onto the vent's sealed corners, his aim steadied down on the grate.

The bullets resonate against the interior of the vent as they hit the back of the shaft. He clicks until the chamber is empty, then he checks the number of bullets in Kevin's own gun. He'd only used that one bullet to shoot into the sky. The rest of the chamber was full. He glances behind him at Kevin. He has to do this now or never.

He stows the empty gun in his belt and yanks the edge of the vent hard enough to loosen the corner. It bends and cracks until the bottom corner pops off. He pulls harder and the bottom corner of the other side snaps, leaving room wide enough for Akeno to squeeze himself into. He climbs into the shaft, feet first, his body landing lightly onto the bottom of the metal vent. He feels its stability and hopes it works. He feels his feet connect and lets his weight drop. At his full height, he's able to adjust the vent back where it was originally, in an effort to disguise his escape route. He isn't finished though.

He jumps back up on the edge of the shaft, his chest leaning heavily on the thin metal lining. The metal cuts into him, leaving a deep impression on his skin with half his weight leaned heavily on it as he positions himself to take him. He reaches his right arm out, Kevin's gun in his hand. He hears the soldiers barging against the doors, the exterior holding true after all this time. He angles his aim at the keypad and unloads his gun into it. The first two bullets miss, but one meets its mark. A red glow emanates on the screen, and then it turns black as the doors cluck to release. Akeno jumps back inside the vent and replaces the cover as feet storm onto the wall.

As he works his way inside the vent, the metal walls grow close. He slides himself down the shaft until he's on all four limbs, his knees sliding against the metal of the vent, his hands sweaty from the damp heat that blows out of it. He can't see the end of the shaft, but he knows it must be there somewhere. From above, he hears the soldiers shouting, their voices angry, bewildered and amazed. They shout a code, and Akeno can hear the words "send for help" and "we got a live one." He exhales with relief and continues to move deeper into the vents.

The path ends at a gaping, black hole. It blows hot air through Akeno's hair, the dirt and dust sticking to his lashes. On the other side of the vertical shaft, the path ends at a wall leading up. It must lead to another vent on the tower's top. It wouldn't be a bad idea to use that as an exit should all else fail. He could always come back, or so he hopes.

He carefully positions himself to slide downwards. He's stretched so that he's hoping to control the descent as much as he can. He lowers himself into the depths. He can't see the moonlight anymore, and it grows immensely dark. His breathing intensifies as he continues to lower himself into the shaft. He wonders what would happen if he just dropped. His muscles ache; his lungs burn, and he can't see. Sweat drips down his back and his hair, his shirt drenched in sweat. He doesn't have a plan, and he tries not to think ahead, tries not to think about anything else except what's right in front of him.

Gabrio would be proud, he thinks. Joanna would be proud. He wants to be proud of himself, but he can't, not yet, not until he's safe. He has to get back to Gabrio, if he's still there, if he's still alive. What happens after this? Will he be safe after tonight? Is this safety even possible within these walls? Perhaps, but only if he's careful. He'll need a good lie for why he didn't check in during curfew. They'll punish him anyway. Maybe he'll take on a new identity, like Gabrio does. Either way, Gabrio knows what he's doing. He'll know how to handle this. He wants to join the resistance. He wants to bring justice to Amity.

The pain in his arms and legs burn at his nerves' core. His muscles are on the verge of giving out, his strained limbs shaking from the effort of lowering himself. He lets himself drop a few feet and stifles a scream. He does it again and again, his heart rate dangerously high as the fear and adrenaline take control of his body.

Just as he's ready to give up, he feels something cool blowing on his face. There's another passage. He stops, strains, and lowers himself enough to feel where he's level with the other shaft. He tentatively climbs inside this one, feeling the cool metal beneath his fingers. It's a relief, his fingertips numb and likely burnt off from the prolonged heat. He lays there for several minutes, his chest heaving in the enclosed space, his eyes closed. He allows himself this time to recuperate. They wouldn't be looking for him here.

As he rests, he realizes this must be the air coming in from the outside. He follows the path until he feels a corner, where there's an intersection of passages. He takes a right, following it deeper and deeper into the wall's interior. He doesn't think anymore, just keeps moving.

He knows he's reached the end when he sees a light shining through a vent. There's no noise coming from the other side. The room must be empty. He creeps to the edge of the vent and peers out, keeping careful not to breathe too loud or move too fast. He's back in the large, interior room. There are no more soldiers, at least not in the meantime. It looks like everyone's cleared out. Akeno can still see the corpses lying on the ground, forgotten in the scheme of events, hidden in the shadows. The interior door is closed from the outside. He takes his chances.

He carefully unscrews the nails holding the vent in place with his fingernails, which haven't been clipped in over two years. They're paper thin from a lack of vitamins. They keep bending under the pressure he applies to the screw. Eventually he pulls a button from his pants and uses that to twist the screws. When he thinks they're as loosened as they'll get, and after several minutes of not hearing a thing, he maneuvers his body so his feet are facing the grate. With one successful kick, the grate falls off the left side. It swings down but doesn't disconnect. He's able to shift the vent and slide out of the massive tunnel system within the walls.

He replaces the cover just as he had done at the top and quietly makes his way to the other side of the room. He sees Gabrio leaning against the wall where he had left him, exactly where he had left him. Akeno fears the worst and chokes on a sob buried deep in his throat. He goes to him slowly, at first on his feet, but then on his hands and knees. His chest tightens from the pain of seeing the paleness of Gabrio's skin.

Akeno bends and places a roughened hand against Gabrio's cheek and feels an immense amount of warmth. He's confused at first but then suddenly relieved when Gabrio's eyes flutter open. "Gabrio?" he chokes out. "Hey, Gabrio, you still there?"

"Yeah, I'm still here," Gabrio whispers. He coughs from the effort, his chest heaving as he chokes out the rest. "Admit it, I'm a great actor. You and those soldiers thought I was dead."

Akeno stifles a laugh, tears streaming down his face. He feels so relieved, but then his nerves kick in again. "We've gotta get out of here,"

379

he says, stifling the feeling of any other emotion. "Any ideas?"

"Don't want to use the front door?" Gabrio asks mildly.

"You think that's a good idea?"

"No, of course not," Gabrio says with a lopsided grin. "There's another room. There should be a side door over there." He vaguely points. "It's the door the soldiers use when they're rotating shifts. We should be able to get out that way."

"You sure there aren't any soldiers in there now?"

Gabrio shakes his head. "The city's on total lockdown. There won't be any soldiers in here for a few more hours." He coughs and spits out a yellow paste.

At least it's not blood, Akeno thinks.

"We'll need a change of clothes," Gabrio says, looking to the darkest corner in the room. Akeno knows what he means, but the thought paralyzes him with fear.

"Come on, we gotta get out of here, right?" Gabrio says, motioning for Akeno to help him stand.

Akeno pulls Gabrio off to one corner. Then he pulls the clothes off of two dead soldiers He strips them of their jackets, their pants, and boots and dons them. Then he does the same for Gabrio. He stows their clothes with the half-naked bodies in the corner. He pulls Gabrio upright and straightens their clothes.

"Can you walk?" Akeno asks.

"Guess I'll have to," he grits. "Let's go."

Akeno helps Gabrio half walk, half limp to the side door, where Gabrio swipes the card. It blinks red. Gabrio leans over the electronic pad on the door and starts typing in a series of codes in numbers and letters. There's a soft clicking sound, and the light turns green.

"I still don't understand how you can do that," Akeno says.

"And you never will," Gabrio says with a half-hearted grin.

They slip inside the other room, which is significantly smaller than the last, more narrow. There's a row of boxes and a bunch of empty benches that allow rest for the soldiers. They move to another door, one that leads to the outside.

"I thought you said we can't walk out the front door," Akeno says.

"This isn't the front door. This is another door." He smiles to himself as he types in another series of codes. The lock clicks, and Akeno pushes the door open. They pass through the interior, and suddenly they're inside a busy house, now a makeshift hospital room.

Within this hospital are a bunch of wounded soldiers, their faces screwed up in pain as they're treated for open wounds and other injuries. Many of them were shouting out in pain as nurses swarmed over them. Some of them lay quietly, their heads turned to the side as they distanced themselves from the present. Many of them are sleeping, or at least feigning sleep, while others groan in pain. The hustle and bustle of the room was pure chaos as the soldiers regained their position on the wall. The resistance had all but completely vanished with the helicopters, or so they believed.

"Excuse me, miss," Gabrio calls to one of the nurses. "Over here," he says with a weak motion of one arm.

One of the nurses hurries over and lays him down on one of the white beds. Two nurses get to work without asking too many questions. To the ones they do ask, Gabrio gives a straight answer, his voice clipped at the end of each sentence. He must be in a lot of pain or feigning more pain than he has. He doesn't finish any of his answers without a humble smile and a grateful compliment to the nurses' aid. Akeno can see the nurses aren't impressed by his flowery language. They're too consumed by the work in front of them.

"You'll be okay," the nurse says evenly. "Nothing we can't fix."

"What about you?" the second asks, eyeing Akeno up and down for blood, scouring him for injuries. "Are you hurt?"

"I'm fine," Akeno says awkwardly. "I found him in a corner."

One nurse notices the marks on Akeno's neck and points at them. "Burns?" she asks, turning behind her.

Akeno reaches up and feels at his neck. From the bomb's explosion on the bridge, he thinks. The wound's tender.

The nurse sticks a wooden stick in a jar of paste and pulls out a clump of it. She hands it to Akeno. "Apply this to your burns, and you'll avoid the scarring."

The other nurse gives Gabrio a shot in his leg, something for the pain, she explains. She marks this in a chart she's had tucked beneath one arm. The first nurse moves on to the next soldier as the other nurse cares for Gabrio.

Akeno sits quietly next to him in a nearby chair, his gaze on the bullet hole. There's still so much blood, but he takes faith in the nurses' practiced hands as she preps his wound. He grunts at her quick touch. The nurse calls for something, and a male nurse walks by and hands her a wooden peg, eyeing the wound on Gabrio's leg. The nurse takes it and hands it over to Gabrio.

"Bite down on this. It's for the pain," she explains.

Gabrio takes it but doesn't make use of it. He grits through the worst of it, his eyes watching the nurse's every move. Once she's done cleaning it, he rests his head on the thin mattress, his eyes dimming as the sedatives kick in. He smiles through the pain.

Akeno watches the nurse work on Gabrio's wound. She's quick and careful. Once she's found what she was digging for, she holds it up in the light, smiles with satisfaction, and tosses the bullet in a separate dish with a grunt and heartfelt pride in her work. She neatly finishes him up with a tight wrap around his leg. Then she leaves them both alone without another word.

"It's gonna be alright, kid," Gabrio says under his breath, his eyes fluttering open to study Akeno. "You look beat. I don't blame you, but I'm worried. It's okay if you can't handle this. It's alright to want to leave."

"I know," Akeno says.

Gabrio nods.

"You've done good today," he says. "I'm glad you're still here. It should have been everybody tonight, but..."

There's a moment of silence.

"Where do we go from here?" Akeno asks. "Do we go back to our lives as usual?"

"It's complicated, but I have it figured out." He shifts in bed.

"What happens to me? What about you?"

"Don't worry. We've got a good cover. Our files say we've been held overnight for breaking and entering combined with vandalism. We'll go back to the block looking as beat up as they expect from those sorts of crimes."

"How'd you pull that?"

"You'd love to know," he says with a twisted grin.

Akeno laughs, and Gabrio closes both eyes with a smile. He gives a nod of the head a few times before finally drifting off. He breathes deeply, and Akeno thinks he's asleep.

"Just so you know," Gabrio interrupts Akeno's thoughts. "There's plenty more work to do. You've no idea what you've gotten yourself into. Not yet. This project's huge."

"I've seen the worst of it tonight. I can do it. I'm ready."

"I know you are." His face slackens, and then he's out, his chest rising and falling with a steady rhythm of someone in desperate need for the release.

Akeno pockets the bullet from the dish, sure Gabrio will want it when he wakes up. He takes a moment to close his eyes and relax in his chair as he listens to the sound of metal clinging, the nurses' whispered assurances to the soldiers stranded here by themselves. He listens to their groans of pain, the stirring of bodies clinging to life beneath thin bed sheets. He thinks about the rest of the day, tomorrow, and settles into himself. He lets it all go as the morning sounds of dawn announce the sun's rise over a new day.